About the Author

JUDITH KOLL HEALEY has a keen interest in France and its medieval history. She has spent her career as a philanthropic consultant to families of wealth across the nation. She lives in Minneapolis, Minnesota.

www.therebelprincessanovel.com

The Rebel Princess

JUDITH KOLL HEALEY

The Rebel Princess

HARPER

NEW YORK · LONDON · TORONTO · SYDNEY

HARPER

A hardcover edition of this book was published in 2009 by William Morrow, an imprint of HarperCollins Publishers.

HarperCollins books may be purchased for educational, business, or sales promotional use. For information please write: Special Markets Department, HarperCollins Publishers, 10 East 53rd Street, New York, NY 10022.

FIRST HARPER PAPERBACK PUBLISHED 2010.

Designed by Rosa Chae

Map by Mary Karen Lynn-Klimenko

The Library of Congress has catalogued the hardcover edition as follows:
Healey, Judith Koll.
    The rebel princess / Judith Koll Healey. — 1st ed.
        p. cm.
    Sequel to: The Canterbury papers.
    ISBN 978-0-06-167356-6
    1. Alix, de France, 1160–ca. 1220—Fiction. 2. Great Britain—History—Henry II, 1154–1189—Fiction. 3. France—History—Philip II Augustus, 1180–1223—Fiction. 4. Mothers of kidnapped children—Fiction. 5. Kidnapping—Fiction. I. Title.
    PS3608.E236R43   2009
    813'.6—dc22   2008020366

ISBN 978-0-06-167357-3 (pbk.)

10 11 12 13 14   OV/RRD   10 9 8 7 6 5 4 3 2 1

To my four sons,
Sean, Paul, Michael Brian, and Colin,
every one worth a risk and a rescue

The enemies of God must die.
They will go up in smoke,
Burn like summer grasses.

—Psalm 37

THE JOURNEY OF THE PRINCESS ALAÏS TO FIND HER SON

(Languedoc and France in the 12th Century)

Paris

Poitiers

Lavaur

Toulouse

Verdun

Laurac

Foix

Alaric

Narbonne

To Santiago de Compostela

Fontfroide Abbey

Mediterranean Sea

Kingdom of Aragon

The St. John Cup Legend

Legend has it that at the Last Supper, Saint John was handed a cup of poisoned wine. He blessed the cup, whereupon a snake was seen crawling from it and the wine was made whole. The Cathars had a special devotion to Saint John the Evangelist, who is believed to have written the fourth gospel and possibly the Apocalypse.

Preface

At the turn of the twelfth century France was a very small kingdom. It occupied the land of the Île de France in the north, but not much more. The kings of France were constantly involved in skirmishes with the Angevin Plantagenet kings of England, Henry II and subsequently his sons, Richard and John. Much of Normandy, Le Mans, and the Aquitaine, which King Louis had to relinquish when his first wife, Eleanor, left him to marry young Henry, were under Plantagenet control.

Philippe Auguste, called Dieu-Donné by his father who had waited long for a son, ruled France. Many powerful duchies surrounded his lands, notably Burgundy and Champagne, which were intermittently friendly and quarrelsome. They operated independently, although their leaders gave homage to the king of France as their overlord under the prevailing system of fealty.

The lands to the south, ringing the Mediterranean Sea, were under the control of petty nobles or viscounts who gave homage to the counts of Toulouse. In those lands the culture was much freer than in the north, the art of beauty more admired and attended to, and the counties smaller than the large northern duchies.

The south, as it was called in Paris, was rich in other ways. Closer to the trade centers, these lands had no shortage of gold, a condition that permeated France, which at this time had to mint all of its coinage in silver. And the ports that facilitated the trade that brought the gold must have looked inviting to the king of France in his landlocked northern lands.

Still, the south was far away from the center of France and busy with its own affairs. At the time our story opens, it must have seemed an unlikely candidate to become part of the northern kingdom.

All of that changed with the advent of a peculiar religious sect that sprang up during the latter half of the twelfth century. These people identified as Christians, and called themselves *"bons hommes"* or *"bons chrétiens,"* "Good-Men" or "good Christians." Their enemies called them "Cathars," or *Cathari,* the "pure ones," and labeled them heretics. Though relatively small in number, they presented a powerful challenge to the church of Rome because of their simple ways, reminiscent of the early Christians. Through debates for some decades in the twelfth century, the Roman church representatives tried to cajole these errant sheep back into the fold of the dominant Christian church, but the new religion only spread and became stronger.

These Cathars were sometimes called dualists, believing variously in two sides of God (the light and the dark) or, in some cases, in two gods, good and evil. It was said the origins of their faith lay in ancient Persia, in the Manichean religion, transported through the Bogomils in the kingdom to the east of the Lombards. Wherever it came from the new belief presented an increasing threat to the church of Rome in a number of ways: The new religion employed wandering lay preachers, needed no official priests, and filled the needs of the faithful without the organization, indulgences, or the quest for gold that characterized the dominant Christian church of the times.

In 1207, Pope Innocent sent his third and final letter to King Philippe Auguste of France, asking him to raise an army and go south to fight the new religion. Philippe refused this demand, although eventually the call of orthodox religion, land, and gold would prove irresistible to the state of France. The Albigensian Crusade, as it came to be called, would become the first religious war that set Christian against Christian. But at the time of our story Philippe of France was not persuaded that he wanted to join the battle.

King Philippe was at his court in Paris when the emissaries of the pope arrived bearing his letter. They were accompanied by his long-time friend William of Caen. With the king was his redoubtable half sister, the Princesse Alaïs, who was anything but retiring. And this is how our fiction begins.

Prologue

The Abbey Church of St. Denis

When I recall how the adventure began, I see again in my mind's eye the abbey church at St. Denis and the remarkable characters that made up my life at that time: my brother, King Philippe of France, my aunt, the dowager Countess Constance of Toulouse, Etienne Chastellain, the king's sinister chief official, and all the people of the court of Paris.

We were attending the high Mass at the abbey at the direction of my brother, the king. He always insisted that we make the hour's journey from our home on the Île de la Cité to St. Denis on feast days. He honored the abbey church which was the burial place of the kings of France. His own father and grandfather, who had placed so much confidence and wealth in this place, now rested here, their souls called to their eternal glory, or so we supposed.

I knelt slightly behind my brother and his

wife, my prie-Dieu less ornate than theirs but still elegant, fitting for the sister of the king of France. We were at the side of the great altar, in our private royal space, where we could see the glorious liturgy and still remain hidden from the prying eyes of Philippe's pious subjects.

A thousand candles lit the cavernous interior and torches dispelled the shadows near the stone walls. The new fashion of filling the windows with stained glass, begun in the king's own Sainte Chapelle only a few years earlier, had reached St. Denis. The bright October sunlight, muted by the colors of the glass, gave a rich glow to the interior. The abbot's flowing gold vestments added luster to the scene. Even the novice choir members wore stoles of bright silk in honor of the feast.

It was during the consecration of the host that peculiar events began to happen. The priest was intoning the Latin, bending over the chalice and murmuring the incantatory prayers. This special cup held ordinary wine now, but soon would hold the consecrated wine, the very blood of Christ. Ripples of the gold and white silk chasuble trimmed in fur flowed over the altarcloth, hiding the chalice even from the view of those in the royal box.

The abbot was muttering words we could not hear, but we knew what he said from our student days. The cathedral school clerks had taught us well. *Hic in enim calyx sanguinis mei.* "This is my blood . . . of the new and eternal testament." The words Christ spoke at the Last Supper, turning the wine into his own blood, or so they said.

He raised high the chalice then, for all to adore, and that was when I noticed something singular. The gold chalice was extraordinary, ringed with jewels glinting in the lights from the multitude of tapers on the altar. It was special not only for the gems that dotted it. St. Denis, with its long ties to the kings of France and their wealth, had many valuable and beautiful sacred vessels, equally bedecked. No, it was something else that captured my attention. This chalice had the longest stem I had ever seen on such a vessel.

Regal, full, tapering from the cup to the round base, it was nearly twice the height of the usual chalice stem. Around it, wrapped like a snake, braided gold wove a hypnotic covering so broad that the abbot needed both hands to grasp it. It was a wonder.

I had no sooner taken in the unusual form than I remembered that I ought to cast my gaze downward. The chalice was raised to be venerated, our cathedral tutors had taught us when we were royal children, but not ogled like a common tavern goblet. I must reflect on my restless soul, my constant lack of decorum in these religious ceremonies which lasted so long and seemed to bring me no nearer to the God I sought.

But as I looked demurely away a soft rustle of silk at my side caught my attention. My aunt Constance, dowager Countess of Toulouse and sister to our late father King Louis, had risen from her prie-Dieu and was watching the lifted chalice with a look of intense concentration. It was not exactly an expression of rapture, but rather one of calculated assessment.

And I was not the only one who caught this striking scene. The king, sitting directly in front of me, glanced back at the noise. For a moment our gaze met. Then a sudden commotion in the middle of the church claimed our attention.

The royal family turned as one toward the center of this disturbance and saw a party of three knights in chain mail clanking forward. They had entered the church still wearing their swords, which was expressly forbidden. They were covered with sweat and even from my distance I could see they were oblivious to everything but reaching the front part of the church. They pushed the standing throng aside as they came forward. As one, they roughly shouldered past the choir pews in the center of the church, where the monks labored valiantly to continue their singing despite the distraction.

The impolite knights reached their goal in the front ranks of the standing worshippers and I could see the king's shoulders stiffen. The king of France was not used to having his worship interrupted, especially when those who entered with such little show of ceremony were coming for his counselor and not his royal self.

Etienne Chastellain, the king's chief minister, stood at the center of a small group in the very front of the worshippers. He turned as the knights reached him, and brushed aside one of his counselors who would have intercepted the visitors. He bent to hear their suit, then suddenly made a dismissive gesture with his hand, a slice downward as if he had heard enough. I saw him snap his fingers and two of the small coterie of men who always surrounded him jumped to his service. They placed their hands on the arms of the knights who had entered the church with such ill grace, and hustled them to the side aisle and back through the crowd of standing faithful.

My attention was reclaimed by the drama at the high altar. The ritual continued in full progress, as if nothing had happened. The acolytes carried the posts of bells and jangled them with joy, the monks swung the censers on their golden chains, releasing the sweet perfume of their burning cargo. All heads bowed in reverence.

The abbot himself came to the royal box to distribute communion. The king and queen, my aunt Constance and myself, were invited to receive the body and blood of our Lord every Sunday. Pity the poor, vast body of other worthy Christians who were allowed the privilege only at Eastertide. Such were the perquisites of royal life.

I tried to put myself into a devout frame of mind, and took my turn after Philippe and Queen Ingeborg had been served the host. But I was consumed with curiosity about the importunate knights and their speedy escort from the public eye. I drifted close to Philippe as we swept from the basilica after the final blessing, hoping to learn something on the way to the waiting litters.

I was rewarded to hear the king issue a peremptory summons to his chief minister through one of his squires as soon as the priest had left the altar. I watched Chastellain receive the messenger, detach himself from his group of counselors and hangers-on, and approach the king as we descended the steps of the abbey church. I was nearly clinging to my brother's arm in an attempt to hear the news, and this was so unlike me it caused the king to turn in my direction several times with a questing expression. But he forbore to reproach me and I continued to hover by his side.

Chastellain bowed low to the king, and then to the queen and finally to me. His bows, I noted, were slightly more perfunctory each time; the bow to me could have been characterized as a bob. We did not like each other, this minister and I. No doubt he sensed I found him arrogant when he was away from the king, and overly solicitous when he was in his presence. But the man dared not show any hint of open disrespect to me, the king's sister.

"Well, Chastellain, what was that all about?" Philippe's impatience had reached his voice.

"Your Grace," the minister began, in exactly that kind of unctuous tone I deplored. He smiled, revealing stained teeth, twisting his hands together all the while as if washing them. "A slight misunderstanding. The knights were part of an advance guard I had sent to the west, to gather news about King John of England's troop movements. You yourself ordered me to find confirmation of our reports last week."

"Yes, yes, but why the interruption of Mass?" Philippe could not conceal his increasing annoyance. "Why did they not come to the *palais* and speak with Us after Our dinner today? What did they have to say that could not wait? Has significant movement in John's forces been observed?"

"A mere misunderstanding, Your Grace. These men had no great news to impart. The situation remains the same as we were told last week. King John's men are in the same place as before. I gave you the briefing only yestermorn." He spread his hands as if to soothe his monarch with his assurance. "The knights thought I would want to know immediately what they had to say but, indeed, matters are no different than before."

"Hunh." With that indeterminate grunt, the king turned abruptly and made ready to mount his richly caparisoned horse. "See that they understand that We do not favor interruptions at the Mass, especially at the point of consecration." Philippe's groom cupped his hand and the king made use of it to spring upon his horse. From that height he spoke again, looking down at his minister. "Such an affront offends my people and makes it appear We do not take religion seriously."

Chastellain bowed his head.

The conversation seemed to be over, so I was now forced to move toward the litter waiting for me. Ingeborg had already left and I surmised we would see her no more until the following Sunday service, where she made a point of joining us to let the people of France see how devoted their queen was to the praise of the Lord.

As I bowed to Philippe and prepared to enter the waiting litter, I heard a final comment in a brusque tone that gratified me. The king's stern voice carried well: "Chastellain, I'll expect a full briefing after the noonday dinner."

When I settled back among the velvet cushions, the scenes from the cathedral replayed themselves before my unwilling eyes: the odd chalice, the way Constance looked at it, the interruption of Mass by the armed knights, the strange response of Chastellain to the king's inquiry. A whisper within me matched the clap-clap of the horses' hooves on the stones of the Paris road: There is more here; there is more here.

BOOK ONE

Intrigue in Paris

1

PARIS COURT, ÎLE DE LA CITÉ

Chambers of the
Princesse Alaïs

The announcement of the courier surprised me. I was sitting at my long oak table, preparing to mix a new bar of ink with water, when the sharp knock interrupted. The door opened, letting in a blast of the cool October air along with my maid, Mignonne. I put down the pitcher with an unsteady hand. Perhaps this was what I had been waiting for.

"My lady, there is a message for you. The runner says it is urgent."

"Well, send him in then." I was unable to keep the excitement from my voice. All morning I had been restless, unable to focus on my needlework, pacing my chamber. The feeling that something was about to happen had been gathering in me since the previous evening. This could be, at last, a letter from William, with news of his next visit. Or it may be something else, something not so pleasant. I knew

I must have patience. This gift of mine, some called it second sight, could not be hurried. Everything would be revealed.

I arranged myself in my largest carved chair, with the heavy tapestry cushions. I sat upright, no smile upon my face. For underneath the excitement lurked a sense of foreboding.

Mignonne soon returned with a young man, still breathing heavily from his ride. He was tall and thin, and moved awkwardly as if he had just grown last week and his body had not yet adjusted to its new height. The young man wore a cloak too thin for our brisk northern air, and I did not recognize the colors of his livery. He immediately removed his cap and went down on one knee.

"Rise, young man. Tell me your business," I said, motioning him up.

"Your Grace . . . umm Princesse Alaïs, I have a message for you from my mistress. She bade me ride here with all due speed."

"And who is your mistress, lad?" I prompted more gently, for I could see the youth was inexperienced in matters of court formality.

"Joanna, Countess of Toulouse, Your Grace," he said, bobbing his head. A flush came over his cheeks. "She begs to be remembered to you, and sends you this letter. And I was to give it to no one else but you."

The youth pulled a roll of well-mashed parchment from within his tunic, and handed it to me. I could see his hand was shaking, perhaps with cold, or with the responsibility of delivering his burden to the sister of the king of France. My heartbeat had slowed. It was not to be news from William after all.

Mignonne, who had been standing aside during this exchange, took the parchment and carried it to me. She made a nice courtesy as she handed it to me, and I saw with some amusement her glance slide to the youth, as if she were instructing him on what to do next. He followed her example with a low, awkward bow, and I summoned a smile for him.

"Mignonne, take this young man below. Be sure he has food and drink and a place to lay his head. It seems he has traveled far, and done his mistress's bidding well. Get him a warmer cloak, as well." I turned to the youth. "I'll see that you are properly rewarded for your work, young man. Meanwhile, you should eat your fill and get some rest." And I brushed the air with my hand, a signal to my maid to make a hasty exit.

The youth bowed again and backed away from me, his long legs uncertain whether to kneel or flee. He tripped, causing Mignonne to grin, but then she caught my glance and immediately became sober. In a moment, they were gone. I slipped from my chair and went to the table, where a sharp knife lay.

I had not had word from Joanna of England since she had married Count Raymond of Toulouse some years earlier. She was Eleanor and Henry's daughter, and had been my dearest friend when we were young. She was the favorite sister of my betrothed, Richard later king of England, and stood by me in the turmoil that surrounded the breaking of that promise.

Joanna's letter also took me by surprise because I had expected any message would be from William. I thought for certain that my unsettled feeling that morning meant that I would finally hear from him. He had not returned at Eastertide, as he had promised. Nor had he come at Whitsuntide. And the long summer, unusually warm, had dragged by without news of him or Francis for months. Now, here was this unexpected communiqué, not from him, but from my long-ago friend.

I slit the red sealing wax with my knife, and unrolled the parchment. My disappointment was matched by my curiosity. Why a letter from Joanna after all these years? And why had she employed the young, untested page, rather than sending the letter through ordinary couriers that came regularly to my brother the king from the court at Toulouse?

As I read the letter, I began to understand.

To: Alaïs Capet: Princesse Royale of France
From: Joanna of England: Once Queen of Sicily and
Now Countess of Toulouse

Dear Alaïs:

I hope this letter finds you well, dear cousin. I think of you often, and hope that the years in Paris at your brother's court have been good to you.

I write now, in confidence, because I need your help in a matter both personal and diplomatic. The court of Paris will soon receive a visit from two very important monks. They are legates of the pope and powerful in their spiritual realms. They are on a mission to persuade your brother to give them arms and men to invade our county here in the south.

Yes, it seems impossible, but that is the truth. They were here recently and were most importunate with Raymond. They told him that if he could not root out the heresy of the Cathar religion from his vassals' lands in Béziers and Foix, his own land of Toulouse would be forfeit. After a stormy session, the leader, Abbé Arnaud Amaury from Cîteaux, threatened Raymond with the armies of the king of France, and then left.

I believe these men are hastening to Paris to persuade your brother to intervene here in the south. I beg of you, do everything you can to keep King Philippe from joining those monks in this battle. I cannot say all that is in my heart, but know that these people in my husband's lands are gentle. Their beliefs are somewhat unorthodox, but they call themselves Christian and have a great reverence for Saint John and his gospel. Trust me, Alaïs. They intend harm to no one. The abbot Amaury is

overzealous. And Alaïs, he is dangerous. Look to your safety if you
tangle with him.

The politics of Rome are involved here, but I try not to concern
myself with these things. Only, I am fearful that if the monks
succeed, we will have war in the south and no one will escape the
carnage. I cannot understand how the peaceful words of Christ
have come to be used as a battle cry for war.

Count Raymond, my husband, knows nothing of this letter.
Tell no one. But please, watch what happens at court and do what
you can to block the monks and forestall a disastrous war. If you
send to me, give the message to the courier I have used here. He is
young and not experienced but his loyalty is beyond question. I hope
one day he will have the opportunity to train and be knighted. His
name is Giles. His father came with me to this court from England.

How fares my husband's mother, the dowager Countess
Constance? I hope for her good health, but I also hope for her
continued stay in Paris. Last time she paid us a visit, it was a
year before my husband's good humor returned!

Yours, with affection and all good wishes,
Joanna R., Countess of Toulouse

Addendum: The Lord William came to our court just after the
monks had left. He did not stay long. I think he was in a hurry
to catch these monks and journey to Paris with them. The Lord
William wishes us well, but he serves many masters.

The large *J* covered the rest of the page. Joanna had learned to
write along with the rest of us royal children raised by Eleanor and
Henry, but she always preferred just her initial. She made the mark
even more distinctive with a large loop.

I rolled the parchment and tapped it against my chin, as I thought about the message. Her note about her good-mother, Countess Constance, made me smile. But her addendum about William was puzzling. Why mention him? Surely news of my liaison with William had not reached the courts of the south! Had they nothing better to do than talk of the royal family in Paris? Or had William known Joanna would write to me, and asked her to mention his departure for Paris?

I walked to the window and stood looking out on the gray October sky. Joanna's letter was mild enough, but I could read between the lines. This man, this Arnaud Amaury, was known to me. William had told me of him at Christmastide. I liked not what I heard. William said this abbot was the greatest barrier to peace in the south, with his hatred of the new religion and his love of war. He was a powerful man, but single-minded. And he was now on his way to our very doors, if this letter was to be believed, to engage my brother in his wrongheaded deeds of violence.

I harbored great affection for Joanna. Her husband, Raymond, was another story altogether, but I would not ignore this plea from my childhood companion on his account. Abbé Amaury would receive no welcome from me. I still had the ear of my brother, the king, but I knew I must move carefully. Philippe was an astute ruler and diplomat. He would notice if I attempted to block his will. I would wait and discern the best course of action to defeat this man who meant harm to my dearest friend.

A sharp knock on the door of my chamber roused me from my musings. I whirled from the window and faced the door, saying, "Enter," in a voice as strong as I could make it. I was to have my second surprise of the morning.

The door swung open, revealing the bulk of Michel de la Ronde, my brother's private secretary and confidant. His black hair was cut straight across his forehead, guardian of his perpetual frown. His person matched his somber appearance, always direct and to the point.

"The king requests your appearance immediately in his chambers," he said, in his voice like gravel. "He begs me to accompany you. He says it is most urgent."

I grabbed a cloak from the chair closest to the hearth, and threw it around my shoulders. This peremptory summons from my brother was most unlike him. Something troubling must have happened. And given Joanna's letter, I had an idea of what it might be.

2

PARIS

The King's
Privy Chambers

My brother's apartments were at the opposite end of the palace from my own. De la Ronde was a man in a hurry and walked quickly, despite his bulk. I matched my steps to his with some effort. My cloak billowed with our speed, allowing sharp drafts that chilled me. As we turned into the hall leading to the king's privy chamber, I saw the corridors lined with all manner of folk, as was usual. Palace guards in uniform mingled with court sycophants in silks and velvets waiting for favors. Honest yeomen in rough leather jerkins seeking redress of a wrongdoing kept to themselves, apart from the grandees. As we hurried past, the guards snapped to attention, like so many human pikes, but I had little interest in them. I was puzzling over what my brother might want from me.

When we arrived at the heavy oak door,

marked on the outside with the large coat of arms the Capets had adopted generations earlier, M. de la Ronde gestured to the men. One stepped forward to knock briskly on the door with the pike staff. We heard an equally sharp reply, one that apparently was interpreted as positive, as the guard swung the door wide. I entered with some trepidation. The king did not sound happy.

This was the king's privy chamber, used for both work and sleeping. The room had always seemed cavernous to me, and relentlessly male. Several large oak tables covered with documents gave the room an official look. The hunting scenes carved into the mantel over the main hearth and dark mauve curtains enveloping the royal bed on its dais at the end of the chamber added to the formality. The same heavy velvet covered the two apertures now shuttered against the autumn air. The entire scene seemed to represent the essence of the warrior knight.

The king was seated at the far end of a long table, which provided a place for all his papers as well as a center for conferring with his counselors. My brother looked up with irritation and dismissed de la Ronde with a wave of his hand and a quick word. He beckoned me toward him, not rising.

"Welcome, Sister. I pray you place yourself here, near me. I want to show you something."

"What is it, Brother?" I made a perfunctory courtesy and then gathered my skirts to sit, pulling up a small chair to the right of the king, where I could see the documents on the table.

De la Ronde, bowing to the king, backed out and softly closed the door as he left us. The king turned toward me and propped his cheek on one hand, regarding me like an owl. He had a swelling on the right side of his mouth. "My tooth hurts like the very devil."

"Let me call for a servant to bring a poultice," I said, imagining a sympathetic twinge in my own jaw. I had had such a pain once and it was not entirely forgotten.

"Not now," he said brusquely. "I have something I want to show you. This was not intended to be the topic of our meeting this morning, but it may be connected. Look what de la Ronde has just brought me."

Philippe had a piece of parchment flattened under his hand. It had severe creases where it had been folded, rather than rolled. Indeed, there were already lines of tearing in the stiff paper. He slid it toward me. It appeared to be a short note.

The writing was spidery, as if the hand that penned the note had a palsy, making it well nigh unreadable. But the simple message could be discerned if one squinted and held the parchment very still.

To the Chief Minister:
You should advise the king to stay in his domain. He has problems
in Paris more pressing than those in the south. Snakes made of
gold are treacherous. Tell him to have a care that the treasures
of St. Denis do not find their way to Toulouse. And tell him to
watch his family closely. Not all are as loyal as they seem.

There was no signature. There was no further writing on the page and nothing appeared to have been blotted out.

I glanced at Philippe.

"How came this to your hand?"

"The note was delivered at the gates before dawn by someone who said he was a messenger from a friend. The note was addressed to Etienne Chastellain. But it's obvious it was meant for me."

"Chastellain." I was immediately on my guard. "And did your chief minister have any comment when he sent this to you?"

"He never saw it. The guard at the gate delivered the note to de la Ronde. All the porters and guards have been so instructed if missives arrive for my counselors."

I looked up sharply. "You do not trust Chastellain, either?" His comment took me by surprise, as I had been careful to avoid sharing my opinion.

The king shifted uneasily in his chair and paused, as if deciding how much he wanted to reveal to me.

"I am aware that there are intrigues swirling in this court. I cannot say yet who is involved, but it appears that information is leaking from my very councils to John of England's armies in the west. When we decide on a stratagem here in Paris, they are already countering it by the time the message gets to my captains."

"But you trust de la Ronde. Why exempt him from suspicion?"

"He can read and write, and his loyalty is unquestioned. We were raised together. He was my companion in my youth, in those years you were in England at Henry's court. I trust no one else for the moment. Until I clear this matter, everyone in my court is under suspicion."

"Surely not everyone," I said with a light tone, but then I saw his face darken and I held back my smile. His next words struck a chill in my heart.

"If you mean yourself, I have no reason to suspect you. But still, I watch everything." Philippe tapped the table impatiently with the handle of his silver knife, the one he used to break seals and pare apples in the autumn. "At the moment, I am more interested in the substance of this note than its delivery."

"Its message is cryptic, that is certain, both about the gold and about your family."

"St. Denis is full of treasures, but it is the king's church. At least until Notre Dame is complete. No one would dare to steal from St. Denis. They would incur the wrath of both church and king," he mused, examining the letter again with the round Italian glass that he kept on his table to enlarge print.

"If they speak of golden snakes, they must mean that odd, jeweled chalice the abbot used Sunday. When he raised it up at the consecration I was astonished. Did you mark it? The overlong stem was braided in gold, wound around like a snake. I've never seen one like it. Wherever do you think the abbot got it?"

"He got it from me." Philippe's tone was crisp. "I brought it back only a fortnight ago. I was most displeased to see it used on Sunday. I sent word to the abbot that the cup was to remain under lock and key from now on."

"How came you by it?" I was puzzled, my early interest compounded now by some note of warning in his voice.

"It was given to me by our cousin Raymond of Toulouse, when I met him a fortnight past at Blois. He said little about it, but his remarks made me think this was the object of some plot in his own realm. He merely asked me to bring it to Paris for safekeeping."

"I thought you went to Blois for the hunting," I said pointedly.

"So I told the court. My real purpose was to meet with Raymond about the difficulties he finds himself in, caught between the pope and these so-called heretics. These *Cathari*, who have invaded his towns in the Toulousain. The pope insists he must discipline his nobles, whose wives seem to protect the heretic preachers. In short, our cousin begged me not to intervene in the south." Philippe threw up his hands in mock-confusion. "I asked him why he thought I would do such a thing, as if I don't have enough trouble with John of England in our west lands. Then Raymond said I could expect a visit from two monks soon, who will say they have the pope's order to recruit my royal troops."

I wondered if Joanna knew of my brother's secret meeting with her husband. I was about to ask what his response was, and to tell him of Joanna's letter, but then thought the better of it. He should not know of my keen interest. Not until I had decided on my own plan to block those monks. Unexpectedly my brother changed the topic.

"Back to the matter of the golden snake chalice," he said briskly, as if I had been the culprit in taking our conversation afield. He fiddled with his pearl-handled knife. "That chalice interested our aunt Constance as well, I noted." He rubbed his swollen jaw in thought.

"I, too, saw her attention. She scarce bothered to hide it. I thought perhaps the attraction of the cup might simply be the flash of its jewels and gold."

"No, not true for Constance," he said. "Gold has never been her weakness. Look at the way she presents herself at my court. Her clothes are so frumpy I even ordered the queen to find out if she had need of new ones." He paused, frowning. "Which the queen probably never did, being occupied with her own appearance to an appalling degree."

"But if she has need of funds to help Raymond?" I prodded gently, bringing him back to our topic. "Constance might think of stealing something so valuable for the ready money it could supply."

His quick shake of the head dismissed the idea even before he spoke. "That makes no sense. It is Raymond's cup. He could have sold it if he needed gold. She must know that. Besides, I am convinced Raymond does not lack for silver and gold. He has control of the shipping ports in the south, or at least his vassels do. No, I cannot image Constance considering a theft."

Philippe tossed his knife onto the table as a child might who tired of a toy. "As for gold and silver, I'm the one in need. You can see it even in my treasured objects." He pointed with his knife to a small statue set on the cedar table next to my chair. I picked it up and turned it in my hands. It was a peculiar cross shape, with a ring around its center, almost like a halo carried too far.

"It's called a Celtic cross," Philippe offered. "The design is from Brittany, and quite ancient. The icon is fashioned in gold but set in a base of silver, an odd combination to be sure. Agnes had it made for me just before she left."

There was a pause, and I did not fill it. I was always saddened when Philippe mentioned his beloved Agnes. The pope had forced him to give up his second marriage, made for love, and resume his first marriage with the dour Dane Ingeborg. Agnes had retired to the south, but Philippe still pined for her. He and his present queen cordially detested one another.

Then he resumed his thoughts. "I had given orders in the court that the use of gold for jewels and display be curtailed. The artisan who made this object dared not complete it in gold, as he had already used his allotment for that year."

"I did not hear of this order," I said, puzzled.

Philippe rose and began pacing as he talked, forcing me to look up from the short chair on which I sat. His steps were cushioned by the Smyrna carpets he had brought back from the Crusades. But still he moved swiftly. His words floated back to me over his shoulder.

"My dear sister, you so seldom ask for jewels to be made that the court jeweler probably thought not to bother informing you of the ruling."

"But what does such an action accomplish?"

The king rang the tapestry bellpull near his writing table, and took a cushioned chair near his hearth. He motioned to me to sit opposite him, on a carved bench with a back and deep, goose-down embroidered pillows. I relinquished the low chair happily but with effort, feeling the pull in my back as I rose.

The king appeared not to notice my stiff movement as I walked to the bench near his hearth and sank into the welcoming softness. Instead he answered my question.

"We cannot afford to make even small treasures out of pure gold. We have need of all gold in our treasury. These sporadic battles in the west with John of England are draining me."

"Was Raymond negotiating to trade gold for your agreement to leave him alone?" I seized upon this practical idea as I settled myself.

"No." My brother gave a short, ironic bark that might pass for a laugh. "Would that he had made such an offer. But Raymond doesn't have enough political sensibility to offer bribes." The king looked up as a servant entered in response to his call.

"Bring us some sweetmeats and figs," he ordered quickly, stretching his legs out in front of him and crossing his ankles. "And some bread also if it is out of the oven." He knew the schedule of the royal kitchens, I thought with some amusement. But then my brother had ever been fond of taking his meals at odd hours, especially when he was locked in discussions with his councilors.

When the servant had bowed and backed out of the room, my brother gave his attention to our conversation.

"But let us discuss this notice just delivered," he said, reaching for it at the table by his side where he had tossed it earlier. He flapped it open again and perused it, then threw it into my lap with an expert toss. "What could it mean by impugning the loyalty of my family, do you think?" He watched me with a keen expression. I could not fathom his thoughts, but I had a sudden moment of disquiet.

"What meaning, indeed?" I answered with some heat. "The royal family is you, the queen, little Louis, and myself. Think you someone questions my fealty to my own brother?"

"How now, Sister," Philippe said, in what passed for a soothing tone from him. "My trust in you is well known in this court and beyond. No one would dare to suggest such a thing."

I wondered if he would say the same about the Danish queen, but decided against voicing the question. And little Louis had reached only four years, scarce old enough to foment treason. I tried for some lightness.

"Let me see. The writer mentions Toulouse. Perhaps our cousin Raymond intends to steal the oriflamme from the altar at St. Denis."

"No," Philippe responded solemnly, "Raymond wouldn't do that. Possessing the flag of our royal house would not make him king of France and it would only succeed in annoying me no end, which he can ill afford to do at the present."

I looked at him and he held my glance for a moment, before breaking into a full grin, restoring humor to our exchange and calming my worries of his suspicion.

"But let us talk now of other matters, the reason I asked you here this morning." Philippe made his fingers into a tent, and tapped his lips. His black eyes, almond shaped as were all the Capets' in my memory, narrowed. I held his gaze without flinching. "I told you I have suspicions that there are agents of John of England here at my court."

"So you said." I waited for more information, or a clue as to where the king was taking our conversation. After a moment of silence I prompted: "Have you information that points to a particular person?"

He regarded me for a long moment. "Who else is in our royal family besides those you have named?"

I shrugged. "Our father's brother, Duke Robert. But he resides in Orleans. And his sisters, Charlotte, abbess of Fontevraud, and Constance, dowager countess of Toulouse . . ." My voice trailed off.

"Exactly," Philippe said, watching the growing look of enlightenment spreading across my face. "Constance, mother of Raymond of Toulouse."

"Why would Constance engage in treason with John of England? Or for that matter, occupy herself with events in Toulouse? She has been in Paris for more than two decades, ever since she left Raymond's father. Surely, if she were disloyal, she would have acted before this." I thought again of mentioning the letter I had received that morning from Joanna, but immediately discarded the idea. Not yet.

At that moment, a sharp scratching on the door caused Philippe to call a distracted command for entry. A servant appeared with a tray piled high with fresh bread, grapes, and oranges from Hispania. The king gestured toward the low table in front of my bench. He then beckoned the servant and gave him another order in a low voice.

I looked around the room. There was a musk smell pervading this chamber, a scent that no woman could claim. I was certain Philippe's wives never came here. He must bed the royal consorts in their own chambers, and his mistresses in theirs. These days, with Ingeborg back at court and the beloved Agnes banished, I doubted he was much engaged in connubial activity.

As I was musing over these indiscreet thoughts, the door closed behind the clerk and my brother rose and strode to one of his long oak side tables. "Cider or burgundy?" he questioned, as he held a pitcher up.

"Cider, at this hour," I said, in my best elder-sister voice.

"Well enough for you," he muttered. "I need to fortify myself against a long and difficult day." He poured from a silver pitcher into one glass, and from an earthenware pitcher into the other.

"First apples from Normandy this autumn," he said, grinning, as he handed me the cup. He sank once more into the welcoming cushions of the royal carved armchair, and added, "And last grapes from Burgundy," as he lifted his own cup.

"And now let us return to the topic of Constance," I nudged.

"Constance, yes." He frowned as he spoke. "News of a set of suspicious meetings held by our aunt has reached my ears. They may relate to Toulouse and heretics or to information leaked to John of England, or perhaps both."

"I cannot imagine any such connection. Aunt Constance is such a mouse here at court. I scarce recall she is even here. I would be hard put to see any mystery surrounding her."

"Let me remind you that 'Aunt Constance' is still dowager countess of Toulouse," Philippe said firmly. He shook his head. "Her son is at the center of the present turbulence between the south and Rome. Mouse, perhaps, but possibly an active one, involved in intrigue to protect her offspring."

"The count's mother she may be," I said, "but rumor has it her marriage to his father was most unhappy."

"Ah, well, a mother's love and all of that." Philippe waved his hand in dismissal. Then he rose again and began pacing the length of the long chamber, tossing his black hair out of his eyes. My gaze followed him as I sipped my cider. "Nevertheless, her meetings are secret, discovered by de la Ronde's men quite by accident. Why would she keep them so private if there was no intrigue about them?"

"A secret assignation? Aunt Constance?" The image of the stubby figure of our elderly aunt rose before me and a giggle escaped before I could stop it. I leaned back against the bench cushions and drew my legs under me, preparing to hear another chapter on our royal family saga that my brother so loved to embellish.

"Not that kind of assignation," Philippe said dryly. "My agents tell me that she has journeyed twice to Créteil, an hour's ride from our court. The coachman who drove her has reported, under . . . um . . . earnest questioning, that there she met two men in the common rooms of a small inn, had the coachman wait for more than an hour each time, and then came directly back to Paris."

"And you are wondering what could be the purpose of such meetings?" I was puzzled. We rarely saw my aunt, though she lived in the drafty wing of the palace just next to my own suite. She was of a naturally withdrawing nature, and so unhappy over the events that had occurred when she was married to the fifth count of Toulouse that she never spoke of her years there. "It may only be that Constance has a sense her son Raymond is in danger. Everyone says the pope's patience is running thin over the count's failure to deal with the heretics. Have you thought that she only seeks news from the south of her son's well-being?"

"Then why all the secrecy?" He paused and spread his hands in question, then brought them together in a definitive clap. "If John has established agents in my very own court, I cannot afford to sleep. Anyone can be suspect in selling state information. Constance may be doing this to obtain gold to send to her son."

"But you said Raymond had no need of —" I began, but he went on, overriding my protestations.

"And there are more disturbing developments surrounding this that make me increasingly suspicious."

"Such as?" I felt a frisson of interest as I plucked an apple from the bowl on the small table near me. As I began to munch, I realized how hungry I was. I had only taken a few bites of the breakfast Mignonne had set before me. Perhaps the promise of a new mystery was reviving my appetite. I rose and began to wander the room, finally lighting on the corner of Philippe's large oak writing table as a good place to sit. I shoved aside a stack of scrolls that skittered onto the floor.

Philippe had ceased his restless pacing and stood facing me, his arms folded across his chest. "When I returned from Blois, I carried a message for Constance from her son. Last Sunday, after Mass, I sent de La Ronde to Constance's chambers with the note from Raymond. He returned to me and reported that her maids said she had just departed for a meeting in Créteil. That it had to do with 'affairs of state.' 'Affairs of state'!" he repeated in high dudgeon, flinging his arms outward. "Whose state, I wonder? The only state here is Ours!"

I closed my eyes momentarily and sighed. When Philippe reverted to the royal "We" in his speech, speaking in his mode of kingship, he often became unreasonable. It was usually a sign that he felt a threat from some quarter, for at other times he was often the most informal of rulers.

He walked to the window and back, apparently to calm himself, then continued. "So I ordered de la Ronde to send two of my best grooms packing after her. They were able to follow her because she was silly enough to use a court carriage for the journey. The trail was easily found."

He stood over me, scowling, one hand behind his back, the other raised in admonition in my direction. "Only one of my grooms returned. I don't like losing men, even varlets. It's unseemly that the king's men should be ill-used."

"Well, I wasn't responsible. Stop shaking your finger at me." I set my goblet down on his writing table. A man dead under suspicious circumstances. Now he had my full attention. "What were the particulars of events at the inn, as you know them?"

"My men arrived shortly after her carriage. They split at the inn, after assuring themselves that Constance was safely inside and her coachman drinking in the common rooms. All this according to the man who survived, who gave this report." Philippe moved toward the table on which I was perched, and glanced down at a roll of parchment, tapping his finger on it, then made a grimace and brushed his hand dismissively across the paper where it lay.

"Who gave you that report? Etienne Chastellain?" I reached to pick up the vellum, but my hand fell short.

Philippe shook his head. "As I said earlier, for the present I trust only de la Ronde. Chastellain knows nothing of this." He tossed the scroll onto my lap and continued his story, planting the knuckles of one fist firmly on the table and the other hand on his hip. "The report of the survivor says that one of my fellows crept close to the window on the side of the building where the common rooms were, and from whence he could hear the voices of Constance and at least three men closeted with her. While the one man was watching, the other went round the back, to see how many horses the visitors had, for they didn't know the number of men and feared for their survival if a fight erupted."

"What does de la Ronde say happened next?" I fingered the report but did not unroll it, concentrating on Philippe's face as much as his words. As if my artist's eye could discern what he thought was most important about what he was telling me.

My brother turned away as he replied. "Well, when the first man didn't rejoin his comrade minutes later, as agreed, the other fellow eventually went to investigate. He found his partner lying on the ground under the window, with his throat slit. The survivor hotfooted it out of there back to where they had hidden their horses. He was shaken badly, I can tell you." The king had resumed his chair and now stared balefully across the room at me. I moved back toward him, my fingers gently cradling the rolled vellum. After taking the chair opposite him, I shook the scroll open.

"What did your man see?" I asked the question absently as I scanned the report, laying it open on the low table in front of us when I had finished.

"My man said they spoke a strange dialect. He could make out some words, but not many. It seemed to be a tongue related to ours, but still foreign. The men kept saying '*oc*' rather than '*oil*' when they were nodding yes."

"The langue d'oc," I murmured. "The speech of the Occitan region. I learned it at the court of Eleanor when we were children in Poitiers."

"And that fact led me to the conclusion that Constance was meeting secretly with someone from her son's county." Philippe ploughed on, unwilling to be distracted in his thoughts by a lesson in lingua franca. "But not necessarily sent by Raymond. He may have known nothing of this, else why send a note through me to her? If the envoys were his, he could have sent a message through them at this meeting."

"Or he used that as a ploy to assure you would have no suspicions about her," I promptly replied, but he shook his head.

"The count loves finery and opulence. And he needs my help too greatly at present to antagonize me by murdering my servants. No, this has something to do with Constance alone."

I stretched my arms upward and clasped my hands behind my head for a moment to relieve my back. "And he certainly would not order such an action after you have just taken the trouble to meet with him in Blois, not a fortnight past."

"That makes these events all the more mysterious." Philippe leaned his head on the back of his chair and stared upward, as if seeking answers from the heavens. "So the question is: Who from the south was present at these meetings, and why?"

The king took a long draught from his own goblet and slammed it impatiently on top of de la Ronde's report, causing some of the burgundy to spill over and make splotches like blood on the white paper. I watched them pool.

"Call for a remedy for that tooth, Brother," I said absently.

"Not now." He dismissed my suggestion with a curt wave of his hand. The conversation lulled as he seemed to collect himself. "The business at hand is more important."

"Well, Your Majesty," I said, "this seems to be a serious affair."

Philippe nodded brusquely, his square chin jutting forward. He moved to the edge of his chair, leaning toward me with an air of intensity. His elbows rested on his knees and his strong hands dangled between his legs, their jeweled rings snapping in the reflection of the candlelight. "There are links to these events—the note warning me about a family member, Constance's attention to the chalice at St. Denis, and the murder of my varlet. She is up to something and I'll warrant her son knows nothing about it. I want your help, Alaïs. We need to smoke out any treachery at our court. Those meetings were so secret someone had to die for them."

.3.

PARIS

The Palace of
Philippe Auguste

I left my brother's chambers that morning with the promise that I would help him discover the secrets that lay behind the mysterious actions of our aunt, Constance. In truth, I knew not how I would do this, but I had confidence that an opportunity would present itself where I might inquire of her, without raising suspicion, about her son and his lands. Perhaps I could make a casual comment about receiving a letter from Joanna, and convey her best wishes to her good-mother (though not the part where my friend instructed me to keep Constance safely in Paris to ensure Raymond's continued good humor!).

Several days passed uneventfully, and my aunt was nowhere to be seen. I was beginning to believe I would have to create an excuse to visit her chambers, when certain events pushed all thought of Constance and the murder from my mind.

The following Friday the court came alive. It was the day before the last tourney of autumn, a grand event that drew knights and nobles from far and wide. The castle had been humming for days with preparations for the many visitors. It was on that morning that I had one of my rare premonitions, a "visitation" as William called my visions. My sleep had been fitfull all night, and toward dawn I started suddenly, sitting upright as if to defend myself. My active dreams had returned, those vivid pageants that came to me from time to time with warnings lodged in their peculiar images. This time I had seen gryphons flying about a room, and an elderly man who insisted that I help capture them and restore them to the glass bowl.

I sat still for a moment, remaining under the spell of those fabulous creatures. I considered whence they might have come, how I had encountered them before. But I could not remember.

Suddenly, without warning, a flash of light flooded the room. I was aware of a throbbing in my head, and felt my palms dampen with fear. I was frightened, wished to flee yet was powerless to resist. I dared not even lie back against my pillows.

The outline of a room was revealed, dimly at first as if there were a lifting fog. I felt the warm air of the south wafting over me and slowly, emerging from the brightness, an oval of thirteen standing men took form. Ten were dressed alike in scarlet robes with wide-brimmed hats of the same color perched on their heads while the other three wore only white. Two figures stood at the head of the oval, like the clasp on a necklace. All faces were turned toward them. In front of each man was a lighted taper, standing in a black wrought-iron holder reaching up from the floor. These candles were like sentinels, forming an inner ring to the circle. The flames licked the air with a smoky hunger.

I peered at the leaders, fascinated in spite of myself. One stood tall with his white hair flowing away from his bronze face, the aristocratic nose marking him as the figure from my gryphon dream. He was wearing the papal tiara, a white, beehive-shaped crown trimmed in gold and jewels, so tall that it would diminish a lesser man. But it only added to this amazing man's force.

The man next to him was unfamiliar, never before seen in my dreams or my visitations. He was robed in white, too, but in a simple style, in the white wool robe of the Cistercian order. His cowl was pulled forward.

As I watched, a tall, slender figure gradually took shape on the other side of this monk. His face became visible and my heart nearly stopped. It was Francis, garbed as a Cistercian, standing silently with a look of wonder on his face.

Suddenly the mysterious monk pushed back his cowl and revealed his face. It was long and fleshy with a chin that jutted out, as if to invite battle. His eyes glittered and the reflection of light off his brow threw into relief the ruddy tone of his face, a contrast to the deep tan of the man beside him and to my son. He had a focused, rapacious expression and I shuddered when he casually placed his hand on Francis's shoulder.

Then the bronze-faced man swung a bell up once, strongly, and at the sound and with one accord all of the scarlet-robed men pulled the tapers from their holders, turned them upside down and plunged them into the dust with a final and vicious gesture of annihilation. The vision darkened and I fell back into my pillows.

I lay there with my eyes closed for some time, captive to the echoes of the bell sound that had triggered the final eclipse of light. That sound seemed to recur in concert with a pulsing inside my head. Eventually both the sound and the throb receded and I was left to such peace as I could muster. I slept again, dreamless this time.

And so my servants found me some hours later. Mignonne, who alone knew of my visitations, made excuses to the others for my dazed state, and fed me watered wine, which revived me. After that, I was able to take some brown bread and fruit sweetened with honey. And I came more into myself.

I spent the morning quietly in my chambers, declining to join the king for his noonday dinner when he sent a note to summon me. I made an excuse of illness, although the ache in my head had ceased after I partook of some nourishment. Instead, I sat at my table, now reading some of the poetry from the south that I loved, now working in a desultory fashion at my charcoal and vellum, trying to draw the form of the fabulous birds who had flown around the room of my dreams.

After I had little success with that task I found myself drawing what I could remember of the scene where the red-robed men plunged their tapers into the sand. I was captivated by the memory of the man with the flowing white hair, and the other man beside him, the one with the fleshy, venal face. Yes, his face was easy to recall. I had it in a couple of strokes. I looked at what I had drawn and was both attracted and repulsed by it. It was a face interested in power, and earthly pleasures. It was the face of strength, and perhaps the face of a killer. But why had this face been sent to me? And what place had Francis in the company of such men? And who or what was to be extinguished? For that was the clear meaning of their ceremony.

I rose and walked to the window for air, tossing the drawings under other scrolls so that Mignonne would not see them when she came in with my bath. My small black cat, Minuit, rubbed against my leg, but I was in no mood for play. I waited. Suddenly a strong urge rose, an inner voice commanding me to leave my chamber.

What moved me I cannot say. These restless feelings sometimes came over me. I accepted these callings just as I accepted that my left hand had been withered from birth, and that I was specially marked in some way. Some said I had the gift of second sight. Not as a witch, as sometimes the Parisian court whispered, but still there were things about myself even I did not understand. Odd dreams, visions, inner movements that gave me direction, such as the one I felt now to go to the highest point of the castle. My feet flew along the hall to the tower at the end, and I climbed the steps quickly, rather more like a girl than the woman I was.

I emerged at the top onto the stone parapet just in time to see a bizarre picture spread before me. Looking down, I gazed upon an extended, winding human snake outlined against the distant meadows. I leaned out between the crenellations to better observe.

The line looked for a moment like a long, colorful, mythical serpent created for the amusement of onlookers at a festival, but soon the flags carried in the front became visible, and the many wagons bringing up the rear rolled into view. The serpent broadened and the moving tableau was defined as an ordinary company of knights and their entourage. With all the adjacent baggage and the many foot soldiers and attendants, it was clearly the train of someone very important.

"You have recovered from your malady?" The deep, rather hoarse voice at my shoulder startled me. Philippe had come upon me with no warning. He stood so close I could sense the heat from his climb up the stairwell. I looked at him, but he remained staring straight ahead at the advancing group, frowning and pursing his lips. I saw he did not expect an answer to his question, for he continued: "So they called you to come, as well."

"No," I said, "no one summoned me."

"Another of your premonitions?" he asked, his brows rising slightly. He didn't take his eyes from the colored autumn fields on the west bank across the Seine, and I turned back to watch with him.

"Yes, I suppose you could say that. Who comes below?"

"It's too early to see for certain," Philippe answered, and for the first time I detected a light note in his voice. "But I suspect we will see the pennants bearing the insignia of the Templars among those in the front rank."

"Philippe"—my heart stuttered in joyful surprise—"William is in this train!"

"So said the advance courier who arrived sweating like a drenched bird only an hour past."

"But why did you not tell me immediately?" A storm of feelings was taking me over, my anger at William for his absence in conflict with my rising joy to see him again. And the happiness that now, finally, I could tell my son the truth about his blood bond to me. I clutched the iron ring attached to the stone rim and leaned farther out, determined to get a better view. "It's been eight long months. I should have prepared."

"Softly, my sister." Philippe took my arm and pulled me slowly away from the edge. "How could we explain to the grand master of the Templars in England that his dearest love fell over the parapet in plain sight of her beloved's train and within reach of her own brother's hand? That incident could start a war!"

"Philippe!" I turned to face him again, only to see him grinning like a schoolboy. Philippe never mentioned my seven-year liaison with the Templar Grand Master William of Caen. What could possess him to show wit about it now?

But he only shrugged and tossed the locks of his dark hair back from his forehead. "Well, all the court talks of you and the Lord William. I suppose we can acknowledge it when you and I are in private."

"Oh, the court again," I said, pressing my fingers to my temples in mock-fury. "Always the court and their endless chatter."

"How now, Sister." Philippe took my hand lightly in his own. "Do not distress yourself. If my courtiers speak of you at all, it is with kindness and with some awe. After all, a man as famous and handsome as the Lord William will draw attention, even if you in your retiring manner do not seek it."

I shook my head, but I could not allow the mention of the silly court to distract me now from the startling news: William, coming home at last! I cast my gaze back to the brilliantly colored train and was astonished to see the group's speedy progress. The front riders were now quite close to the bridges of the Île de la Cité. The colors were coming into view, and I could make out four distinct flags.

"I see the Templars' flag now, the white with the red cross, and the brilliant blue—that would be William's house. But there are two I don't recognize."

Philippe squinted against the late afternoon sun, shading his eyes with his hand. "You would not. They are seldom seen in Paris. This pair of flags signals little good. They represent the pope of Rome and the abbey of Cîteaux. They announce the two monks I told you of, those who come to persuade me to war."

"Cîteaux, the Cistercian abbey?" My eyes closed as I saw once again the sinister white-robed Cistercian monk of my visitation, and my son Francis standing next to him. "You did not say they were Cistercians."

"The leader is called Arnaud Amaury. He is abbot of Cîteaux. The other, the lesser in power I think, is named Pierre of Castelnau." My brother continued to watch the advancing party, even as he spoke. "Why the interest? Have you heard these names before?"

I shook my head, for in truth Joanna had not mentioned the names of the monks. But there was no doubt in my mind. These were the two bent on mischief in the lands of Toulouse. "Mere curiosity, Brother. Nothing more." I paused. "And why does William ride with their party?"

Philippe sighed and turned toward me, casting a baleful glance in my direction.

"God himself only knows, but the sense of the letter delivered only an hour past from William's advance courier is that he met the monks' party just north of Poitiers and made it his business to travel with them to Paris. No doubt he intended to garner information on the journey, under the pretense that they were both coming to our court to discuss the same problem . . ."

"Namely, the heretics in the south," I interjected. He nodded, and turned away again, saying no more.

I knew better than to press the subject, and waited a moment, watching the progress of the colorful snake as it made its way across the bridge onto our little island. When next the king spoke, his tone became more agreeable.

"I did not ask you when we met: Have you had news from William recently?"

"I've not had anything since Whitsun. Last December the pope promised to release William from his Templar vows so that we might marry after he performed one final mission. When I agreed to this, I did not know that final mission would take the rest of his natural life! I will be glad of heart to see his diplomacy end soon." I didn't bother to keep the irritation from my voice.

Philippe motioned to me as he moved toward the opening of the narrow stairwell that led down the turret. I followed him, as the passage was too narrow to accommodate both of us. He kept talking over his shoulder as we descended. The steps were so steep and rough that I nearly tripped when a small cat ran across my path. They were slippery as well, and I had need of the iron rings in the wall from time to time to steady myself. The moss growing on the walls added to the gloom.

"William has confided in me his plan to marry you and return to Ponthieu as soon as he concludes his present business." He paused, one jeweled, slippered foot rotating on the white stone step, and turned upward to me. His voice held an uncharacteristic softness as he continued: "I told him he had my permission and my blessing." I was oddly moved, for the second time in this interview, by my brother's affection. I placed my hand on his shoulder, which he touched briefly before continuing his descent.

"When did you have this conversation, Brother?" I asked, suddenly suspicious.

The king, never one to show emotion for long, resumed his brisk tone. "William was with me when I met with Count Raymond in Blois these few weeks past."

"You did not say!" I burst out. "Why did you not tell me William would be meeting you? I would have come!"

"I did not wish to raise your hopes. Until the very last, he was not certain he could be in Blois in time for the conference." The king paused and cast a look upward at me. "It was William's request that I meet with Raymond in Blois. And his direction that I not tell you the purpose of my journey. You must ask him why." He spoke with finality, as if disposing of a troublesome diplomatic situation by delegating responsibility to someone else, which of course he was.

When he turned to make his way down the remaining steps, I was grateful that my brother could not see the dismay that spread over my face at his words and guess at my deep consternation. It was not William's habit to keep secrets from me, and that alone was disquieting. It seemed our relationship was changing, that the distance between us in miles was reflected in our spirits. How would this affect my son, who was so attached to William?

We fell silent for a few moments, though the echo of our voices continued to bounce off the rocks of the tower stairwell. Each of us was occupied with our own thoughts.

At last we reached the bottom of the winding stairs, and the broad white-stone expanse that led to the oak doors of the Great Hall. The porticos were empty now, except for the occasional page leaning over the balustrade to watch the melee in the courtyard below. To one side we could see what appeared to be the entire palace population milling about in the courtyard below us, noisy with the preparations and excitement of welcoming the grand train of visitors.

We stood in front of two arched openings in the wall facing the west, and I saw that the sun was racing toward the horizon. The busy courtyard below would soon lie in shadows, perhaps even before

William's party arrived. Philippe put his hands on my shoulders and turned me to him.

"It was William who told me about the treachery in my own court. When we met at Blois, we had private conversation, as well. He had information from the Templar network that John knows every move my armies make in advance. John's captain recently set up an ambush west of the Vexin that lost me threescore men, key archers from the Berry region." Philippe ran his hand through his black hair, a habit of distress since he was a child. "The devil of it is, I am not certain who is involved in leaking this information, nor how widespread this treason is among my courtiers."

Before I could reply, my brother moved closer to me. He looked around before speaking. "Have you thought further on our conversation of mid-week? About Constance? What is your plan?"

I looked past his shoulder, speaking in a low voice to match his. "I am waiting for the right time to speak with her. I have not seen her in these days, and I did not want to seek her out." I could feel his breath falling on my cheek in measured waves as he leaned closer, now his voice nearly a whisper.

"There will no doubt be opportunity enough in the next days. Two state dinners, a tourney, important guests." He gripped my shoulder. "She has to appear sometime!"

It was not a request, it was a command. "Yes, you are right," I said. "These days will provide the opportunity." Then, just as suddenly, his mood changed.

As he released my shoulder, he gently tapped my chin with his knuckle, in a teasing gesture only a brother would make. "Meanwhile, you will want to prepare yourself for William. If we tarry here in the corridor our guests are in danger of descending upon us as we are. They are nearly at our gates as we stand here chattering."

After a swift touch of his cheek to both of mine, a gesture he rarely made, we turned in opposite directions. In truth I was eager to ready myself for William's arrival, feeling suddenly disheveled and unwashed. But I was not ten steps away when Philippe called out to me. I retraced my path.

"Sister," he said, his voice dropping as he looked around for listening ears. "Study our monastic guests well tonight. I shall be keenly interested in your observations."

I nodded, puzzled. What was I to watch for? But he was already off and I was left frowning. Then I thought, with some humor, that my brother was only instructing me to do what I had planned already. He had no idea how interested I was in our monastic guests.

I paused, with my hand on the balustrade, and looked out over the stone to the courtyard below. Suddenly, the import of this event, the arrival of my beloved William and my son Francis, came home to me. At Christmastide William had agreed that I could at last inform Francis of his lineage: that he was my own son, and that his father had been the great Henry, King of England. The first Plantagenet king. William had insisted I hold off the telling because of the unstable political situation, but promised the time would be right when next he came. Then Francis would know the entire story and we would be mother and son to all at last.

The shouts of welcome in the courtyard below grew more raucous as the first horsemen rode through the open gates. Suddenly my feet grew wings and I could feel my heart lightening, despite the somber conversations with my brother and Joanna's cryptic note. William, home at last! And Francis with him.

PARIS

Chambers of the Princesse Alaïs

I arrived breathless at my chambers to find my maids gone, lured by the excitement in the courtyard. Fortunately they had heated the water for my bath in the large wooden tub near the fire. Glad was I to have trained them always to help me bathe before any public court appearance. I slipped into the still-warm water with gratitude.

The softness of my own apartments welcomed me. Here the tapestries were of animals and forests, but with references to peace and tranquility, not the hunting motifs my brother adored. The quiet blues and greens of the Toulouse tapestry-makers were soothing as I settled in the bath and contemplated the birds and flowers in the wall hanging before me. I could hear the fire crackling in the hearth as I laid my head on the cushion at the rim of the wooden tub, grateful for the moment of warmth and serenity. My irritation that William had not come to me for these long months was receding. I remembered only that I loved him once, and loved him still.

I was sinking into a reverie of William and me lying together in a sun-washed grain field outside of Poitiers when I heard a commotion in the hallway. Alarmed, since my wing of the castle was out of the way of common traffic, I reached for the robe that had carelessly been flung over a stool near the bath. Before I could do more, the door burst inward and William himself stood framed in the opening.

"Woman, where do you dally?" came the bellow of an army captain. "Is this the welcome I get after being away for three entire seasons?"

"William!" I shrieked. "The door!" Several curious male servants crowded behind him, but they quickly fell back just before he kicked the heavy oak shut with his heel. "Have you brought Francis back to me?" I called out as he came toward me.

"You know I have, love. I made that promise."

I shot from the water without another thought and threw myself into his arms, whereupon he shouted with feigned annoyance, "Wife, you are soaking wet and stark naked. Is that the proper way to greet a dusty, tired, ravenous knight, who has been away chasing dragons for months?" He swept me up and carried me to the bed, providing his own laughing answer. "Yes, it is the proper way, and you, as only you would, knew that truth." Tossing me on the bed, he stripped off his own doublet and hose with expert speed. Soon he was on me, and dust and water, fatigue and desire, mingled as we had our fill of one another like wild animals caged too long. All my choler against him for his long absence disappeared in the magic of his presence and his touch.

Afterward we lay facing each other, covered against the chilling evening air. I traced the deep lines that ran down each side of his face, from inner eye to the edges of his smile, thinking them the very illustration of his intense zest for life. Then he followed the outline of my cheek with the back of his finger and said: "Sweeting, I missed this face every hour that I have been away. These green eyes, like cat's eyes," and he touched gently the outer corners of each eye with his finger, "this full mouth," and he bent to kiss it softly, "and the billows of this dark hair which I dreamed of winding around my hands."

"And I, too, recalled your face and drew it with my charcoal more times than I can count." I stroked William's dark, iron-laced hair that swept back from his brow, well behaved even now, after all his exertions. It never fell in an undisciplined way over his forehead as did Philippe's. Now his cool, piercing eyes seemed to search out my soul and I felt that, indeed, he looked there for the mirror of his own.

"When I am in the south, everywhere I see men and women with your bronzed skin, and they make me ache for the sight of you."

"Ah, so you like those southern women!" I laughed.

He drew me to him gently, his hand behind my head. "Only your beauty moves me now, my love, none other," he said, loosening my hair and ruffling it as if I were a child. "But because King Louis took a bride from Hispania, and they had a daughter with bronze skin like her mother, when I am in the south I am ever reminded of you."

We both were silent for a moment. I thought on the dark-skinned princess, the mother I never knew. How strange that I carried her with me in my coloring, my black hair, perhaps my very soul.

He lifted my withered left hand and kissed it, a veneration as if it were the relic bone of some saint. It never failed to touch me, this warrior's gentling of my hand that had no feeling of its own. Only with William could I let it be as it was, feeling no shame or anger when he touched it, though it lay in his palm more like a claw than a hand.

"I have a surprise for you," he said in a quiet voice.

"I could wish for no other surprise than yourself and my son," I said.

"No, no, you will not say so when you hear." Now he pushed himself into a seated position, looking down at me with a warm smile.

"Francis has been knighted. By no less a personage than your brother, King Philippe, when we met with Raymond in Blois not a month past."

I scrambled to sit up next to him, surprised and delighted. "William, why did you not tell me immediately? How wonderful. The king did not say a word to me about Francis."

William shrugged. "Why would he? He knows of no connection between you and the lad. To Philippe, Francis is simply my former clerk, my squire. Because I made that vow to you at Christmastide to keep him safe, I had Francis always at my side." He chuckled for a moment. "Philippe must think Francis is my natural son, the way I never let him out of my sight."

I clasped my hands around my knees and shifted to watch his expression. The torches on the wall behind the bed illuminated my own features but cast his somewhat in the shadow. "William, I am so proud of Francis. Now that you have returned, we can tell him he is my son. I can scarce wait to see how he accepts the news. I am so fond of him. And I would love to have my brother know this fine young man for one of his own family!"

His face turned slightly away. I regarded him as he sat upright against the pillows. I could not read his feelings, but the brief hesitation before he spoke told me everything. My joy dimmed, like a candle flickering in a draft.

"Princesse," he began, and his use of my title brought on a feeling of foreboding. This was to be an official speech, not an exchange between lovers. "There have been some new developments since last I saw you. I do not believe it safe yet to tell Francis of his heritage."

"But you promised at Twelfth Night, before you left . . ." I could hear the whining child begging to surface in my voice. I pressed it down.

"I know, I know," he said, casting aside the linen sheets and furs and making ready to leave the bed, which movement also conveniently allowed him to turn his back to me. But I caught his arm and pulled it with all my strength. He was forced to turn and face me, half out of the bed though he was.

"Hold, Lord William," I said strongly, mimicking his formality by using his title. "Stay and explain what has caused you to change your course of action. I shall not be put off on the matter, sir."

"All right." He sighed mightily, resettling himself with an air of resignation. Now I edged around in front of him, sitting with my legs crossed like some young page. "While in Rome, I received a number of messages concerning the future of the English-French conflicts over land in the west. These came from various sources. But in at least three cases, I was told directly that a son and heir to King Henry had been found, that the news was spreading. At last, a challenger to King John has been identified. No one seems to know who this person is, but the rumors of his existence have spread as far as the court of the Holy Roman Emperor."

The beat in my chest had quickened so that I was certain William could hear it, and I put a hand up to still the sound. I was no longer playing the coy mistress. "My love, who could know? It has been such a carefully kept secret all these years. Only you and I have the history."

Now William looked at me full in the face and his mien was grave. "It is said the rumors are coming out of the court at Paris."

"But who, here . . . ?" My thoughts were racing and the panic must have shown in my expression. He reached out and took my hands in his.

"We do not yet know. I have men in three countries working on this gossip, to track the source. We will eventually find the men who started this. But the mere fact that such notions are in play means danger to Francis." He tightened his grip on me and his voice became urgent. "It may be only a matter of time before someone from the past, someone from Henry's court or someone who knew you when you were young, puts two and two together. They may remember that years ago you bore a babe at King Henry's court. And recall the gossip of the time."

"To make Francis a party to the secret could add to his danger." I spoke reluctantly, by way of talking to myself as much as to reassure William.

"You can see what a burden it would place on him." He fell back against the pillows once again and studied the dance of shadows on the ceiling. "But sweeting, we cannot let this news overshadow our time together. As long as Francis is with me, he is safe. And if he is ignorant of his heritage, he is unlikely to place himself in any danger, albeit unwittingly."

"And how can you keep him safe? And when will I be able to tell him I am his mother? And when will this wretched diplomatic business end and the pope give us our dispensation to marry?" The news had unsettled me more than I could say. Once again, I must put my own desires aside for politics. Only this time, politics meant the safety of my son. Suddenly I recalled the visitation of that morning and the premonition of danger to my son. "And when shall I know Francis is safe?"

"Alaïs, you never change. You are shooting questions at me like arrows. Cannot you restrain yourself for just a moment?" William propped himself on one elbow, arching his brow.

"And cannot you stop reminding me of my shortcomings?" I threw a pillow at him, trying to appear lighthearted. I must think on this matter later, when I was alone. For the time being, I would set it aside. To see my son would have to be the assurance of his safety for the present. "But where is François? I want to see him now."

"And so you shall, momentarily." He caught the pillow expertly, brightening at the sign of my returning good humor. "He is seeing to our lodgings here in the castle. He has that bright young English knight with him, the one he brought to court here last winter."

"The young man from Exeter—I think he is called Geoffrey. I remember him. The one with the large, dark eyes and the easy smile. He has a babe's open face, so at odds with a new knighthood."

"You have a good memory, lass. The two young men are alike, strong and courageous. They have become inseparable in our travels, and they have such ingenuity that I believe together they will be able to arrange all matters here in your brother's palace to their satisfaction. And no doubt to my own, as well." William chuckled, tousled my hair, and then added, "I thought to encourage the friendship. If young Geoffrey is with Francis night and day, there is less chance of any mishap, intended or otherwise."

"An intended mishap?" I echoed. I had thought of the possibility of my son injured in war, or a tourney, as such things happen in our time. The thought of other malicious events, less random, that could occur, was a new one. "Who would . . . ?"

"These are dangerous times, my love. Even though Francis's true identity remains yet unknown, he still belongs to my household. Not everyone favors my efforts to make peace in the south. I have received veiled and anonymous threats myself." William stretched upward, then casually put his hands behind his head, elbows out. He spoke calmly, but his words created a flutter in my heart. "Even the two monks who rode in with me, who think they are appointed by God and not the pope, could turn on me, wish me or mine harm."

"Ah, yes. The papal envoys. Philippe told me about them." I thought again of Joanna's letter. I had not yet decided what I would tell William about her request, but prudence whispered that I should hold back for the time being. At least until I had met these monks.

"With the pope's known protection, your household should be as safe as the court of the king of France," I countered, keeping the conversation in its channel.

William dropped his arms and folded them in front of his chest, his features assuming an ironic expression. "As safe as the court of your brother? Well, it may be so. But how safe is that? I told Philippe at Blois that there are foreign agents at his court. Some of your brother's own advisors may be corrupted. He cannot be certain of his own *sûreté*. Think you Francis would be safe where the king of France is not?"

I recalled Philippe's comments of treachery in his court and fell silent for a time. Finally I asked: "Where, then, would Francis be safe?"

"Within my sight, sweetheart, as you also would be safest by my side. Or should I say, instead, under me." William caught me and pulled me to him. I was off balance and helpless to resist. He moved onto me with such a swift motion it took my breath away. But it was only to run his hands down my body once, before he freed me. "But we must collect ourselves. I instructed Francis to give me an hour with you, and then to come with the servants who are bringing my fresh clothes."

"Oh, you are maddening." I scrambled from his grasp and quit the bed. "You arrive unannounced, interrupt my bath, and now you've taken over my chamber for your *toilettage*." I threw back the doors to the armoire and began to riffle through my robes. Where was the Lincoln-green wool, William's favorite? "Next you'll be taking over the bathwater itself."

"An excellent idea," William said. He rolled over and leaped off the bed in one motion, deftly catching his footing as his feet hit the floor. "I had intended that all along." He stepped into the tub. I watched his tall, broad-boned body and marveled that—at his age—he still looked as fit as young Francis when last I saw him. "This bath is not very hospitable, sweetheart. *Au contraire*, it is now quite chilly."

"And whose fault is that, Sir Lover?" I asked, and received a hearty laugh for my saucy comment. "As for me, I'd like to have my maidservants in to do up my hair, but I suppose it would give them scandal to see you lolling in my tub." My hair was disheveled, but, truth to tell, I was expert at catching it with my good hand in a band of ribbons I had made especially for the purpose. I pulled a loose robe over my head before I busied myself with this task, but could not forbear at last to express my pique at his long absence.

"So, Lord William, tell me. Why has it been these many long months since you have found time to make your way back to the court of France? One would almost think you had forgotten me. Only a handful of letters. And no news that you were meeting with my brother at Blois just weeks ago. I might have joined his party."

"That meeting was clandestine, my love. If I were free to tell you of it, I would have done. But Philippe swore me to silence. He came with only a few men, under pretense of hunting. He did not want anyone to know he was seeing Raymond."

I recalled Philippe's comment that it was William who demanded secrecy for this meeting, but I forbore to say anything for the moment.

"And what was the result of this all-important meeting?" Although I had not yet found the gown I sought I left off searching the garderobe and leaned against the door, my arms folded, waiting to hear what I could be told. I was behind William and he could not see my face, but I hoped the tone of my voice conveyed my serious intent.

"Philippe wants to avoid war with his cousin in the south, and the pope seems intent on pushing him into it. Rome has already sent two formal letters requesting arms and men from Philippe to threaten Raymond. The king thought a personal conversation with the Count of Toulouse might help to resolve the situation, make Raymond understand the gravity of his position if he continues to support these heretic nobles of his." William adopted a casual air in these remarks, which did not fool me one whit. I knew the well-being of William's mission depended on such diplomatic meetings.

"And was the king successful?" I pursued the topic.

"Not exactly." William now spoke tersely, as if to end the discussion. "It was not clear at the end what Raymond would do. He promised Philippe nothing, but he did reiterate his loyalty as vassal to the king of France." William reached out to the little oak table next to the tub, and snatched a handful of grapes from a bowl. He popped them into his mouth one by one talking all the while, as he deftly changed the subject.

"By the by, your son has decided he prefers his Anglo-Norman name, Francis, and has instructed us all to call him that, although he probably will make an exception for you if you prefer the French." He chuckled.

I could not suppress my smile at that sally. Francis was truly fond of me, of that I had no doubt, and the mention of my son lightened my heart. "Have a care, my lord, in making free with my scented soaps and oils. You'll have every woman in the Great Hall trailing you tonight if you are so liberal."

"Good, if it will make you sick with jealousy," he replied, sinking into the tub, oblivious of the waves of water spilling out onto the rushes. "The holy father was quite taken with Francis and all his talents." William surveyed the ceiling thoughtfully, his head cushioned on the back edge of the wooden tub as mine was earlier. "Philippe is not the only one who thinks Francis is my natural-born son. The pope is curious, as well."

"Ah, well, in a way, I myself think you are nearly his father." I came to sit on the edge of the tub and, catching up my sleeve, soaped his shoulders with my right hand. "Henry sired him, I birthed him, but 'twas you who saw to his care and upbringing."

"Only because you could not do it," he said, catching the fingers of my good hand and bringing them gently to his lips. "Have you forgiven me for having kept news of his safety from you those many years?"

"My love, there is naught to forgive. I have only gratitude that you raised and guarded my son. All else was beyond our control."

"Alaïs," William said thoughtfully, "I have a serious question to ask. I have been giving this some thought."

"My lord?" I asked, moving to a more comfortable wooden stool but still within his reach. We could have been any domestic peasant couple in a cottage at the end of the day, talking comfortably while the man washed the dust of his work away. I needed only his hose to darn to complete the picture.

"Do you ever wonder what Francis will say when he finds out what we have kept from him?" His voice was thoughtful, and I searched my soul for an answer.

"Do you fret over this? You have been his guardian for so many years. I cannot think he would be angry with you about aught." I spoke slowly, thinking more on William than myself.

"Indeed, I am of the same mind." William's voice became more robust. "I harbor no fear that Francis will bear me ill will for my part, for he has a kind heart and has ever been well disposed toward me since he was a small lad." William reached a long arm for a towel from the stool near the wooden tub. "He knows I care for him. And I want to reassure you that you should have the same confidence."

"In truth, I do have a lurking fear . . ." It was so difficult to put into words, even to William who knew the secrets of my heart. "Perhaps that is why I am so eager to get past the telling, to say to him all the things I must say as a mother. And to help him understand . . ."

"Because you think he will blame you for not holding on to him when he was a babe?" William shook his head, water sprinting from his mane of hair. Then he wiped his face with a *serviette* that I handed to him. "You know better than that. He considers you a kindred soul, though he does not know how truly kindred you are! Do you recall when you first met Francis as a young man, when he was my clerk? You did not know yet who he was. We were all traveling together. One night in Chinon you and the young lad, unbeknownst to the other, escaped my men to have an adventure. I had to spend my time looking for the pair of you, and found you both in the same crowded square—watching the town players. Living for illusion, the pair of you."

I had to smile at his feigned irritation. "Too bad, for the mighty Lord William, having to search for his family!" And I was rewarded for my impudence by a splash of water that dampened my gown and made me cry out with surprise.

"William! Will you never grow up entirely?"

"But now, do be serious," he said, as if it were I creating the frivolity. He took my hands, offered to help him from the bath, but he did not move. "I want to tell you, my dearest heart, that when we can, when it is safe to tell Francis who he is, we will support him in his choice of action over his claim to the throne of England. But we shall also offer him the chance to do nothing but stay with us as our son. Because by that time, pope or no pope, we shall have spoken our vows as man and wife."

Before I could give voice to the several responses crowding forward inside me, there were three loud knocks on my chamber door. William responded with a hearty, "Enter," and the door flew open. The tall, comely youth stopped short on the threshold, his cheeks flushing at the sight of his master in the bath.

"Forgive me, Princesse Alaïs," he said, with some confusion. "My Lord," he added, beginning to back out. Behind him three round-eyed menservants, each carrying an armful of wools and silks of the deepest reds and blues, stopped short also and the young, newly made knight was in danger of tripping over them. For indeed it was my son, the young knight Francis.

"Come in, lad. Please," I said, as I extended my hand to him, giving way to a broad smile from my heart.

"Put those clothes there, on the bed, and leave us!" I issued the order to the menservants in quite a different voice, gesturing with my gloved left hand, and then turned my attention back to the young man before me.

Francis went down on his knees but I raised him up immediately. "No, no, Sir Knight," I said. "Come, give us a proper greeting." His merry grin returned as I embraced him heartily, brushing each of his cheeks with my own.

"You look well, Princesse. I am happy to see you again."

I held him at arm's length, and saw with amusement that he was blushing. "And I am pleased to see you looking so hearty." I nodded to him. "More than you know, Master Francis, as I understand you wish now to be called." He bowed again, obviously pleased.

When he turned to address William I had an opportunity to observe the changes the last months had wrought in my son, for he had been away since Christmastide. He had spent the time well, growing broader shoulders. There was a look about his body now that was more manly, less the stripling youth he had been when they had set out the previous spring. His profile had changed, too, his bone structure stronger, his face wider as if even his features had decided to settle into adulthood. A scattering of youthful freckles was still visible, but they had grown faint under the tan he had acquired riding the roads of the south. And a full head of auburn hair, King Henry's coloring, *certes*, still framed his dear face.

For just one moment, I smiled to myself to think that William and I should have discussed his safety as if he were a callow youth. He looked every inch a man and could no doubt well care for himself should the need arise.

I was charmed to hear him, with all dignity, addressing William as if he were sitting in the Templar grand master's chair and not splashing about in my bath. "Lord William," Francis was saying gravely, "I bring you news. Abbé Amaury and Pierre de Castelnau are asking for an audience with King Philippe immediately. I think you should come now. Such a meeting should not take place without you."

"Do not fret, Francis. Papal envoys or not, Philippe will receive the monks when he pleases and not one minute before. And that will not be until the dinner hour tolls. I know how he manages things." I smiled as I spoke, although the mention of our other newly arrived guests called to mind Philippe's hostile response to them. I was not looking forward to sharing their table in the king's presence.

"But they say they have an urgent letter from His Holiness, Pope Innocent." Francis may have looked older, but he still had the insistence of youth. He swiveled his head to keep William in his sight as he spoke.

"I know, I know." William began to rise from his bath, throwing water everywhere like a mythical sea serpent frolicking in the ocean. I tossed him another large towel without ceremony. Francis glanced at me, the corners of his mouth twitching with humor as if in tune with my thoughts. "But of course they have a letter from His Holiness. And I have one too, as fine as theirs. But all in good time. *La princesse a raison*, Francis. Philippe knows I am here, and the king will not formally receive the monks without my presence." He winked at the youth. "The Templar seal still counts for something, even at the court of France. And if it did not, the king will yet operate in his own interest, which is to include me in the meeting. He has no intention of acceding to the demands of these monks, and he knows I'll help him out of his difficulty."

"So you and the king have already devised a strategy to deal with these messengers?" I dropped into a well-cushioned oak bench, and motioned for Francis to sit opposite me.

"After I met with Philippe and Raymond in Blois, I sent to the monks and asked that we gather north of Poitiers. I knew they were coming to Philippe's court, and I wanted to discover their mission, how they planned to approach the king." William perused the garments on the bed and, with his usual flawless taste, selected a deep, smoky blue wool tunic, gray hose, and an overcloak of the same lined in silver silk. Not being royal, he could not the wear the scarlet fabric made from kermes dye. But with such an attire, and his own regal bearing, he had no need of it to impress the court. "And take their measure, so to speak." He struggled with the closings on his tunic and

Francis leaped to aid him. My one good hand would have been of little assistance, I thought ruefully.

"And engage their trust?" I cocked my head to one side and he bent to stroke my cheek as he passed me by. "They must be dense as pigs not to see that motive."

"Ah, but it's no matter if they see it or not. They had no choice but to travel with me. After all I, too, am on the pope's own business." He picked up his sword, dropped on the floor in his earlier haste to bed me, and buckled it on, casting an amused glance in my direction. "And once we had joined, and conversed, I sent a courier on to Philippe with the knowledge I had gleaned, and some suggestions about how to handle these two minions of God who come seeking silver to make war."

"What sort of man is this Arnaud Amaury?" I rose now, moving toward my large garderobe to choose a gown, and my question appeared casual. "He has certainly made no friend of my brother, with his constant messengers begging for arms and men. Philippe is not happy to have him here."

William turned slowly toward me and caught my arm as I passed him. His gesture took me by surprise, as did his next words. "The abbot of Cîteaux? The venerable successor to the saintly Bernard? The former abbot of Fontfroide Abbey? Why, sweetheart, I think you will find he is the very model of the Prince of Darkness himself."

I was arrested in mid-motion. My face turned toward him and I knew my astonishment was written there. It was the controlled violence in his voice that startled me.

"Do you say so?" I made an effort to keep my voice unconcerned. Out of the corner of my eye I could see Francis sitting upright, perfectly still, as one might watch a storm roll over a hill on the southern moors of Henry's island. His face betrayed a surprise that told me he was startled by the vehemence of his master's response.

William recovered his composure as quickly as he had lost it. He shrugged, donning his cloak. He spoke in measured tones as he fussed with the closing of it. "Perhaps I should not speak so of God's representative, but there it is." He paused for a moment, then continued.

"Amaury was a knight and fighter when he was young, quite a good one it is said. Now he is known as a warrior of words, a heretic-fighter in the south where the great debates have been raging between the bishops and those who defend the new religion. Amaury has burning religious fervor, some say a bit too much for a priest. He is capable of killing anybody to defend his idea of God. Harsh words. No compassion. No mercy. And a swift sword promised to those who disagree with his view. But I should not predispose you." He finished with the clasp on his cloak, and brushed his hands together, like Pontius Pilate. "Meet him and judge for yourself. Then tell me what you think."

"How could you predispose me when you express such neutral views on the man?" My tone was light, but I turned back to my gowns to hide the expression on my face. I did not want him to see that I had more than a casual interest in his words. "By all the saints, I care little to meet this person, abbot or not . . . Although, on the other side of the coin, perhaps I should want to meet someone who inspires a show of emotion from one usually so controlled."

"You think it so?" William was suddenly at my side, his arm around me. "Come, give us a kiss, and I'll show you my control." And he planted his mouth on mine without waiting for my acquiescence, his arm stealing around me.

"William." I pulled away, annoyed. He had never been so free in front of the youth before. "Francis is here."

"Ah, Princesse, no more pretense. I have told our young Francis we will be married, as soon as this business in the south is finished. He has given us his blessing." And the grand master of the Templars in all of England winked over my shoulder at the young knight as he released me. Francis had a droll expression on his face, as if he were caught enjoying a bawdy play in the town square. I thought again of Chinon and had to smile myself.

"Enough, from both of you," I said, with all the firmness I could muster. "Out now, I say. My maids will help me prepare for the festivities. I'll see you in the Great Hall." And so saying, I threw open the oak doors. A page appeared and I motioned for my maids, who clustered at the end of the long corridor, where they dallied pleasantly with William's men.

"Your Grace," Francis suddenly said, stopping in front of me as William was hustling him out the door. "I beg leave to escort you to the banquet tonight. I would have you meet my friend Geoffrey of Exeter, who has been traveling with us. We were knighted together."

"I would be delighted, Sir Francis. Give me only a short time to prepare myself and return then with young Sir Geoffrey."

"Good plan," William said, clapping his hand on the young man's shoulder. "He shall enjoy a cup of ale in my chambers, tell three tall tales of his valour on the field to his friend, and return here in the space of an hour."

Mignonne and two of the younger maids slipped into the room and crossed behind the two men, swinging their small hips. William glimpsed them over his shoulder and turned back to me smiling. Suddenly he performed an exaggerated, sweeping bow to me, assuming a propriety that was almost comical given the bantering that had preceded it. Francis, flashing me a grin, followed his master's movements exactly. And I, shaking my head at their nonsense, was left to doff my gown and immerse myself once more in the bathwater, now tepid and somewhat clouded with sweet-smelling soap.

.5.

PARIS

The Great Hall

I chose the new white wool for the formal dinner, with the scarlet slashes in the long sleeves, and the tapered skirt with the elegant train. I counted myself lucky that my dressmaker had harried me into several new garments during the previous long winter. My interest was not usually lodged in paints and pots and gowns, but I was moved this evening to make my *toilettage* carefully, and not only for William.

I wanted to impress our guests while I was assessing them. They must see me as a person of power, not dismiss me as a decoration of this court, a useless royal, female bauble. I wanted them to consider what it might cost them to cross me. After I had taken their measure, I could better form my plan to block their every wish.

These thoughts raced through my mind as Mignonne finished braiding and wrapping my hair. She held the mirror up and rouged my cheeks and lips to my satisfaction, her own full lips dancing as she fought the urge to tease. I had not been so careful making my *toilettage* since William had last been to court and we both knew it.

"Do not dare to say what you are thinking." I rose and turned toward her, tapping her shoulder with my mother's pleated, hand-painted fan. Mignonne had been my maid for some years now, and there was much familiarity between us. "I have more in mind than just Lord William. I want to make an impression on the king's important visitors, as well. They must see me as a *princesse royale* if I am to have any weight in the coming discussions."

A smart knock on the door with a sword handle interrupted us. I threw a light fur over my shoulders against the damp autumn night air, and opened the door. There stood young Francis, splendid in a cape of deepest sea blue over a matching tunic. His hair was swept back and he had found the time to shave the stubble that earlier had marked him as a traveler. At his side was an equally dapper young knight cloaked in burgundy, the round-faced Geoffrey of Exeter.

"Francis!" I exclaimed. "You look every inch the knight you have become." My remark was met with a broad grin. Both young men bowed gallantly.

"Your Grace, permit me to present to you my dearest friend, Geoffrey of Exeter. We were knighted together, and have pledged our life-long friendship." He looked at me earnestly. "Perhaps you remember Geoffrey from his stay here at Christmastide?"

"Indeed I do," I said warmly. The young man began to kneel, but I reached down and placed my hand under his elbow to raise him.

"No need for such ceremony here," I said. "I have heard you are Francis's good friend. As his friend, I welcome you to Paris with all my heart."

"Thank you, Your Grace," the young man said gravely. "I am pleased to be here, and to be in Lord William's train. He is a great man. I seek to be like him someday."

"And so you shall, if you nurture your soul in valour as well as your body," I said. I then took the arm Francis offered me, and walked with the two young men into the night air.

The castle was arranged so that the primary apartments all opened onto flagstone corridors, which in turn were rimmed by low walls, balustrades, and pillars, but mostly open to the outside. Only the servants' quarters on the lowest level underground had no access to open corridors. The night air that brushed us briskly as we moved from my apartments to the central halls was most refreshing but by the time the three of us reached the Great Hall I was feeling a chill. Still, one benefit for me would be flushed cheeks and bright eyes that William might find attractive.

As we approached the massive oak doors that opened onto the Great Hall I talked gaily to Francis and Geoffrey, whose heads were bent low to hear me. I was making light of the various modes of flattery that they would shortly observe at the dinner we were about to attend. So engrossed was I in entertaining my young companions with somewhat ruthless imitations of courtiers vying for the king's attention that I failed to notice a small party approaching from the opposite direction. These men were also deep in conversation, and had the same hurried step. We arrived at the portals at the same moment, and nearly collided under the bright torchlight.

"Your Grace," exclaimed the man at the head of the group, pulling up short, as startled as I. "*Je suis désolé.*"

"Chief Minister!" I stared suddenly into the hooded eyes of Etienne Chastellain. Those eyes that gave nothing away. "Good even to you."

"Your Grace, we beg your forgiveness," he repeated, as he bowed deeply. "We were discussing an important topic, as you observe, and did not see your party." He gestured to the two men with him. I recognized one of them from my brother's conferences, Chastellain's chief scribe, Eugene. The third man was unknown to me.

Chastellain was a short, stocky man. A stranger could be forgiven for taking him for a peasant. His people were from the Burgundy countryside, I had been told, and his origins showed in his appearance. His balding head and broad shoulders spoke more of the former army captain he had been than of the role of steward, which his father and grandfather had played for years to the dukes of Burgundy. Hence their name, for they were the castellans of the dukes. Chastellain had risen in the ranks, however, through his military service to my brother, and eventually had been knighted. This, and a certain male bravado, gave him stature among the other ministers and their assistants.

The men with him tonight were lean, ascetic-looking clerics, trained in the law at Rome and later transplanted to the court of Paris. Chastellain's secretary, Eugene, in contrast to his master, was tall and thin, a floating sort of clerk with a permanent expression of disdain on his narrow, pale face, perhaps the result of having to look down on most people who approached him.

"And to the young men, greetings." Chastellain was bowing again, excessively polite to the young knights. When he had finished, he examined Francis closely. "Ah, I see you wear the insignia of the household of Lord William. You must be François, his former secretary and now, I hear, a knight of his household."

A chill swept over me at these words. I felt like a mother sparrow watching a raptor sweep past my nest. *Certes,* Chastellain knew all the secrets of the court. Francis had visited Paris with William at Christmastide, so the spymaster would have made it his business to know about him. The comment could be only a passing and casual reference. Still, I liked not his remark and liked still less the familiarity with which the minister dared to address those in my company. And then a new and dangerous thought appeared: Could the chief minister have a hint that Francis was of my own blood?

A quizzical smile played on Francis's lips. He appeared surprised that the king's minister could call him by name. When he bowed and seemed about to respond, I intervened hastily.

"As you can see, Sir Etienne, we are late for the affair." I smiled and nodded as I motioned to the guards, and they immediately flung the doors wide. "We may not dally, as tardiness annoys my brother, the king." I edged Francis forward into the room, and Geoffrey trailed after us, looking over his shoulder with curiosity at the small group of men who followed us at a respectful distance.

As we swept into the Great Hall the trumpets sounded to announce my arrival. Everyone turned at the signal of the horn's high notes. I was so proud to be on the arm of Francis, who looked every inch the knight he had become. Tall and auburn haired, he seemed to have developed the regal bearing that came naturally to the Angevins. In his manner he was so like his natural father, King Henry.

The company was splendid, as befitted the court of Paris the day before a royal audience and tourney. The miracle of Bruges dye had created a panoply of color around the room, the dark reds and blues vying for dominance as the court women had the first opportunity to wear their new finery this autumn. Deep-colored wools, the woad blue and weld yellow dyes, and the new brushed fabric called velvet, were everywhere. The silk veils of the women floated after them as they turned their heads, clouds of pleasing color.

I scanned the room quickly looking for William but then my attention was drawn by a small cluster of noble ladies close to the giant hearth. It was the curious headdress of one in the center of the group that captivated me. Her veil was extended in height by the use of a beautiful jeweled comb, the way that my mother wore her veil in my earliest memories. I had not seen this look in Paris since, excepting only my aunt Constance of Toulouse. I wondered who this visitor was. To judge from her dress, the woman must have come from somewhere in the south.

William was standing with the king on the other side of the largest open hearth. A small circle of knights and nobles ringed them, listening to the king who was talking with great animation. I saw my beloved look up at the bustle that surrounded our entrance, pleasure spreading across his face when his glance caught mine. The crowd, which had paused only briefly in its conversation as we made our way toward the group around the king, resumed their chatter. The hubbub began to mount.

Philippe was in the midst of telling one of his hunting stories, which he felt compelled to illustrate with sweeping hand gestures. The men appeared riveted. Several faces were familiar to me, nobles from surrounding counties who had come for the tournament. Others, appearing tanned from the sun, must have ridden in with William's party earlier that day.

As I neared the group those facing me gradually took their eyes from the king and followed my progress. The largest of the men, garbed in a deep maroon tunic edged in gold, had his broad back to me. He turned to see what distracted his companions and I momentarily recoiled. I recovered quickly, but not before I saw his heavy eyebrows rise slightly in response.

For, indeed, at this moment I looked upon the face of the man central to my morning visitation, one of the two leaders in the strange ritual I had been shown. His was the figure I had seen at the head of the circle of men as they plunged their tapers into darkness, the cowled monk whose long and fleshy face was revealed to me just before the darkness fell, the man who put his hand with such familiarity on Francis's shoulder. And the eyes that stared at me now were anything but friendly.

As I approached I noted the same jutting, aggressive chin I had seen earlier, the same ruddy skin and jowls. Now I saw the unruly tonsure which had been hidden by the cowl in my vision: the short, thick black hair curling around the bald spot as if in protest against the cloister's demands. The heavy brows framed rather small eyes that glittered as I drew closer, catching the light in a sinister way. Joanna's letter and my vision came together. This man and I were born to be enemies.

"Abbé Amaury," I said with a clear voice, moving now without hesitation to where he stood. I offered my right hand and he took it with his own flaccid paw, oddly soft for so renowned a warrior. I tucked my withered left hand into the pocket I had sewn into all my garments especially for that purpose.

"Of course, the famous Princesse Alaïs," he drawled, his deep, raspy voice rippling with authority. He bowed low and I felt the brush of his full, wet lips on my hand. I suppressed a brief desire to shudder. When he raised his head I removed myself from his touch though I met his gaze without flinching.

"So, you know me even without my monk's robes?" His gaze was searching. "Yet I do not think we have met before."

"No, I should remember if we had," I answered.

"Sister, welcome," my brother said, more quickly than seemed necessary. He sensed something uneasy in the air. "Then you already know the abbot of Cîteaux?" I could tell he was puzzled, no doubt recalling our afternoon conversation in which I had appeared ignorant of the abbott and his mission.

"Only by reputation." I smiled, striving for a dazzling effect. "Abbé, we are honored by your presence here. I have heard stories from many of your remarkable valour in opposing heresy." I kept all irony out of my voice, but William, sensing mischief about to happen, hurriedly intervened. He moved with lithe steps across the space of the circle to edge himself between my person and the abbot.

"And you must also meet Pierre de Castelnau, Princesse, Abbé Amaury's companion in service to the pope, and the court's good guest." He gestured to the ascetic-looking man in the Cistercian monk's white robes with whom he had been in deep conversation when I entered the hall. This man moved forward and it was with relief that I noted he, at least, had not played a role in my morning vision. Then I looked into his remarkable face and was astonished. The wide eyes of Pierre de Castelnau were deep and dark, and seemed to me glowing with pain. Suddenly I realized how occupied I had been with the person of Arnaud Amaury, with never a thought to his companion. His demeanor was humble as he bowed deeply to me. I gave him my hand without reserve.

"I suggest, Your Majesty, that we move to table now that the Princesse has arrived. I know my companions"—and William gestured to several of the men, including the abbot and the monk Pierre in his sweep—"are as famished as I from our long journey." He looked expectantly at the king, and Philippe, his chain of thought from the previous conversation now firmly broken, shrugged and nodded. The king offered me his hand, and I placed mine on his in the manner of courtesy. We moved toward the dais.

Francis and Geoffrey had disappeared from my side as I was absorbed into the king's circle, and I noticed that they had attached themselves to a group of younger courtiers standing near a trestle table, one of whom was the petite woman of the remarkable headdress. My son was in deep conversation with her. The woman, uncommonly beautiful, drew my brother's attention as well when we passed.

"We regret that the queen is not able to be with us tonight." The king was speaking to his companions, even as his glance lingered on the young woman. We advanced through the parting crowds to the high table where the plates of silver were already set out. "She would welcome you herself, but a recent illness has left her weak and she begs your forgiveness for her absence."

"Your Grace," William responded, "since there is a place set at the high table that the queen will not occupy, perhaps you would indulge me and allow my squire and knight, young Francis of York, to sit with us." He smiled winningly in my direction. "Princesse Alaïs is quite taken with his manners, they tell me."

Philippe nodded good-naturedly as we began our ascent of the stone steps. "But of course, if you wish it."

William scanned the room and located young Francis. I followed his glance and saw that my son had just seated himself next to the young woman in the unusual veil arrangement, and their heads were already bent together. Young Geoff was on the other side of the woman, engaged in intense conversation with yet another lovely maid. It amused me that my brother's court lacked no opportunity for young love to blossom.

William snapped his fingers and a page appeared, bending to hear the murmured order. The youth, his short cape a streak of burgundy, ran through the tables to where Francis was sitting. A brief exchange brought the young knight swiftly to his feet and he looked up in my direction. Our glances met, or so it seemed to me. Francis reached our party as we mounted the dais, attaching himself to William as if waiting the next instruction. I was touched by his quick response, and wondered, briefly, if it were for me or for William that he came with such alacrity.

"The queen's presence would have graced us, surely," Pierre de Castelnau was saying with no trace of irony in his voice, when I returned my attention to our group. "We hope for her improved health."

The abbot of Cîteaux grunted in agreement. He must be wondering how Pope Innocent's interference in the king's marriage could damage their request for his help.

At my brother's direction, I took the chair to the right of the king, the one usually designated for the queen. Philippe motioned for William to sit next to me, but then the king turned away. William directed Francis to take that seat instead. As always, he knew what to do and how to do it.

The abbot of Cîteaux set himself down heavily on the other side of Francis and William took the place next to his, while Pierre de Castelnau took the last seat in the line, beside William. To my brother's left side sat his current favorites, the Duc de Brabant and the Count of Champagne, the latter a former enemy with whom a satisfactory peace had recently been concluded. Philippe turned his attention to his nobles with a jest that caused them to laugh uproariously. It appeared that those of us sitting to the right of the king would be left to our own conversational devices. I guessed Philippe desired no casual dinner conversation with his monastic guests prior to tomorrow's audience.

After the king had seated himself, the others in the crowded hall took their places at the long tables laid out below the royal dais. Cushioned chairs and benches for the nobility were provided at tapestry-covered trestles on the lower level, and farther down the grand hall the lesser knights and their ladies who made up the bulk of the court were seated in slightly more crowded, if still festive, table arrangements. From our perch above it all I saw that they created a colorful panoply of deeply dyed blue and red wool, of silver threads and forest-green capes, of rubies and emeralds occasionally flashing in the light of a thousand torches and candles. The assembled court appeared to be a flock of exotic birds gathered for the king's royal entertainment.

The jongleurs and minstrels were filing into the hall now, bowing to left and right as they threaded their way among the tables. Conversation fell to a low buzz. When the serving began, there was a pause that allowed Philippe to turn to our side. He seemed puzzled to see the seating arrangement that William had reordered. Little did my brother know why I rejoiced to have the young knight seated next to me.

A small stage was set up for the jongleurs' performance, near to the main hearth and opposite and slightly below the royal dais. I spied a familiar face at the place of honor nearest that stage.

"Look, Francis, there below in the bright yellow cloak." The young knight followed my gesture. "That is Gace Brulé, the king's new favorite trouvère. Lately he has been performing his own songs for the court, and I suspect he will sing this eve."

"Is that the man from Nanteuil lès Meaux?" He peered over the crowd. "I heard his name, in Toulouse. He is nearly a legend. I am pleased to see him in the flesh."

I had to smile. "You will be even more delighted when you hear him. I understand the nobles from the south cannot believe we in the north have songs of *courtoisie* in our own langue d'oïl. They tend to think their troubadours are the only performers of this fine art. You must correct this impression when you travel there with Lord William."

"Do your trouvères sing their own songs?" Francis was still interested in things aesthetic, I noted with pleasure.

"The maker of the song always sings for the king, if he is present. Philippe expects it as a mark of respect to the crown. Is it not also done in the courts of the south these days?" It had been many years since I had spent summers in Poitiers with my stepmother, Queen Eleanor of Aquitaine. Sometimes I sighed for the gracious life there, especially when the winters in the north grew long.

Francis smiled. "Lord William and I were in Toulouse only for a short time in the autumn. But at the court of Raymond, the troubadours who were not of noble blood performed regularly. I heard myself the plaintive and beautiful poems of Pierre Vidal, '*le protégé du Comte Raimond soi-même,*' as he titles himself. They were exquisite songs of love." A look of pleasure crossed my son's face, as he bent forward to hear the plaintive love lyrics of the sweet-voiced singer.

I thought again of the young woman in the elaborate headdress and, without considering the consequences, I asked Francis: "Who was that young beauty sitting next you when William sent for you to join us? The one with the jeweled comb holding the veil, in the southern mode of dress."

Francis couldn't hide his sudden discomfort, visible to me in the light of the torches. I instantly regretted my overly direct question. He responded gamely, however.

"She is the sister of the Count of Foix, a small viscounty south of Toulouse." A smile spread slowly across his serious face. "Her name is Esclarmonde. It means 'light of the world.'"

I wanted to say I knew the Latin, but forbore to speak, so serious was the youth's expression.

"She is most interesting," he continued, absently stroking his chin in an unthinking imitation of William in deep thought. "Not like other maids I have known."

"How so?" I asked, now carried along by the conversation. I was driven by the prick of envy that defined me as the mother of a son old enough to love other women, and yet I was mildly amused by it withal.

"She talks of important things, not court gossip. She is concerned for the safety of her brother's land in the south. She is here to beg the king to resist interfering with her family's rightful heritage." He paused, his earnest words labored. "She has such intense beliefs. It is unusual in a woman and . . ."—he paused, glancing my way—"when she speaks with her great passion, her beauty shines forth."

The young man's candor and obvious feeling made me suddenly blush to question his private life. To cover my feelings I turned my attention back to the stage below. A simple murmur directing his attention to the revelers ended this portion of our conversation.

The servants had begun to serve the food and conversation had fallen to a low buzz to allow the music of the minstrels to be heard. My attention strayed as a Breton *lai* was begun, telling a new, albeit short, story of the adventures of King Arthur's knights. The lute's plaintive notes fell on the air as I contemplated the profiles of the monks seated near me.

The difference in their appearance was striking. The ascetic Pierre in his simple, white habit, lean but not hungry looking, watched the innocent spectacle with flickers of admiration on his long, thin face. It was difficult to see his form under his monk's robes, but there was no doubt from the way his facial bones jutted that he was lean from fasting to the point of danger. His mysterious dark eyes had moved me when we met at close range, and now I could see that his hands, placed carefully one over the other in front of him when not in use, had not one extra ounce of flesh on them. Yet I had to admit his expression had a sweetness that spoke of generosity and self-denial. I marked the outline of his face, and would attempt to draw it with charcoal at the first opportunity. Perhaps it would reveal more to me under my own artist's memory than it did now.

This monk seemed genuinely to enjoy the ferocious physicality of the entertainers, who did handsprings to amuse us between the rounds of ball juggling that Philippe so adored. I liked the look of laughter that passed over Pierre's face when the lead juggler tripped backward and deliberately dropped his many colored balls—one after the other—retreating in exaggerated embarrassment. I had the feeling that if the jongleur were truly embarrassed, the monk Pierre would give him all due sympathy.

Amaury, on the other hand, watched with a bored look on his face, fidgeting from time to time by shifting his bulky body or locking and unlocking his meaty hands impatiently as they rested on the table. His luxurious garb displayed his love of court finery. Did he enjoy dressing up, like some morality play actor who put on a costume to impress his audience? Or did he take a sensual delight in having the silk next to his flesh, rather than the harsh wool of the Cistercian robe? Or did he think himself royalty, entitled to the ermine worn by kings? I found my thoughts wandering into a field of wonder about his manhood. Was he celibate, as priests were now required to be? Or did he take his pleasures wherever he found them?

Suddenly the object of my attention swung his head around and looked past Francis, and directly toward me. I made an effort to assume a blank expression, which was difficult given my thoughts at the moment. Abbot Amaury stared as if he were sending me a hostile message. He leaned forward and our eyes locked in the bright candlelight between us. I raised my brows in a cool fashion, as if to inquire the meaning of his intense and somewhat disrespectful attention. He was the first to look away. I then continued to ponder his face for another full moment, searching for clues to this man's soul and his place in my private visitation of that afternoon.

Philippe finally waved the entertainers away, and began a more serious conversation with the nobles at his left side as the main service of the meal commenced. At almost the same moment, William initiated an exchange with the churchman seated next to him, leaning forward to include Francis and myself.

"So, Abbé, tomorrow you present the pontiff's letter of request to the king for an army to settle the matter of the south, yes? And if he agrees will you lead this army yourself?"

Amaury was caught unawares by William's question. He was in the act of moving his heavy jaws to work on the roast boar. He nearly choked, but in a moment had recovered himself enough to swallow and respond. "The Lord William honors me with his interest in my mission." There was a pause, during which the abbot threw down another gulp of port. "As you already know, it was only recently that I was named the papal legate to the good people of the south. Yes, the holy father begs the king of France to help me to restore them to the true faith. And if the king agrees to help, yes, I myself shall lead the army."

"And why do the people of the south need this restoration?" I asked innocently.

"Because they have fallen into error, Princesse." The abbot's sonorous tone recalled many leaden sermons I had been forced to attend at St. Denis. These tones must be the official voice of Rome, I thought. "They are consumed as a people with the rapidly spreading Cathar heresy."

"Surely, my lord Abbé, heresy is a weighty matter. It can and does exist. But why pay particular attention to the heresy of the south? I have heard tales of so-called Good-Men as far north as the lowlands. And were there not heretic burnings in Lyons, even in the memory of men still living?"

Arnaud Amaury was prevented from speaking for a moment as he attended to another silver plate set in front of him, this time turnips in spiced cream. I waved my own portion away as I waited for his answer to my inquiry.

After a moment Amaury looked up. His mouth was partially full as he waved his two-pronged Italian fork in my direction and spoke. "Yes, it is true. There have been many recent instances of heretics in other places. But the south is a veritable hornet's nest of them, madame. And where others may be isolated instances of holy men—or madmen—preaching here and there, this time the belief has spread across the populace. Every village is infected. And Rome has had enough."

He paused only long enough to wipe his mouth carelessly with his hand, a soldier's gesture. "The *Cathari,* or '*bons chrétiens*' as they call themselves," he added contemptuously, "pretend to want to purify the church, but they defy Rome at every turn. There have been many debates and many attempts to squelch this filth, but, far from killing the heresy, every effort to address these fallacies of belief has served only to encourage those who take part. New adherents are reported daily. A stronger approach is needed."

"But Abbé," interjected Francis unexpectedly, "everything I have discovered about this strange sect is to their credit. They seem to want to return to the simplicity of the early years of the church. How can Rome object to those who wish to adopt practices that follow the gospels and the example of the early Christians?"

We all turned to look at the young man, who glanced from one side to the other with a mildly quizzical expression. William leaned forward expectantly, a smile spreading across his face.

The abbot, who had addressed his earlier comments to William, now swung his strong jaw in the direction of the youth.

"And who are you to take up an issue with me?" he bellowed, causing my brother to interrupt his conversation and glance briefly in our direction. "You young puppy! How dare you speak to your betters on matters of which you are ignorant!"

I opened my mouth to defend young Francis, but William was already voicing a firm rejoinder.

"My Lord Abbot, permit me to introduce Francis of York, my former clerk and now a knight of my household." William signaled the footman behind him for more wine for the abbot. "He is educated and well traveled. He has spent much time traveling across the domains of the south with my retinue, as we have been exploring ways to avoid an armed conflict between north and south. He resided in Rome with me two years past, studying swordsmanship and theology."

William paused to allow the abbot to take in his comment, but before the man could speak he added, in a quiet voice: "Francis has the protection of my office. And the holy father was quite taken with his interest in diplomacy these past months." William turned his broad shoulders so that he was directly facing the abbot. I could see my beloved's face as he spoke. His eyes had narrowed and there was a warning edge to his voice. Francis, on the other hand, seemed unconcerned by the exchange as he continued to exercise his hearty appetite, but he kept glancing at the abbot between bites as if he still expected a response to his comments. Finally the abbot spoke.

"Young knight, even though you are protected"—there was a perceptible softening in the abbot's tone, although he bit off the end of this last word with menace as he leaned toward Francis—"you must learn to be careful. The situation with the heretics is complex and perhaps not quite understood by many. But these rebels present a real threat to Rome." Here he paused as if searching for *le mot juste*. "And those who defend heretics could find themselves accused also."

"Here, here, Abbé Amaury," William interjected firmly. "Francis is a knight known for his piety and his adherence to his faith. The issue of the *Cathari* beliefs as heretical is still far from settled. And you must admit, young Francis has the right of it when he talks about their imitation of early Christian simplicity."

"I'll admit no such thing." The abbot had returned to his dinner, tearing at his pheasant with a vengeance, as if it were the challenging young Francis under his pudgy fingers. I observed the exchange impatiently, wanting to speak. But for once I bit back my words, knowing that I was not the person to defend Francis. I was too close. And I did not want my care of him to be noticed. The abbot did not appear to miss much. Besides, my son appeared to be the abbot's equal with his next comment.

"As I heard it in the port taverns of Rome this summer, the main threat to the church of Rome is that the new beliefs will put many priests out of work, and then the gold they generate may cease to flow into Italy." The abbot was taking a swallow of wine and he sputtered as Francis spoke, which gave the youth the opportunity to add, rather playfully I thought, "Not that I support that view. My duty as a knight certainly lies in defending the faith of my fathers."

The abbot was not amused. He wiped his mouth and answered: "Do not cultivate insolence in your discourse, young knight. Pope Innocent has had enough of the pretensions of the people of the south, gold or no gold. They are not exempt from the faith as defined by our pontiff and the church councils. There have been dialogues for four decades and the Cathars still have not explained why they can call themselves Christians when they spurn the dictates of Rome. The time has come for action."

"And what actions do you propose, lord Abbé?" I asked in a naïve voice.

"They will bend to the will of Rome, or they will feel the sword of

God." Amaury smacked his hand on the table, and then downed the remainder of his red bordeaux, motioning for more with his other hand. My gaze met William's, and his eyes narrowed for a moment. He pursed his lips and shook his head firmly in my direction. Discreet though his gesture was, his message to me was unmistakable. Let it go. I smiled again in his direction. I could almost feel the thrill of bear baiting, but I forbore to challenge the abbot further. Not at this time, nor in this place. We would have another opportunity for exchange, I was certain.

"What is this loud talk?" My brother ceased his exchange with his *copains* and turned his full attention to the conversation on our side, causing us all to become suddenly subdued.

"Your Majesty, we were simply talking of tomorrow's audience, where we will present somewhat differing requests for your attention to the situation facing the south." William clapped his hands and rubbed them together, as if to end the discussion. "We shall each make our best case, and you will decide. Meanwhile, did I not hear that your own favored trouvère, Gace Brulé, was to perform at the conclusion of this fine feast?"

The abbot ignored William's cue and leaned around him to catch the king's attention. "We hope Your Majesty will not be deterred from sending arms and men to the south just because Raymond of Toulouse is your very own cousin." I felt a prickle of fear. The abbot was courting disaster. My brother did not like to have politics interjected into his feasts when he entertained visitors. He also did not favor veiled threats. His royal answer was sharp and immediate.

"We trust our cousin, the Count of Toulouse, implicitly. We have had numerous exchanges on this matter of the heretics with him. He is managing this matter." Philippe's voice had dropped to a lower tone, one I had come to respect as somewhat ominous. "The fact that he is our cousin is of little moment. On the other hand, the fact that he is our sworn vassal is compelling. He has our protection."

Parry and thrust. Take that, Abbé Amaury, I thought to myself, as the royal gauntlet went down unexpectedly.

There was a moment of blessed silence as everyone within earshot turned to look at the abbot, who sat back, finally speechless. I glanced to my right, and saw young Francis with the ghost of a smile on his face. I could not see Amaury's expression as his face was now hidden by Francis's broad shoulders. But I doubted that the abbot was smiling.

William interrupted again, this time with uncharacteristic abruptness. "My lord Abbot. If you please, we will delay this discussion until the morrow. His gracious Majesty has arranged further entertainment for us, and it would be churlish to continue this talk of worldly affairs."

"Quite so." Philippe picked up the cue quickly. "Tomorrow we will meet on these heavy matters in public audience in my presence chambers. You will have an opportunity to present your suit, Abbé Amaury. I will hear your arguments and give you my answer at that time. Meanwhile, let us attend the festivities without distraction."

With that, Philippe waved a casual hand in the direction of Gace Brulé, who had been awaiting the royal signal. The tall, lean singer was cloaked in elaborately embroidered forest-green silk, which he casually tossed back over his shoulder as he stood. He made his way to the hearth, and pulled a bench close. Then he placed his foot on the bench and began strumming a few chords on his lute. Suddenly the chords formed a melody and he began a mournful *lai* telling the story of the end of the great King Arthur's court. A grave quiet settled over the crowd. Philippe himself listened attentively through the first moments of the performance. I could see his clenched hand, resting on the arm of the chair, ease as the music calmed him.

Finally he placed his elbow on the wide oak arm of his royal chair and jammed his fist into his cheek as the servants approached quietly with more platters, this time of the mulled wine, fruits, and cheeses from the countryside that signaled the end of the feast.

Suddenly my brother turned to me and said in a low voice: "You see now what we have to deal with in these importunate monks. I want you at the public audience tomorrow, when I officially hear their request." He tapped his fork emphatically in front of me, adding abruptly, "And do not be late!"

I bent my head close to his and murmured the thought I had been turning over in my mind: "Brother, these monks bring a serious request to you. If you are set on denying them, perhaps the scene tomorrow in the presence room will be . . ."—I searched for a word— "difficult. Do you still plan to hold the tourney afterward?"

"Sister," he replied, his tone as dry as autumn leaves underfoot, "have you ever known me to cancel a tourney once the knights have gathered and wagers have been laid?"

"No, Your Majesty. Never." Tournaments were as dear to the king's heart as my drawing was to my own. I could not disguise my amusement as a smile spread across my face.

"Then why in the name of the Virgin's mantle would you think I would consider canceling tomorrow's joust?"

"Yes, Your Majesty," I replied demurely. Perhaps he was right. The festivities would take the edge off any unpleasantness that might occur when the monks were denied their request.

Philippe added: "Besides, Amaury is a bloodthirsty old reprobate and he, at least, will enjoy the carnage."

"Hunh. Let us hope when you have finished with him, he does not feel he is part of it," I muttered, causing the king to grin as he turned back to the badinage of his laughing nobles.

I scanned the faces around me. William was now engaged with Pierre de Castelnau in what appeared to be an amicable conversation. Amaury's face was flushed with the evening's wine. He glanced at the entertainment from time to time, but his expression was that of a man occupied with distant thoughts. The folds of his heavy face were traced by the dancing candlelight. Only Francis seemed to be watching the entertainers perform. Yet though he laughed, his brow was furrowed. He suddenly looked my way and gave me a reassuring smile. But I was not fooled. Something was troubling him.

Gace Brulé finished his long and mournful song, and bowed low in the king's direction. The crowd in the hall cheered. Taking the opportunity, the king rose and waved his arm to Brulé in a gesture of appreciation, then turned to leave. The Count of Champagne and the other nobles at the table stood also, still chatting together. The entertainers bowed and scattered, as was their custom when the king made ready to depart. William, now also on his feet, crossed behind the monks and offered his hand to me. I placed my hand on his right willingly. I was glad for his courtesy, yet I felt the evening was ending prematurely. *Certes,* there was more to be said on many topics. My spirit was far from tranquil as I bid the young Francis a hasty good night.

.6.

Chambers of the Princesse Alaïs

William made a show of leaving me at the door of my chamber, a charade of doubtful effect. I did not for one moment believe it fooled the guards stationed at the top of the stairwell nor the maids inside, shortly to be ordered from my room. When I entered, I found the fire had grown low in the hearth. My maids added wood at my direction. Then I sent them to retire and sat alone, watching the flames rise to lick the logs. My head was spinning with all of the strange events and mysteries that had passed this day.

Finally I blew out the great candle on the stand near the door, doused the torches near the hearth with the iron cup, and crawled into the recesses of my goose feather bed to watch the last flames. Just at that moment the door creaked. I was not alarmed. William had the habit of waiting until much of the castle was asleep before he came to me. It was a futile subterfuge, since most of our servants knew of his visits, but it preserved his sense of honor and his discretion amused me.

Tonight, however, I was impatient to quiz him about the events of the evening. He wasted no time coming to my bed, doffing his tunic and robe as he slid in beside me, under the furs. Although the embers were still glowing in the large hearth, the room had gone chill. I could feel William's cold feet at the same time as he surrounded me with his arms.

Suddenly he caught me and pressed his mouth hard on mine. It was some moments before I could breathe, and extricate myself from his close embrace.

"Hold, sir, if you would. Identify yourself, please!" I mocked him.

"What, you wanton? Identify myself? Have there been others in your bed, then, whilst I was away?" And I saw that he would not be denied, and so we laughed and made love that was no less intense than it had been earlier, for being less frantic and much more inventive.

At some point, as often happened, the rhythm of our lovemaking slowed. Without words, as if by mutual consent, we paused and lay quietly in each other's arms.

"My love, why . . ." I was the first to speak, and it was almost as if I were just breathing rather than giving voice to my thoughts. But William picked up the thread.

"Why can't we just stay as we are?" He knew me too well. "Together, quiet, apart from the outside world. You see, I know what you want without your words."

"But we were happy that way, at Ponthieu these two years past, until you were called away by the pope. And just when Francis was coming back to live with us after his knight's training. And we were to be married."

"And all that will come to pass again," he said, caressing my cheek with the back of his hand. "You need only a soupçon of patience."

"So you said when you accepted the invitation from Pope Innocent to go to Rome." I was insistent. "And yet here we are a year later and no closer to blending our lives."

"Yes, and I have been on horseback on the dusty roads ever since. Do you think I prefer that life?" William pulled himself to a sitting position and leaned his back against the wall. He pulled a small fur around his shoulders against the cold as he spoke. I heard a warning note of irritation in his voice, but I had a task that would not be put off.

"When you could be in domestic bliss with me, instead!" I said it playfully, but I could feel him stiffen.

"Alaïs, to continue to remind me of how happy I am with you, and how difficult it is when we are apart, does no earthly good. I made a commitment to assist the holy father to settle the problem of the Cathar heretics and Count Raymond's lax oversight of his petty nobles, and I must hold to that. You only create more unhappiness by introducing this topic over and over." The room lay in shadow, but I could make out the outline of a frown as the moon cut a path across our bed and caught his face in the light. I edged up to a sitting position as well, so we were once again side by side, though far from an embrace at the moment.

"I am sorry to press you. I just wish . . ." My voice drifted off for, in truth, my only wish was that we could be together again in his lands on Ponthieu with Francis near. The thought of my son brought another pang to my heart, a needle spreading the heat of fear.

"I know you are not happy here at court." William was speaking, but I scarce attended him. "Nevertheless, I want you to stay with Philippe until I return in the spring. Then, I promise you"—and again his arm encircled my shoulders—"what we both wish for will be accomplished."

I did not move away from his embrace but I said nothing. He continued, as if the matter were settled.

"Now I have a question to put to you, something that has been puzzling me for hours." He took his hand and placed it under my chin, turning my face up to his own. "I thought you said you never met the

Abbé Amaury. Yet, when you approached our group tonight in the Great Hall, you walked right up to him as if you knew him."

I sighed. "I had a visitation this morn."

"One of your waking dreams, as you are wont to say." William nodded.

I swallowed, remembering the feeling of being pinioned against my cushions as if in bonds, unable to move, the strange half-light surrounding the figures who gradually became visible.

"The abbot's face was plainly visible in the scene that was given to me. When I saw him again this evening, I was transfixed. I could not keep myself from confronting him."

"In the visitation, what happened?" William understood my gift of second sight, and knew from experience that, no matter whence they came, these visions carried meaning.

"I saw a ring of thirteen men. One of them was in the white habit of the Cistercians, and he had the face of Amaury. It was a vivid apparition and unmistakably the abbot. Ten of the men wore red hats. Another had a tiara and one next to him wore the Cistercian habit. When the monk's cowl fell back his features were revealed. It was the face I saw when I came to the king's group of knights. You recall the *abbé* asked if we had met before. I told him no. That was a truth, as he had never seen me."

"There is something you are not telling me." William took his arm from around my shoulders and turned full to me. I met his gaze.

"I would I need not tell. But you must know. Francis was in the circle as well. I saw him clearly."

"What transpired in the vision?" William's staccato questions were those of a captain quizzing his lieutenants.

"The men stood in an oval. When a bell tolled, the man in the tiara gave a signal. With one accord all the men in red hats plunged their torches into the ground."

"And Francis? What of his role?"

I shook my head. "He only stood there. As if he were a reluctant guest, taking no part." I paused. "But as he was standing next to Amaury, the abbot threw his arm around Francis's shoulders, as if he were a possession."

William suddenly cast off the furs and threw his legs over the side of the bed. This time he did rise, muttering more to himself than to me. He retrieved his hastily discarded cloak from the floor and threw it on. Then he began his habitual restless pacing.

"This vision is a confirmation of what I suspected," he said. "Amaury will go to any lengths to get what he wants." He turned back to me when he came near the bed again, where I still sat clasping my knees. The moonshafts behind him illuminated his broad shoulders, but the shadows around us frightened me. "Amaury considers this business with the heretics a war. And he is capable of using any stratagem to obtain his ends. He sees me and my diplomacy as an obstacle. He would not be above taking my knight as hostage."

"William!" I was stunned that he had voiced my deepest fears. "Then you must leave Francis with me. Here, where that man cannot touch him." In my agitation I, too, began to climb from the high bed, sliding my feet into the warm beaten-wool slippers, pulling a robe from the end of the bed around me, tying the sash. All these ordinary acts were performed with a kind of frantic madwoman haste. "You must leave him here."

"Alaïs, I've already explained there are agents at this court who are in the pay of John of England. If John credits the rumors about an heir surviving Henry, he will know it might involve you. You are at this court. This would be the first place he would look for that heir."

"So Francis will not be safe from John if he is with me, but he might be in danger from Amaury if he is with you." I placed my hands on my hips. "And if the odds are even, then I believe the mother's heart must win."

"You might think it so. But I tell you in this case I must assume the responsibility. I have men at my command, fast horses and willing swords. I will keep Francis always at my side. That is the only way to assure his safety." William talked more rapidly than was his habit, as if to forestall any comment I might make. The silhouette of his hand in the moonlight made stabbing gestures, as if it were already wielding a sword to defend my son.

I turned and picked up a small fur from the oak bench to wrap around myself, feeling the night chill as William had. Then I proceeded with deliberation to light three candles nearest the bed with a taper put into the only one burning. This act created only a small circle of light, but the bed and its surrounds were illuminated. The dark, earlier so friendly to our lovemaking, now seemed threatening. I took a cluster of ribbons tied in a loop from the table and came back to sit cross-legged on top of the bed. There I wound my hair expertly into them whilst I considered carefully my next words. William began to pull his wool tunic over his head to ward off the chill. I knew now there would be no more lying together for us this night. But in truth, I was so disturbed that my desire had fled.

Finally I made my decision. "There is something else you should know," I said with firmness. I had his attention. "Something odd occurred tonight, an accidental encounter. Or so it seemed at the time. But perhaps it was less chance than I thought." I paused. I was about to tell him something that would bolster his case for taking Francis away, but I knew it was necessary. If I were to think of the safety of my son, I knew I must confide in this obstinate man, who after all desired the well-being of the young man we both loved.

"What came to pass?" William had pulled on his hose and reached for his sword. But he seemed to pause, and let it drop again. He came now to sit next to me on the edge of the bed, with the easy manner of one who believes he has won an argument fairly.

I pushed past my annoyance at this and tried to recall the details of the meeting at the door of the Great Hall. "Francis and Geoffrey were with me. We were coming into the Great Hall for the feast. As we approached the door we were involved in talking, heads bent and that sort of thing. Suddenly we nearly collided with Etienne Chastellain in the company of three clerks." I paused. "I don't like that man, nor the clerk who seems stuck to his side, that tall one, Eugene."

"Go on with the story." William made an impatient, brushing motion with his hand. "What caught your attention?"

"Chastellain knew who Francis was. He greeted him and made reference to his place in your household. He made a point of saying it and seemed to enjoy my surprise." I watched William's face in the moonlight and could see the outline of his pursed lips. He tapped his finger against them, thoughtful.

"And one more thing. My brother told me this very afternoon that he does not know which of his counselors to trust in this court. And that includes Chastellain. What if the chief minister is in the pay of King John? And what if he has already heard the rumors about Francis? He could be in league with Amaury, each working with the other for his own ends here at court."

"Alaïs, all of this simply confirms my earlier decision. Francis would be safest with me, where I can defend him if need be." William clapped his hands together with maddening finality, making as if to rise.

"Perhaps." I put my hand on his arm and paused until he turned to me once more. "But beware. You heard him challenge the abbot this very night at the king's own table. I doubt that Amaury will forget his name, nor your defense of him. Now we have two enemies who are watching Francis."

For a moment we fell silent. Then William rose and, taking one of the tapers, padded to the hearth where sparks still lingered among the embers. He lit it from the dying fire and used it to bring several wall torches to life. Then he came back and flamed all the remaining candles near my bed, as if to dispel the fears I had voiced with the darkness. He edged me over on the bed and sat beside me.

"Tell me more of what you suspect about the treason here at court. Perhaps if we can clean the court of corruption in the king's own council, Francis would be safe here." Lest I perceive an opening for renewed argument, he added hastily: "Later, that is. After this next journey."

I rubbed my brow. "Chastellain makes me uneasy. I do not trust him. And Philippe has said that he has a matter that he wants me to look into, a conspiracy here at court, and I am not to tell anyone. Not even his chief minister. Surely that is a signal the king does not have full trust in him, either."

"I confess I must take responsibility for putting that thought into Philippe's head. We discussed the matter when we were at Blois, after Raymond left." William, restless as ever, now made his way to the long table, pouring us each a goblet of spiced and watered wine, ever-present in its earthenware pitcher bearing the royal mark of the Capet family. "Based on what the Templar agents tell me, John knows every move Philippe's captains make in the west before they even have their orders. There is someone at this court who is feeding them information. Some person who is privy to the king's highest discussions. Chastellain is one possibility."

I thought for a moment. "Last Sunday at St. Denis there was an interruption right at the consecration of the host. Three knights shouldered their way to the front of the church to see Etienne Chastellain, and the king was in a choler about the interruption."

"And did Etienne then leave the church before Mass ended?" William now seemed oblivious to all thoughts of leaving my chamber.

"No, in fact he seemed annoyed to have the interruption. Perhaps because he knew the king would be displeased."

"And would ask questions Etienne did not want to answer," William countered.

"So he dismissed them immediately and later told the king there was no reason for the interruption."

"Well, it could have been any number of things." William raised his cup to his lips, his voice thoughtful.

"I don't think Philippe believed him," I said, frowning as I recalled the scene in front of the abbey church. "And there was another strange event at that same Mass. The *abbé* at St. Denis used an unusual chalice, one I had never seen before. It had the longest, thickest stem surely ever made, braided round with gold. The cup was studded with jewels, but of course many are made that way for the great churches. It was the length and broadness of the stem that drew attention. My aunt Constance rose from her kneeler. She was riveted by it when the priest held it up for veneration of the host. Even my brother took note of her strange reaction. Then he told me later that Raymond himself had given him the chalice to take to St. Denis for safekeeping."

"Did he so?" William sat down again on the edge of the bed, facing me. "He said nothing to me of this." He looked puzzled.

"I surmised when he told me it was some deep secret that Raymond did not want bruited about. But what do you think is the provenance of this dazzling chalice?"

"I heard tales in my youth during the wars in the Holy Land about a sacred chalice that belonged to Saint John. It had such a stem of braided gold."

"Saint John called the Baptist?"

"No, the other Saint John, the young one who was close to Christ. John, called the beloved disciple. He who is the author of the fourth of the gospels."

"So what was the story of this chalice?" I drew my knees up for warmth, and William tucked the furs around my legs.

"The legend is that at the Last Supper Saint John was given a cup of poisoned wine. He—"

"Wait," I interrupted. "Who would give Saint John poison? It was Christ they wanted out of the way."

He waved away my question. "This is a legend, Princesse. Yours are questions for university faculties in examinations. Do you want to hear this or not?"

I nodded and held my tongue.

"It appears that Saint John recognized the danger in drinking the contents, blessed the cup, and a snake crawled out over the edge and slithered off."

"Heavens above!" The story brought a smile to my lips. "What a story. And that same chalice found its way to Toulouse?"

"Yes, it was brought back by some of the southern knights, along with the story of its provenance, when they returned from the wars in the Holy Land. It was held in Béziers for a time, in the residence of the Cathar bishop there. Then it disappeared, some said into the safe houses of the Cathar bishops. Suddenly it turned up again in the Toulouse cathedral, no one seemed to know how. After that it was venerated there as a true relic of Saint John by the faithful, including Raymond, Count of Toulouse. And well guarded it was, by the cathedral sextons."

"Was it ever out of the church?"

"Once a year it was taken on procession for a month throughout the towns of the Toulousain in the summer. This past year, I heard reports that it was stolen while in procession between the towns of Albi and Carcassonne."

"So it was taken by the count's own vassals? The Cathar nobles?"

"So it would seem. But perhaps not. The south is a mysterious place just now. Any number of persons could have a motive for stealing this chalice." William frowned. "It may simply be that someone stole it to bring it north, to sell it for the gold." He paused. "But if it were in the hands of Raymond's churchmen all the time . . ."

"Perhaps it wasn't stolen at all." I finished the thought.

William moved his head from side to side, as if considering all the possibilities, and screwed up his face in thought. "What could be his motive?"

"Raymond may have staged the theft so he could dispose of the chalice for his own purposes."

"I cannot think he means to sell it. Raymond is many things, but he is not that devious." William stroked his chin in thought. "No, this object has some other value. Raymond must know what it is, and he means to secure it by sending it here."

"And what do you make of the attention of my aunt Constance to this chalice during the Mass?"

"She may have recognized the object from its days when it was shown in the Toulouse cathedral for veneration by the faithful." William was making ready to leave, rising with obvious reluctance and reaching for his sword belt. "These are events we must ponder, but I must take my leave, *ma chouette*. I have some preparations to make for our audience with the king in the morning, and we both must sleep."

As he bent low to kiss my lips, I grasped his hand and pulled his head closer to me. Taking my chance, I said: "William, truly, is it not possible that I tell Francis I am his mother before you leave? If he were sworn to secrecy . . . How would telling him change anything in his circumstance?"

He straightened, looking down on me. "Alaïs, please do not ask me this again. He cannot know at this time. It would increase the danger to him, and that is already grave."

I know William spoke to impress me with the reasons for his adamant denial. But the sound of the words made my heart go cold.

"All right," I said. "The day is yours on this topic. But mind, you must keep him safe. If anything should happen to him before I have the joy of telling him I am his mother, I shall never forgive you."

I had never come close to making a threat to William before. He looked into my eyes, for now it was I facing the moonshafts. He took my face between his hands, searching as if to discover some secret there, but he did not kiss me again Then, abruptly, he turned and left my chambers.

The King's Presence Chambers

The next morning dawned gray and foggy, not a good omen for the tourney to be held that afternoon. But before the entertainment, we were all required to suffer one of those interminable public audiences that royal life demanded. This one would decide the fate of the monks' mission to obtain men and arms to fight the nobles of the south.

I had been warned not to be late, so I presented myself in a timely fashion in the awe-inspiring presence chamber of the king of France.

The liveliness and pageantry of the royal receptions were always appealing, but even more so in the declining days of October, when days were often clouded with mist and rain. And this gathering would not disappoint. The woad blues and madder reds mixed with weld yellows in the festive gowns and capes worn by the courtiers.

In one end of the room, the jugglers Philippe found so entertaining were informally tossing balls and standing on their hands, drawing amused onlookers from the small groups crowding into the room.

Philippe, whatever his personal inclination for privacy, was a master of the public ceremony. His royal guard were lined in rows against the tapestries hanging on both sides of the chamber for warmth. They stood stiffly at attention, and although they were not in chain mail (Philippe was more subtle than that), the Capet emblem was prominently displayed on their tunics. I noted that swords, usually not worn in the royal receiving rooms, were visible in their scabbards. Their presence constituted a fine point of implied power that would not be missed by the papal legates.

I saw Francis against the far wall, in animated conversation with three other young knights. Young Geoffrey looked up just at that moment and, recognizing me, gave a generous smile which I returned in kind. William came to my side immediately, to escort me to the front of the chamber.

I moved toward the king's dais, nodding to the courtiers as I went. It cost me nothing to be pleasant, even though I knew they gossiped about me at every turn. Still, I was pleased to be on William's arm, as he always created a great stir. As Princesse Royale I stood apart from the others, near the platform that bore the king's throne. I felt no lack of comfort in my solitary status. The court allowed me solitude, whether from fear of my sharp tongue or because of my closeness to the king, or perhaps out of the old superstition that I was a witch because of my withered hand. I would not be drawn into conversation if I did not signal my desire for it, and today, tired as I was, the respite was welcome. William had left me after a low bow and a murmur of, "We'll have time alone later, *ma chouette*," that (I was thankful) could not be overheard. He joined the two monks as they were standing near the throne, preparing to present their credentials and their suit for men and arms to take to the south.

Philippe's vassals and knights stood clustered in groups about the large hall, each in splendid and colorful array of dress, each surrounded by his own men and, in some cases, women as well. Brightly colored pennants with various family emblems were standing in the center of each small group like so many plumed birds, held by pages dressed in their patron's colors. After the formal part of the program, various groups would mingle. But for now, it was clear the court was organized for a display of power.

The vast room sparkled, in contrast to the gray October day outside. All the torches were lit, and the huge rings of candles hanging by chains on wooden tiers from the ceiling beams created dancing light. The woven Damascus carpets that Philippe had brought back from the Crusades ran the room from one end to the other, masking the sound of our steps, and muting the rising buzz of talk among the courtiers. The tapestries on the walls, with their fine scenes of the nobility's hunting and domestic activities, softened noise even while they colored the scene.

The women without men were there, also, the wives of the nobles and knights gone to war against King John, fighting even now somewhere in the west. Widows of nobles long dead formed a small group of their own, no less formidable for the lack of men, as all who were not still in black were arrayed in the jewels and richly colored velvets of their station.

Also present were the priests of the court, and some from the city of Paris, in their clerk's robes. A large group of monks from Cluny were gathered, identifiable by their black Benedictine robes, the tall abbot in their midst marked only by the heavy jeweled cross hanging from the large gold chain around his neck. The abbot of St. Denis in his full, gold-thread-trimmed, purple regalia holding his crozier was talking with the newly appointed bishop of Paris, vying for glitter award with his own glistening trim.

I was amazed that Philippe could put together such a vast assembly to impress our guests on short notice. But then I had the thought: Their visit must have been timed to be this day, the day of the last tourney before the winter set in. No doubt Philippe had given William private orders as to the very day when he should arrive with his companions, so as to impress the papal legates with the full spectacle of his court.

Close to the dais on which Philippe's throne was set, but on the opposite side from where I stood, a cluster of five men had positioned themselves apart from the others. These men were the members of the king's privy council, his closest advisers. They wore longer robes, not the tunics and hose of the knights, and most were clean shaven, in contrast to the short-bearded style of most Frankish knights. While their robes were of the finest wool, the colors were severe and formal, ranging from forest green to deep burgundy.

The short, muscular figure at their center, however, was robed to be noticed. He wore deep crimson rimmed in silver, as if to deliberately set himself off from his more sober colleagues. It was the ubiquitous Etienne Chastellain, surveying the room with a sardonic expression on his face. As I recalled how easily he had identified Francis the night before, and how quickly he managed to let me know, my heart chilled. My own gaze went momentarily back to my son, who had now been joined by William and several other knights. I returned my attention to the chief minister.

Chastellain looked formidable this morning in his opulent robes, the brilliant red silk sash of his office crossing his broad chest. That, and his commanding look as he scanned the room, set him apart from the crowd of ministers.

Etienne Chastellain, chief minister to the king and his known confidant. The court called him "the wizard" behind his back because, it was said, he could make people disappear. I think he knew this name and was pleased with the notoriety. When he saw me he nodded slowly, as if somehow we shared something. Not quite a bow, I thought, but more than a passing glance. I forced a slight nod in return, while I pondered the king's rising lack of trust in this counselor. Then I turned my attention again to the assembly.

And, *mirabile visu*, not twenty paces away stood my uncle Robert, Duke of Orleans, marked by his height and the way he carried himself. I knew him even before he turned around to look at me, and gave me his most dazzling smile. The grand master of the Knights Templar in France, my uncle rarely came to court unless summoned by Philippe. He cared little for my brother's current counselors, and today he stood apart from them, but equally near the throne. He was surrounded by his men, who provided a great contrast to the pale-faced ministers. Duke Robert's men, hardened by travel, had faces bronzed by the sun. They were boisterously regaling one another with tales that generated shouts of laughter that made even me smile.

As my gaze swept across the room's tableau I spied my aunt Constance, standing with a group of women off to the side opposite me. I was astonished to see her wearing a magnificent green and gold silk headdress. It was quite tall and held up with jeweled combs, according to the southern style that had crept into Toulouse from Navarre. The Paris ladies, with their hair bound and covered by uninspired veils held in place with golden circlets, had no match for it. Her dress, too, appeared nothing like her ordinary modest apparel, being made of a rich green wool trimmed in matching velvet at the neck and lining the long, pointed sleeves. What was the occasion that prompted her to cast off her usual drab garments?

As I watched my aunt, I recalled the strange look on her face the previous Sunday, at St. Denis, when the chalice had been raised, and I wondered again at the source of her interest. Suddenly someone standing in front of her moved slightly to the side, and I had a better view.

Even though her eyes were downcast, I could see her wizened face folded into an expression of pain and boredom. She tapped her closed fan against her hand as if waiting for it all to end. She had grown stout and was unhappy and her finery could not make up for all of that.

The women about her were mostly her own retainers, brought with her when she returned to the court of Paris, and their dark, southern faces were somewhat familiar. But when Constance leaned forward at that moment to murmur something to a companion, her fan opened to keep the words close between them, I saw the beautiful young woman who seemed to hold appeal for Francis the previous evening.

This young woman appeared even more attractive in the light of day. She wore no distinctive headdress now, indeed no headdress at all. Her hair, piled on her head in the fashion of the Occitan, was laced with jewels. So also sparkling stones decorated the points of the fan she carried so that when it opened they caught the reflected light of the hanging candles. Her vibrant clothes and jewels identified her as nobility, her style of dress as a stranger in this northern court, her dark skin as a woman of the south.

Then I saw my son, Francis, detach himself from a group of young knights and move toward the bevy of women who surrounded my aunt Constance. I was puzzled by this, for I did not know that Francis and my aunt were acquainted. But the object of his real attentions soon became clear. He gave the countess a perfunctory bow, kissed her ring, and quickly proceeded to turn his charm in the direction of the little beauty by her side.

"Your Grace, I was asked to deliver this message to you." My thoughts were interrupted before I had time to enjoy again the slight mother's jealousy that had pricked me the evening before. One of my brother's personal servants, tall, slender, and composed, stood before me. I nodded my thanks as I took the note in my right hand but before I could inquire from whence it came he melted off into the crowd.

I saw my brother nearing, as he slowly made his way down a center aisle marked by the royal carpet. He was bowing to this and that knight or group, and his progress was slow, but I had only a moment to decide whether to examine the message I had been given before I need speak to him. My curiosity overcame me.

I worked the wax seal open as quickly as I could with my good hand and glanced down to see a single line scrawled. While I could not be certain, it appeared to be the same spidery hand that penned the note that had so upset my brother at our recent conference. I read the short phrase with astonishment:

If you would understand the mysteries of this court,
follow the golden thread to the south.

I stuffed the note into the pocket on the left side of my gown (always awkward to cross the right hand over and find the opening), and slipped my withered hand back into the space as well, further crushing the parchment.

The king was now mounting the dais to assume his throne. I tried to look unconcerned, despite the flush I knew suffused my face. In the name of the Virgin's mantle! What was the meaning of these bizarre warnings and who was behind them?

The queen's throne, next to the king's but on a slightly lower level, was empty. The court had grown used to seeing it so, since Ingeborg had not once taken the chair since her return. This was her way to show her displeasure with Philippe, and no doubt the whole of France. Still, the kingdom churned onward, doing its business despite her absence. And so it was this day.

I was just musing that Philippe and Ingeborg were in accord on at least one item, her regular absence from his court, when I saw the king turn and beckon to me, clearly meaning me to mount the royal dais after him. Puzzled, I advanced slowly. I had no desire to be singled out, but the royal gesture could not be ignored. Conversation slowed as the court shifted its attention to me.

I made a low ceremonial courtesy before the king. He then reached down to take my right hand, and guided me to the throne at his side. A quiet descended over the murmuring court from the front to the back, like a cloud, as courtiers strained to see what was occurring. Philippe carelessly dropped into his own, larger throne, resting his elbow on the arm and his chin on his hand, as was his wont, his right foot thrust casually out in front as he spoke to the court in his strong voice.

"As you see, the queen is unable to attend our court. I have asked my sister, Princesse Alaïs, who is renowned for her—uh—wisdom to aid me in considering the requests that are presented here today."

No one could have been more surprised than I at that moment. Although the king had often sought my advice over the years, such meetings were always in private. I suspected that he feared my withered left hand might cast a shadow over my counsel, even that he might be accused of consulting a witch. Why he should choose now, and the occasion of the visit of these bothersome monks, to indicate that he listened to me was not clear. I assumed an expression of benign indifference as I sank into the chair of the absent queen, hiding my sense of excitement. Chance had given me the opportunity to aid Joanna in a way I had not anticipated.

The herald announced the petitions that would be heard, and the formal audience began. Chastellain and his coterie stood off to the side, watching. An air of expectation had settled over the room.

At first there was much droning, beginning with formal introductions of the dignitaries made by the court herald. Then Amaury and William each presented a scroll of credentials. Chastellain stepped forward and took these, as the king's chief minister. There was more bowing on both sides through this part. Chastellain then brought these scrolls to Philippe, who merely glanced at them and waved them away.

William, tall and regal-looking in his black tunic with his short cloak of matching wool and fox tossed carelessly across one shoulder, nodded to Amaury to begin. A wise stratagem, I thought, since it would give William the final word of the audience.

The court herald called in a loud voice: "The papal legates Pierre de Castelnau and Arnaud Amaury, abbé of Cîteaux, request permission to address the king of France."

"I understand you have letters from the pontiff in Rome with a request for me," Philippe said. "You have permission to speak."

The two monks moved forward, with Amaury a few steps ahead of his comrade.

"Your Majesty." Amaury's bow was low, but then his voice lifted for all to hear. That sonorous churchman's voice again. Observing him from the side as I did, I could see his jowls quivering, but whether from fear or passion I could not tell. *Certes,* he did not seem to be a man who would be possessed by fear, even in front of the king of France.

"We carry a request from the pontiff to aid him in correcting the grave situation in the south. You have already heard from us how the Cathar heresy is spreading. Christianity itself is in peril. The pope asks, nay insists, that you commit men and money to stop the spread of this plague." Amaury stopped and ran his tongue over his lips. A few courtiers took the opportunity to cough.

"Our holy father says events are even more ominous than when he wrote you last year. He both begs and commands your material support to put this disease to rest." Here the abbot paused again, as if gathering strength.

Then he resumed in a voice that echoed in the rafters of the hall: "He asks that you lead an army alongside us to the south, to threaten the Cathars and their protectors with extermination if they do not give up their heretical beliefs and practices." Amaury stepped back, extending his hand to his companion, yielding the attention to him. "And so says my brother in Christ, Pierre de Castelnau."

Pierre de Castelnau had no choice but to move forward and speak as well. His words, however, were delivered in lower tones calculated to be heard only by the king and those standing closest to him. When he spoke, his comments were surprisingly restrained.

"Your Grace, we beg you to consider our request. Use your best judgment as to the worthiness of our cause. We stand for honor and for the best interpretation of the gospels of Christ Jesus our Lord."

The monk of Castelnau then stepped back beside his partner, who cast a quick, fierce look in his direction, obviously displeased with his colleague's vague and passionless statement. Both men bowed again to the king, as court protocol demanded.

Phlippe nodded brusquely to the two monks and then motioned them aside. He gestured to William, who had remained standing respectfully at a distance.

"Lord William, we will hear you now." The king sat forward, his hands firmly placed on the arms of his throne, indicating to all that his full attention was given.

A slight whisper, like the rustling of dry leaves, ran through the room when the herald called out, "Lord William of Caen, grand master of the Knights Templar of England." The whisper gradually turned into an audible buzz. While many courtiers knew of William's visits to the court, or had seen him in the company of the king, few except the king's counselors knew he was grand master of the Knights Templar in England. Still fewer knew he was also a lord in his own right, with lands in England granted by King Henry when he was still living. Yet no one but I knew that the lands were a reward to William for keeping my son Francis safe for all the years of his youth, years when I thought the boy had died.

William did not often promote his title, but he was not above using it when needed to add to his diplomatic weight. Clever William. Clever Philippe. I had an utter certainty that Philippe already knew what William was about to say. It seemed as though I were watching a carefully scripted morality play.

William stepped forward showing the confidence I knew so well.

He extended his arm in the direction of the throne as he began to speak, as if inviting the king to listen. His voice was strong and could be heard, I was sure, to the far reaches of the presence chamber.

"Your Majesty, the holy father did indeed ask for arms and men to help in the south but the letters he sent with his honorable legates presented here were written some months ago." William paused and, with almost exaggerated courtesy, bowed to the two monks.

Then he continued, not a trace of mischief in his lifted voice. "However, the pontiff is aware of your own difficulties in defending parts of your land against John of England. After some discussion with me, and further thought, the pontiff wrote a later letter to the king of France, one that offers an alternative."

Here William, with his fine sense of drama, moved toward the throne and proffered a large rolled scroll with a seal visible as a splash of scarlet that could be seen by all near him. Chastellain moved forward with the speed of a fox chased by hounds, and nearly snatched the scroll from William before he could hand it to the king. Chastellain then turned to the king, but Philippe motioned him away impatiently, continuing to focus his gaze on William.

"The holy father has entrusted these good monks with a mission." William gestured politely in their general direction, while keeping his gaze on the king. "That general mission, to settle the matter of theological disputes in the south, is still in force. However, as to your own role, the letter I bear suggests another course of action than do the good monks. The holy father asks you to withhold your men and arms for the time being, in order to give diplomacy a chance for victory. He desires one more meeting between Count Raymond and the papal legates here, to see if some agreement can be reached. I am directed to assist such a meeting in Toulouse, as soon as it can be arranged."

I was beginning to enjoy this audience. Perhaps I would not have to battle Amaury at all to assist Joanna. At least not in public, nor with my brother.

Arnaud Amaury made an almost imperceptible movement forward, but Pierre de Castelnau, standing on his other side, placed his hand firmly on his colleague's arm. Amaury's face darkened, but he held his tongue. It was clear the abbot had had no warning that the pontiff had sent William to Philippe with a compromise, an excuse not to commit his men to Amaury. I recalled with amusement what William had told me; the good abbot had not shared his mission with him on their long ride to Paris from Lyons. Why should William have shared his message with the abbot? Turn about—fair play, as the children say.

Philippe pursed his lips, his habit when he was displeased. He scanned the room, then came back to rest his gaze on me. I thought for a moment he would address me, but to my surprise he turned back to the assembly.

"I would hear any of the rank of knight or above who choose to address me on this matter." I tried to keep the expression of astonishment from my face. It was not Philippe's habit to consult his subjects on major decisions.

The room fell silent. Either his courtiers were stunned by the offer, or no one wanted to risk a comment that might run counter to their sovereign's wishes.

"Your Grace!" Hervé de Donzy, Count of Nevers, pushed forward and stood in the center of the room. William fell back slightly, as if to give the count space. The papal legates did not move.

"We will hear you, Count of Nevers," Philippe said.

I disliked this noble heartily. He was a tall, sinewy reed of a man, clean shaven except for his black moustache which he kept carefully turned upward with the aid of boar grease. Only ten short years earlier he had been a minor knight in the *Nivernais*. But through warring on his overlord—a clear breach of his oath of fealty—he took both the man's daughter and his title. I reckoned him among my least favorite courtiers, vain, greedy, and without redeeming grace. He stood now before the king, exuding confidence.

"Your Grace, I bear a letter from Duke Eudes of Burgundy, telling me of the tales coming into his court from the south, of the spread of heresy and the danger to holy mother church. He instructed me without delay to bring this news to you, and to beg you to name an army of a thousand men, with Your Royal Highness at its head and the duke and myself to assist, to go to the south and grind this new heresy out of the people. And now, here we have the same urgent message from these good monks." The Count of Nevers paused to wipe his brow with a square of linen that he produced from his sleeve before he continued.

"But Your Majesty, if you will not go yourself, or send your armies, permit my humble self and Duke Eudes to represent you, to take our own men and go south at our own expense. I have a score of knights and a hundred yeomen, my own vassals led by Simon of Montfort, my liege man, who are willing to go to the south and fight for Christ and the pontiff of Rome." The count's voice trembled. "Permit us to take our own men and conduct a campaign for the glory of France and of our holy mother church."

The count, seemingly overcome with emotion, went down on his knee and bent his head as if he were a docile child. I was close enough to see the beads gathering again at his temples. One could never be certain how the king of France would take such importuning. He was as like to fly into a temper at such a request as he was to cordially grant the boon. The count was playing a huge game of chance.

Philippe regarded the bent figure thoughtfully, tapped his lips with his forefinger, and then looked out over the crowd as if the count were not there at all.

"Are there others who would be heard?" A silence filled the chamber. After a moment, it became palpable. There were few present who wanted Philippe to engage an army to go to the south in Rome's cause. All knights and liege men would be required to do service if the English threat in the west widened. Should the king engage an army of mercenaries to fight in the south, it would drain the royal treasury. But the audience waited to see which way the king would move.

Suddenly drama appeared from an unexpected source. The strange and beautiful diminutive woman in my aunt Constance's retinue, she who had been conversing with my son Francis so intensely, stepped into the center of the room. She advanced until she was standing next to the still-kneeling count. His knees must ache by now. It appeared that Philippe had forgotten to bid the man rise, but I knew that was not the case. Philippe forgot nothing in the royal public appearances.

The woman made a low courtesy, then rose and looked boldly at the king. "Your Majesty, if I may speak." Her voice was surprisingly full for one so slight. Her bottom lip trembled as she spoke, and I knew Philippe could see it. If she only knew how the king reacted to such tactics from women she might have exercised more control. He cared not for such womanly manipulations. Or so I thought then.

"Who are you?" Philippe barked. I wanted to put my hand on his knee, which was within reach, to counsel patience. But I dared not. He was, after all, the king and we were at a court assembly.

"I am Esclarmonde of Foix, sister of Raymond-Roger, Count of Foix, the vassal of Raymond of Toulouse and thus Your Majesty's vassal also."

"And what is your suit? What have you to do with these issues?" But Philippe must know exactly what she, a noblewoman from the south, had to do with these issues. A shadow of suspicion rose in me. I recalled the king's lingering glance on her at the banquet the previous evening. Could Philippe have planted this woman, like a rose in a cabbage patch, to do his work here? What game was he playing?

"I beg Your Majesty, do not respond to these men who would have you send barons and knights to the south. We of the south are a peaceful people. We do not prepare for war. We are farmers and keepers of animals. Our villages are full of people who are not learned, and who mean no one any harm. We are not heretics. We know a few among us hold unconventional beliefs. But these people are good Christians. Their only difference with Rome is that they want more simplicity in their lives. Protect your friends, the people of the south, Your Majesty. Our overlord, Count Raymond, is your liege. Honor that relationship. Do not send wolves to devour us."

After this long speech, the young woman turned boldly and glanced at the two monks standing to one side. The abbot returned her look with an impassive face, while Pierre de Castelnau looked down at the floor to avoid meeting her eyes.

In the silence that followed, the Count of Nevers's head slowly turned upward and the expression on his face was almost comical. His visage registered disbelief and anger and defeat all at once. For he now understood what I had grasped a moment ago. He had been trumped by the little woman from the south.

"Rise, Count of Nevers, and return to your standard. I will announce my decision in a moment." Philippe finally seemed to take notice of his subject. Hervé rose, somewhat awkwardly due to the length of time Philippe had kept him on his knees, and backed away from the throne until he was some distance from the king. Then he melted into the small group gathered around his pennant, still visible by his height to those who sought him.

"Princesse Alaïs." The king unexpectedly turned back to me. "You have heard what has been said. You are known for your wisdom. What is your sage advice?" Philippe lifted one eyebrow in question. I sighed. Why did I have the utter certainty that Philippe knew exactly what I was about to say?

"Your Majesty." My tone escalated and rang out with great clarity, a voice calculated to be heard by all the court. "You have more than six hundred men engaged now outside Chinon, holding back John of England's forces. I believe any further deployment of the knights and arms of France should be to defend or expand your own borders. On the other hand, if you hired soldiers—not of France—to go to the south, it would deplete your own royal treasury. More important, such action would violate feudal law and custom, since our cousin Raymond of Toulouse is your liege man. Once such violations begin, no one will be able to trust the bonds between vassal and lord, for everyone will then do only what is convenient."

"But what of the letters from Pope Innocent?" Philippe was pushing the boundaries of my good humor. He wanted me to come up with his reasons for rejecting both the pontiff's request and Count Hervé de Donzy's impassioned proposal that men from the north be permitted to go south.

"But Your Grace, the holy father himself must understand that Count Raymond is your sworn vassal. Supporting an attack on your own liege man calls into question our entire system of fealty." I paused, then my voice rose even more as I had an inspired thought. "To countenance such action as king could shake the foundations of feudalism. If a vassal cannot count on his king's vow to protect him, the king will no longer be assured that his liege men will keep their vows to him." There was spontaneous applause when I had finished, an event that startled me more than it did the king! Certain groups pounded their standards on the wooden floorboards, creating a great racket, which took some moments to subside.

"Oh, Your Majesty, heed the wisdom of the Princesse Alaïs," the brilliant little Esclarmonde said as the last of the noise drifted away. She was speaking without invitation from the king, in defiance of all court protocol, as she sank to the floor in a deep courtesy.

Philippe suddenly stood, but I no longer feared that he would humble the noblewoman from the south: indeed, she was his accomplice in this little scene as much as I. And I had the uncomfortable thought that while I had been an unwitting assistant, she may have been more prepared.

"You have all heard the Princesse Alaïs," Philippe intoned, sweeping his hand to take in the entire congregation. "Truly, *elle a raison.*

We will take no action at the present time. Nor do we now countenance our vassals to join any conflict in the south. We will, however, watch the situation carefully. The people of the Toulousain must be united with the church of Rome. They must not allow any heretical preaching to flourish."

Philippe's tone was stern, as he looked down upon the petite noblewoman from Foix, now nearly prostrate on the floor. She had all but submerged herself under her cloak and skirts, her long, pointed sleeves spreading gracefully to the side as she knelt before the king. "Take that message back to the Count of Foix, and to all the nobles of the south." He added softly, "And now, madame, you may rise."

An audible sigh swept the room. The crisis seemed to have been resolved. The king was still in good humor and, somehow, both the royal treasury and the safety of the knights present had been preserved, despite the best efforts of the church's official representatives.

"And now, to our tourney and then the feast afterward that has been prepared for all of you." Suddenly the room broke into cheers, which caused a smile to spread across Philippe's face. Leaving me behind, he swept down from the dais and raised up the southern beauty with all the grace and elegance he could assume so well when he desired. Then, smiling and nodding to each side, he led her through cheering ranks of courtiers.

Protocol demanded that I follow, and I would have done so with ill grace had not I found William immediately by my side on the dais, his eyes dancing as they could when he was amused.

"Quite a scene, that," I murmured, forcing a smile as we passed through the crowds.

"Don't say a word, my dearest love, and before you say what you think to your brother count twenty blessings he has provided for you in this life." He offered his arm, and I took it, shaking my head.

"I suppose you both think you are quite clever," I remarked, and he broke into laughter so infectious it caught me up. If I could swallow the medicine so injurious to my pride, I could see the humor in it. And they both were counting on that. "Well, the next time you two decide to use me as your puppet, tell me ahead of time."

"But you would not have played your part nearly as well," he said. "You know you cannot dissemble, you are honest to a fault. You would have given the game away at the outset." And as we nodded to courtiers on either side of us and made our parade into my brother's private rooms, I knew that what he said was true.

And I also knew what neither William nor Philippe could know: that the little scene just played out accomplished my own ends of blocking the monk Amaury completely. And, doing the will of the king, I had given nothing of Joanna's role away. Still, a small voice lingered in my head with an ominous message: You and this monk have not finished with each other. Not yet.

.8.

The King's
Privy Chambers

Philippe was occupied in bantering
with the beautiful Esclarmonde
when we entered his private chambers, and he refused to meet my
glance when I passed directly in front of him.
Only wait, Brother, I thought, until I have you
alone! But William pressed my hand, which
rested on his arm, and I gathered my wits about
me. What was done, was done. And it was ever
said I could enjoy a joke as well as the next
man—or woman. After all, it had turned out
well for matters that concerned William and
myself. William's diplomatic mission from the
pontiff was saved as my brother was not going
to commit France to war, and I could look forward to the end of my beloved's task and our
marriage and retirement to Ponthieu. Or so it
seemed for the moment.

Everyone of our small group seemed to
breathe more easily after escaping the crowded

assembly room. The long, private chambers, while still cavernous compared to my own modest quarters, were far less intimidating than the reception rooms. And filled with chattering crowds, as it was now, the room seemed much less formidable than it had only days earlier, when my brother and I had conferred here. The many windows allowed light, the smaller alcoves gave room for tête-à-têtes, and the rich velvet bed hangings provided color. Even the tapestries, though filled with hunting and jousting scenes, were now merely ornate backdrops to the rhythm of happy chatter and occasional boisterous bursts of laughter.

All of the hearths had fires, and large oak tables were scattered about the room filled with silver pitchers of the best wine from the Loire Valley, from Burgundy, and even as far away as Bordeaux. Half a dozen minstrels strolled about the chamber, and there was a general air of relief evident in the open greetings and knightly clasping of strong hands to renew old friendships. Put aside, if not forgotten, was the tense exchange of not an hour before in the public rooms. The crowd made ready for the tourney with great good cheer.

My uncle Robert strode over to the window embrasure where I stood alone, William having departed to secure goblets of wine for us.

"Good morrow, Uncle." I greeted him warmly as he bent to kiss both cheeks, for he was a great favorite of mine. "It is a surprise to see you so soon again at court."

"The tourney is always entertaining, Niece. And I have some important business with the king." Even as he spoke, his gaze drifted over the room, pausing at the small group surrounding my brother's chief minister. I knew from William that my uncle trusted that man not one whit. Etienne Chastellain was in deep conversation at that moment with his scribe, Eugene, his head tilted in a manner almost flirtatious toward the younger man. I thought of the court gossip about their private relations. Many were amused, since the king's counselor's face was already lining with age, while Eugene had yet to grow a full beard! Eugene was a tall reed of a youth so that stocky Etienne must look up to him when they talked.

As I watched, the Abbé Amaury worked his way through the crowd to the side of the chief minister. I saw Chastellain turn with alacrity, and the younger man, as if on hidden signal, drifted away.

"Now what do you suppose the king's trusted counselor could have to say to the fiery abbot?" My uncle voiced my own thoughts unexpectedly. "I did not know they were acquainted."

"It bears reflection," I responded, my eyes narrowing as I watched the two engage in an intense exchange. I turned back to my uncle.

"What think you of this morning's entertainment, Uncle?" I had scarce voiced the question when William appeared at my elbow followed by a page bearing our wine. The two men, grand masters of the Templars in England and France respectively, bowed with great ceremony. Then they laughed and embraced heartily, for my uncle was genuinely fond of his younger colleague, even though they sometimes disagreed vigorously.

"Yes, Duke Robert, did you like the theatricals?" William's crooked smile had something of the elf about it as he took the hammered-silver goblets from the tray and handed one to me.

"Everything came out well in the end. Philippe always manages it somehow." Duke Robert shook his leonine head. We all turned in Philippe's direction, but he was still deep in conversation with the noblewoman Esclarmonde. I wondered if he were planning to bed her. And then it occurred to me that he may already have done so. I recalled with a pang the picture of Francis in deep conversation with the lovely girl just before the drama of Philippe's audience. I breathed a prayer that my son would not have his heart lanced in his first love, especially not by the hand of his own uncle!

"We cannot have outside interference in the south, not just yet. We must take any measures to avoid that." William was speaking to

Robert with vehemence, gesturing with his free hand. "King Pedro is sitting in Aragon like an eager hawk, waiting for some movement on the part of the north to set his armies forward. He would be happy to gather his formidable troops and be in the langue d'oc country within days if there is any concerted move by Philippe into the area. The slightest excuse will do. The spoils for Aragon in such an invasion must be well nigh irresistible. Then we would see battles joined that would make mothers weep." He paused, seeming to gather himself. "No, Philippe is taking the right path. His counselors argue otherwise, but Philippe is determined to stay out of a conflict in the south. He is wisely choosing his own way this time."

"His counselors?" I interjected. "You mean Etienne Chastellain and his little band of puppets have encouraged Philippe to go to war?"

William nodded. "So I hear."

Duke Robert threw his head back and gulped his wine. He passed the back of his hand across his mouth and shook it out, as if the act could erase the idea of Chastellain and, indeed, the entire privy council. "This group of advisers has not given the king prudent advice for some time. I don't know why Philippe tolerates them."

"What?" I said to them both, with some mischief in mind. "The counsel of Etienne Chastellain and his colleagues is not to your liking, gentle nobles?"

"You know I have never been fond of that man. I think his advice to the king is always shaped to accomplish some end that furthers the career of the chief minister himself," Duke Robert snapped. "He surrounds himself with lackeys trained in Rome who parrot Chastellain as if he were the pope himself."

"And I"—William cast a considered glance in the direction of the minister and his colleagues—"do not trust the man, either. He cares too much for his own power. I also believe Chastellain is playing a game right now with regard to the affairs in the south, but I don't know quite what it is, nor how it benefits him." He rubbed his chin thoughtfully with his thumb and forefinger.

"Why do you say that?" I turned to him, intrigued.

"His response to all of what we just heard is too smooth, too restrained." William shook his head. "I would have expected him to offer some public counsel to the king just now, to support yours, Alaïs. Or to argue against it. But he said nothing. Just watched the interplay with that false smile. It's troubling. It makes me think he might have some other, private plan to interfere. Hidden from all of us and thus doubly dangerous."

I glanced again at the king, and noted that he was now engaged with the Count of Troyes. The groups around the king had reconfigured, and Francis had managed to obtain the side of the fair Esclarmonde who was now in the center of a group of women. I may have been wrong about my brother. His connection with the young woman of the south could be nothing more than that she served his political ends. Perhaps I should meet her and judge for myself.

On impulse I excused myself to my uncle and William, and made my way to the group chatting around Esclarmonde.

"Your Grace," she said, dropping a deep courtesy to me, as did the other women. Francis bowed as if we were strangers, which amused me.

"My dear Lady Esclarmonde," I said, raising her up immediately. "I have been wanting to make your acquaintance since last even, when I saw you in the suite of my aunt Constance. You did very well today. I admired your courage in the audience with the king. You spoke out for your beliefs."

"Indeed I did," she said, looking at me without wavering. "And everything I said was for one end only: to protect my homeland from invaders and those who would do us harm." She cast her look downward for a moment, then met my glance again. "I meant no disrespect to the knights and monks who would persuade the king otherwise. But for us it is a matter of life and death."

"I hear good reports of your life in the south, of the sweet air in the mountains and the love of beauty in dress and song. I would enjoy visiting you some time in the future."

She grinned as she gave me a rejoinder, a sunny, artless look coming over her face. "If you did come, I know you would be welcomed, Your Grace. Especially in my brother's court at Foix, but also in the surrounding towns. We are blessed with strong women, and you would find shelter and hospitality in Laurac or Lavaur, our neighbors as well. They are households run by friends of my brother's dear wife, Philippa. Please do visit us sometime."

I returned her smile and gave her my hand. As I made my way back to William, I mused. So that self-possessed young woman had engaged the interest of my son. This could very well be a friendship worth watching.

William had scarce time to inquire what I had to say to the Lady Esclarmonde, when the heralds appeared and let fly their high, joyful notes, announcing the king's departure for the tourney field across the Seine, and the beginning of the court's progress. The three of us moved toward the door behind the king's retinue.

"Speaking of mothers' tears," my uncle said, "I wonder how the lists have formed." We were talking as we wound down the grand stone staircase. "Do we look forward to good sport this day?"

"I think we shall see some valor, Duke Robert. My own clerk, who once fancied himself an actor, is now taking to the field to prove his mettle in arms."

"Oh, William, not Francis!"

He caught my elbow and pressed it hard. He wanted no clues that might lead anyone to suspect that my interest in Francis was special. But I was as timorous as any mother at the thought that my young lad would enter the lists and possibly be hurt—or worse—by the end of the day.

"Alaïs has developed a great fondness for my young knight," William explained. But Duke Robert, who was anyway hard of hearing, continued to descend the broad stone steps ahead of us. He was completely oblivious to both my exclamation and William's comment. "Fear not, Princesse," William continued in a lower voice. "Francis has been well prepared. I have seen to it. Much of his training for the tourney has been at my own hand! And his friend Geoffrey has enlisted also. It should be good sport."

Still, I was not happy. So caught up had I been in the drama of the morning that I had forgotten the tournament to come. These displays of manly courage, often at the expense of broken bones, held little charm for me. I had agreed to attend today only because Philippe had requested it, and because William was here. But my heart was unquiet to hear that my son would be among those at risk.

At the bottom of the castle steps horses had been assembled to take us across the Seine to the fields of the west bank, where the tents had been raised for the knights. From a distance the red and yellow flags of the various nobles' houses appeared to be so many butterfly wings pinned to the white pavilion peaks. Our horses pawed the ground impatiently, but we were forced to wait for the king, who had stepped aside on the balcony at the top of the stone stairway, and was engaged in an animated conversation with the Count of Champagne. Finally he turned and bounded down the remaining steps with his athletic stride. The crowd, assembled to see us off, cheered their king. The air of anticipation in our entourage was palpable.

We rode swiftly, for the audience in the Great Hall had cost the tournament precious time. Though the October breezes were still warm under the noon sun, we knew that the games must be finished in a few hours, for the sun's slide at the end of the day was precipitous at this time of year. And there must also be enough time left in this busy day for the grand victory banquet.

I noticed ahead of us in the train the two Cistercians, accompanied by their flags and their many retainers. Whilst we had been refreshed in my brother's privy chambers, they had used the time to change out of their austere white wool monk's habits and into cloaks and tunics of blue and green that made them indistinguishable from the rest of the court.

"Note well my erstwhile travel companions ahead. I see they have decked themselves out for the games. One might almost suspect they enjoy such frivolities." William's smile was grim. "You know Amaury was a soldier before he became abbot of Cîteaux."

"So you have said. It would seem, however, he has just exchanged one bloody career for another."

William turned to me, clearly startled. "Do you know something you have not said to me about this affair?" he asked rather roughly. "Have you some premonition about how this will all end?"

"I don't know. But something about those men, about Amaury in particular, disturbs me. When I know more, I will tell you." I was dissembling, for I still held the secret of Joanna's letter.

"Perhaps you ought to draw him," William said thoughtfully. He knew my hunches were often better revealed through my art, though I might not know what would come when I picked up my charcoal. "When you see him in your mind's eye, you may yet discover something we have overlooked."

"It may be so," I agreed. But privately I was not at all certain I wanted to know more about this importunate churchman.

In the Pavilion

hen we reached the field, William took hold of the reins of my horse, for the crowd was a milling squabble of animals, knights, squires and nobles, pages and stableboys looking to earn a coin. The courtiers who had been so civil at the audience in the Great Hall were now acting like a horde of Huns. All was confusion, with the horses kicking up great clouds of dust from the dry land. I pulled my veil over my face to avoid choking. Pages were running everywhere with pails of water from the river to dampen the ground. Gradually the dust settled and the passage to the royal quarters became bearable, although we were still buffeted by the churning crowds. I rode my favorite palfrey, kept for me in Philippe's stables, while William rode a much larger destrier and so had an advantage in this whirling melee. He led the way, carving a path for us through the crowds.

The standard of the royal house fluttered over one group of pavilions, set up in the meadow adjacent to the tourney field. The smaller tent next to Philippe's was mine. Queen Agnes used to have her own quarters at these events, but Ingeborg never came and now the servants did not bother to set up a shelter for her. Thus there were only three in the royal group: Philippe's, mine, and that of our uncle Charles. Constance could have had her own retreat also, but she refused to attend these festivals.

William led my horse to a stop and slipped to the ground. He waved the groom aside and helped me dismount himself. As we made our way inside the tent he held my elbow, as if somehow I might fly away. It amused me, this need he had to touch me whenever we were together. I wondered if that need would remain once we were man and wife, and he—retired at last from the Temple order and its demands—stayed at home by my side.

When we entered my pavilion it was as if we were suddenly absorbed into a separate world from the noisy, dusty one we had just ridden through. Heavy Smyrna carpets had been spread and reclining seats set up for our rest. Colorful tapestries hung on the walls, cheering the interior. I chose a favorite couch and made my way there, slipping my cloak from my shoulders. William caught the garment before a servant could spring to my side, and handed it to the young man. He then pulled a deeply colored burgundy wool shawl from another chair and tossed it over my lap and legs when I was settled. I smiled my thanks for the added warmth.

He joined me in an adjacent couch, so that we sat side by side, our legs stretched out comfortably in front of us. I was glad for the steaming cups of mulled wine the servants brought, for my bones were chilled. Although the fog had lifted and the sun had finally graced us with its light, there had been precious little warmth from it on the ride across the Seine.

"Well, sweetheart, the first part of the day has been adventuresome. Here's a toast to the second part, with the hope that it will be less exciting."

"William." I leaned my head back against his arm outstretched along the back of the couch. "Is there truly a need for me to witness this joust? Could I not just stay behind here in the pavilion?"

"I fear not, love. The sister of the king of France would be sore missed, especially after your role today in the public audience. Besides, did you not say that Philippe expressly asked that you attend today?"

"Yes, but I don't know why." I ran my finger around the rim of the cup. A thrust of strong wind shook the tent, and I could hear the standard overhead flapping on its pole.

"Perhaps it has to do with your role as his adviser. I believe he wants the court to see his confidence in you."

"But why?"

William shrugged. "Philippe keeps his own counsel, as you may have noticed. He confides in me, sometimes in his uncle, less and less I believe in his privy council, but many things he does not share. I don't blame . . . ah, there you are." William leaped to his feet at the sudden entrance of young Francis and his companion, the sweet-faced Geoffrey. "I was afraid you were lost on the way. What delayed you? Could you not find one of the three royal tents?" he joked.

The two youths were splendid in their flashing tournament garb, robust and healthy and looking well nigh indestructible. Their chain-mail shirts somehow made them appear older than they had in the palace reception rooms, as if the very act of dressing for combat added years.

"Princesse." Both youths dropped to their knees, but I motioned them to stand.

"Please, young knights. Do not stand on ceremony with me when we are not in court." I looked at Francis, and could not keep the pride from my voice or face, but I addressed them both. "You look wondrously ready for this adventure. How long before the king takes his place, do you know?"

"We were told that we had only a short time to make our courtesies to you, Your Grace." Francis grinned as he bobbed his head.

"Lord William said we must see you before we take to our horses. He said it would bring good luck." Geoffrey clapped his companion on the shoulder as he spoke.

"And are you both ready for this test?" I asked, amused at their excitement.

"We've practiced so long," Geoffrey said. "I've only been knighted for half a year, and already I've been in the lists in three tourneys." He stopped for a moment. "Or rather, two before this one. This is my third tourney," he confessed. "But I intend to bring honor to Lord William's household!"

"I am certain he is already proud of you," I said, willing all my good spirit onto these two earnest young men.

The flap to the tent door opened again just then, letting in a shaft of light. Then a shadow fell across the room. It was only a figure blocking the slanting autumn sun, but a chilled breath sped across my heart when I saw who entered.

"Your Grace." Etienne Chastellain, resplendent in a fox-lined cloak of deepest green, bowed to me. I nodded curtly, making no move to welcome him. He turned immediately to the two youths standing awkwardly to the side, their faces registering some surprise to have the king's chief minister appear so casually.

"Young knights, they are calling the lists even now. You'd best be on your way." His voice was commanding and I bristled like a forest animal at his impudence.

"You came to fetch the two young knights?" My voice dripped honey. "How considerate of you."

"I came to have a word with you in private, Princesse," he retorted smoothly.

"Lord William," I heard Francis say, "come, put your name to ours on the list as our sponsor."

"I don't think . . ." William looked quickly from me to Chastellain, a frown gathering. There was a roar from the direction of the field.

"Yes, William. Do go with the young knights," I urged. "And please tell Philippe I will be in place shortly. I hear a commotion from the direction of his tent and I fear he is making his way onto the field now." I knew from the sound of the crowd the king had stopped on the field to receive the welcome of his people on his way to the royal box.

Casting a glance in my direction, William hustled the two young knights from the room, saying over his shoulder, "I'll send one of your grooms to accompany you."

"Now, Sir Etienne, what is your business with me that is so private?" As I spoke I occupied myself with arranging the folds of the wool shawl William had thrown over my lap when we first arrived.

"Your Grace," Chastellain said again as he sighed and pulled a small stool forward next to my couch. He perched unsteadily, his bulk being unsuited to the small seat. He was now on a level with me, his eyes boring into mine. I did not recall giving him leave to sit in my presence, but I decided to overlook that breach on his part. He made me uneasy, and I wanted to hear what he had to say and dispatch him as quickly as possible. In the back of my mind lurked the ominous shadow of our encounter the previous night. What did he know about Francis? Could he know that he was my son? That his father had been king of England? My heart beat so loudly I thought sure he must hear it.

"Continue, please." We sat eyeing each other like stray tomcats.

He glanced sideways and began to fiddle with his chain of office. Another small noise, almost a grunt, preceded his next remark, as if he were shifting the burden of his thoughts to me.

"Your Grace, it pains me to have to ask you this, but I require your help at this time."

"On what matter?" I still regarded him steadily.

"This morning . . . uh . . . you heard the request of the two Cistercians, their plea for the king's assistance in overcoming the heresy of the south." Chastellain's demeanor and voice underwent a change as he spoke, softening like the tone of a young man courting in the spring. He leaned toward me and I could smell wine on his warm breath.

"Please, Etienne, get to the point." I deliberately used his first name, denying him the respect his chain of office demanded. If he didn't make haste I'd address him in the familiar *tu*, like a servant!

"Your Grace, I am trying to say what I must with as much finesse as possible. But as you will." He straightened his back and faced me directly, once more the man of business. "I require your aid, as I have said. This morning it was clear how much your brother trusts you. Before the entire court he asked you to judge, as a veritable Sybil, on the matter of giving arms and aid to the Cistercians."

"I am aware of the events of the morning." My impatience was evident but I cared not. "*Certes,* you did not come here to test the reliability of my memory!"

"No, Your Grace, but there have been some later developments that I thought might cause you to reverse your position."

"How could there have been time?" I was incredulous. "We only left the assembly rooms an hour past."

"Events are moving swiftly," Etienne said pompously. "The long and short of it is that I am here to ask you to intervene with the king in these matters."

"In what way?" If he knew me at all, he must have an idea how dangerous this conversation was to him. What he was asking bordered on treason.

"Nothing improper, Your Grace," he said, holding up his hands as if to ward off my recriminations. "In point of fact, His Majesty this morning did not say he would forbid his liege men to fight with the monks at some time in the future."

"Go on." I drew the words out, clipping the ends of them as if with a knife.

"Hmm, yes. But here is a problem." He was fiddling with his chain of office now, twisting it in his fingers. "The need is urgent. If the king delays in sending aid it may be too late."

"You heard the king this morning. He is not in the habit of changing his opinion, once given in a public audience."

"Ah, but he could change it if you asked. Just this once. And he would not have to go with his own army. He could allow Nevers and Burgundy to take their men and go, just as de Donzy requested. Such an action need not affect the royal treasury. It would even offer the king an alternative to fighting one of his own vassals, Count Raymond." Chastellain paused. "I thought . . . I've noticed your high regard for young Francis of Lord William's household, and I thought perhaps, to ensure his ongoing safety with the help of my men, um . . . you might be willing . . ."

His words sent a cold shaft through my heart. I threw back the shawl and rose abruptly, nearly knocking the prime minister off the three-legged stool in the process and putting a sudden end to his vile speech.

"Sir Chastellain, I have tarried too long in this conversation. The king will be wondering where I am. I hear by the noise of the crowd that the first knights are ready for the contest. You heard the king's decision at the morning audience. France will not countenance war in the south, no matter what the wishes of Rome or their legates. I would not presume to intercede with the king when he has made his decision so clear." I paused, then continued with clear enunciation. "The king wants neither his armies nor his liege men involved in this matter. Not now."

Chastellain rose also. He was so short that his eyes were still level with mine. He came closer to me but I edged sideways. I turned and picked up my cloak, busying myself as I pulled it about my shoulders.

"Your Grace, the Count de Nevers is intent on going to the south." Chastellain was speaking quickly now, aware that the time to make his case was nearly finished. "He rode with me to the tourney here today. He feels it is a matter of his immortal soul, that he must make reparation for the sin he committed when he made war on his wife's father. He begs you to intercede so that the king will allow him and the Duke Eudes to take their men and go with the monks to fight this heresy."

These words came tumbling out of the chief minister's mouth while I occupied myself with fastening the jeweled clasp of my cloak. I allowed a pause, long enough to be uncomfortable, before I looked up from my task.

"Yes, I understand the Count de Nevers has much to atone for. I wish him well in his quest to do so. But my brother has good reasons for not wanting the knights of France involved in a war. You heard him this morning. I will not importune him further on the subject." I turned to go.

"Your Grace, this is not wise . . ." Chastellain began, and I whirled on him, this time deliberately stepping quite close. Now it was he who was forced back a step.

"Sir Chastellain, by no means! Do not dare to tell me what is wise for me and what is not. And never, ever again bring a private request to me to intercede with the king, nor bring mention of the Lord William's household into our conversation." I narrowed my eyes with unmistakable hostility. "Do we understand each other, sir?"

The little man had no alternative but to nod, once, reluctantly.

I turned and went swiftly from the pavilion. Outside, as William had promised, a groom held my restive palfrey. Another appeared and cupped his hands for my foot. I could scarce see for the tears of anger blurring my vision. I rode off without a backward glance.

.10.

On the Field

I cantered along the turf past the nobles' boxes, paying little heed to their turning heads and dropped jaws. The king's pennant flew from the largest of these units, in the center of the long row. The masses of townspeople and guilders were on the opposite side, in makeshift bleachers. On one end was a huge open space, where the peasants from the country could stand and watch the jousts. The participating knights would ride in from the opposite end, where the marshals and heralds were already milling about in their midst.

I rode boldly in front of the crowd. The man assigned to ride with me had been left quite behind as I sped onward alone. Any woman without escort in public was an unusual sight, and to see a royal female without a knight at her side must be astonishing to the king's subjects. My performance would provide grist for gossip in the taverns that night! When I reached the royal box, the king's grooms leaped forward to help me dismount.

William and Philippe were standing in the back of the box, talking intently. A footman recognized and assisted me, clearing the way through the crowd. William looked up as I entered and broke off his conversation with my brother. He hastened to my side.

"Alaïs?" He could see my distress. "What has happened?"

I had conquered my urge to cry like a rageful child and composed myself. But I still did not trust that my voice would not tremble. I shook my head.

He tried for a light tone: "The two bright red spots on your cheeks give you away." I was in no mood for teasing so I merely shrugged.

"What did Chastellain want in his private interview?" he persisted, now more seriously, sotto voce.

I finally spoke. "He pressed me to intercede with the king on behalf of the monks' suit."

"He dared that?" There was true surprise in his voice. "What reply did you make?"

"I said on no account would I do so. And William . . ." I was about to tell him of Chastellain's final comment, the veiled threat about Francis, but at that moment the king looked up and beckoned us to our seats.

William nodded, and handed me into my chair, which once again was beside my brother. The king stood at the front of his box, waving to the crowds, the townspeople and serfs from the surrounding villages freed for the day and festive as happy pigeons around grain. Philippe adored appearing before his people. He was a natural-born monarch. I found such crowds and displays stifling, but then again, I was not a ruler in search of the love of my subjects. Meanwhile, the marshals were having hard work of it to clear the field of stragglers so the games could begin.

Philippe acknowledged my presence with a brief nod just before he sat down.

"What are the rules of the day?" I asked, forcing a casual lilt. "It will be arms of courtesy, will it not?" Fresh from the interview with Chastellain, I feared for the safety of Francis. Harm could come from any quarter.

"The heralds are just now starting the announcements." The noise lessened as the horns sounded. "Yes, arms of courtesy. I've put a ban on tourneys with unblocked lances again," Philippe said. "Too many young men are dying on the fields of France for sport." He was watching the field intently, as the knights assembled for the first round of charges.

I breathed a sigh of relief. Because of the blunted lances no one would be gravely injured, although a knight could sustain broken bones if he were unseated too industriously by a challenger.

After a shrill blast of trumpets the lead herald rode forward to pro-claim the rules for the tourney. Five challengers were to be selected by lot from the lists, and any knight from those assembled could then propose himself to fight against these knights. After five lances were broken, the king would declare the winner of that joust.

The heralds completed their task, and were showered with gold and silver, as was the custom. I looked around the cheering crowd and beyond, to the brilliantly colored trees that surrounded the field and the deep blue sky above. The fog of early morning had burned off, and left us with a sparkling late-autumn day. Even I, loath as I was to be here to witness these war games, admitted that the day lacked nothing to be perfect for open-field festivities. Why God should bless the lashing and grunting of a tournament with such beauty of nature was beyond me.

"You know, if they didn't organize war games, the knights and younger sons would be fighting among themselves in every field and byway. The overall consequences would likely be even more dire. This way, at least, they are supervised." William's voice was in my ear. Once again he had read my thoughts. I was about to give him a rejoinder that sometimes youths died on the tourney field, and what, pray, could be more dire than that, when suddenly Francis pulled up before me, riding a magnificent warhorse. I recognized it as William's own.

"Princesse Alaïs." The young knight smiled and lowered his lance until it was level, the tip quite close to my breast. His strong young shoulders were visible under the chain metal tunic as he struggled to hold the impatient charger. "Will you give me the honor of wearing your colors in the lists?"

I found myself blushing, to William's apparent delight, as I unraveled my favorite green silk foulard from my neck and wound it on the end of the lowered lance. "My compliments, Sir Francis," I said, acknowledging his knighthood. "And I wish you fortune's favor for the day."

He laughed then, and rode gaily off. William pressed my hand briefly. I couldn't look at him, but neither could I stop the smile that would rise to my lips.

"He's a brave lad," I said, my voice full of the feeling for which I could not find words.

"Yes, he is indeed. And so also is his friend Geoffrey, who has joined the lists with him."

"Both are gallant young men," I murmured absently, watching the field.

Now the heralds rode forth to read out the names of those who were on the lists. My heart fluttered when I heard Francis's name, along with the Count of Nevers and three others unfamiliar to me.

Philippe stood and raised his royal arm, bringing it down like a broadsword. "Let the games begin," he shouted, and the heralds repeated the order down the line, as they galloped off the field.

My motherly qualms subsided as I watched Francis time after time take on the challengers and unhorse or disarm every one. I was of a

mind for a brief period that he would be victor of the day, although he was surely the youngest knight on the field. But close on the end he faded with fatigue and finally was bested by another, losing his seat on the remarkable warhorse. He retired from the field to an uproar of support from the sidelines, a cry from those who saw how young he was, and how valiantly he had fought through the hours. And though he lost the lance, I saw him scramble to retrieve my favor from the field, where it had fallen in his mishap. He scooped it up and stuffed it back into his doublet as he was helped across the mangled turf.

As the afternoon sun lowered in the sky, the rays seemed to increase in intensity, casting long spikes of light across the field. The crowd became ever more jolly, as if anticipating the happy conclusion of the day, the awards to be given out, and the alehouses to which they would repair later to replay the events. The cheery noise had the opposite effect on my spirit. I felt a premonition. Something was not quite right.

To my surprise, I looked up to see the two monks approaching the king. Amaury, who always seemed to thrust himself into the lead position, bowed low. "Your Majesty, my compliments for a fine exhibition here."

The king took his eyes from the field momentarily, frowning at the interruption. The monk continued quickly: "My colleague and I request permission to withdraw at this point. We have not yet said our daily office, and must attend to our prayers if we are to make a showing at your feast."

Philippe waved his hand negligently. "I understand, Abbé. You have our permission to withdraw." I suspected the king's friendly tone was an attempt to smooth over any ruffled feelings that were retained as a result of his refusal to fall in with the monks' request at his audience that morning. "But I fully expect to see you both this night. After all, the festivities are in your honor."

The monks bowed again, and made their way down onto the field. I followed their progress as they signaled for horses. Amaury mounted expertly, Pierre with more effort. Then they rode quickly from my sight. Something about their early exit bothered me, but my gaze was drawn back to the action on the field.

The next round was about to begin, and I was met with a jarring sight. As a seasoned knight made ready at one end of the field, a familiar figure took his place opposite, at the other.

I exclaimed loudly, "Oh, no. This cannot be."

"Alaïs, what causes you distress?" William, whose gaze had been fastened on the field, was immediately solicitous. "Are you ill?"

"No, *pas du tout*," I exclaimed, unable to take my gaze from the field. "It's the boy. Francis's friend Geoffrey. He is so young, and he faces Hervé de Donzy, Count of Nevers! The count is much older and more experienced. And he is known for his brutality on the field."

"But, Princesse, you know the lists are settled by chance. They cannot be altered at this time." William looked around. "Speak softly. Do not draw attention."

"Why, you are afraid I will create a womanish scene!" I turned to him with vehemence. "But what of this young man's fate? He is younger than Francis by at least five summers. And look at de Donzy." William's glance turned just in time to see the frontispiece of the helmet clamp down over the scowl of the older knight. "Can you imagine how angry the count is after this morning? His plea was dismissed by Philippe. He was refused in front of the entire court while he was on his knees!" And then I was struck by another thought. "Perhaps the Count of Nevers knows I refused Chastellain's request. He may hold a grudge against me, and his anger may fuel violence here."

William shook his head. "There is nothing to be done."

I could not keep the pleading note from my voice. "You have the ear of the king. Can you not stop this?"

"Alaïs, Geoff is a knight who entered the lists here. He wants to prove himself. He will be fine. They are fighting with blunted lances." William sought to soothe me, but I had a sudden terrible feeling that the sunny afternoon was about to turn dark. I saw young Geoffrey as a mirror of my own son, and a son without a mother here to protect him.

"I will ask Philippe to stop the joust." I said this with determination, and half rose. But William placed his hand on my arm.

"You cannot do that without humiliating this young man," he countered quickly, his voice stern. And I knew what he said to be true. The youth would not thank me for interceding for him, even if Philippe were willing to call a halt to the games. And there was no certainty the king would honor my request. I turned back to the field to watch.

The first pass was in progress. As usual, it seemed primarily a test of mettle between the combatants. Did one knight flinch? Did the other give way? Was there a weak spot to be pressed in later passes?

The townspeople and peasants cheered, as much to encourage the knights to greater boldness as a response to their mild actions. The knights reached the end of the pole and pulled in their horses, circling them around to begin again. At the sound of the horn they commenced riding. The second pass was more lively, with each knight making a serious attempt to unhorse the other, the long bar between them. The third held even greater action, with a valiant attempt by Geoffrey, giving a thrust that nearly unseated de Donzy. Then there was a long pause as the two knights readied for the final test. It seemed de Donzy had asked the marshal for consideration so he could slip from his post and tighten the straps. His horse pawed the ground as he remounted and settled himself. Eventually the baton fell, the horn rang out, and the final run began.

The two men rode hard, the hooves pounding on the ruined field. The figures blurred slightly before my eyes, merging for a moment into one. Every part of my body gripped inward. I knew with certainty the awful outcome before the happening.

The crowd must have sensed what I already knew, for a strange silence gradually descended upon all, like a calm that precedes a storm. I averted my eyes. Then I heard a crash followed by a roar. I looked up quickly, but I was blinded by the sun's rays bouncing off the helmet that lay in the middle of the field.

I shielded my eyes against the light with my good hand, but still I could not see what had happened. "William?" I questioned.

"It seems the young knight has been unhorsed," he replied. "De Donzy's lance struck him in the forehead."

"But that is expressly forbidden," I cried out.

"The count has dismounted. He comes quickly now, to beg forgiveness of the king."

"And the young man?" I had risen. The king was distracted by the event, and the approach of the Count of Nevers, and did not notice.

"He is not moving," he said quietly. "The marshals are attending him."

I swept past William and made quick work of the steps to the field without looking back. When I reached the fallen knight I knelt beside him. He was pale and bleeding from the wound in his head. Blood was trickling from his mouth, as well, and I knew he was lost. Then his eyelids flickered and opened. I bent closer. He spoke in a whisper.

"Princesse, I am so sorry to disappoint . . ." And he faded away. I took off my mantle and covered him with it, smoothing it over his face and shoulders as his mother would have.

When I stood William was at my side. I placed my hand on his arm to steady myself, but there was no need for words. In a moment I turned back to the royal box and saw de Donzy kneeling in front of the king. Philippe listened, head bent, and then waved him away, a gesture both contemptuous and forgiving. The marshals had taken Philippe's wave to de Donzy as a signal to end the tourney, and the closing horn notes rang out. The king, morosely slumped in his chair, made no move to stop them. De Donzy bowed his head and slunk off.

I nearly ran back to the royal box, arriving breathless, and stopped abruptly at the railing in front of the king's own chair. I leaned up to speak to him, almost shouting in my distress, my arm extended to catch his attention: "Is no one to be held to account then? No responsibility assigned to snuffing out the young, promising life of this youth?"

He shook his head and said with a brittle tone I rarely heard: "Leave it for now, Sister." Then, leaning toward me, he spoke again in a low voice: "I understand what happened here. This shall not be forgotten. Come now, resume your seat for the awards."

The marshals dispersed the few knights who still waited to joust. There was some muttering, but the crowd seemed to have had enough. No one called out to continue the contests. The death of the young knight had cast a pall on the entire affair. Morover, it was nearing dusk, and Philippe must yet award the title of victor for the day, and the prize of a great warhorse that came from the royal stables. De Donzy was out of the running, having committed a violation of the tourney's rules by aiming at the head. The victor came forward now, the grizzled knight of Blois who had unhorsed Francis. He was experienced in tourneys and, indeed, in war itself, and this was not his first tourney victory. He bowed low to accept his prize, and then led his horse in a victory promenade around the outskirts of the field, to a subdued crowd that could muster only scattered cheers.

When he had finally exited, and as if on an invisible signal, a great swell of townspeople surged onto the field, followed by another wave. Rising clouds of dust from the movement of horses and humans, and a constant undertone of muttering noise, created a sense of controlled violence. The marshals, holding their batons sideways, were valiantly trying to clear a way through the swarming masses for the king's party, even as our horses were led toward us by the royal grooms. We descended from the king's box and made ready to mount.

Philippe's groom handed me onto my horse and my brother mounted even more quickly, as if anxious to quit this place. The rising mood was dark. His beloved subjects were fast becoming unpredictable rabble. We started across the field, the king and I riding side by side, but we said nothing. The crowds parted for the king's herald, riding just in front of us with the royal standard. Philippe sat straight and looked neither to the right or left. I knew it would be futile to speak of de Donzy. The king would deal with him in his own time. But I seethed with inner anger, all the same.

Philippe interrupted my thoughts, turning to me unexpectedly. "Where is William?"

"He is still with the young knight's companion, Francis, I believe." I looked over my shoulder. We were nearly to the edge of the field, almost to the road that would take us back to the bridge across the Seine. I scanned the horizon. Finally I made out the dim figures of Francis and William, standing with a small cluster of knights around them. "Yes, there I see them." Then I saw William detach himself from the group, jump on a horse, and gallop toward us.

"Here he comes now," I said, pulling on my reins. Philippe followed suit, raising his arm to signal a halt for those behind.

As we waited, Philippe made a curious comment. "The monks left before this mishap. I'll wager it was Castelnau who insisted on leaving. Amaury would certainly want to stay."

"Yes, he was once a soldier, William tells me," I replied absently, my gaze tracking William's advance.

"Quite a good one, if all the tales are but half true. It's odd . . ." My brother's voice trailed off.

"What say you?" I thought the wind had taken his words, but then I saw he had simply paused.

"I feel that his passion to eradicate the Cathars is one way for him to resume the field. That he could go to war again if he could persuade someone to give him arms and men, only this time for Christ."

"Rather for Pope Innocent and his imperial designs than for Christ," I retorted. Philippe smiled.

"Sister, you must guard against cynicism. It was ever your weakness."

William pulled in his charger, turning him to stop abruptly in front of us. "Your Majesty," he said, as he bowed. Then, without further ceremony, he turned to me. "I've a message for you, Princesse. Young Francis is with Geoffrey's body. He is asking for you. Please come."

"My Lord?" I turned a questioning face to the king.

"Of course you may join him," Philippe said, as if it were the most natural thing in the world for William's young knight to be asking for the sister of the king of France. Philippe signaled to his party to resume the progress back to the Île de la Cité and I bowed low as he passed me.

I followed William somewhat reluctantly, dreading to see my son in his grief. By this time attendants had moved the body and we found the circle of young knights surrounding Geoffrey behind the stands that had been hammered together to provide rough seating for the town crowds. Several marshals were directing servants who had just arrived with a stronger litter for the body. The setting sun threw long shafts of gold between the wooden slats cobbled together to make the stands. Light lay in stripes across the somber group. Always the light with the dark, I thought. Always.

I dismounted quickly and went to Francis's side, placing my hand on his arm to let him know of my presence. He turned to me, his face ravaged by his shock. His tears had stopped, but their remnants were still on his face, and his eyes were red-rimmed. He looked, suddenly, much older.

"I am so sorry, lad." I shook my head. "This should never have happened."

"The man who did this, the man who pleaded before the king this morning, is he just going to walk away?" A fierceness appeared now. It took me by surprise, for I had never seen Francis angry before this time. "It was a clear violation of the codes of chivalry. Will no justice be done for my comrade?"

"I don't know what will happen," I answered truthfully. "The king will decide. The man broke the rules. I'm certain there will be consequences." I spoke all this with a strong voice, although privately I wondered. A young, unknown knight, a powerful noble with a temper just denied a boon: the king might decide to delay any action, hoping that everyone would forget the incident.

"But you can implore the king. You can make him call this knight to account. He not only broke the rules of the tourney, he has broken the rules of knighthood." He paused, his jaw taking on the peculiar set I remembered from his father, King Henry. "This was no accident. The Count of Nevers intended to kill Geoff."

I put my hand under my son's elbow and led him apart from the others. I could feel his arm shaking. I knew I must speak plainly. This was no time for soft words.

"Listen to me, young Francis," I whispered urgently. "Do not voice such suspicions where others can hear you. There is more involved here than you think. The king is aware of conspiracy in his court. This rough action may be a part of an effort to plague the monarch." I glanced around to be certain we were not overheard. William stood some yards away, deliberately engaging the rest of the group in conversation.

"What conspiracy?" Francis's voice rose. "Geoff and I have nothing to do with such things."

I put my hand on his arm. "Softly, lad. I am saying this may be part of a larger pattern of acts. And when all is made clear, I know the king will seek retribution for this deed. But you must be patient."

"Then I'll seek my own revenge." A hard edge in his voice startled me.

"I don't think—"

"Just don't talk to me about the folly of revenge." He moved his hand back and forth, palm outward as if warding off evil spirits. "I couldn't bear to hear that right now." He had lowered his voice, but not its intensity. He flexed his fingers, opening and closing his right hand, his sword hand. "Geoff was my constant friend, my comrade in arms. He was like a brother to me. You know his killing was no accident. Revenge may be all I have."

"I'm not going to say you must not take revenge. What I am about to remind you is that a man must be alive to take revenge. Do you understand me?" I hissed. "The first rule: you stay alive. Then you think about revenge."

He looked directly at me, startled. "You talk like a man—I mean, with the courage of a man," he amended quickly.

"I talk like a practical person. Mourn all you want, but keep your demands for justice soft for the present. There are more ways to find justice than through the crown. And you know not who may be listening in this court, nor who is friend or foe. It will do Geoff no good for you to fall also, a victim of some other 'accident.'"

We stared at each other for a long moment. There was no need for further talk. The bond between us was palpable. I had a sudden urge to tell him the truth, right then and there, to tell him I was his mother and that he was the natural son of a great king, Henry of England. To warn him he had enemies. To counsel him to take care. But a chill gust of wind blew autumn leaves up in a swirl around me, and the moment passed. There was too much to explain and not enough time.

Suddenly William was between us. "Francis, Geoff is being taken away. There is no need for you to go with them. A priest has been called and tomorrow there will be private prayers for him."

"There will be no funeral Mass at court?" Francis looked up at the older man, the only father he had ever known.

"Nay." He shook his head. "That is unlikely for many reasons. But you have my leave to join your other companions tonight. There is no need for you to be at the king's banquet."

"I had not thought . . . no, of course not. My gratitude, Lord William. I don't want to see anyone at court again. I can scarce wait until we leave Paris and I hope it will be soon." He turned to me. "Princesse, my thanks to you for your words. I'll not forget."

I wanted to tousle the auburn hair as he bent low over my hand, but I could not. And anyway, he was a man and not a boy, as he had just proven with his anger.

William watched him walk away. "You are going to have to tell him soon," he said. "There is too much feeling between you. He needs to know the reason."

"I agree. That is what I have been saying."

"But now is not the time," William said firmly, as he took my elbow and began steering me back to the cluster of men and horses waiting for us. "Let us leave the chaos of the tourney and hasten to the chaos of the banquet given by the court of France, my love. At least with Francis away tonight, I won't have to worry that he will challenge the evil Count of Nevers to a duel of honor."

"Mother of God," I exclaimed. "That never occurred to me."

.11.

Chambers of the
Princesse Alaïs

We rode in silence the rest of the way to the palace. When we entered the courtyard, the grooms left off their gossip and sprang to help us. William and I immediately became more guarded in our exchange. We parted in the corridor outside the Great Hall, and I went off to my chambers to refresh myself. I waved away the servant who appeared at my side to accompany me. I had need of time alone, and I did not fear for my safety in my brother's castle.

Nor did I think William would visit me before the dinner. He had seemed occupied with other thoughts as we rode back from the tourney and he merely brushed my hand with his lips in a perfunctory gesture before we parted. Indeed, last glimpsed, he was at my uncle's side, speaking with some urgency into his ear. But I was too tired, hot, and dusty to give either of them much thought as I hurried to my rooms.

As I made my way up the stone staircase, I thought on the events of the day and was mightily saddened. But when I passed the corridor that led to the wing next to mine, to the chambers of my aunt Constance, I had a sudden idea. Perhaps a surprise visit from me at this odd hour would be a spur to sharing confidences. I might learn more about her peculiar meetings and why the chalice at St. Denis had so captured her attention.

On this whim I turned left instead of continuing to my own apartments. I was thinking on the death of young Geoff, and what meaning this had for my family, when I came upon a most astonishing sight. The scene before me caused me to stop completely, and drift closer to the wall to avoid being seen.

A tall arch at the end of the passage framed the deepening blue sky of dusk and set in relief against it were two clearly outlined silhouettes. I couldn't have been more startled at the sight that met my eyes. Tall combs holding the veil of my aunt's unique headdress were apparent on the shorter of the two. She was leaning forward as if to catch every word that her companion, bending down, was uttering. The second figure was even more surprising. The bulk of the shoulders and the height indicated a man, but not one I would have suspected my aunt would engage for a minute. For I could make out a monk's long robe, loosely belted, and a hood resting across his shoulders. And it wasn't the thin, ascetic form of Pierre de Castelnau I saw outlined before me. No, my aunt, the dowager Countess of Toulouse, was in deep conversation with none other than Arnaud Amaury, enemy of her son.

As soon as I had identified the couple, I melted into the shadows and slipped around the corner. For the moment, I had no thought of what this clandestine meeting might portend, but I did not want the abbot to know I had seen him talking with my aunt. The very same aunt who introduced Esclarmonde to the court. The very same Esclarmonde who this day begged my brother to oppose the abbot's demands!

It was darkening by the moment, and that worked in my favor. I was certain I had not been seen. As I turned and hurried toward my own apartments, I reflected that the monk and Constance could not have identified me in that descending dusk even if they had observed my figure at a distance. For I would not have known it was my aunt and the abbot without the outline of the hair combs and the cowl to show me. But what did their private rendezvous, outside of all court formality, mean?

Then another thought struck me. I would be well advised to take care in what I said to my aunt until I understood her connection to the sinister abbot. I recalled my aunt's mysterious meetings at Créteil on the outskirts of Paris. The disturbing scene I had just witnessed was a warning to have a care in how I proceeded in my investigations.

So deep in thought was I that a movement at my right elbow startled me into a soft cry. A shadow had detached itself from the wall and materialized into the tall, slender figure of Pierre of Castelnau. For the second time within the hour I was riveted to the spot with surprise. It seemed as though the Cistercians were intent on invading my entire evening.

"Père Pierre." I spoke first. "What are you doing here?"

Pierre de Castelnau looked around, furtive as a night thief. "I need to talk with you, Princesse," he whispered. "Could we find a place where there is no danger of servants overhearing?"

I pulled open my chamber door and motioned for him to follow. Mignonne had laid a fire in the great hearth, and I gestured to my guest to take a cushioned chair set before the the comforting warmth. The monk nodded and sat without comment. Then he began wringing his hands as if all his fear could be dissolved by this action. I stood, leaning my back against the mantel, my left hand jammed into its pocket, my right hand on my hip, waiting.

I had a perfect picture of him in the dancing light of the flames. As the monk pushed back his cowl, I noted that his lean face and tonsured head were damp with perspiration. At that very moment he quickly took a cloth from within his sleeve and mopped his brow, as if he were in tune with my interior observations. He stared at the floor for a long moment. His balding head seemed somehow suddenly vulnerable.

Finally he raised his head and noticed I was still standing. A frown appeared. "Please, Princesse, please sit. It is not right that I sit in your presence while you stand."

"No matter, Father. We need not observe ceremony here. Please tell me what is so important to discuss that you must lurk about my door like a common cutpurse rather than address me in public." I was tired and would truly prefer to be left alone. But I must confess my curiosity had been piqued.

"This is difficult for me," Pierre began, and I noticed a slight tremor to the voice that had been firm in the morning's pleadings for arms and men. "I must talk with you, as I know your brother listens to your advice." He paused, starting again, stammering like the fool jester Philippe occasionally favored in his court. "I find this hard to say, but I don't know any other words to use, although you may think me disloyal." He paused again.

"Pierre of Castelnau, this has been a long and trying day." My patience was about to snap. First Chastellain, now this monk. Would everyone at court beat a path to my door begging me to intercede with my brother? "I must ask you to state your business and then to leave me to my rest before the dinner hour."

At that, the man seemed to pull himself together. "You saw me stand with my colleague this morn, in front of your brother, and beg for men to march to Toulouse and clear the land of the heresy that is rampant there." I nodded when he paused. "I did so because I was forced to. But I do not believe such a course is the solution to the problems of the south," he blurted out.

I was so surprised that I did suddenly sit down, taking the chair opposite him. Beads glistened again on his forehead, but he plunged gamely onward.

"My colleague, Abbé Amaury, is headstrong in the extreme. Because he was a soldier in his youth, he sees a military answer for every problem. I do not agree with him, especially in this case."

"But why do you not, then, address this with the abbot?" I asked, not bothering to hide my annoyance. "Why is this conflict between you monks, from the same holy order and with the same charge from the pope, dragged into my chambers?"

"Princesse, hear me out. I can see you are impatient, but things are not that simple." There was an urgency to his voice, almost a pleading.

Some inner counsel bade me hold my temper and listen to him. I recovered myself with a sigh, saying gently: "All right, Père Pierre. Just tell me the story." I leaned forward to observe him more closely.

He rubbed his temples with the finger and thumb of his right hand, then spoke more strongly than before.

"I am a man of peace, and a man of God. I do not believe in war and killing as a way to spread the gospel of Christ. But I am in a difficult position. I have remonstrated with Amaury about the rush to war over this matter. But he answers that we are appointed by the holy father to deal with this problem. He says that to speak publicly for peace at this point would give comfort to the heretics, and perhaps prevent souls coming to Christ. That we must be strongly in favor of force, that the mere threat of force will bring them to heel, like hounds in the hunt."

"Do you believe that?"

"No, *pas du tout*. I think the dogs of war have a life of their own. And I believe that Amaury wants war for himself and he will let nothing stand in his way." The monk stopped again and hauled himself to his feet with apparent effort. He was clearly distracted as he paced around his chair and toward the hearth like a restless colt. As he talked, however, his voice became increasingly clear.

"Amaury has threatened me. If I do not support him in calling for war, especially in this suit to King Philippe, he said he will bring harm to me and my family." He stopped and made a sound, as if clearing something from deep in his throat. "You saw the anger on his face this morning, when he did not believe I was firm enough in what I said."

"Yes, I saw that anger. But what has brought you here to me, and just at this moment?"

He sat down again and looked at the floor. "I cannot stand by and watch what is happening without telling someone. These things are not right."

"You mean the killing of young Geoff today," I said quietly, as the truth dawned.

"Yes," he said with simplicity. "You must know that was no accident."

In my heart I had known all along.

"Amaury managed to have a brief conversation with de Donzy as we crossed the field before the games. Chastellain had already informed him of the outcome of his request to you in the pavilion. They knew you had refused to interfere, and they wanted to send a message to you and, God help us, to the king himself." The monk, whose hands had lain in his lap, began to clasp his fingers as if imploring God himself to hear him. I rose and placed a hand on his shoulder as I passed him. I thought of young Geoff fading from life as he tried to apologize to me, and of Francis flexing his sword hand in frustration, and I felt the cold breath of death brush my neck. I shuddered.

"And that is why you left the field before the end. You knew what would happen."

He nodded. "I do not know how they manipulated the lists to have de Donzy fight the youth, but I heard Amaury make a comment of satisfaction to Chastellain. 'Now,' he said, 'they will see that the great Lord William's house is not invulnerable. The smallest will go first.'"

"But how can Amaury harm you?" I returned to him with a cup of mead from the side table. He took it with shaking hands, and put the cup to his lips as I resumed my seat opposite him. "You are joint legates of the pope. Neither of you is above the other. Surely if the pope knew of this threat to William, or to you, there would be strong consequences."

"I have a half sister in Béziers, a noblewoman of the name Beatrice." He set his cup down and rose again to pace, his fluttering hands showing his agitation. The fire spat a few cinders on the hearth, narrowly missing his slippers.

"Ah, yes, I have heard her name." I managed a smile, hoping to calm him. "Her beauty is legendary."

"She was once married to Count Raymond's father. But she was sent away from his court when the count wanted to marry Constance, the sister of the king of France. Now Amaury says he has evidence that my sister, Beatrice, is connected to these Cathar heretics, that she has given their preachers shelter. He has said he will see her burn as a heretic, and also her family, if I do not do as he directs."

"I see." And indeed, unbeknownst to the monk I did see, but what I saw I could not describe to him. In a lightning flash came the morning scene in my brother's presence chamber, and the retiring Pierre de Castelnau saying little, but standing straight beside the florid abbot. Another tall, equally slender figure stood next to him, face shadowed by her falling cascade of graying hair. She was so thin I thought she must be brittle, could break easily. The abbot pointed an accusing figure at his comrade, but it was the woman who was suddenly engulfed in flames. I closed my eyes, but the vision persisted for fully another moment. I swayed slightly, and caught the carved arm of the chair to steady myself.

Silence filled the chamber. Finally, I stood and spoke, trying to push the sadness of my vision away and bring hope to my voice. "You heard my brother. He will not countenance sending his men and arms to the south at this time. So you are in the best possible position, Pierre of Castelnau. You have performed in public as Amaury required, your family is safe, and still what you secretly want will come to pass. There will be no interference from the crown of France in the southern situation at this time. What else would you have me do?"

"My family is not out of danger. Amaury is persuasive. The king may change his mind. But worse than that, I feel impotent. I cannot prevent this impending disaster from happening. I know there will be war and carnage. All will be swept away before these terrible armies." As he spoke, he flung out his arm and cleared the small table in front of him, sending the bowl of fruit and the cup of mead clattering to the floor. "My sister will die in flames, and I am helpless to prevent it."

Then Pierre de Castelnau slumped back into his chair and held his head. I could think of nothing to say. Indeed, what could I do to ease this monk's mind? I knew, with excruciating clarity, that all he said was true. It would come to pass as he saw it.

"I cannot sleep at night. Whatever I do, I know it will matter not. I see the crowds of knights on horseback and hear their hoofbeats. I see them advance on my sister's city. I watch the flames and hear the screams of the people as they burn, trapped in their church. Then I wake." His sobs took him over as his voice broke.

I leaned down and peered closely at Pierre. I saw an ascetic man, perhaps a holy man, but more than that. I suddenly recognized another such as myself, one who had the gift of second sight. I knew well that in his realm, in those things that concerned him directly, he could see the future. I recalled my special vision the day the monks arrived, the strange circle of men who ritually plunged their torches into the ground. I felt the power of the church as I knew Pierre felt it also. It was temporal power, but something more than that.

"How would you like me to help?" I said finally, willing to place my gifts in his service.

After a moment, the sobbing ebbed and he lifted his tearstained face to me. "I have two requests," he snuffled as he gradually gained control. "First, use all your influence with your brother to help him hold to his resolution not to get involved in this malicious business."

"Easily done," I said, seating myself once more, this time on a stool in front of the saddened monk. "I share your view against war in the south. And especially that it should not come by the hand of France. And the second request?"

"If anything happens to me, find a way to help my sister."

I reached out to him, not as a *princesse* of the royal house of France, but as a woman who had had a sister once and now had none. My right hand covered his and I felt how cold were his fingers. "Why do you think your sister is in danger?"

He looked me in the eye without flinching. "She may, in fact, have done what Amaury says. But she is a good woman, nonetheless."

I held his hand deliberately for a time, and then I rose. I went to the fire and gazed into the flickering flames for a long moment.

"I will help you, Pierre de Castelnau," I finally said when I turned. "I will help you because I think Amaury's venture is woefully misguided. And because I like him not. And because I, too, once lost a sister."

I moved back to him and stood directly in front of him. "But I will help you in every way I can most of all because I despise fanatics. And your colleague, with his devotion to arms and power, seems to be altogether more fanatic than any so-called heretic."

The monk rose with a stiff movement and bowed low before me. "If you were not a princess, and I not a priest of God and legate of the holy father, I would embrace you for what you have just said. I know you have the courage to keep your word, and I give you thanks with all my heart."

For a moment I stared at him, and then I amazed myself. I, a royal princess of France, lifted my good hand to this monk's shoulders and reached up to brush his cheeks on either side with my own. Then I stepped back.

"Ah," he said with wonder in his voice, "you have the healing touch. You are one of us."

"I embrace you also with my spirit," I said, nodding to him. "Go with God. Be of good heart." But my own heart was heavy as the door closed behind him. I felt great sadness at the monk's grief for what he had seen of the future.

As I reflected gloomily on recent events, my puzzlement increased. Where was appearance and where truth in these scenes? What was the meaning of the conference I had observed between my aunt Constance and Abbot Amaury? The monk, Pierre, who seemed an ally to the evil abbot, was not; and my aunt, who seemed his enemy, might not be what she appeared, either.

I scarce had time to ponder these thoughts before Mignonne appeared at my door. She was a whirling storm of movement and a glad distraction for me. Her ministrations brought me back to the present. Hot water had been ordered from the kitchens and I was glad to shed my dusty gown and sink into the warmth of the oak tub. My hair felt dusty from the tourney field, and I wished for time to soak it, too, and smooth it with oil, but I knew my presence was required in the Great Hall soon. Tonight I would wind my tresses into braids with jewels and coil them on the crown of my head and wear the scarlet gown and pearl-laced velvet redingote and William would be most pleased. But even that thought could not push aside the fears that were gathering in my heart.

12

The Great Hall

t was not an hour later that, dressed and composed, I entered the Great Hall. Whilst we had been at the tournament lackeys had brought in huge oak tables and set them on trestles, then covered them with colorful woven cloths. The trenchers the servants had used for their midday meal were replaced with silver plates and platters and all looked ready for another festive evening. Clusters of nobles and their ladies stood everywhere between the tables, talking and taking goblets from the trays Philippe's liveried servants carried as they circulated among them.

All of the visiting nobles, their knights and ladies, were invited to dine with the king. I knew that their retainers were having their own fill of meat and wine in the bowels of the palace, dressed in their daily leather jerkins and no doubt happy with their lot. But this hall was filled with jewels, rich robes, color, and laughter. I marveled at the cheer spilling around the room as if nothing dire had occurred at the tourney only a few hours earlier. For myself, I could take no part in it; Geoff's pale face was still etched before me.

My gaze swept the room, searching for William. With surprise, I saw my aunt Constance making a low bow to my brother. What, I wondered, had propelled this hermit into the company of the court twice in one day?

William usually watched for my entrance, coming to my side before he lost me in the crowd. Tonight, however, when my glance alighted on his tall figure, he was already occupied. I was startled to see him deep in conversation, and with no less a personage than my aunt Charlotte, abbess of Fontevraud! When had she arrived? She had not been at the tourney, nor did Philippe tell me she was expected at court this autumn.

I paused for a moment. Their conversation appeared intense. I noted what a handsome couple they made—my tall, elegant aunt with her utter disregard for abbey protocol, dressed as she was in deep green velvet and mauve silk robes, the hint of cream silk slashing her long, pointed sleeves, and William in his own court finery and broad shoulders. I knew that my aunt had been chosen to attend some of the debates between Cathar believers and churchmen of Rome in the south and I wondered if she brought news for William to aid his mission.

Charlotte saw me first. She broke from William, and came to greet me with great affection, and I returned her embrace right willingly. My gratitude for her recent role in reconciling me with my stepmother, Eleanor of Aquitaine, was still strong. And I so admired her style!

William came after her, and made the customary bow over my right hand. My withered left hand, gloved as usual in public, slipped into my pocket after I embraced Charlotte. Both Charlotte and I began to speak at the same time, then we laughed and she held up her hands in surrender. I began again, more slowly this time.

"Aunt Charlotte, what a delight to see you. And what brings you to court? We had no word you were coming, or at least none I heard." As soon as the words were spoken I regretted them. I hoped my greeting did not sound like a rebuke.

"Alaïs, I had no time to send ahead. I arrived only this afternoon. I have received news from Moissac Abbey that I thought Philippe should hear. And I wanted to bring it myself."

"What news, pray, Aunt?"

"The abbot at Moissac has paid a visit to the court of Count Raymond at Toulouse and encountered rude challenges from some of the nobles, who appear to follow the new religion. Charlotte thought Philippe should have the letter from the abbot that describes the painful confrontation." William responded for her. "It will be a help for me to know, also, what news there is before I leave on my mission."

As if on cue my brother joined us, providing a temporary distraction. "We have been waiting for you, Princesse, before we take our places for the feast. Pray, let us tarry no longer." Philippe took my elbow in a way that brooked no resistance, and we led the group to the table on the dais.

"Did you know of Charlotte's coming?" I dropped my voice, so as not to be overheard.

"No. There was no message ahead of her arrival. She whispered when she greeted me that she carries a letter from the abbot at Moissac. She doesn't trust couriers. She seemed quite secretive."

"What could be in the letter? Have you seen it yet?" Philippe was handing me up the steps to the high table and I turned as I spoke, keeping my voice low.

"I had no time. She just walked into the hall before you. I told her I would see this missive tomorrow morn, before the hunt. No sooner were the words from my mouth than William joined us and eased her away for a private conversation."

"Have you found out more about Constance's clandestine meetings in Créteil?" I whispered so the footmen standing along the stone wall would not hear.

"No, and I don't want to talk about this where others may overhear." Philippe smiled as he spoke, looking beyond my shoulder in that annoying way he had sometimes of appearing to search for more interesting company while talking to me. He nodded at someone and I turned to see the two papal legates mounting the dais. Amaury appeared refreshed, apparently recovered from the trauma of viewing combat that afternoon. Pierre's eyes were downcast and he did not meet mine, though I tried to give him a reassuring gesture. My brother beckoned the page to assist me into the seat left vacant, once again, by the queen.

I prayed Philippe would not motion Amaury to the seat on my right, longing instead for William to take it. But it was not to be. A royal motion sent the abbot to my side and I turned to make a quick grimace to my brother's back. On Philippe's other side sat my aunt Charlotte, then William, then Pierre de Castelnau.

With surprise, I saw my aunt Constance being led to the place on the other side of Amaury. Well, well, this might prove interesting, indeed. Perhaps through listening to their casual dinner conversation I would gain some clue as to the meaning of the earlier, more intimate, meeting I had stumbled upon. Evidence was mounting that my aunt Constance, who appeared so seldom in public, had a remarkable affinity for more personal conversations, and not only at Créteil.

I turned in my chair to greet my aunt as she passed behind me, led by one of the king's pages. We were not on such close terms that we embraced. Still, her brother had been my own father, so I gave her my hand and accepted her slight bow of courtesy to me (she was, after all, now only the wife of a deceased count and sister to a deceased king whereas I was a reigning king's sister and a *princesse* in my own right).

"You are well, Aunt?"

"Yes, I have been so. I saw you in the presence room this morn, Niece, but we had no chance to speak. You did well with the role the king assigned you."

Did I mistake her look, or did her eyes narrow somewhat as she spoke? But then she continued in her throaty voice, "You must come visit me. It has been too long since we have spoken." This was the invitation I had waited for. I glanced at her, observing her closely. Her wizened face, small and expressionless under the lace mantilla held in place by the tall combs, gave nothing away. At such close range I noticed the wrinkles of age. And the thin lips, tightly drawn, that gave her face such a forbidding expression. She had the almond-shaped eyes of the house of Capet, though, no mistaking them, and they shifted warily from my own to the figure of the king next to me.

"I would be delighted to do so, Aunt. Mayhap tomorrow, shortly after the noon meal? The nobles will have departed by then, and the castle will be quiet." I was pleased that she had made the offer. When we met I could probe for the answers to the king's questions at my leisure. The burden of the conversation would be on her.

"I think not on the morrow. I will be much fatigued after the festivities today. And the morrow is *dimanche* and there will be the Mass in the morning. But the day following would do." She lowered her short, rather stout body into the assigned chair, and now the abbot's bulk was between us. He acknowledged her presence by rising slightly and producing a half-bow. She looked up as he resettled himself. Even seated, he towered over her.

"Abbé Amaury," she said in a manner not at all friendly.

"Countess." He gave a perfunctory nod.

"I wonder that my nephew seated us together. It cannot be comfortable for you to find yourself next to the mother of your enemy." I stared straight ahead while overhearing these words, glad a servant's efforts to pour wine hid my surprised look.

Philippe had given the signal and the trumpets sounded the entrance of the roast boar, which was carried on a huge slab of wood, shoulder high, by six stout servants. The crowd, which had grown hungry, shouted its approval. The boar, already sliced, was set on a table in front of the dais and a flock of servants descended on it and carried away platters to all corners of the hall, serving first the king and high table. The trumpets announced the entry of the kid, the next course. The pageant was repeated, and the crowd finally fell silent as platters of meat were placed on every table and the courtiers proceeded to the business of hearty eating.

"Countess"—I could hear the abbot's gravelly voice as a break occurred in the noise—"I do not blame you for Count Raymond's shortcomings. Nor do I bear your son any ill will."

"Yet you seek from my brother's son, the king of France, arms and men to use against my own son." Constance spoke in tones laced with bitterness.

"Madame, I seek to do the will of God. I have no intention of harming the count or any of his vassals." The abbot slammed down his goblet. "But he seems unable to stem the tide of disbelief in his realm. We intend to help him. I have no doubt that the sight of the good men of the north, loyal sons of Rome all, coming to aid him in persuading his nobles to reform their ways will be welcomed by Count Raymond."

I was increasingly puzzled by this conversation. Had I not seen these two erstwhile enemies not an hour earlier deep in intimate conversation framed in twilight streaming through the arch in the castle wall? But here they were, trading jibes as if they had not talked before. Was it for my benefit?

Without warning the abbot swung his powerful bulk in my direction, his beetle brows coming together fiercely over a strange half-smile. He managed to appear both sardonic and ingratiating. I waited for his opening sally.

"I suppose you think the performance you gave at the king's audience today was quite successful. You no doubt believe you have blocked my mission here at court?"

"I don't understand your meaning, Abbé," I replied, busying myself by tasting the soup that had just been set before me. "I merely gave an honest opinion when the king asked for it. My advice has nothing to do with you. My brother's realm is my concern."

He placed his elbow on the table and propped his chin with his hand, affecting a focus on me that was meant to be disconcerting. His tone was low, intense and provocative.

"I don't know what your motive is, my lady, but I knew from our first encounter last evening that you have designated yourself my principal adversary here at court." He pursed his lips thoughtfully. I glanced at him and saw hostility written broad upon his face.

"But I know you and those like you. Your faith is weak and you will not triumph in the end. They say you have special gifts. But we know the source of those gifts, don't we?"

Now I stopped eating, and turned to look full at him. I let the silence between us run to an uncomfortable length as I waited for him to fill it. Finally, as I had hoped, he went a step too far.

"Perhaps you can exercise your so-called special gift, and help the king see where his interest will lie in the future, now that John of England has him on the run in the west. He needs all the allies he can get, my lady. He should not be making enemies at this time. You, who can tell the future it is said, should know that."

The abbot turned back to the table and appeared absorbed in stirring small pieces of dates into his almond cream pudding. So casual was he that I wondered, for a moment, if I had heard the words correctly. Then he added: "Just as you no doubt knew ahead of time, through your special gifts, what would befall the young knight of Lord William's household today at the tourney."

The servant set a plate of sweetmeats before me, giving me time to take a long breath and gather my wits. The last question had caught me off guard. The memory of young Geoff was still raw, but I held in my anger and did not respond. Carefully I brought a piece of raisin cake to my mouth, chewed it thoughtfully, and washed it down with a splash of wine before I answered.

"Special gifts," I murmured. "I don't understand what you mean by such a term, Abbé."

"Well, let me be clear then. Rumor has it that you have powers most of us ordinary mortals lack." ' He ran his tongue around his lips, as if savoring some special delicacy. "It is said that you are marked, that you can see things others cannot, visions and such." He made a rolling motion with his hamlike hands. "I thought perhaps you could see what will happen if the Cathars are allowed to run free in the south. What a threat . . . "—here he paused for effect—"the war that is sure to come could pose to a France already weakened by the English armies' victories."

I had a flash of desire to ask him how he knew about the English victories, but chose the other path. I knew this exchange would define our future dealings. With just a little more effort, we would finally have honesty between us. Then there would be no going back.

"Well, Abbé, I lay claim to no such a gift as you describe, a gift I believe is known as second sight. To admit that I had this gift, as you must know, would surely be a danger in these times."

I pulled my malformed hand from its pocket and removed the glove from it. I deliberately laid my arm in front of me along the edge of the table, so that the claw almost touched his arm, resting on the table. "If I did have such a gift, I could never admit it. Holy mother church might look upon me as a witch, an aberration just as she looks on the heretics of the south. And we know the fate of witches and heretics, do we not?"

I looked straight into his eyes. He held my gaze, but I could feel his bulk pull back slightly. I knew he had glanced at my withered hand when I laid it before him. He must know the peasants thought such a misfortune to be the sign of a witch. The abbot was using every part of his will not to stare at it. A man of learning, he still had just enough superstition to be slightly afraid.

"*Je crois que vous avez raison, Princesse,*" he finally agreed. He scanned my face, then added: "It is surely not a gift you would want to flaunt, not in these times."

"Let us understand one another, Abbé," I leaned my head closer to him, as if I were about to impart a state secret of immense importance. "I am a *princesse* of the house of Capet, a daughter of the kings of France. I am not an ignorant farm woman to be cowed. Nor am I afraid of men. You have your realm of power, and I have my own. Let us each respect the other's province." I carefully pulled the glove back over the withered hand, looking all the while at the prelate. "Or let us openly declare war." I withdrew the hand out of sight and laid it in my lap, sitting back in my chair.

I had seen him flinch and that was enough for me. I turned away and made an effort to take no further notice of him.

A servant came between us to pour wine, and in that instant my aunt Constance demanded the abbot's attention. I looked out over the table at the milling crowd, nursing my thoughts. I had been brave, nay perhaps foolhardy, to set that discussion in motion. Still, we had taken the measure of each other. I had now been introduced to the real Abbé Amaury, a driven and unscrupulous man, one willing to threaten obliquely and perhaps powerful enough to breach the protection of the crown. And he was now, officially, my declared enemy. I didn't need the gift of second sight to tell me there was a feeling of apprehension gathering in the pit of my stomach.

Suddenly my morose musings were interrupted and all thoughts of Amaury fled. I saw de la Ronde, who had just entered the hall with three men, nearly running toward the king's dais. He clutched a scroll and had not even taken the time to doff his hat. I placed a hand on my brother's arm, and nodded toward his aide. When de la Ronde reached us he bounded up the short distance and came directly to the king, falling on one knee. Philippe's attention was fully engaged.

"De la Ronde, what is the meaning of this interruption?"

"Your Majesty, this message just came for you. The page carrying it says it is urgent. It is from your head counselor, Sir Etienne Chastellain."

Philippe motioned de la Ronde forward and took the scroll, frowning.

"Shall I see an answer delivered to the chief minister, Your Majesty?" De la Ronde's face was grave.

Philippe held up his hand as he shook open the scroll. His lips tightened as he read the contents. Amaury and my aunt brought their odd exchange to an end as their attention was drawn by the disturbance.

When he had finished reading, the king rose and motioned to William, who came immediately to the king's side. They moved a bit apart from the table. On impulse, I slipped from my chair and joined them. William put his hand on my shoulder and drew me closer as my brother was speaking in a low tone.

"William, would you see what this means? I can scarce credit this news from my chief minister." Philippe handed him the rolled message. Those at the king's table had momentarily ceased conversation when the messenger arrived, but the hubbub slowly began again.

William scanned the note, glanced at me and then at the king. "What would you have me do, sire?"

Philippe looked briefly at me before he spoke to his friend.

"I want you to go to St. Denis immediately, this night, and see what has happened. If this message proves true, I order you to leave for Toulouse at dawn."

"What is so important that you must send William away? He has scarce arrived at court." My rising voice betrayed my concern as I suddenly thought of Francis. He would go with his lord. Must he now, so soon after our reunion, be separated from me? And on the day of his friend's murder on the field!

"Raymond must hear of this matter directly from my personal envoy." The king's tone was stern. "There is too great a chance for misunderstanding if it were otherwise. Alaïs, we are trying to avoid war. I am sorry for it, but this is no time for personal consideration."

"But what could be so important?" I persisted.

The king shook his head, his face grim. "Etienne writes that a theft has taken place at St. Denis."

"A theft? Why would they disturb you at dinner for a simple theft from the abbey?"

Philippe leaned closer to me, and spoke so low I could scarce catch his words. "The chalice we talked of earlier, the one with the gold braid wrapped around the stem."

"The cup of Saint John? The one Raymond gave you for safe-keeping?"

"Yes. Well, it's gone. And the sacristan on duty, who may have seen the thief, was killed in the event."

"Murder in a sacred place!" While I had no love for the fanatics of religion, I was a great believer in spirits. It was not wise to tempt them with such acts.

"There is some political aspect to this, I know it." Philippe could not hide his distress. "This theft and murder is an effort to divide Raymond and myself even further, but I don't know who is behind it."

"That explanation assumes the thief knew that the chalice belongs in Toulouse," I said sensibly. "We don't have evidence of that yet, Your Majesty."

"That's why you are to investigate now, William, and leave immediately for the south if the report proves true. The disappearance of the chalice could affect the success of your diplomatic mission to Raymond's court, as well, and destroy all Our efforts to avert war. Someone wants you to fail and they want to see France weakened.

We must discover who or what conspiracy did this dastardly act."

I recalled the abbot's words, uttered moments earlier: "What a threat the war that is sure to come could pose to a France already weakened by John of England." My sense of foreboding increased as I watched William move swiftly through the hall with de la Ronde. He would be leaving and so I would lose Francis yet again. I was certain of that. But, for once, I could summon no vision, no picture that might help me know what was to come after.

13

PARIS COURT

Chambers of Princesse Alaïs and the Courtyard

ater that night, I was roused from a sound sleep by a familiar voice.

"Your Grace! Mistress! Princesse Alaïs!" The thin, sweet voice rose as it called each new title. The wave of sound was moving unmistakably closer to my ear, and I could no longer ignore it, although I could scarce pull myself upward from my deep slumber. I had been dreaming of a flock of doves, pure and white, flying low against a blue summer sky. I desired to join them and began to float upward. One dipped low and brushed my forehead.

"Your Grace, you must attend. Please, wake. Please!" I opened my eyes and saw my maid's sweet face hovering over me, unaware that the end of her soft veil was brushing my face. Her own countenance, seen in the uncertain light of the candle she held high over my head, was the picture of dismay.

"What is it now?" I asked, sleep crowding

my voice. "Have I not just begun my rest for the night?" But I struggled to sit upright with her help. Even in my half-awake state I knew that Mignonne never disturbed me without good reason.

"Princesse, you are needed at once in the courtyard." She was breathing heavily, as if she had been running.

"The courtyard? At this hour? Have you gone mad, Mignonne? It is quite the middle of the night. Even the moon has gone to sleep." I was still brushing the cobwebs of dreams from my eyes with the back of my hand.

"No, my lady. It is the Lord William who sent for you. His man is even now standing at the door, waiting to escort you."

I glanced to the still-open door and saw the outline of a burly man of some height, holding high a torch that flickered in the gusts of air that swept through the open spaces along the outer wall. His cloak danced around him.

I sprang from my bed, throwing a fur robe around my shoulders, stuffing my feet into the felted-wool slippers that stayed always by my bed. They were a protection against the cold stone that could be sensed even through the rushes covering the floor.

"Run ahead, Mignonne, and tell the Lord William that I come in haste." As I entered the outside corridor the winds that flew through the palace in the winter, especially at night, clipped my face. Mignonne, fleet-footed always, flew on ahead while the man with the torch stayed just in front of me.

I used the wall along the way to steady myself, my right hand sliding over the moss that lined the stone stairway, the flickering light of the torch held overhead providing little help in the narrow, winding passages. Even though there were rough stone edges jutting out from the wall, the slime that covered them did not allow for a good hold for my hand. I was forced to feel each step with my toe before proceeding, which slowed my progress considerably. A mouse squealed under my foot and, no doubt as startled as I, fled.

Why was William sending for me at this odd hour? Something must have happened. Perhaps he had changed his mind, and was willing now to let Francis stay! I hardly dared to hope, but what else could this summons mean?

As I came into the courtyard I spied him immediately, always nearly half a head taller than the knights who surrounded him. I ran forward.

"William!" I called out. "Will you let Francis stay after all?"

He was busy shouting orders to the right and to the left, and his groom was saddling his horse with dispatch. William turned at the sound of my voice. He appeared oblivious to my question.

"Alaïs, you have come. Good," he said, in the terse manner he adopted when he was commanding his men or his servants. "Come, I must talk with you where we will not be disturbed." So saying, he drew me to the side of the courtyard, where there were no men or servants, and very little moonlight. It was impossible to read his expression, but somehow I knew my initial guess had been an arrow well off course.

"William, why did you send for me?" He was pulling me along, in his hurry, to a place where a bench sat against the outside wall. The milling men and horses were only two stones' throw away, but I blocked the noise so as to focus on what he had to say. After drawing me to sit near him, he hesitated, seeming to have trouble finding the words to speak.

"Alaïs, it's about Francis," he began. My heart leaped.

"Oh, William." I placed my hand on his arm. "You will let him stay with me after all." He stared at me for a moment, as if I had lost my senses.

"Changed my mind?" he echoed, then shook his head with some impatience. "Christ's blood no, the very opposite. Alaïs, listen to me. I could not leave without telling you. I know you will hear the news at first light from someone in the court."

"Hear what?" I leaned closer as his voice had dropped.

"Francis is gone."

"Gone?" I repeated the word like a village idiot.

"He should have been waiting for me when I returned from your chamber tonight. I had sent him his instructions before I left for St. Denis, and it is unlike him to be late. He knows my impatience. Still, I had preparations to make, so I took little note when he was not in my apartments." He pressed his temples with his thumb and fingers, as if to erase an ache that lurked there. "When my preparations for the journey were complete and he had not appeared, I sent two of my squires to fetch him. They were back in minutes to summon me. They said I must see what they found."

"What they found," I said. This time it was not a question. A cold feeling, as if I were touched by ice, began to take me over. I shivered.

"It appears that Francis has been abducted, Alaïs." William threw his arm across my shoulders as I began to sink backward, a sudden grayness overcoming my vision, a buzzing in my head. "I wanted to tell you myself before I left," he added stiffly, as a soldier would give a report from the field to his captain. His words sounded hollow, as if they had traveled through a great tunnel to reach me.

"Alaïs." William was shaking me, now reaching around to lightly slap my cheek with his free hand. I could feel the sting.

"Tell me what occurred," I said with an effort. "How do you know Francis has not simply gone off to have some time on his own? Has this aught to do with your plans to take him to the south? Perhaps he does not want to go." As the questions crowded forward I felt the cold of a moment earlier giving way to the warmth of anger. My back stiffened as I pulled away from his touch, and I could feel his arm around me loosen.

"We don't know exactly what has caused his disappearance," he responded. When I said nothing in reply, he cleared his throat. "This event, coming close on the heels of the tourney this afternoon, may be a warning intended for my house. I will discover what lies behind it, and I will find young Francis. I pledge that to you."

"Francis was despondent over young Geoff's death. Perhaps he needed time to think, to collect himself." I rambled on, ignoring William's words. I knew I was grasping at wheat stalks, but I cared not. "Or it may be that he decided to ride into the forest."

"In the middle of the night?" William asked, incredulous. "I think not." His voice was firm in contrast to mine. "It would be unlike Francis to go off on his own without telling me, when he knew we were to travel at dawn. And there is more. We found signs of a struggle in his apartment, papers scattered about, his travel *sac* tossed in the corner. Not the sort of thing one would find if a considered journey had been undertaken." He paused as he took a small roll from inside his clothes. He held up the item, shaking it out so I could see. "This was left, or dropped, at the scene."

"I can't make it out in the dim light," I said, feeling desperation creep over my body. In truth, my eyes would not focus on the page.

"It's a map of the area around Toulouse. And it is not crafted in the hand of Francis." He drew me from the bench to stand under a torch fixed into the wall. "And look, there are several towns near Toulouse circled. There they are." He jabbed a finger into the document. The vellum rustled in the predawn breeze. "Foix, of course. And Lavaur and Laurac. These towns must have some meaning for those who took Francis."

"So you think someone dropped that map accidentally as they took Francis?" I looked him full in the face as I flapped a hand dismissively in the direction of the map. The torch behind me threw his face into relief and I saw the lines in his forehead and around his mouth deepen. "I find that highly doubtful," I muttered.

"Why so?" He folded the map and tucked it into his doublet.

"Because I don't believe those who abducted Francis would be so careless as to leave behind a map showing where they intended to take him." I announced this boldly, forcing myself to a spirited stance.

"So you think someone left this to deceive us as to where they have gone?" William's voice was becoming more formal, a bit crisp. I noticed his arm had now dropped from supporting me in response to my contentiousness, as if to say that I was now on my own. "I don't think you understand how confusing an abduction scene can be."

"And I suppose you do know how confusing such a scene is. You have abducted men yourself, no doubt, in your role as leader of the Knights Templar in England." I heard my baiting words but it was as if someone else were speaking them. I had no control. I only knew a fury was rising within me.

"Alaïs, let us not quarrel now." William's tone indicated our conversation was at an end. He looked down on me. "I must be off on the king's business, to tell Raymond of the theft of his chalice and to fulfill my diplomatic responsibilities while I investigate the murder of the monk at St. Denis. But I shall make the search for Francis my first task. I will not fail in this. He is as dear to me as to you."

I looked up to meet his gaze. "William, I must join you. If you think Francis has been taken to Toulouse, I will accompany you there and see for myself. My maid can bring clothes in an instant. Look, she stands yonder waiting."

He shook his head with determination.

"Please, I must go with you." I was ashamed to hear the pleading that entered my voice, so firm only moments before. But I was desperate to take action, any action, to find Francis. Anything would be better than dithering among the fools in the royal court whilst my son was in danger. "I must find Francis. He must know that I am his mother!"

"Alaïs, there is no possible way . . ." William's hand came up to catch my elbow, with an iron grasp, a gesture meant to reinforce the finality of his tone.

I shook mysef free. "Very well. If you are set upon your road, so be it. But you force me to conduct my own search, with my own methods."

"Princesse"—his voice was more intense than before—"I must warn you that there are sinister forces connected with this affair that you know nothing about. I have certain information . . . This action is intended as a warning only for me. Let me attend to it." He paused, as if he already regretted saying too much. After a breath he continued, in a more restrained tone. "I will do everything in my power to bring your son home to you, but you must stay out of this. You would only complicate matters, and place yourself in danger doing so."

"I must do what?" My back straightened as I took in his final words. I stepped back slightly, tilting my head upward to meet his look. "How dare you issue orders to me, a *princesse royale* of the house of France!"

"This is a matter for men, Princesse! Leave it!" William's tone was now angry enough to draw the attention of his knights in the middle of the courtyard. The group ceased their milling and preparations for mounting, and fell silent, casting mute glances our way.

William looked in their direction, and said, more discreetly: "Have a care, Princesse. We draw attention ourselves."

"I care not, Lord William, whether or no we draw attention. I tell you I will not be ordered about by anyone." My own voice was ringing out. "And I will use every means in my power to find young Francis. Every means! Whether it is to your liking or not."

I turned and stalked away, flinging my final comment over my shoulder: "And when I find Francis, I will tell him the truth about his lineage. You shall not prevent me this time!" I was gone from the courtyard before he could answer. I did not look back.

I could not know how I would come to regret my rash exit from our conversation nor how different the circumstances would be when William and I should finally meet again.

.14.

The King's
Council Chambers

I pushed myself up with a stiff arm, and looked around. All seemed in order in my chamber, and I wondered if I had dreamt the noise that had awakened me. Or perhaps I had not latched the shutters closely last night, in my distress, and a gust of wind had caught them.

I reached for the bell that sat ever at my bed-side, and rang for my maid, who always slept in an alcove off my room, except on the nights when William visited. She appeared quickly, as if she had been waiting for my summons.

"Mignonne," I said, throwing back the furs on the bed, "help me to rise and prepare myself. And find a page. I would send a message to my brother."

"Yes, my lady." And the young thing sped about her tasks with her usual dispatch. I held up a silvered oval to my face, and saw therein the ravages of my quarrels with William, my anger, and my sleepless night. In dismay, I tossed it aside.

"Mignonne, as soon as you have found the page, come to my table and help me. Today, after we braid my hair, I would have you get out the pots of powder for my face."

"My lady?" The maid nearly stopped in midair as she was hopping about her business.

"I know. I never use those creams and powders during the day. But this morn I must look my best. I intend to have an audience with my brother, the king, as soon as possible." I glanced once more into the oval. "I need a boon from him. And to look at my appearance now, I couldn't persuade a blacksmith to invite me to supper."

Of course the king of France could scarce deny me a visit, when I had been so helpful to him only the day before in his public audience with the monks. But still, I would take all care so that he would not stand in the way of my plan.

So it was with a firm resolve, a slightly elevated heartbeat, and a face powdered and painted to hide the lack of sleep that I bade his guard announce my visit, waiting not at all for him to return with permission but rather following the man into the chamber.

Philippe was closeted with several ministers when I burst in unannounced. My brother sat at the head of his long council table, parchment rolls scattered in front of him, the inevitable great seal of France near his right hand. He looked up from his intense conversation with Etienne Chastellain at the sound of my voice calling his name. He did not look pleased.

"Sister? What brings you to my council room, unsummoned, at such an early hour?" His voice registered his irritation. He didn't rise to greet me, as he would have done ordinarily, although his counselors did so. It was well for them, for Philippe was a stickler for court protocol. "I sent word that I would see you later, after the noon dinner hour."

I held out my hands in supplication, sensing he was not yet done with his tirade.

"What is so important that you must interrupt a council on state matters?" he barked as I advanced toward him. He blinked when I came close, surprised at either the fatigue or the paint. "Are you ill?" he asked, his tone softening.

"Brother, I have matters of grave issue to discuss with you now. Immediately. And in private." I gave him a low courtesy and he, as I knew he would, gave me his hand and bade me rise.

"Could this matter not wait until my council has adjourned?" He was peevish, I could tell, but coming round.

"Your Majesty." I made my voice firm. "There are certain items I must discuss with you that may have an impact on your future decisions. They concern matters we spoke of recently." I cast a meaningful glance in his direction. If theft and murder were significant enough for him to send William shooting off like an arrow for Toulouse, the king most certainly should be interested in my own plans to depart for the south, for that is what I now intended. However, my absence would slow the investigation my brother had asked me to undertake. And, in any case, I did not dare leave the court without his permission.

"Very well." Philippe's response was grudging. But no matter. "Counselors, wait in the antechamber. I will summon you when I am ready to resume our meeting."

The six counselors had remained standing throughout this exchange, Chastellain shifting from foot to foot with scarcely disguised impatience. Even as Philippe spoke the others began picking up scrolls and quills from the table and packing smaller papers into leather *sacs* brought for that purpose.

Only Etienne Chastellain dallied. We had not seen each other since our irascible parting at the previous day's tournament, after the chief minister had pressed me to intervene on behalf of the monks with my brother. Now he spoke, his hands moving in that nervous, washing motion he employed when addressing the king: "Your Majesty, do you wish me to remain and record?"

Impudent rascal. We stood on either side of the table, the king seated between us. My gaze met the chief minister's. His was the more wary, and he looked away quickly. He wondered what my business with the king was. He had every right to worry.

But this was no time for me to address the issue of Chastellain's loyalty.

"Your Grace," I said smoothly to the king, "my audience with you is on private matters. They do not concern the court or the chief minister." As I uttered this, I detected a slight flicker of relief crossing that man's face. "And I do not think you will need a record of proceedings from our meeting."

"Very well," the king said, making a brushing motion with his hand. "Wait in the antechamber, Etienne, with the others."

"Yes, Your Majesty." Chastellain was now gathering up a stack of his papers and shuffling them into the case. "Your Grace." He bowed stiffly to me, then raised his head and confronted my gaze directly. I returned his brazen stare in kind. He turned and left without a word.

"Now, Sister, what is so important?" Philippe waved me into a chair. His demeanor was abrupt. "Have you news of Constance and her strange activities?"

"I know that I promised I would investigate the strange activities of our aunt Constance," I began carefully.

"But you may not know," he interrupted. "I have some disconcerting news on that score." He riffled the papers in front of him, and pulled out a small, folded square of parchment.

"What is it, Brother?" I was impatient to make the request for my journey, but the king must not be rushed.

"Constance has abruptly left our court." Philippe was tapping his quill on a blank piece of parchment, watching my face. "Do you know anything about this?"

"She has left court?" I had had little sleep the night before, with all the dramatic events, and so felt I had not heard correctly. "No, I had expected to meet with her tomorrow. She gave the invitation only last evening at dinner."

"Well, if you want to meet with her, you'll have to ride like the devil to catch up. She is gone, left early this morning, with only a note to my royal self. She says she is going to visit our half-sister Marie, in Troyes."

"You say that as if you don't believe it." I folded my arms on the table, leaning toward him. "I must admit I am puzzled that she left without sending me word after inviting a rendezvous. But why Troyes?"

The king shrugged. "It does seem passing strange that she chose Troyes. She dislikes the count, who also has just left for his home. If she were joining his family for a visit, why did she not ride with his party? And you know she and the Countess Marie do not have a cordial relationship." He shook his head. "So I had her followed. The two men assigned to her came back with interesting news. She took the road south after she crossed the Seine, not the road to the east."

"Are your men still tracking her?" I asked.

Philippe shook his head. "No. My instructions were only to discover the route she took, south or east." He smiled cannily. "If she is going south, there is no doubt she intends to join her son in Toulouse. But why lie about it to me?"

Suddenly the king frowned, as he recalled his interrupted council meeting. "But what is the reason for your demand on my time this morn? I sense the subject was not to be Constance."

I took a deep breath. "I must leave court, Brother. I beg your permission to do so. And I must go now. Today."

"Leave court? For what purpose? Where would you go?" My brother was rubbing his palm on his cheek, and it occurred to me that his tooth was giving him little rest. But I had no time for sympathy with his infirmities at the moment. Yet I dared not interrupt him as he produced a catalog of complaints in a rising voice laced with irritation.

"We don't want you to leave court. We need you here to assist us. We made that clear in our last meeting. We are no longer certain whom to trust. There is a new riddle now, a treasure stolen and a murdered monk. And Constance is gone. We need to know what mischief she wrought here, and whether she is part of the treason with John of England. And anyway," he added as an afterthought, "you still haven't told me why you want to leave."

I didn't point out that he had not given me an opportunity to respond. I merely took a deep breath. "Brother, all of those items notwithstanding, I tell you I must depart now for the south. William left last night on your orders and I have decided to accompany him, to follow him, to overtake him."

"Oh, he would like that not, Sister," Philippe said with surety, shaking his head. He picked up the royal seal and tapped it on the table nervously as he spoke. "William is on a dangerous mission. He must work for peace. He has orders from the holy father, and Raymond's situation is worsening. And William has an urgent assignment from me as well, to report the loss of the chalice Raymond entrusted to me. We believe the chalice theft is related to the Cathars and we want to prevent Raymond from doing something rash to make the situation more volatile."

"What could Raymond do to make things worse than they are?" I was nonplussed.

"He could publicly accuse the Cathars of the theft of the chalice and the murder of its guardian. The new sect feels persecuted enough now. Any challenge could promote open hostility and roil the land further. There may be war in spite of Raymond's promises at Blois." The king had taken to thumbing through his papers, as though searching for something that may or may not have relevance to our discussion.

I hadn't thought of the looming war, so wrapped up had I been in my personal loss and fear for Francis. But suddenly I made a decision to be honest with my brother.

"William now has yet another purpose in the south, one which came up later in the evening, after you had dismissed him," I said firmly. "It is more important than all the rest."

"And that would be . . . ?" Philippe looked up with interest.

"To find his former clerk, the young knight Francis, who appears to have been taken by force from his chambers just before William's party was to leave in the early morn hours."

"Taken by force? In my own palace? How can a knight of such an important household disappear?" The king drummed his fingers on the ink-stained oak table. "Well, well, that is unfortunate, but it changes nothing No doubt the lad will turn up. You must not concern yourself with William's business."

"Philippe, I don't think you understand. There were signs of a struggle in the young knight's chambers when William sent his men to look. A map was left, whether in haste or by design, that seems to indicate he was taken to the Toulouse area."

"You are fond of this lad, are you not?" Philippe suddenly focused, his look boring into me, that occasional disconcerting concentration that always made me uncomfortable. I glanced down. He leaned back and balanced his chair, his knees propped against the table. "And your next words will be that you, yourself, must go to Toulouse and find this young Francis."

I opened my mouth to agree, but before I could speak he cut me off.

"Don't even think of it, Sister. I will not allow it. And that is final." And for emphasis the front legs of his chair hit the ground. It was the firm sound of a royal denial.

"Brother, I will go to Toulouse." I slammed a fist on the table to get his attention. "Whether or no you will give permission."

Philippe's chin snapped up at my rebellion, a great frown taking possession of his handsome features. "You most certainly will not!" he exclaimed, and with such force my heart sank. His chair fell backward as he jumped up, towering over me, the king of France in a fury. For once I was wordless.

"You go to the south? At this time? I cannot credit that you would even suggest such a thing. I say again, I will not allow it, Alaïs! The journey would be far too dangerous." He thumped his knuckles on the table and the ink pots jumped. "The entire region is a seething cauldron. Anything can happen down there. Violence could be done to you, and we'd not know for weeks. And make me no argument," he added, as I opened my mouth to speak. "This is not just about you."

He wagged a finger in my face, leaning toward me. "You represent the royal house of France. You could be abducted by one or the other of the parties in this religious dispute and held for ransom. Or worse! I tell you, I will not allow it."

"Philippe." I took a deep breath. "You do not understand. This is a matter of my heart, my very life."

"Princesse, I know your love for William is exceptional," he shot back. "But these romantic feelings are no excuse for putting the house of France at risk. I say again, there is no way I will let you leave court now." The king strode away, his hands clasped behind his back.

"This is not about William." I was near to gritting my teeth to keep from screaming, but I kept my voice in check, turning my head to keep him in sight. "It is about Francis."

"I know you are taken with that young man." He cast these words over his shoulder as he busied himself at the long oak side table, shuffling papers, pouring wine from a pitcher. "Last spring, when he was here with William for the Easter celebration, I watched you together. I thought you overfond of him then. He is William's ward, not yours, and William can see to him far better than you." He added hastily: "Not that you are not capable—"

"Stop!" I stood up, knocking over an inkwell in the process. Leaning across the table as far as I could, I shouted at the king of France. "Stop talking!" Then I let out a long wail at the top of my lungs. It brought Philippe's diatribe to a halt.

He turned, looking both angry and amazed, whereupon my voice rose higher from sheer frustration. "I cannot listen to you lecture me for one more moment, when you know nothing of this matter."

"You may not speak to me like that. We are the king," he said, mixing his references as he was caught off guard. Then he added in a matter-of-fact voice meant to calm me, I am certain, "And you, the king's sister, are falling into a fit!" But there was no holding back my feeling now. I opened my mouth and took a deep breath, preparing to give vent to my frustration in a primal way.

"All right, all right, calm down," my brother said, looking around as if to find help, then moving toward me quickly. He put his hands on my shoulders firmly and shook me, then administered a gentle slap of my cheek, whereupon I came to my senses and closed my mouth, shaking my head as I got control of myself. Spasms ran through me, but I swallowed hard and willed them to stop.

"There, that is better," he said, quite pleased with himself. He resumed his chair and gestured me to do the same. I obeyed, trying to still my tremors.

"Now, you may speak, but only if you become reasonable." My brother knew he would have to tolerate what I was about to say, or risk another round of screams or worse, which might force him to call his guards. I gathered in my feelings, wrapping my arms around myself and praying that my voice would steady as I spoke.

"Francis has been abducted. I must find him and make sure of his safety. You do not understand the reason. He may be William's ward, but he is my own, natural-born son." My words were uttered slowly, precisely, as I knew they must be for their full import to be understood.

"What say you?" The king's self-satisfied expression disappeared and his face blanched. His head snapped up, like a deer that has just heard the step of the hunter. "That cannot be!" But even in his statement of disbelief I heard a note of doubt creep in. I could almost see memories crowd behind his eyes. He had noticed how, when Francis was present, I watched him always. He had heard the gentle banter about Francis when the king and I were alone with William. In his deepest heart, he must have harbored a glimmer of suspicion. "What say you?" he repeated.

"He is my son and he does not know it." I was mortified to be possessed at this moment by huge involuntary gasps, but I soldiered on. "He is in danger now and I will go to him. He must not die without knowing I am his mother." Suddenly I found my strength. My voice became calmer. "Philippe, I am his mother. And you are his blood uncle. Francis is also of the royal house of France."

Philippe stood and whirled away from me, the ends of his royal cape flying. For a moment I knew fear. He was, after all, the king of France. And I could sense rage, even through my own distress.

The choices raced through my mind. He could forbid me to go. If he wished, he could have me transported to the Louvre and thrown in that newly finished dungeon of his. If he forbade me the journey, then I would have to decide if I would obey. Would he actually have me restrained? I wasn't sure. But I knew enough to hold my tongue while he absorbed the news I had just broken to him.

Philippe reached the large windows and planted his fist firmly on the stone windowsill, stretching his torso outward as if to gather air and breath. He looked down upon an enclosed stone courtyard. I knew the royal market was busy this morning with the small farmers' stalls set up to sell to the royal provisioners for the week. All manner of victuals and goods were available. Would the king be distracted by the scene, his temper cooling? Or did he look without seeing as he contemplated what I had just said, allowing his anger against me to build. I waited.

Finally he turned back to the room, but he did not move to close the considerable space between us, a bad sign. He leaned on a stone pillar that framed the window, one hand propped against it.

"I scarce know where to begin," he said, and the irony in his tone was not promising. "Who is this Francis and who is his father? And why have you kept this important news from me all these years?"

"Philippe, the indiscretion was many years ago. The lad is, after all, old enough to be knighted." I sat upright, as if rooted in my chair, surprised, though, at how my fingers were tingling and my heart racing. I had courage, but my short breath now was all for my son's danger. That, and my fear that I might never see him again.

"It was when Eleanor was imprisoned and I was forced to live at King Henry's court. The king and I lived . . ."—how to describe that long-ago passion? I made a witless circle with my hand in midair—"together. It did not last long . . ." I tried to keep any emotion from my voice by taking one deep breath, then another. "There was a child. I was told it died."

"By God, so the rumors were true! That is why Henry would never let you marry Richard. He took you for himself." He flung himself away from the window, kicking a small stool out of his way as he stomped down the room like a petulant boy. "And with the fates of England and France in the balance, when we last met with Henry, Richard was willing to forgive everything if only his betrothal to you could be carried out. But Henry refused, yet all the while claiming there was nothing to the rumors of his taking you. And I believed him," he said, his voice ringing with bitterness. "When I was defending your honor for all those years, you were carrying on with him. When we were on crusade, Richard and I came to personal blows over you. I was deceived entirely."

"Oh, for the sake of the sweet, suffering Christ," I shouted, causing him to stop and turn around. "This is not all about you and who deceived you! You talk about how *I* carried on! You men all carried on, Richard and Geoffrey and John playing games to outfox their father, the old king. And you fomenting their family feuds, switching sides when it pleased you. You wanted their land and they wanted revenge on their father. And old King Henry died alone and cold in a strange castle, because of it." I paused, catching my breath.

"And France is in a weaker position because of everything that happened," Philippe said, tossing his black hair back from his forehead in his defiant way, striding back to where I was sitting, standing over me. "At the time, your marriage to Richard would have been to our advantage. But we were foiled by the old king lusting after you." Philippe shook his head, offering one final insult. "Richard probably would never have taken you after that, even if the king had allowed the marriage."

"And whose fault is that?" I countered heartily. "You men are all the same. No one had a thought for me. You used me as a pawn. And many died on both sides when you got your battles." I flung both arms outward. "You were all so manly, so wonderful, making war, acting as stupid as a pack of village idiots, and far more dangerous with your arms and your men." The words tumbled out of me, a stream I could not dam. My reason seemed on the edge of tearing.

After a moment I gained some control, and continued in a more restrained voice.

"But your games then have nothing to do with me now. I want to find my son, and I will do so with or without you." My sudden change of voice, more than anything, seemed to calm my brother's temper. There was a pause, and the waves we had created between us with our loud voices seemed to dissipate.

"Does your son know who his true father is?" Philippe eyed me suspiciously as he sank back into his chair. I instinctively moved slightly away from him.

"No, of course not. He thinks he is an orphan of all the wars you were so quick to inflict on your peoples. He was told by William when he was young that he was rescued by him in a war of King Henry's in the north, near York."

"Isn't that the same as William's own story, of his rescue by William Marshall near Caen?"

"Yes, I suppose he thought the story believable enough to convince Francis it was his own."

Philippe surveyed me with an expression that was glum. "Why haven't you told him yet?" he asked, in a voice slightly less hostile. "There has been no lack of opportunity. He has been with you many times."

"I wanted to but William forbade it." I deflated like a bellows, my righteous anger deserting me suddenly. My cheek sank onto my hand, my elbow propped on the table. "He says the times are too unstable politically, that this news could put Francis's life in danger if his legacy were known."

"What did you plan to do?" The king's voice betrayed no emotion now. He was eyeing me as if I were a wolverine about to sprint forward at any moment. "When would you tell him of his parentage?"

"William thought Whitsuntide next, when his diplomatic tasks are complete. Many political things may be resolved then. We thought we could safely tell him if he were with us, under William's protection. William felt then he could advise Francis on any course of action he might take."

"Like what?" Philippe was quick to interject.

"Telling King John, for example, that he was his half brother." I looked up. "Telling you he was of your own blood. Or perhaps not telling anyone anything."

"I see." Philippe's tone was flat.

"Francis looks upon William as his father, although he knows he is not. We wanted to make a family for him. You know we planned to marry next year, when William's service to the pope was finished. William would then have time to devote to Francis and his situation." The more civil tone of our exchange was having a calming effect on both of us.

"So he does not yet know who his true father is." A thoughtful tone crept into my brother's comment, almost as if he were talking to himself. I knew he was thinking now like the king of France. What advantage or disadvantage this situation might present to his realm.

I could see the mole at the side of my brother's mouth twitching, which meant he felt the same stress as did I. But I had no time for pity. My every effort must be to bend him to my will and allow me to go in search of Francis. Even though Philippe was a young king to have so much responsibility, scarce thirty summers, I would not sympathize. I would press any advantage. I could not take on his problems, as well.

"So you see, I must go." I sat up with a quick motion, and forced firmness into my voice, as if the interview were at an end. I made as if to stand and continued, before my brother could interject a word. "It doesn't matter what happened in the past. This is my son. He is in danger, and doesn't know it."

"Hold a moment, Sister," Philippe said, pointing to my chair with his finger. "Sit again. We are not finished." I sighed, but I sat. He was, after all, the king.

"We don't think you realize the implications of this for Our royal house. You had the bastard son of the late King Henry, half brother to John now reigning. He is also . . . or could be in the future . . . a threat to Our own throne here in France."

There it was again, the royal We, a person who inspired my impatience more than anyone I knew. All his thinking, his decision in this matter, would be driven by what he saw as the advantage to himself as king. I put my hand to my forehead and closed my eyes as I listened.

"Perhaps it is better if you do not tell Francis of his parentage. It is certainly better for Us if the world doesn't know. And what rights might he demand of me as king of France?" He began ticking off the possibilities. "Perhaps he will want some villages in the west? I haven't any counties to give right now. And how can I be sure he will not grow up to threaten my son? Little Louis is so vulnerable, with his mother sent from court by that wretched pope. The pope could even intervene if he knew—"

"Oh, God's teeth, Philippe," I finally broke in. "Get a grip on your thoughts, Brother. This is my grown son we speak of. He has a life of his own. He has earned a knighthood and he travels with William on his diplomatic missions. Even the pope was impressed with his learning last summer. He is not going to importune you for a benefice. He would defend little Louis with or without my direction, because he is a sworn knight. He will probably be mildly amused that he is related to you. He is my son, not some sycophant courtier. I tell you, Philippe . . . I *will* go to find him." Now I rose with determination, forcing the king to look up at me. "With or without your blessing. Though I should be sorry for the rift between us," I added, when I saw the look on his face.

Philippe blew out his breath and for a long moment he looked past me, out through the large windows cut in the stone wall of his state chamber, and to the blue sky beyond. "Well, well. I suppose you must go." He returned his gaze to me, a look of defiance on his face. "But I have to think of everything. That is my job as king, to anticipate what will happen, to protect my royal house, and my people."

I wanted to remind him that his past practice of anticipating had not been a raging success, especially where the Plantagenet princes had been involved, since he had lost nearly all the major battles over territory to them. But that remark would rub salt into his royal wounds. So I forbore to speak.

Then he said, almost plaintively: "How can you go to the Toulousain? You do not even speak the language!"

I smiled a bit weakly, reluctant to remind him again of my past life. "Brother, ignorance of the langue d'oc is one barrier I will not have."

He frowned in confusion. "But . . ."

"You know that before you were born, Eleanor and Henry's heir, the young king Henry, was betrothed to our sister Marguerite. At that time King Henry and our father ordained that I would marry Richard, the second son, and sent me to live at England's court. Richard was to rule the Aquitaine, his mother's land, and it was planned that I would rule with him. Queen Eleanor herself taught me the langue d'oc, the tongue of her own youth. Richard and I learned it together, tutored by his mother." I tried to keep my voice steady, and to push down the memories that intruded. For, in truth, the humiliation of my failed betrothal to Richard still made my heart sore.

My brother regarded me with a long look, no doubt remembering again how that betrothal had come to naught, partly through his own doing in conspiring with Henry's sons against the old king. Then he picked up his quill and began to dash off a note in his own hand, which I took to be a safe conduct for me.

"Who should go with you to protect you?" he finally asked, as he signed with a flourish. "You cannot travel with less than five knights into this dangerous land." He spoke now with the firmness of someone used to giving orders, stamping his just-finished note with the royal seal. "When you went off to Canterbury those years ago, you had four knights, and that was not enough to keep you from being abducted by John."

"I don't want a gaggle of knights to slow me down." I slapped my open hand on the table to catch his attention. But he only continued writing, after which he rolled the parchment and dripped wax on it from the candle-heated silver container that was never far from his side in this privy chamber. Then he applied his ring to the soft red wax and handed the roll to me. "Hold this carefully until the wax is firm," he said, as if I were somehow lacking in practicality.

I bowed and made ready to leave.

"Stay, Alaïs," he said with firmness. "We have not finished. I said I will allow you to go, but only if you are properly protected. Do you have a preference as to knights? Or shall We assign them to you?"

Philippe had donned his kingly role again. Given the display of his famous temper that I had just witnessed, I knew I was lucky to get permission for the journey at all. I didn't press him further.

"I'd like that strong young knight Roland to be with me again. Also Marcel and Thibault." I shrugged. "Any more can be at your discretion. But I am satisfied with those three." I paused. "And Tom of Caedwyd, if he feels fit."

"One-eyed Tom? King Henry's valet? He is old, Sister." Philippe frowned, as if assessing a horse that had outlived its usefulness. "You need brawn for protection. You are riding into a hornet's nest."

"Tom of Caedwyd is canny, and still strong," I said, with all the firmness I could muster. "And he is immensely loyal to me. I do not fear for my life if he rides at my side."

Philippe nodded. Loyalty was something he understood.

"How about your personal comfort? You should have one or two of your maidservants with you. It's not fitting for a *princesse royale* to be rattling around the countryside with only knights for company." Philippe stood now also, his hands on his hips, a challenging look on his face.

"Philippe, Mignonne is the best of my maids. And even she would slow us down considerably. Young women servants have never been taught to ride horses for speed, as I was." I was arguing calmly, but inside I was turbulent. This could turn into a disaster if Philippe took control of my plans. "If I take a maid, we'll be at greater risk. Our party would then be so large we might draw attention when we stopped to rest, or change horses."

Philippe saw the wisdom of this, and nodded. Then he suddenly laughed, taking me by surprise. "Someone should have seen that your maids learned to ride, as part of the training needed for your service. Come. I have something for you."

He turned and signaled me with a careless movement of his hand to follow. He led me to a tall cabinet at the side of the chamber. It was broad, made of carved oak, and there were four distinct doors, each with a set of large locks on it. Philippe pulled a key from a ring hanging from the belt at his waist, and opened the center doors. He reached down and extracted a jumble of scrolls. It took both his hands to hold them. Edging the door back into place with his foot, he motioned to me with his head to turn the keys hanging in the lock. Then we moved to the conference table in the center of the room and he opened the largest scroll, placing small stones to hold the four corners.

I looked at the vellum, moving the candle on the table closer to it. What I saw made me draw in my breath sharply. He opened several others and laid them out in a similar manner.

"Philippe, where did you get these?" I riffled through the sheets and saw the most detailed maps of the towns of the southwest, country towns ruled by lesser nobles, towns that had been accused of promoting the Cathar religion. They included the towns in the map William had waved at me, the map left in the disarray of the chambers of my missing son.

"Their provenance is of no importance, Sister. I am going to let you copy these documents to aid you on your journey. You have drafting skill and you have about an hour while I distract my counselors with food and wine." He was pulling the cord of the bell impatiently to summon the servant even as he spoke.

"Here is parchment, here is charcoal." He pulled blank sheets for me as he spoke, and tossed several new chunks of charcoal on the table. "The ink, alas, has been spilled," he added dryly.

"Sorry for that, Brother," I murmured making my voice uncustomarily meek with an effort.

"Copy this set of maps," he went on. "Pay attention especially to the map of Toulouse, the one on the bottom that shows the defenses and streets from the inside. And don't forget the maps that show the towns of Saissac and Foix and Laurac. These are the strongholds of the viscounts of Raymond's land. If your lad is not in Toulouse, he may be hidden in one of the mountain towns."

I leaned forward eagerly, scarce listening, my elbows covering Toulouse and Narbonne on either side as I examined the land between them. In one of these small towns I would find my son. I was certain of it.

Philippe paused for a moment, then placed his hand on my arm.

"I have a message for William if you encounter him in Toulouse, but I do not want to commit it to paper. Tell him we have need of him in Paris. I do not want him to tarry in Raymond's court. I am concerned with the treachery we have here. When he has informed Raymond of the theft of the chalice, I would see him return with all haste."

"Philippe, you must have a care. I am convinced Amaury and Chastellain are plotting together, and the goal is to put armed French soldiers at the gates of Toulouse. Please, watch for your own safety."

The king gave me a quick glance. "Why do you say so?"

"I was importuned by Chastellain only yesterday to intervene with you on behalf of the monks' suit. I do not know all the threads of this, but I think your chief minister does not have the best interest of the crown in his heart." I paused, uncertain as to whether I ought to tell the king of Amaury's veiled threat to me, or of Pierre de Castelnau's distressing revelations in my chamber.

But the import of Joanna's letter stilled my desire. It was best I not complicate this conversation with too much information for my brother. My goal was to leave the court and search for my son. The rest would have to wait.

So all I said was: "I believe these two, Chastellain and Amaury, intend to create mischief not only in your court, but for William's house as well."

Philippe was quick to catch the inference. "Do you think they are involved in the disappearance of your son?"

"I cannot rule it out," I said grimly.

"It is well you have warned me. This confirms what I suspect. And makes it all the more imperative that William return soon to Paris. If he can help Us, We may solve our problems here and aid in keeping war from the south. I cannot fight on three fronts at once, John in the west, the Cathars in the south, and Chastellain in my own court chambers. We must have peace."

"God grant it may be so."

I closed my eyes and saw an image of the chalice and a monk lying next to it in a pool of blood. The skin on my neck prickled. But I knew I must hide my fear from my brother.

The servant Philippe had summoned appeared in the doorway, entering after a brief scratch. It was the dwarflike Miguel, a dark-skinned manservant of the south whom Philippe had inherited from my own mother's Spanish contingent of servants. Miguel was ancient now, but—for his wisdom—closer to Philippe than any other personal servant.

"Miguel, recall my counselors. We were interrupted earlier, but I would dine with them now in my outer chamber. Summon them immediately and bring us bread and cheese, cold venison and wine. I'll join them directly." He thought for a moment, then added, "Bring an abundance of wine."

"Philippe, my brother, my thanks from the heart." I placed my good hand on his arm. "Not just for the maps, but for your blessings on my trip."

"Why, Sister," he said, a gently mocking tone creeping into his voice, "I know you would have gone with or without my permission. I might as well keep some semblance of command over you." But his eyes belied the slight testiness of his voice and he leaned forward to brush his cheek against mine on either side.

"Godspeed you, Sister," he said with great warmth. "With all this religious turmoil, you are going into the very heart of the beast on your journey. But I know your own mother's heart calls you to do it. Send word as soon as you can as to your well-being. Greet William for me and tell him we need his wise counsel here, as soon as he can return."

"I shall carry your message, brother."

"And Alaïs." He paused, looking thoughtful. "After you tell young Francis that he belongs to Our house, bring him safely back. I watched him in the tournament yesterday. He would make a splendid tutor for my son as he prepares for his kinghood. Our family must build its strength." And a smile spread across his face like the sun.

"You may depend on me, Your Majesty." I made a low courtesy and when I rose and met my brother's almond-shaped Capet eyes, for a brief moment I knew I saw a mirror of my own. And I forgave him all his faults.

In the Heart of the Beast

On the Road
to the South

We made a brave start of it at dawn, my knights and I, moving west and south out of Paris. At Philippe's insistence, I now traveled with a party large enough to wage a small war. Along with Tom of Caedwyd, who assured me he felt fit for the journey, and Roland the young, came Marcel and Thibault, longtime denizens of my brother's house. They all thought that my purpose was to join with William in Toulouse, to deliver a special message from King Philippe.

At first we had easy traveling, with innkeepers happy to help those who spoke the langue d'oïl, even though we quickly left the boundaries of my brother's realm. On the third day we came into lands controlled nominally by John and his agents. We became more watchful, although for a time things continued to go well. We found refuge at night from townsfolk outside of Tours who were suspicious of the new English king and his expanding ambitions. These townspeople valued their independence and liaison with Blois for protection. They were not unfriendly to France, no doubt looking to the future and the hope that they were close enough to Paris to be more than a neighbor one day, particularly if Philippe's forces continued to outperform those of the English king.

In Châtellerault a merchant provided beds in his own house, taking us for itinerant weavers. This error was understandable, for my knights wore garments of ordinary travelers to disguise themselves, their swords wrapped in their traveling bags and strapped to their horses. Neither did I now wear any insignia that identified me as royal, although I carried in my *sac* a small cloak that had such markings. Indeed, I was dressed as an apprentice, with my hair done up under a cap, as I had done when I rode to Canterbury with this same group of knights some years earlier on my first search for my son.

We did not disabuse the good-natured merchant of his notion, though when he asked about the new dye from Bruges I enjoyed a smile at the discomfiture of Tom of Caedwyd, who was posing as our leader. He could no more discourse on the merits of wool dye than I could, but he mumbled something about fatigue, and the good host shrugged and showed us to a room in his attic. I was surprised at the cleanliness of the muslin thrown over the straw bed, and pleased that no vermin were clinging to my doublet when I arose in the morning. We paid him well, and left him puzzling over how a troupe of weavers could afford the silver he was holding in his palm.

We continued moving south and soon found ourselves in Aquitaine country, Eleanor's patrimony. We also found the turbulent chieftains there had little interest in the safety of strangers, and that their peasants and townspeople were downright suspicious of our little retinue, especially my men with their northern accents. I was certain they could understand my men well enough when they asked for food or rooms, but often they pretended they did not. I began to take the lead, using the langue d'oc I had learned in Eleanor's court. At first the words came laboriously, like water out of a rusty pipe that had not been used for years. But soon I got back into the rhythm of the speech and innkeepers began to respond more amicably to us.

When we could not find lodging, or if the winter sun dropped low when we were still far from a town, we took to sleeping in barns, chewing bread and drinking wine we bought from—variously—kind or greedy villagers. The daytime weather warmed somewhat as we moved south. I washed in streams when the opportunity presented itself, my knights careful to stay around the bend and I always careful to be hidden by rushes.

I fell sick as we came near Poitiers, and we sought refuge at a small convent of nuns, Benedictines who knew of my aunt Charlotte and revered Fontevraud. I was feverish for some days, and could tolerate no food. Gradually, as the body often does, I began to heal myself. I will not say the herbs and potions the nuns concocted were harmful, though. Indeed, I believe they aided my speedy recovery.

My malady cost us nearly a week of time, but, truth to tell, my knights were glad of the rest. After the first days, they went out from the convent where the nuns gave us hospitality, and frequented the markets and public houses to hear any news they could of the situation in the south. But there was no market talk of value to us, except of the endless religious debates in the Toulousain. The practical *Poitevins* did not think much of this expenditure of vitality. When I felt strong enough, we packed and continued our travels with fresh horses.

It was farther south, in the region of Périgord, that I suddenly announced a change in direction. We had stopped in a rustic roadside inn for the night, a building that was little more than two stone structures cobbled together with a drafty wooden hallway. It was there that I made a decision that surprised my men.

Because I was beginning to tire, I had insisted that we stop at an early hour. There was a brook running behind the inn, and I took myself down to the banks and prepared to wash my face and hands. Then, on an impulse, I stripped my doublet and leggings and plunged into the cold stream, washing the dust of many days from my body.

I wrapped myself in my cloak and sat by the side of the stream, musing on the events that had brought me thus far. I could see my son's auburn hair in my mind, and willed myself to picture him wherever he might be, to know he was safe at least, but nothing came to me. Then I recalled my final argument with William, and I played again in my head my tart words in our last exchange: "I will use every means in my power, whether it is to your liking or not." I would I was able to call back those severe words. A trickle of regret entered my heart as I pondered that scene. All my years of commanding as a *princesse royale* had accustomed me to a certain hauteur. I did not expect anyone to gainsay me, and certainly not someone who had held me in his arms so many times and pleasured me with words and touch.

Now, perhaps, I had ruined all with my harsh words. I thought again of the map William had waved at me, and my dismissal of his assessment that it was a clue to the mystery of Francis's disappearance. If William was right, then there was some meaning in those towns that had been circled. The only way to discover the truth was to go to those towns and see for myself what they held.

So it was that after a supper of stew and country bread, I told Marcel and Thibault they had permission to retire, and I summoned Tom and Roland into my chamber. I spread the maps that Philippe had given me on a table, and sat on a low, rough bench in front of it, so I could easily show my men the plan. The others sat opposite me, their attention fastened on the papers in front of them.

"You know that our purpose eventually is to join with Lord William in Toulouse," I began carefully. They nodded gravely in response.

"But I have not been completely forthright with you," I said. "I also have another mission. I told you the first night we traveled about the young knight Francis, who was abducted from his chambers just before he was to accompany Lord William to Toulouse."

"The youth who fought so valiantly in the tournament." Roland looked up, interested. "You told us of his disappearance, but did not say a search for him was part of your plan."

"Indeed, it is my first task. I promised Lord William I would look for his young protégé." Inwardly I squirmed as I thought of how I was bending the truth and what William would have to say, could he but hear. I hastened on, hoping they would not ask too many questions as to why I wanted to find the lad. I was not yet willing to share the volatile information of his heritage, not even with these trusted friends.

"And in pursuit of that goal we are changing course somewhat. We are not going directly into Toulouse," I announced firmly, as I traced the route we were taking that led south with my finger. I stopped at a small dot on the map, some distance to the east of Toulouse. "Here is our first destination. Lavaur."

"But Princesse, why the change? And why Lavaur?" Roland looked puzzled. "I thought our plan was to continue south, and pick up the trail into Toulouse by following the Garonne River."

"On the map that William's men found in Francis's chambers the night he disappeared, three towns near Toulouse were specially marked. Lavaur is the farthest north, the first we will encounter." I looked at my men across from me, their faces dancing in shadows the candles threw. "If William is correct in thinking that the map was left by mistake then each of those towns must have some meaning to the abductors."

"You told us about that map. But I thought you had doubts that the *carte* was left accidentally. You said it was a ruse to mislead us." Tom pursed his lips.

I shrugged. "I have thought about it often, and decided I may have been too hasty in my initial assessment. It is all we have now to help us in our quest. We must begin with what we know."

"But what do you know about Lavaur?" Roland was pushing again. "If the map was intended as a trap, perhaps we would be playing into the hands of the abductors if we seek the young knight in the towns where they bade us go."

I sat back on the straw cushions that lined the bench, leaning against the rough wall.

"I talked briefly to the young lady whose brother is the Count of Foix," I said, "on the day of the king's audience where she spoke so passionately for France to stay out of the business of the southern counties."

"She who is called Esclarmonde?" Roland brightened. He had ever an eye for a beautiful lady.

"Indeed. The very same. When we chatted, she made a point of telling me that I would be welcome at Laurac or Lavaur as well as Foix. It was almost as if she were giving me a message." I paused. "She was quite specific. And she made a point of mentioning the women in these towns."

Tom raised his brows. "Quite a coincidence that they would be the three towns circled on the map that was found."

"My plan is to seek hospitality in one of these towns and begin our investigation of Francis's disappearance by questioning these nobles, if they seem friendly to us."

"Will you tell them at Lavaur that you seek the young knight? What excuse will you give for your appearance? Will you let them know who you are?" Roland, with his penchant for hurtling one question after another, suddenly became animated.

"I have not yet decided any of that. We shall see what the reception is at Lavaur, for our poor traveling group of . . . um, shall we say weavers." I grinned at Tom. "But we should get more information on Bruges dyes at some tavern before we hazard that disguise again."

Tom looked chagrined, but he chuckled. Then he turned serious: "Something else draws you to Lavaur, Princesse. What is it?"

"You know me too well, Tom, after all these years." I smiled at my old friend with his one good eye, and remembered how young I had been at King Henry's court when I saw the raptor claw his eye out while he was training the royal falcons. And how the king had made him a fast friend from that moment forward. Tom had been kind to me through many trials. He deserved to know my thoughts.

"I have a feeling, after watching la Esclarmonde, that women play a strong role here. Not like the Paris court where most women are merely decorative."

My knights looked at each other with comical expressions.

"Well, yes," I said, guessing their thoughts. "Perhaps that description does not fit my performance. But if I am guessing correctly, the women here may have something to do with the spread of this new religion. Their role interests me. And if they are in touch with traveling Cathar preachers, they may have news of young Francis. The lady Esclarmonde was passionate in her defense of the south when she spoke in front of the court that day. Whether it was out of loyalty to her brother, the Count of Foix, or whether she herself is sympathetic to the Cathars, I could not say. But her people may be of good use to me in my quest to find the trail of Francis."

The two knights fell silent, and then Roland broke into something like a soft laugh. "Ah, well, if nothing else, perhaps in the south country we can pick up the trail of the missing chalice of St. Denis and the murderers who took it. The abbot and the king must surely be willing to pay if we are successful."

I was lost in my own thoughts for the moment, and almost passed over what he said. But his words hung in the silent air for a moment too long.

"How did you know about the missing chalice?" I asked, slowly turning my head to look at him.

"Oh, it was all the talk in the palace stable the morning that we left Paris, as we readied the horses for the journey. The beautiful chalice, the cup that everyone says was to bring the abbey of St. Denis blessings, has disappeared." He laughed. "'Tis said there is a fat reward for the lucky man who finds it."

I saw again in my mind's eye the chalice lifting during the Mass, and the rapt attention of my aunt Constance following the jeweled cup. Surely the disappearance of the chalice and Aunt Constance at the same time was more than coincidence. Philippe was right: Constance was up to something, and the chalice was part of her intrigue.

"According to the tale you heard, how did this crime occur?" I addressed Roland because he seemed to have the corner on court gossip. Tom, from Wales and not always accepted in the circle of Frankish knights at court, would be the last to hear.

"The theft happened just that night, right after the great tourney. The stable lads were abuzz because it was said the sacristan was killed when the cup was taken. He must have come when he heard a commotion in the sanctuary."

"And how did the stable boys know this news?"

"Well"—Roland shrugged—"it was said they heard it when they were all down in the courtyard helping Lord William of Caen and his men prepare their horses for the ride. You were there—" Roland stopped as suddenly as he had begun, and his flushed face could be seen even in the candlelight.

"Yes," I responded dryly. "I'm certain the stable boys saw me there as well."

"Anyway," he continued, recovering with the aplomb of the young and thoughtless, "that's where the news was bruited about. It was said Lord William must leave for the south to explain something about the chalice to Count Raymond. By your leave, Your Grace, I must stand for a while, or my knees will never more guide a horse."

And so saying, Roland pulled himself up awkwardly from his sitting position. His tall body unwound with the stiffness of the traveler and I was put in mind of the late hour. "You know, when the cup appeared some weeks ago, it was said it came from the Holy Land, and all felt it would bring the abbey at St. Denis, and the king of France, good luck."

The young knight's face was maturing, taking on the fullness of manhood, much as the face of my son Francis was changing, I reflected. They must be about the same age.

"Your Grace?" Roland asked uncertainly, and I became aware that I was staring. I looked at the young man with fondness. "Nothing, Sir Knight. Only that the hour grows late, and we must begin our journey early in the morning." So saying, I offered my hand to Tom and he jumped up to help me rise. My bones were as stiff as a lance from the ride. And I longed for my bed, however humble it would be.

"Sleep well, my men, and we shall meet in the courtyard of the inn at dawn for the next leg of our journey." I added an afterthought: "Keep your tale of the missing chalice to yourselves for now. It is safer to reveal nothing as we travel." And so saying, I nodded to them and each bowed gravely in return. Then, without another word, they were gone and I was left to close my eyes and seek not the strong profile of Roland, but the tousled auburn hair and pale, freckled skin of my own son. And I could not hold back the tears this time.

.16.

The Castle at Lavaur

Gradually we worked our way farther south, and blessed the Virgin for the mild weather that made our riding days pleasant and allowed us nights full of gentle sleep. Finally, after three days, we stood at the bottom of a ravine looking up at the castle of Lavaur, a stone fortress lodged in the side of a hill. The land around it looked savage with rocks and stone everywhere. There were scattered blots of green on the hillside, but these were scrubby bushes scarcely growing. All in all, the picture did not appear inviting.

"Your Grace, I still don't know why we are here instead of going to Foix. It can't be more than half a day's ride from here. And consider: Foix is a much larger demesne and could offer us greater hospitality and perhaps a warm bath." Roland was at my elbow, importunate as ever. I turned to look at his face, no longer clean shaven, and the lines that clouded his sunburned brow. Even though it was November, the sun in the south was much stronger than we were used to on the chilly Île de la Cité. During our hard riding days on the road it had painted us all with its warm color.

At that moment we were joined by Tom of Caedwyd, who had returned from checking the trail around the first curve. Tom, with his canny sense and his wise head, was the perfect counterpart to Roland and his impetuous youth and quick temper. On the other hand, I was happy to have Roland's strong sword arm at my side in this journey.

"As I told you, I have taken a notion to see the dame of Lavaur, Roland." I could see his puzzled expression out of the corner of my eye, as I pretended to examine the small castle before us. "I feel she will aid us in our search for Francis. Now will you see if these good people will receive the sister of the king of France?"

"Oh, Your Grace," he said, laughing. He shook his head as he rode away to explore the road up the hill into the castle, saying loudly to his horse, "No bath, not at this time, Galant. But at least they will know she is a *princesse* and we will be fed." I could hear him whistle as he rounded the boulders that plainly marked the entrance to the path uphill that led to the castle. Marcel fell in alongside him.

I swung down from my horse and walked a bit at the side of the road, my palfrey strolling patiently behind me. Despite my leather leggings, my thighs ached with the rigor of days of riding and I needed to straighten them before they became permanently fashioned to the shape of the horse. I recalled Henry's bowed legs in later life, and smiled. He would roar with laughter if he thought I was going to imitate him in that. I could almost hear him shout: "God's blood, Princesse. Keep your feminine form and show your mettle some other way!"

Strange, I thought, how the spirit of the dead King Henry, once my lover and my lord, sometimes brushed near me when I was alone. It was as if he were riding at my side or standing just behind me, whispering in my ear. And I would hear not only what he had said in the past, but what he would say if he were in the here and now. And this even though I had found the true love of my life, Lord William. Yet I did not feel unfaithful to Henry, nor to William. It was as if I had two loves with me now, one a ghost and the other true flesh. Perhaps the best of both worlds.

Tom dismounted and followed a bit behind as I walked.

"Your Grace expects a warm welcome here?" Tom's voice, just over my left shoulder, reflected his skepticism. I thought a moment before answering.

"Esclarmonde promised that the lady of this fortress welcomes women," I finally replied. "I know her only by reputation, but I think we will be offered good hospitality." We both knew that being a sister to the king of France, in these days and in this region, was no guarantee of any welcome at all.

The clop of hooves receded, and I was aware that the sun was beginning its downward slide. I recalled that the sunset came quickly in the mountains, then wondered what reception Marcel and Roland would receive from the castellan, whether he would take their message to the Lady Blanche with speed, and how much longer until they returned.

Tom had reverted to his taciturn self, merely holding our horses and looking off into the distance. Thibault waited discreetly some distance behind us. He was a short, stocky man, gruff of manner and the least talkative of the group: a man's man, and a hardened campaigner. He often seemed uncomfortable when in my presence alone so I gave him his privacy when the others were not around. My thoughts wandered to Francis. I wondered where he was now. Perhaps closer than I knew. If only I could have a sign. The chirping of crickets broke the stillness. Suddenly Roland and Marcel reappeared from around the rocks.

"Your Grace, we have approached the gates of the castle on the upward side of the hill. The guards immediately sent to the lady of the castle. The message she returned was that we are welcome to all they have, although she warns she is not prepared to entertain a royal *princesse* of France in the manner to which she is accustomed."

I mounted my horse before his words were finished and Thibault was right behind me. We were all anxious to find safe haven before the night set in. The mountains, so friendly in daylight, could turn ominous at dusk, their looming shadows pockets of the unknown.

The path to the castle door was a circuitous route up the mountain, so that the guards in the castle turrets would have ample time to see strangers approaching. It made my mind easier to know we had already been assured of a good reception and would not be subject, even accidentally, to a barrage of arrows from the battlements as we wound our way up the hill.

And a warm welcome it was, or as warm as this chilly castle could offer. The autumn sun was not strong enough, nor the days long enough, to chase the dampness from these stones. A servant clad in a doublet of good wool and leggings stood inside the door slightly behind the guards as our horses clattered across the small moat, which was more like a little stream at this time of year. Still, the intention of the drawbridge to defend was evident. The servant bowed low as we entered the castle courtyard, and spoke before we had even dismounted.

"My Lady Geralda welcomes you and begs me take you to her in the Great Hall." The servant spoke in the langue d'oc, and showed a slight surprise when I answered him in kind. Then he smiled broadly.

Three grooms took our horses from us as we dismounted. Another servant, dressed more humbly, appeared and announced that he would show my men to their quarters and see that they were well fed. It seemed suddenly strange to me that our small group had shared quarters intimately, if respectfully, for a fortnight and now we were to be separated by our station in life, but that was the way of our world.

I followed the well-dressed servant into the Great Hall. We passed the fireplace and mounted a set of stone steps at the far end, and through a door at the top.

As we passed under the portal, the warmth and pleasant air surprised me. The chamber was not grand, but spacious enough and it was cheerful in a way that one seldom found in outlying fortresses. Torches everywhere flooded the room and candles were hung overhead by means of a multilayered wooden apparatus. Layers of rushes lined the floor and dried herbs were scattered overall. Sage must be burning in the fireplace also, I thought, for a fine, light scent filled the room as the fire crackled.

I paused at the door to take in the scene, and to prepare my answers for the questions that would surely come.

The fireplace and hearth along one wall were clearly the center of activity in the large room. Over the hearth was an enormous iron kettle, swung inward to keep its contents warm. I saw no oak tables laden with manuscripts, such as we had in Paris. Instead I saw a semicircle of cheerful women seated before the hearth, comfortable in colorfully cushioned oak chairs. Some had spinning staffs, others crewelwork in their laps. Still others worked on small frames of embroidery, their needles flying, chattering like a flock of magpies.

The servant with me cleared his throat, and then said the first words I had heard him utter since welcoming us in the courtyard: "Lady Geralda, Lady Blanche, honored noblewomen, I present the Princesse Alaïs, sister to the king of France."

All words suddenly ceased. Fingers and needles were suspended in the air as the women turned in my direction. I felt my travel-stained garments were a drawback to my royal image, not to mention the smudges I knew lined my face, but I had to make the best of it.

With one accord, the group rose. The silver-haired lady at the center of the group, tall, slender, with a grace of movement even my aunt Charlotte could envy, came toward me. Both her hands were outstretched in welcome. Just behind came a larger woman, younger but with a resemblance to her. It was as if she were drawn with broader bones in her cheeks and forehead, wider shoulders and less fluid movements.

"Your Grace, I am Blanche of Laurac, widow of Sicard," said the elder woman, "and this is my daughter Geralda, mistress of Lavaur. She is also widowed. Please accept our welcome for you and your companions. We are honored to have you with us." She made a deep courtesy to me. I could hear the fine wool of her sky-blue gown rustle as it brushed the dried wheat shafts on the floor. Her daughter, likewise, bent her head and her knee.

I was touched by their humble manner, and the gentle serenity I saw on both their faces. I raised up the Lady Blanche myself and embraced her, touching her cheek on both sides with my own. "My Lady Blanche, you are most kind."

I turned to her daughter and was surprised that I must look up to her. I am tall for a woman, and there are few that tower over me, but Mistress Geralda was one. Still, despite this, she was fine to look at, a noble head that one could draw with delight. But then a premonition passed by, between myself and the daughter, and I frowned. It might be only the fatigue from the road, but I saw, for a fleeting instant, Geralda's head bowed in pain as it was struck from above by a falling rock. I prayed in an instant this would not be her end.

"I thank you for your hospitality, Mistress Geralda, and wish you good fortune all the days of your life." I forced myself to speak this and, as I did so, my sight cleared entirely. I stepped back to look at both mother and daughter.

The Lady Blanche had an oval face that was nearly perfect in the arrangement of its elements. She wore the starched wimple of the widow, and her skin—like porcelain—echoed its pallor. Still, there shone from her something of the vibrant aura of one younger and brimming with vitality.

And the daughter was equally handsome in a much different way.

She must have forty summers, and yet had rose suffusing her cheeks like a maiden.

"And I welcome you to it with all my heart," Geralda replied, her large, brown eyes suddenly brimming with fun. "Come join us at the hearth. We have already taken our evening meal, but you must have hunger from your long travels, and you must be tired. Sup first and meet my dear friends and then I will have you shown your chamber."

With these words, the daughter took over as the mistress of the castle and the mother retired to sit with her companions.

I nodded at the invitation, although I would sooner have retired and had the meal brought to me in private. I was vastly fatigued and did not know if I could remember on the morrow one name or face of anyone I met just now. But I gave her my arm and let her guide me to the small group, who had fallen so silent I wondered if they would ever chatter again.

"*Mesdames,*" I said, inclining my head. At my approach they all made a polite but not exaggerated courtesy to me. It was clear they wanted to make me welcome, but they were not effusive. I was aware of my position and that of France, as an outsider in this land.

I took my place in the high-backed, oak-carved chair Blanche had vacated, when she motioned me to do so. I sank gratefully into its goose-down cushions. She herself took the chair at my side. Geralda bustled past me, and spoke rapidly in langue d'oc to one of the women who wore white muslin tied around their waists. She began to ladle something steaming from the kettle hanging over the hearth. Another woman appeared from out of nowhere, and set a small table at my side, and yet another brought a pewter goblet. Geralda busied herself directing them, while talking to me all the while.

"Your Grace, we give you our best wine, and I confess it is very good, indeed. It is from the harvest of two years ago, and you will not

find fuller taste anywhere, though you search the surrounding countryside. And our region is known for its wine!" She laughed, a hearty
laugh for a woman, and despite my tired body I had to smile.

"I thank you, Lady Geralda. We have traveled far, my knights and
I, and I must confess to being sore weary with fatigue, but I would be
glad of some refreshment now."

"And you shall have it. And your good knights as well." Geralda
turned to one of the women in a pinafore and nodded, and the servant
dashed off, no doubt to see to the comfort of my men.

"Princesse, these are my kinswomen and my friends. Ladies, please
introduce yourselves." Blanche swept a delicate hand around the circle
in a gesture of invitation. It was becoming clear that, while Geralda
was the lady of the castle, Blanche was the leader of the women present. None had resumed any of their needlework or spinning since I
had interrupted them.

"I am Philippa, wife of Count Raymond-Roger and Lady of
Foix," said the woman next to her, an open-faced woman with full,
bright cheeks and dark, sweeping eyelashes. The sister-in-law of Esclarmonde! I viewed her with interest.

My gaze, moving around the circle in tandem with the voices, suddenly froze. For the next woman had a face I knew. Older, surely,
and more lined than I remembered. But nothing could disguise that
slightly upturned nose, the high, aristocratic brow, the expression of
irrepressible merriment that even now threatened to break into full-
blown laughter as she waited for a sign of my surprise. I was stunned.

"Joanna," I cried, starting from my chair as she rose also. I nearly
knocked down the poor Lady Blanche who stood at the same time, as
if to calm the two of us as we threw ourselves into each other's arms.

None of the onlookers said a word, but there were many knowing smiles, for each must also have had dear friends from childhood
they thought were lost to them. Blanche wound up gently patting our

backs as my long-lost childhood companion and I held each other in a breathless clutch.

"Oh, my dear sister, *ma chérie*," Joanna was saying over and over again and I found my own face wet with tears.

"What are you doing here?" I said finally, when, by some tacit emotional agreement, we loosed our hold on each other. We were each rather breathless, myself from surprise and feelings that came racing out of my past, and Joanna, no doubt, from the same emotions.

"The hardest part was not to fly at you when you came through the door," she was saying, half in laughter and yet through tears running down her face. "When your men arrived and they said you desired our dear lady's hospitality, I nearly rode back down the hill with them myself. But the Lady Blanche cautioned me, and said the surprise would be so much sweeter if I waited."

Again I pulled Joanna to me in a great hug, although I gradually became aware that the others were sitting in amused silence. I began to feel my royal dignity might be compromised if I carried on much longer.

I released her and looked her up and down, feasting my eyes on her dear face and figure.

"You look so fine, Jo," I said. "Just as you did when you went off to marry the king of Sicily."

"Ah, you need not fear honesty, Alaïs. I know the years and my travails lie heavily on me." Joanna screwed her still-lovely features into a comical face, a trick that was so like the young, sassy woman I remembered that I laughed out loud. "Not to mention the difficult husbands that have been foisted on me."

I turned to the group of women, who watched with warm expressions. "This noblewoman is my childhood friend, and she is like my sister. We were raised together at the court of Henry of England and Eleanor of Aquitaine, and pledged our lifelong friendship." Tears began to crowd my throat and I could not continue.

"Did my letter of warning find you, Alaïs?" Joanna asked, as I put my hands to her shoulders and held her away from me to truly look at her.

"Indeed it did and I made my best effort to fulfill your wishes," I said. "And, I must say, with some success, although it was not difficult. My brother's will was in concert with ours."

"I knew you would help. You have the thanks of my heart," she said to me, as we embraced yet again.

"Come, sit next to your kinswoman," Blanche said, with what I was beginning to see was her customary kindness and authority. "I will take Joanna's seat closer to the fire. I am in need of warmth against this damp night. And you must be so glad to have found each other."

Someone cleared her throat, and the elderly woman who had been sitting next to Joanna drew Blanche's attention.

"Your Grace, this is Ermengarde of Narbonne, a distant kinswoman who now makes her home in my humble fort." I had resumed my seat, and smiled at the elderly, thin-boned woman coiled in her chair, her lined face framed by the immaculate widow's wimple. She nodded and her face lit up in a generous smile.

Next to her sat a large, rawboned woman with a crooked nose and heavy brows, a peasant, who had jumped up to wait on me, ladling the stew which even now sat cooling on the small table next to my chair. I noted that she had a white apron pinned over her gown, and that she was not spinning but carding wool, pulling it through the holes with a vigor that indicated she had done this all her life and still enjoyed it.

"That is Guillemette, my maid, who comes from the mountain towns to the west, and these . . ."—Blanche gestured to the other two who had hastened to help settle me when I arrived—"are my other maids, Brune and Raymonde, also from our villages."

I nodded to the servants. Blanche then introduced me to the three women I had not yet met who occupied chairs to my right. They were noblewomen of minor demesnes, every one a viscountess or lady of her own household. One by one, they nodded: Fabrisse of Saissac, Gaillarde of Fanjeaux, and Grazide of Montauban.

"My greetings to you all," I said, finally turning my attention to the cooling stew at my side table, which turned out to be quite tasty, especially when washed down with the red wine, full and pleasant as promised.

"I suppose you are wondering why so many noblewomen"—my hostess leaned forward as she spoke—"and why we are all gathered here."

"No, not at all," I replied untruthfully. I raised my wine goblet to Joanna on my left, and she toasted me back with her own cup. "Although it has always struck me that there are a fair number of noble titles in a small space of land here in the south."

"That's easily explained," the deep voice of Geralda intervened. She spoke with the same tone of authority that characterized her mother, although she had about her a certain earthiness that the wraith-like Blanche lacked. 'Twas often thus with mothers and daughters.

"If you understood our system here, you would see how humane it is. We do not, as you do in the north, turn out younger sons and leave everything to the eldest. We divide our lands, and make a place for each to have his own nest, his own opportunity to thrive. In the north, younger sons must hire themselves out as paid soldiers and leave their families to take up life on the road of fortune."

The tone of superiority in her remarks annoyed me. "There are many reasons for the practice of primogeniture, madame," I said, a cool touch to my response. "Yes, it is frequently difficult for our younger sons in the north when all of the land goes to the eldest brother. But some go into the church, and others find their way in the world as knights. And some are trained as scholars and become the clerics to the courts of Europe." I raised my brows slightly. "Many people do not have their security arranged for them, and they come out of it well enough in the end." I tore a piece of bread and bit on it definitively.

"Geralda merely meant to explain our differences, Your Grace. Do not take offense," Blanche said. "Our lands have been divided and subdivided, so our counties are quite small. The noble families of Foix, for example, or the Trencavels in Béziers, have diminished lands to govern as time goes on. And subsets, such as Saissac, Laurac, and Montréal have then their own rulers." Blanche motioned the maid called Brune to tend to the fire, which had subsided to a glowing mass. "Of course, the *petits nobles* owe fealty for their lands to their overlords," she added with a nod to me, "but you have that system in the north as well."

"Indeed," I said, thinking of King Henry and his proud sons doing homage at various times to my father and brother for their lands on the Continent.

"So, Your Grace, what brings you to our fair country? You are a long way from Paris." It was the round-faced Lady Philippa of Foix who raised the question. Suddenly all of the women were attending to their needlework and their spinning, and the maidservants began carding wool as fast as they could, as if none wanted to appear too interested in my response.

"I have cause to journey to Toulouse on personal business for my brother, the king of France," I said, affecting a casual air. "I had the great pleasure of meeting your husband's sister Esclarmonde at the court of Paris, and was intrigued by her. She told me I might find hospitality at Foix. But she also mentioned this place as one that would welcome me, so we thought to stop here and rest."

"But I am so glad you are here at Lavaur, as I would have missed you entirely if you had continued to Foix," Philippa said, adding quickly, "though Foix is open to you whenever you care to come. And I shall be leaving here within the day to return to my home, and would be glad of your company if you care to travel with me."

"I would like to journey with you," I countered. "But I fear my affairs demand that I visit Toulouse soon. I must see Count Raymond and I should not tarry here long."

"Foix is a considerable distance south of Toulouse," the Lady Philippa murmured. "I can see that it would be out of the way, if you have pressing business in the city."

"I have another purpose," I added, after a moment's silence. "I have a message from the king for Lord William of Caen. He departed Paris for Toulouse, just ahead of me." I paused, wondering how eager I should appear to find William. "I wonder if any of you has heard news of his arrival in this land?"

Joanna looked up quickly. "Yes, he did arrive in Toulouse, but—"

She was not to complete her statement, for a door flew open and a blast of cold night air invaded the room. We turned as one to see what had caused the interruption and there was an audible, collective intake of breath at the sight.

A tall man with flowing dark hair and beard stood in the doorway, in dusty, simple clothes that bespoke a long journey. He had a staff, and a knapsack on his back, and the way of his dress struck me as peculiar, a rough-woven green wool robe belted at the waist, much longer than the tunics and doublets I was used to seeing. It was the dress of a shepherd, but of a distinctive, forest-green color. His face also had the hard lines of a man who spent much time in the outdoors. He clutched to his side a worn, leather-bound book.

The man with him was shorter in stature, and ruddy faced. He was dressed in the same-colored robe, and he, too, carried a staff. Perhaps they were shepherds who had lost their way, I thought. But how peculiar that they were not announced, almost as if they were familiar to this household. And why the dark green color when most shepherd's robes were bleached wool? And why the exact same robe for both men?

The Lady Geralda was out of her chair as if she were an arrow loosed from a bow.

"You must have become confused in your direction," she said to the men quite firmly, as she moved toward a bellpull. "The hospitality for travelers is offered below. Meals will be served to you in the Great Hall. I'll call a servant and have him take you there."

The taller man looked startled for a moment, and then his roving gaze moved to me, sitting in the chair of the mistress, and a look of alarm spread over his face.

"A thousand pardons, my lady," he said, backing up. "The gate-keeper gave us wrong directions to the travelers' quarters, and when we saw the stone steps to this room, we thought this was the garret for our sleeping."

The man who had led us to this room entered behind the two men and a look of consternation invaded his face also. "Lady Geralda," he began, but she interrupted him.

"Pedro, these travelers were misled and came into this room by mistake. Please take them with you immediately, see that they get some refreshment, and then show them the loft in the outbuilding where they might sleep. Be certain they have what they need against the cold." And she used her hands in a sweeping gesture, as if to scoop up the three of them and deposit them outside the door. As if she could erase the entire interruption from the memory of our cozy gathering by so doing.

I watched this scene with a rising sense of perplexity. Something was odd about it from start to finish. The women were too stunned at the interruption, almost fearful, the travelers were too surprised to see me, and Geralda was too loud of voice in her instruction to the servant, as if there were some meaning behind her words, some secret signal to her man.

After the departure of the two men, which took but a quick moment with Geralda's bustling instructions and motions, the women seemed to release the tension with a collective sigh.

"Well," said Blanche, as Geralda settled back into her seat, "now shall we sing?"

"Sing?" My eyes slid from side to side as my brows furrowed. Joanna, who caught my droll movement, laughed in her familiar bell-like tones.

"We often sing together, especially toward the end of the evening," she explained with a smile. "It seems to give us contentment as we depart for our night's rest."

"Ah," I said, waiting to see what came next.

"We know you must be tired, Your Grace. Such a long journey. Indulge us for one song, and then I'll show you to your chamber. Alas, you must share with the countess, as we have no other private rooms here. My other kinswomen will sleep with me in the larger room."

"I am delighted to share a room with the Countess Joanna." I spoke truly. "It has been too long since we have had the opportunity to be together."

Joanna produced that sunny smile that was her hallmark. And then, with no warning, five amazing, bell-like notes from Geralda filled the room for a moment. It began with a high, clear note, like that of a meadow lark, and then a trilling spiral downward where the entire group met her and took up the melody with harmonies so practiced I was in awe.

I listened with an aching heart, for the song was one the traveling singers used to perform at the court of Poitiers. The music made my eyes brim with tears as it reminded me of the childhood Joanna and I had shared, and brought with it the poignant memory of my first youthful infatuation, her brother Richard of England.

This group had sung together before, and often, and I let myself be lulled by their beautiful tones. As the song filled me, I felt keenly a sense of passing, as if this moment would never come again. Suddenly there appeared, in place of the present scene, a vision of walls of a besieged castle, cracking under attack, finally giving way. A whole piece of time itself crumbling into smoke and rubble. But the image was gone as quickly as it had come, and the last notes of the song died away at the same time.

The Lady Geralda moved first, rising with an elegance that belied her broad frame. I saw her anew at that moment, as a woman blessed with peace about her life. Even the manner in which she pulled the bell rope to summon a servant was calm. My earlier sense of impatience with her faded.

"Your Grace, please accept our poor hospitality. I will have my servants show you to your chamber, where hot water from the kitchen will be brought for you to wash. Should you want anything further for the night, the servants will provide."

I rose also and, with Joanna at my side, bade my adieu to the group. The women filed past me with low courtesies and I took each by the hand as a sign of sisterhood. Some hands were warm, from the fire and from the wool they had been spinning. Even the maids, who were still with us, made a low bow. And I took each of their hands, as well.

"Come, Alaïs," Joanna said, as all stood aside for us to pass. "You must be fatigued unto death." And we followed the Lady Geralda's servant from the room.

At the door a slight noise caused me to look back. I saw a strange sight: The remaining women flocked into a circle with Blanche at the center, bowed their heads, and began murmuring in the tongue of the south. Some shared prayer, I thought, as the door swung shut.

Joanna touched my elbow. "The servant waits," she said. And I followed, thinking of Lot's wife. What silent, closing ritual had I just observed?

17

The Chambers of Countess Joanna

The chamber to which the servant led us was comfortable enough, though simple. Numerous candles in wall brackets provided good light, although they flickered whimsically in the breezes that drifted at random through the cracks in the stone. The furniture was minimal, consisting of a small cedar table which held a basin and pitcher for washing, and also a small tray with bread, cheese, and wine for our comfort. Against the far wall stood a large oak garderobe, which contained, I knew, chamber pots for our convenience, as well as garments that Joanna's servants may already have packed away for her.

I surmised this had been the lady Geralda's chamber when her husband was alive. The bed resembled a large boat, and was so high there was a small ladder to assist in achieving the top. It looked amazingly soft, however, with goose-down feather beds layered one over the other. It would play good host to me and my longtime childhood friend, and I was grateful.

I turned to Joanna and embraced her once again with all the strong feeling of our years of friendship.

"Ma chérie," I said from my heart. "It has been so many years. Let me look at you." I held her at arm's length and saw then something I had overlooked in our earlier encounter. Her face was lined with worry. As she doffed her veil and wimple, I saw her hair was marked with silver. Two gray wings flew up from her temples, and though the effect was one of striking beauty, I knew it signaled the loss of her youth.

"You see me as I am, no longer young and no longer beautiful," she said, as if she could read my mind. The bitter tinge in her voice saddened me and for a change I had no tart rejoinder. I felt only sympathy for her loss.

"Joanna, what are you doing here with so many of the nobles' wives?" I spoke after a moment's pause, as I moved toward the bed and busied myself shaking out my belongings from my worn leather travel *sac*. I pretended a casual manner.

"I arrived here only hours ahead of you today," she answered. Then, as if she knew the deeper meaning of my question, she added: "Does it strike you as odd that so many of us should chance to be here together, all at the same time?" Joanna watched for my reaction even as she moved to take a robe from the large chest that stood against the far wall.

"One might think it." I nodded as I stepped out of my leather riding hose and stained doublet, and slipped a shift from my *sac* easily over my head. "So many noblewomen in such a small *redoute*. Strange indeed. But to find you here among them is even stranger."

She stopped fussing with her robe lacings and looked at me. "You have always had acute powers of observation, Alaïs. But tell me what you see that causes you to question us."

"Joanna," I said, going to her and taking her hand. I drew her to the expanse of the bed, which was the only resting place in the room large enough for two. "Please sit with me a moment. I want to talk with you." After the slightest hesitation she nodded, using the small ladder to climb up after me. We sat facing each other, legs folded under us, as we had when we were children playing guessing games with one another.

"First, in truth, I know why the women are gathered here. From Lord William I learned that women are at the heart of this new religion. From Esclarmonde of Foix, who went to great lengths in front of the court to dissuade my brother from sending arms and men to the south, I learned of the connection among the noble houses in this area. So what could be less surprising than to find those related noblewomen gathered around someone like the venerable Lady Blanche of Laurac."

Joanna paused for moment before asking: "Do you think we are here to conspire against the church of Rome?" she asked suddenly, trepidation in her voice. "Do you mean to betray these good women?"

"Oh, for the love of St. Winifred's well," I snapped, throwing up my hands. "To whom would I betray you? The king of France? He just wants the pope and all problems of religion to disappear. He's not interested in prosecuting anyone on behalf of Rome, and certainly not a gaggle of women tucked away in some southern stronghold. Or the Abbot Amaury? I'll wager his spies have already identified this area, if not this very *domus*, as sympathetic to the Cathars. To the Count of Toulouse? But he's your husband, and if he doesn't know what is going on under his nose, I have better tasks than to enlighten him."

"I'm sorry, Alaïs. I did not mean to provoke you," Joanna said, turning her head away for a moment. I reached out to put my hand under her chin and turned her face toward me in time to see two large tears wander down her cheek.

"Joanna, dear friend. I am the one to be sorry. Forgive my impatience." I silently cursed my quick tongue. "I seldom consider the effects of my temper until it is too late. I would not for the world have made you cry."

Then a sudden thought struck me. "Dear heart, are you enceinte?" I had not seen any noticeable swelling, but it was true she was fuller in the face than I remembered, and she had loose gowns belted higher than was the fashion.

"Oh, yes, a plague on all men!" And Joanna's tears began in earnest at my question. "I hate it. I hate being pregnant. I feel so vulnerable and awkward . . . And to be caught like this when my hair is gray, when I should be enjoying my *petit-fils*. And . . . and it makes me so weepy."

I moved to sit next to her and pulled her head to my breast. As she began to sob, I rocked her, murmuring reassurances as if to a child. For several minutes she cried, and then her sobs gradually receded, as I knew they would. Joanna might be physically prone to weeping because of her condition, but the brave and impish friend of my childhood would soon reassert herself. Of that I was confident.

And indeed, it was in no more than the spin of a child's top that Joanna was snuffling, as if to finish the storm. She sat up and gave me a rueful look. Then a smile, somewhat uncertain, broke through the clouds.

"There," she said bravely, shaking her head, drying her face on the sleeve of her robe. "That felt quite refreshing."

"I take it you are not happy about your condition," I said rather tentatively, risking another outburst.

"Oh, Alaïs. If you only knew!" Joanna fell backward on the bed and threw her arms overhead, in a gesture of mad abandon. I waited, sitting patiently with folded legs. After a moment, she half sat up and propped herself on her elbows.

"The count alternates between being a lecher and a saint. One moment he is chasing women, drinking too much wine, and playing at dice with his nobles, and the next he is biting his fingers over the worry that the pope will find some reason to ruin his land and persecute his nobles, and running to church to pray it will not be so."

"Well, Raymond always did lack gravitas," I commented mildly. "I think Constance spoiled him when he was young."

"Constance!" Joanna, ordinarily so gentle, spat the name back at me. "Don't mention that woman to me."

"Why so angry at the mention of Constance?" My back was growing tired, so I wriggled my body over the feather beds until my back rested against the wooden headboard. "You haven't seen her for years. She's been with us in Paris." Until recently, I thought, but did not give voice to it.

"*Pas du tout,*" Joanna stated. "I just left her in Toulouse. Constance arrived a week past, and has been strutting about the city ever since, as if she were the countess, not I." Joanna flounced off the bed, and began to pour the water in the basin for washing. She splashed her face with vehemence, as if it were Constance she was dousing.

"Constance in Toulouse?" I tried to hide my amusement. Troyes, indeed! "She left the Paris court suddenly just before I did, and she sent a note to the king saying that she was going to Troyes to be with our sister Marie."

"She did not go to Troyes, evidently," Joanna responded pertly, toweling her face with verve, as if the very thought of her husband's mother demanded action. "She came south to plague us."

"Well, she is the dowager countess," I murmured. "Raymond is her son."

"Yes, but she has been absent for many years. Suddenly she appears, and demands Raymond reinstate her as dowager, with all of the benefits of that station. All must rise when she enters, she presides over dinner next to Raymond . . ."

"But surely she has not displaced you as rightful countess?"

"Not exactly, but she is an impossible woman, always thinking of herself. Very demanding. Anyone but Grendel's mother would be overshadowed by her. And she bullies Raymond mercilessly."

I had to laugh at Joanna, recalling the long hours of learning in the English court when we were children. Joanna hated the Nordic sagas that the Anglo-Saxon races held dear, but King Henry insisted we must learn the stories of the people we lived among, and none dared disagree. His queen, Joanna's mother, Eleanor, turned up her nose at the patrimony of the English, but we children dutifully learned their myths.

"Did it not impress Constance that you are to produce an heir from this marriage?" I knew from the last time we had met, some years earlier, that being childless had been difficult for Joanna. "Surely she must respect that accomplishment."

"I think she is jealous. Raymond was her only child. He was born just before she escaped back to her brother's court in Paris." Joanna had come back to the side of the bed and stood facing me, her lips pursed in thought. "And she keeps talking about some golden chalice, the one that was stolen from our cathedral."

"The St. John Cup," I interjected sharply, suddenly attentive.

"Yes. That's the one. She said she saw it at the abbey of St. Denis, but before she could claim it, the thing was stolen."

And how would she know about the theft, I wondered, since it only happened the night before her departure? In a flash, the picture of Constance in the abbey church of St. Denis, staring at the raised chalice, came before me. So she had identified it as I suspected, the day we were at Mass.

"Why would anyone steal it?" Joanna peered at me. "What do you know of this?"

"The news of the theft, and the murder it prompted, was delivered to the king the same night. We were all at the feast after the tournament. Constance left mysteriously early the next morning. I thought perhaps she had managed to get a hold of the chalice." I forbore to mention Philippe's role in keeping the chalice safe, nor the possibly duplicitous role of Raymond, who might know even now the whereabouts of the chalice. One could believe anything about Raymond!

"How odd. Constance arrived in Toulouse with great fanfare announcing that she knew where the chalice was, that she could have it returned to our cathedral for a ransom. The news of the chalice was her excuse for reappearing after all these years." Then, as if the thought had finally presented itself through the web of self-concern that was always Joanna's way, she suddenly moved closer to the bed, lifting a candle flickering on the bedtable to examine my face.

"Alaïs, what is the real reason you are here in the south? What is it that brings you to this small castle, to the Toulouse area? You are not seeking the chalice, are you?"

I paused a moment while I conducted an inner debate on whether I should tell her of my son. Much as I loved my childhood friend, how did I know I could trust her? In her current state of irritability, could she keep my confidence? What would happen to my news when she returned to Toulouse? But I felt such a strong need to tell someone about Francis. I had kept my fears to myself for too long. Except for the interview with my brother, and the cursory information I had given to my knights, I had told no one of my quest. It was especially painful to recall my parting argument with William, as he would be the one I would ordinarily seek out when troubled.

"Come sit beside me, here." I patted the bed. Joanna replaced the candle in its holder and climbed up once again to sit beside me. When she was settled, I said quietly: "Joanna, I have a son. One born many years ago."

She started to speak, but I held up my hand. "No, I do not want questions about him, or his parentage. Only know that I lost him as a babe, but in recent years we have been reunited. I had hoped that he might come to live with me at Ponthieu, where William and I will make our home when his service to the pope is completed." I felt a pang of remorse as I uttered this statement, recalling our final argument and William's anger. Our happy life together at Ponthieu seemed so far away. It may have been only a fantasy, another dream ruined because of my impatience and bad temper. I sighed.

"I would be so happy for you if that should come to pass," Joanna said, with heartfelt emotion, not noticing my sadness. "But you said 'hoped,' as if it were unlikely now. What has come to interfere with this plan?"

"Just before I left Paris, my son was abducted in the middle of the night, taken from his chambers." There, now I had told another person besides Philippe that Francis was my son.

Joanna's hand flew to her throat. "Such things can happen in the palace of the king of France?"

"Indeed. Many strange events occurred in the few days before I left, including the murder of a king's man outside Paris. A conspiracy in which Constance was implicated."

"Constance! Murder! Oh, really, Alaïs, that is too much. Even for Constance."

"I was charged by my brother to find the truth of the matter, but the disappearance of my son put all else out of my mind. This is my entire life, now."

"And you think your son was taken here, to the langue d'oc region?" Joanna propped her head on her fist, her elbow resting on pillows. I could see she was beginning to drift toward sleep, despite her interest in all of the surprises she had been subjected to in my report. She, too, had traveled far that day.

"William showed me a drawing that was dropped in young Francis's chambers. A map, showing the Toulousain. Several surrounding towns were circled. At first I did not think that it was a valid clue. But with my urge to find my son, and with no other information to go on, I have come to this area."

Joanna came more awake. "Which towns were circled?"

"Lavaur, Foix, and Laurac," I responded quickly. "I wanted to see if there was some information, some thread here that might lead to my son." As I spoke these words, I thought of the note I had been given at my brother's audience: *"Follow the golden thread to the South."* Francis had not yet disappeared when that note was delivered. Yet it had stayed in my mind. Did the note refer to the missing golden chalice? Or to something more valuable, more golden, the life of my son!

"I believe I have an idea that may help you," Joanna said quietly.

"And I believe I know what it is," I echoed, with the beginning of a smile. "The women gathered here are those who preside over the ruling houses in those villages. This is a mighty coincidence."

"And you have already figured out what they are doing here?"

"Joanna, it would take an unobservant, nay, simpleminded, person *not* to conclude that the two men who stumbled into our gathering tonight were Cathar preachers. They were alarmed to see me and happy to depart with Geralda's servant. On another evening, they would have been welcomed into the circle of women. Your friends are known to honor the new Cathar religion, and it is obvious you came together to hear your shepherds."

The countess let out a long sigh. "These three castles are the stronghold of hospitality for the Cathar preachers. There are not many believers in the towns, but the number is growing. And the women here are committed to give the opportunity to any who want to hear, so they offer the preachers, the *perfecti*, food and board, and safety. These men travel constantly over our southern land. They may have heard news of your son in those journeys."

"As I thought," I murmured. "But Joanna, turnabout is fair. Let me ask you again: What are you doing here, with these women?"

"Fleeing from my husband, at the moment," Joanna said, tossing her hair free of the braids that she had unwound. "You said Constance spoiled him as a youth. Spoiled does not begin to describe the count.

I curse the day my brother King Richard married me to this incompetent fool."

"Joanna!" I was astonished at her careless talk.

But she only shook out her long, full mane of hair and continued in the same tone. "Oh, mine was to be a marriage of convenience, Richard said. He thought he could consolidate the southern end of his kingdom, putting Raymond and the Toulousain solidly in his camp by putting me solidly in Raymond's bed. What even Richard failed to see was Raymond's utter confusion, his inability to hold the center of his county." Joanna was rendered momentarily speechless as she pulled her robe over her head and tossed it off the bed. "His inability to even *find* the center of his county," she added, as she quickly crawled under the furs in her shift.

"God and the Virgin know I have tried to help. I have counseled my spouse, I even sat with his advisers and offered my opinions as to what they can do to protect their people from dangerous interference, from Rome or from France." She cast a quick look my way. "Sorry, but it's true. Still, these men heed me not." She was sitting up and so pulled a silk shawl around her shoulders to protect her from the rub of the rough furs. "They believe women are to be decorative and provide beauty for the court setting. And that is supposed to be the end of our aspirations."

"So, you are retreating into the Cathar mysteries out of pique with Raymond and his court?" I gently teased as I began to unbraid my own hair.

Joanna looked startled for a moment, then burst into a peal of laughter. "Cathar! *Moi?* Don't be amusing, Alaïs. I cannot abide religion in any form. I was in the Holy Land with Richard and his troops, for sweet Saint Mary's sake. I saw ancient churches and mosques burn. I saw the bones of the Christian empire builders bleached upon the Saracens' sand. I even . . ."—she tilted her head in my direction knowingly and lowered her voice to a conspiratorial whisper—"saw a piece of the one, true cross itself."

"Careful, Joanna," I said, made uneasy by her tone of ridicule. "You know not who listens at doors. It is best not to make fun, whether a believer or not. One must put caution first when one is among strangers."

"Be of good heart, my dear friend. This house is safe. No one here will report us to that wolf, Bishop Foulques. Even the servants here are of the new religion." She shook her head. "But can you imagine? Beseeching Saladin for a piece of the true cross? As if a piece of wood could have survived for twelve hundred years and still be identifiable." She laughed, a high trill that belied any true amusement. "The Saracens must have thought us all fools. But they gave us what we wanted."

Then Joanna suddenly turned serious. She looked down at her clasped hands for a long moment. "Truly, we are fools, Alaïs. I saw so many men die in the Holy Land that I wanted to die myself. To this day, I cannot drive the noise of the battles from my mind some nights. I hear the shouts and screams of the men when I sleep at night, and feel myself drowning in their blood. I awake drenched, but it is always my own sweat only, as if I had been the one fighting. And all over religion. God save us all as we fight and kill in his name."

I could think of no reply. Instead, I moved to the edge of the high bed and carefully lowered myself to the floor, making my way to the small table that held the washing basin. I splashed my face in the water, now cooled considerably by the autumn breezes coming in through the wall openings. I was further prevented from responding for a moment as I dried my face and hands. As I climbed back up to take the place next to my dear friend, I saw her face crumpled with sadness. I reached out with my arm, and drew her head to my shoulder. She folded into my embrace, like a weary traveler sinks into the bed when he finally attains it.

After some silence, I spoke again, and briskly.

"Still, one may believe what one likes, but one should be discreet." I felt as preachy as Abbé Suger, our father's adviser from St. Denis, but better safe than dead. "You are much too careless, Joanna, you know you always were. I hope you are more restrained with your words in Toulouse. Foulques may be a wolf, but he is still bishop. We know not where all this rattling of religious sabers will end."

Joanna had placed a small silver plate on the bed, and we shared the bit of bread that had been left to us, brushing the crumbs to the floor as we finished. I determined to turn her thoughts from the bloody wars she had recollected moments earlier, and so I said, "Tell me more about this new religion."

My friend, who had always shown amazing resilience, came alive again. She so obviously cherished her friendships with the women I had met that very evening.

"What Foulques does not understand is how the Cathar faith is growing in the countryside, among the peasants. He thinks if he can stamp it out in Toulouse, or in the houses of the minor nobles, that it will go away. But he doesn't take in what appeals to the people about this way of practicing faith."

"And what is that?" I asked.

"We are tired of the complexities of Rome, of indulgences and priests who lord it over us. The religion of the *bons chrétiens* is a way of returning to the early Christian purity and simplicity. Most of us just want peace. And now it appears that peace will be denied us."

"So what do you intend to do?" I saw that I had forgotten the candles, so I slipped off the bed and began snuffing them out one by one. Then I climbed back up to her side and we both wriggled down under the covers and clasped each other for warmth, just as we had when we were girls at the court of Henry and Eleanor in drafty old England.

"I am leaving the south. I can no longer be a wife to Raymond, and I fear greatly the war that is to come, a war that is the result of his own folly."

"You are leaving him for good?" This bit of news caused me to sit up in the dark.

"Please get back under the furs, Alaïs. You are creating a draft," Joanna said sensibly. She slid farther down and pulled the coverlets to her chin. "Yes, I am even now on my way north to join Queen Eleanor at Fontevraud."

"But your mother is so aged. I heard she was near death." I closed my eyes and the picture of Eleanor, bent and palsied as I had last seen her, came before my eyes.

"She knows I am in great danger, and she fears for my unborn child. This poor little child, the unexpected fruit of a night in which Raymond, having drunk too much wine, came to my apartment and scattered my serving women with his shouting and belligerence," she said bitterly. "I fought him. I had not lain with him for two years, because of his drinking and womanizing. But he had his way, and this is the result."

"And what does the count think of the coming child?" I could not forbear asking. "Will he not be furious that you have left?"

"When he thinks of it at all," she said slowly, "he is quite pleased that he could beget a legitimate heir when we are as old as we are. But I have been Queen of Sicily, survived prison locked up by my husband's nephew, that dreadful Tancred, and marched with my brother Richard on the plains of Acre, and I tell you, as I told Raymond, I am no man's breeding cow." She paused, her voice echoing around us.

"Joanna!" I turned to her in the dark. I could see the outline of her face turned upward to the ceiling by the light of the stars and moon that crept through the narrow windows.

"Well, it's true, my friend." Her tone was almost petulant. "And further, I am most fearful of this gathering storm here. I will not subject a child of mine to the machinations of Bishop Foulques, who stalks suspected heretics and goads his sheep into violence, all in the name of God. I will not birth my child here. I tell you, it is no longer safe in the south."

"I suspected that," I said. "And you have problems you don't yet know about. The monk you warned me about, the famous abbot of Cîteaux, Arnaud Amaury, is a dangerous and evil man. The 'sword of God' they will call him someday, no doubt. He'll make Bishop Foulques look like a rabbit."

"Alaïs, do you still have visions of the future?" Joanna turned suddenly on her side and put her hand on my cheek. "Can you foresee what will happen to me?"

Most of the time, when someone asks me to see for them, my heart hardens. I do not use my gift in this way, as if I were a merchant of goods for sale. But this was my childhood friend, and we were alone in the dusk of candlelight. If I could help her, mayhap I should. I forced myself to concentrate on Joanna's face in my mind, looking for patterns of images that might arise to speak to me.

As I lay, I saw an image of Joanna, *débraillée* and in childbed, tossing and shrieking, noises that grew into faint moans. Then her form disappeared, and there was only the empty bed before my mind's eye. The covers were now settled, as if no one at all had lain there. The picture faded. A shudder went through me.

"No, dear friend. I believe I have lost that gift with age. I rarely see now, and when I do, it is by happenstance," I lied. I could not relate my unhappy vision to her.

"Ah, well. It was worth the asking." And I smiled even in my distress, for Joanna was always as easily turned from her purpose as she was quick to engage in it. Her voice was fading with sleep, and I felt her body start to turn away from me, then stop.

"But dear Alaïs." I sensed her form turn toward me again, and felt her breath now on my cheek. "I have been chattering so about myself. I nearly forgot what I was telling you when we were interrupted by the *perfecti* earlier this evening. The Lord William is even now in Toulouse. Do you not wish to join him? He may have news for you about your son."

William, now so near again. What would be his reaction if I appeared in Toulouse? Would he create another dramatic scene? Or worse, make the bitterness of our parting in Paris final? Or send me back to Paris under guard of his men?

"I am not certain what to do next," I said. "Perhaps I will ask your preachers if they saw anything unusual in their travels."

"Oh, yes, do," Joanna murmured, already drifting into sleep. "They can be trusted, I swear to you."

"I will ask about the Lord William first," I said, the plan forming as I spoke. "That will allay suspicion. It may be that they can then be drawn into giving me news that relates to Francis."

"But you already know . . ."

"That William is in Toulouse," I finished for her. "Of course I do. You just told me. But such a query will provide a cover for my true purpose."

"Oh," Joanna said. "I see."

"After I talk with them, I will decide my course of action." I made every attempt to sound assured. "So for now, since we can plan no more, let us sleep."

And then Joanna, creature of impulse that she was, leaned over and kissed my cheek, before turning to her side to sleep, as she always had done as a child, facing the wall.

18

The Great Hall of the Castle of Lavaur

The next morning the women were already gathered when Joanna and I arrived at the castle's Great Hall, where a crackling fire burned against the early morning chill. Stone fortresses never really warmed inside, even when the sun shone. And it was, after all, early November.

"Good morrow, Princesse. And to you, Countess." The Lady Geralda bowed to each of us as we entered. "I trust you slept soundly?"

"Indeed, my thanks for your good warm furs and the feather beds that served us so well," I said, responding for both of us. "I don't intend to impose on your hospitality too long, Lady Geralda. I will tarry only another day so that my knights may rest."

"You are welcome to stay as long as you wish, my lady," Geralda said graciously, although I thought I detected a faint note of relief in her voice.

The women stood in a circle around the fire, in front of the same chairs they had occupied the evening before, with Blanche in their midst. They made their courtesies and then, at my gesture, resumed their seats. Each picked up her spinning and needlework and a scattered conversation began. A small boy of eight or nine summers came into the room and sat on the floor next to the Lady Philippa of Foix. He was dressed in a warm wool doublet with a short cape, and his cheeks were red from the cool air outside.

Blanche saw my eyes go toward the boy. "Princesse Alaïs, this is Roger-Bernard, Countess Philippa's youngest son." The boy stood and made a deep bow when presented. He had been taught well.

"Lady Blanche, let me speak plainly." I had remained standing, the more to give authority to my remarks. I now addressed them to the Lady Blanche, as she was so clearly the leader of this group.

"You have two travelers in your house who arrived last even. I would speak to them. I seek to ask them if they have come across my Lord William of Caen, who is on a diplomatic mission for the holy father and my brother, the king of France. As I told you last night, I have a message from the king to deliver to Lord William."

The Lady of Laurac paled at my words.

"Don't worry, Blanche, Alaïs has already guessed they are Cathar preachers," Joanna said casually as she swept to the oak table and picked up a sweetmeat from the platter. "She said she would have to be simpleminded not to have known them for what they were when they appeared last evening." She was licking the sugar from her fingers in between her words.

"I see," the Lady Blanche said slowly. "Need I plead that you keep our secret here, Princesse?"

"I would not think of breaching your daughter's hospitality, Lady Blanche. But tell me, surely it has not yet become a crime to receive Cathar *bons hommes* into your homes and castles? There is no law against the new beliefs. The church itself is sponsoring debates all over the south to discuss openly the differences these people have with the church of Rome."

"Your Grace, it is no crime yet. But we are watched. The very stones have ears. We do not know who our friends are. And we fear bloodshed as tempers are becoming increasingly volatile." She smiled faintly. "We hear of an abbot from Fontfroide, one Arnaud Amaury, who has a hatred in his heart for anyone who does not believe exactly as he does. He is said to be preaching war against us. Almost, one imagines, even to think differently is a crime. But I shall send for the Good-Men. I believe they would be glad of a chance to talk openly with you."

Surprisingly, the door opened while she was yet speaking, and the young heir of Foix, who had slipped from the room unnoticed, led the two strangers into the room. They had taken advantage of the night to rest and clean themselves, and they had obviously taken nourishment. They did not look like fugitives, nor did they appear guilty of any secret. No doubt the furtiveness of their movements the previous night was due to their surprise at my presence.

"Princesse, this is Guillabert of Castres and Benedict of Thermes. They are our honored guests. Messires, this is Princesse Alaïs of France. She is a friend to us, and will keep our confidence." The Lady Blanche rose with her customary purpose and elegance and extended her hand to the men as she spoke. The men bowed to me, then waited.

"Good sirs. I seek news of Lord William of Caen. He left Paris for the south some weeks past. Did you perchance encounter news of him in your travels?"

"Indeed, we have not, Your Grace," the man called Guillabert said. He stood at a sort of tilt, putting more weight on one foot, as if one leg were longer than the other and he must compensate. I had noticed earlier that he walked with a slight limp. Perhaps from his months and years of walking the mountain slopes, like the shepherd he imagined himself to be, he had shortened one leg. "We have just come from Narbonne, where the religious debates took place. We have not been near Toulouse. We would not go that far, as it is not safe for us in the city."

"Narbonne! You must have walked day and night to come here from Narbonne in seven days!" I thought momentarily how much time we had lost in Poitiers because of my illness. It had cost us dear.

"Oh, no, Princesse. Do not be concerned for us. We fell in early with a caravan of merchants bringing spices and cloth to Toulouse overland. And they were happy to allow us to ride part of the way in their carts. For a small consideration, of course," he said, an elfin smile coming to his lips.

"The merchant who owns the carts believes as we do, in the purified religion." The man called Benedict took up the story here, as if they had the habit of speaking in tandem, so long had they traveled together. "So we made an agreement that if Benedict and I would preach around the night campfires, the merchant would allow us to ride with his group. We stayed together almost until Foix. But then he deemed it not safe in this country to show his sympathies. We are still too close to the troublesome Bishop Foulques of Toulouse, may he soon find his proper reward."

"At the religious debates, did you hear any news of the Paris court? Of the theft of a chalice that once belonged to the Cathars from the abbey of St. Denis?"

"No, my lady." Of the two men, Benedict seemed the more inclined to talk. "We heard no gossip from the north. Everyone was focused on the points made about religion by those who came to Narbonne."

"Forgive me." I hesitated, unsure how to address these two men. "I have kept you standing. You must sit with us." And I took the carved chair at the center of the semicircle before the hearth that had been given me the previous evening. "I have one more query of you."

They seemed grateful to take two chairs hastily set before my own. I was uncertain how to ask the question uppermost in my mind, but they waited patiently for me, expectant looks upon their sun-brushed faces.

"I am also searching for a young man, one . . ."—how could I phrase this without giving too much away?—"one who was of the Lord William's household in Paris. He disappeared some weeks ago, and it was thought he may have come south."

"You want to know if we have seen him?" Guillabert's tone was grave.

I nodded and opened my hands, which had been clasped on my lap. "Seen any sign of a young, northern knight. You would know him by his tongue, for he speaks only the langue d'oïl." I smiled. "Or was there anything you saw that might have been unusual in your passage here?"

The preacher looked at me steadily and I observed his face fully for the first time in the burst of sunlight streaming into the room. His visage was lined with the marks of outdoor weathering, but his eyes were an amazing black color, and his gaze bored into me, as if he knew secrets I had told no one.

"Something unusual has happened, has it not?" he asked, almost as if he knew my thoughts exactly.

"Yes," was all I said. He thought for a long moment.

"When we passed the abbey of Fontfroide, outside of Narbonne, there was excitement. A large retinue was pulling its carts into the abbey road, and it was clear there were many knights. We heard northern accents. He might have been among those in that party. There appeared to be more than a hundred knights, and much baggage."

My heart skipped over, then settled. "Whose pennants flew from the train?"

"The papal flags, and those of Cîteaux Abbey." He spoke these words without expression.

"Amaury!" I exclaimed, rapidly assessing this information. "He must have left Paris within days of my departure." I uttered this last more to myself than those about me.

"Yes, the Abbot Amaury." Guillabert repeated the name softly. "He who would take us to war over our beliefs."

Suddenly I was drawn out of my own cares and thought of the dangers visited upon the men before me. "I hope he did not see you! Your lives would not be safe if he did!"

Benedict and Guillabert both smiled, albeit grimly. Benedict spoke first: "Princesse, we know who means us harm. Once we identified the flags of Cîteaux, we stayed within the wagons and instructed the merchant to keep out of the way of these knights. We carried books, you see. Books that would not please the venerable Abbot Amaury." And he waved his right hand, which held the worn leather volume I had noticed the night before. "We feared if he recognized us as preachers of the new faith, he would not let us pass unharmed."

"I believe you were wise," I said, my respect for these two growing. These were not country roughs, playing at preaching for gullible women. They seemed calm, sensible, and articulate. I wished I could tarry long enough to know them better.

I rose from my chair and walked to the opening in the wall, needing some air. Leaning out over the wall, I felt as though I were tottering on a precipice. The drop from this room, at the back of the Lavaur château, was direct. The outside wall merged into the steep hill, which fell away in a jumble of brush and dirt. It was a great distance down to the road below.

I tried to summon a picture of the Abbot Amaury, to discern where he might be, or in what state, but I could not reach him. When it came, the vision was not of Amaury, it was an image of my son. I saw a figure alone, standing halfway up a hill. Behind him, in a valley, stood a great church, a bell tower, and a set of other stone buildings. Francis seemed uncertain which way to turn, looking down, and then up. Suddenly two slavering mastiffs entered the picture, galloping up the hill toward him. Abruptly, the image disappeared from my sight, as if a curtain had been dropped. I sighed.

"Joanna, I have made my decision." I turned to my friend, who had been silent, and who now watched me with apprehension. "I am going to Fontfroide Abbey."

If I had said I was going to Jerusalem Joanna could not have looked more surprised.

"Alaïs, you cannot go to Fontfroide. It is four more days of traveling and you and your knights have scarce rested!" she exclaimed.

"True, but I will go. There is a reason Amaury left Paris. I cannot help but think it is tied to Francis's disappearance, and the only way I can discover the connection is to go to Fontfroide and confront Amaury."

"Princesse?" The Lady Blanche was looking at me, her expression a mélange of curiosity and concern. "I thought you said you had a message for Lord William. What, in truth, has drawn you to the south?"

"My search for this young knight, Francis," I said simply. "I fear for his safety. That concern is more important than finding the Lord William, at least for the present."

"This young man. He is very special to you, is he not?" Blanche looked at me keenly.

"More than I can say," I replied softly. "And more than that I cannot say."

There was a pause, for the space of a heartbeat. Then Blanche spoke again.

"But to go to Fontfroide, with only four knights, if the abbot means you or this young knight harm . . ." Blanche had risen to emphasize her words. "This action would put you in danger and do nothing to help the young knight."

"I am not afraid," I retorted. "Please ring for someone to alert my men."

"Your courage is not in question, madame," Blanche said quietly. I turned to look at her, rather astonished that she would speak so to a *princesse* of France. "Perhaps there is another way."

Instead of reprimanding her, which had been my first impulse, I waited to see what else she would say. For I knew she spoke the truth.

"Why not go in disguise?" Geralda spoke over her shoulder, as she pushed the embers on the hearth into new life. "That way, you can discover what you need to know without putting your own life in danger."

"Yes, what a good idea." Philippa clapped her hands. "We could go as pilgrims, perhaps as women from a religious house. They would have to take us in. We could say we were on our way to Santiago de Compostela."

"That is quite the other direction from here." The practical Geralda stood up, brushing her hands together to rid them of the soot from the fire iron.

"But the abbey monks won't know from whence we came," the woman who had been introduced to me the previous night as Grazide of Montauban murmured without looking up from her needlework. I turned to look at her, a pale-faced retiring young woman who sat on the edge of the circle. Those were the first words she had spoken since I had arrived. "That's the point of a disguise. You can be anyone."

I was thunderstruck. What a wonderful idea. I would never have thought of it. I made a silent pledge to myself to rein in my impatience in the future, and search instead for the most creative plan.

"Hold a moment," said the ever-thoughtful Blanche. "Philippa, you cannot go. The Count of Foix would have my head if I allowed that. You know this is not a journey for those of us with graying hair."

Philippa frowned, but I could see common sense overcoming her original enthusiasm.

"But I could go. I have no husband, nor children," Grazide said.

"And I too," Fabrisse of Saissac said. "My father need never know. He thinks I am staying here at Lavaur until he comes to fetch me at Christmastide."

"And I could go as well," Gaillarde echoed.

"Wait." Geralda held up her hands. "We must think this through. Gaillarde, your father has entrusted you to me until the spring, when he returns from his own pilgrimage. I cannot allow you to go on this journey. You are too young by far."

The younger woman's face fell. "But you may stay here with my mother Blanche and help her manage my château until I return."

Gaillarde's thin, pale face lit up. "Will I really help manage the household? Will I learn what that is like so that I can surprise my father when he returns?"

I had to smile myself at her eagerness, and how easily she was turned from one plan to another, a habit of the young.

"I fear this will mean danger, and I would not put you all at risk." I felt I must say this. "I think I should make the journey alone."

"Nonsense," Geralda said. "It has already been decided. You and I, Grazide and Fabrisse will go. We will help you as sisters would." She turned eagerly to her servant. "Guillamette, hurry and find some bolts of black muslin for us. I think we have some in the loft, bought from traveling merchants last Christmastide. I had meant to send it to the monastery at Moissac, but now we can put it to better use."

"We cannot take my knights. If Amaury is yet at Fontfroide when we arrive, he would recognize Roland and Tom for certain." I began to pace. Her excitement was contagious. "So we must leave before dawn tomorrow alone. I will tell my knights that we plan to stay one more day, in order that I may rest. They will think we are moving on to Toulouse."

"But when they discover you have left, they will come after you, I fear," Philippa said. "They can ride faster and would overtake you with only a day's advantage."

"That's easily prevented. Blanche can tell them that Geralda has been called away by her brother in Montréal, and that I have fallen ill with a fever again. I was recently ill in Poitiers, and they will find that believable for at least two or three days. Then they would have a more difficult time to catch up, even if they knew which direction we had headed."

"But what will they do when they discover you have gone?" Gaillarde was no doubt seeing that managing the château might be more challenging than she had thought, with angry knights crashing about the place.

"I will leave them a note, telling them to join William in Toulouse, and that I will soon be with them." I grinned. "What can they do at that point but obey?" William will be furious, I thought, but it would be just deserts for him. He should have taken me with him when he left Paris, as I had demanded.

"And we have the day to stitch the simple garments we need. The black of the Benedictines, and their white wimples, will hide our identity even as we leave this castle." The young Fabrisse was becoming excited as well. A bold spirit seemed to fill the room, even as the sun invaded through the windows.

"I wish you well on your search, Your Grace," Guillabert said, rising and bowing. "We also must be going, as we may not stay in any one place too long."

"Will you bless us before you go, Brothers?" Blanche asked, with great dignity.

"But of course," Benedict said. "Since time is short, we will read from the gospel of our beloved Saint John. That will suffice for this time. We will be back within the month, and hope that you will have returned by that time."

"Can you not stay one more day?" I asked suddenly. "I feel my friends have been cheated of your visit because of my interruption."

"No, Princesse, do not think it. We must always be on the move.

It is dangerous to stay more than one night in any place." Guillabert looked at me with great kindness. He placed his hands on my shoulders, and I felt more than saw that his black eyes mirrored eternity. "Your coming to this place has meant a great deal to these women, and friendship is one of the greatest blessings we can have."

Then he seemed to come to himself and quickly removed his hand from my shoulder, bowing as he did so. "I pray your mission will be successful, Princesse," he said.

I placed my own hand on his arm, to reassure him I had taken no offense at his familiarity. "And yours, also, my Brother."

And so this amazing scene concluded with all of us seated in a semicircle while Guillabert, standing before us, read the gospel of St. John in his deep baritone, accompanied by the birds twittering outside the open windows. All the while the deep autumn sunshine washed over us. And I listened as I had never listened to the words, opening my heart to the meanings behind them, as I thought about the rescue of my son:

> *In the beginning was the Word. And the Word was with*
> *God. And the Word was God . . . And the light shineth*
> *in the darkness, and the darkness comprehended it not.*

19

A Pilgrim Hostel
Near Verdun

Our leave-taking the following morning, well before the November sun had peered over the horizon, had all the character of a furtive, criminal act. Although I could scarce sleep for the excitement of taking action to find my son, I also felt compunction at deceiving my knights, and something else, a vague sense of lurking danger. It was not for myself that I feared, but for Geralda and the young women who would accompany me.

And there was one niggling thought that I did my best to keep at bay, but it persisted in rising to the fore: What would William say to all this when next we met?

But then I thought of Amaury, how nonchalant he was after young Geoffrey was killed in the tournament, and his small, glittering eyes the last night as he challenged me to show him my gift if I dared. I thought of his veiled threat against Francis and my growing certainty that he had abducted my son and I stiffened my resolve.

Joanna bit her lip and hugged me, and Blanche and Philippa cried, and even the aged Ermengarde, who had risen from her sleep to send us off on our great adventure, sniffled. I was pained to part from Joanna, feeling that I had just found her again. But she was bound for Fontevraud Abbey and a reunion with her mother, Queen Eleanor, and in no condition to join our adventure, though she desired it. I bade her farewell with a sad heart, knowing we might never meet again.

Our little troupe looked like a flock of ravens in our Benedictine black, our heads wound tightly in white wimples that had been cobbled together from the cloth of the serving girls' aprons. Our cloaks were black as well, and our horses were soberly covered in the darkest and most ragged blankets they could find in the stables, so that we would appear as the poor pilgrims we pretended to be.

Our story was that we had joined the crowd at the theological debates in Narbonne before continuing on our pilgrimage. We would say that the horses we rode had been loaned to us by the Trencavel viscount in Béziers, so that we would pray and offer reparations for any misdeeds he had committed or might commit in the future. This last seemed particularly odd to me, but Blanche reassured me that it was quite a common prayer for the nobles of the south. They were a turbulent group, apparently, and wanted to achieve heaven without the necessity of changing their improvident actions here on earth.

Our plan was to approach Fontfroide and ask for hospitality, saying that the ride had tired us. We even decided to offer to work in the abbey in exchange for our bread and a roof over our heads. That was Geralda's idea, as it would provide an excuse to roam the abbey grounds, listening for any clues to the fate of Francis.

We led our horses down the hill from the château at Lavaur until we were well out of earshot and then all of us mounted and cantered onward.

The trip was less arduous than I had thought it would be. The Knights Templar, who for the past one hundred years had encouraged pilgrims to journey to the Holy Land, also provided hostels for pilgrims who were bound for the sacred shrine of Santiago de Compostela in Galicia, in the northwesternmost part of Hispania.

We took the less-traveled roads, and passed by the towns of Montgey, St. Felix, and then east to Verdun. After that we dropped down to travel along the Aude River and came to the town of Alaric. We looked for Templar hostels and stayed in them when we could. Our story for these good monks was that we were on a journey to the Holy Land, for we were making our way east at this time.

But on the third night that we sought hospitality, I was heartily surprised. We were lodged in a hostel near Verdun, a group of wooden and stone buildings that had once been a small monastery. It had a large room at the center of two wings, sufficient to serve dinner to the pilgrims who were gathered that night. We were always offered a hot meal of some kind, before the hospitaler showed us to the dormitories that were designated separately for men and women. I knew the sleeping would be cold as the night deepened, so I resolved to savor the heat of the refectory fireplace.

As we sat demurely at the wooden trestle tables, without cloths, eating stew from ordinary trenchers like peasants, and listening to the reading of the holy epistles, a monk approached our table. I watched him advance with purpose, but his hood prevented sight of his face. There were thirty or more of us at that evening meal. The monk who sought me out surprised me, and I started when he called me by name.

"Princesse Alaïs." Though he spoke my name softly and close to my ear, I uttered a small cry of surprise.

"Sweet Jesus' crown of thorns," I said under my breath. "What are you doing here, Pierre of Castelnau?"

"Do not say more. I must talk with you, but not here where we may be seen. I will leave this room now. In a moment, rise and follow me. There is an alcove outside in the cloister walk where I am certain we will not be disturbed. Turn left when you have come through the door."

I had never before taken an order from a monk, but what he recommended seemed a good plan if we were to talk. Once I recovered from my surprise at seeing him, I was ravenous with curiosity to discover what he, a papal legate, was doing in a Templar's pilgrim hostel.

I leaned over to Geralda, who had become my good companion and who, I had discovered, had a remarkable sense of humor, and murmured to her: "I have been identified by a monk of my acquaintance. I must speak with him and ensure that we remain anonymous."

Geralda nodded, rightly assessing that we should have a minimum of whispering while the holy lecture was read. We did not want to draw attention to ourselves. But I could not resist one more comment.

"Please bring an extra cake for me, if any is offered at the end of the meal."

She cast me the look I deserved for that, and returned her attention to the reader, and the epistle to the Corinthians, leaving me to slip off the edge of the bench and drift toward the door Pierre of Castelnau had indicated.

"Princesse Alaïs." The familiar voice came from the shadows just outside the door.

"Pierre de Castelnau," I said, "what are you doing here? Why are you staying at a simple pilgrim's hostel when you are a papal legate?"

"And I might ask the same question of a *princesse* of France," he replied, chuckling softly. "And why in a nun's habit?"

It was an unexpected flash of lightness and I replied: "Well said. It seems we are both traveling in disguise. Shall we each leave the explanations for another day?"

"Yes, we have more important things to discuss," he said, now serious of tone. "It is a stroke of luck to find you here. I have been anxious to talk with you ever since we parted in Paris."

"Whither are you bound?"

"I go now to Toulouse. I have just come from the religious debates in Narbonne. I prefer to travel alone in these uncertain days. I attract less attention that way." I heard a note of fear in his voice. "Amaury likes to tout the fact that he represents the pope, and he travels with a retinue that could storm Jerusalem, but I have other inclinations."

"Tempers seem to run high over religion in this region," I said, in some sympathy with the papal legate's position. "By the by," I said, attempting to sound offhand, "where is your colleague, Abbé Amaury, now?"

"He has decided to visit the monastery of Fontfroide where he was formerly abbot. I encouraged him to come to Toulouse with me, but he was adamant. He seemed to have some business at the monastery that he did not want to discuss with me."

The blood surged to my cheeks, and I was glad for the shadows that hid my color. So I had made the right decision. If Amaury would not even tell his fellow legate why he must go to Fontfroide, his purpose must be sinister indeed. Perhaps something very like concealing an abduction.

"We are to have a high conference in Toulouse." Pierre's words continued to fill the silence created by my interior reflections. "I have instructions to confront Count Raymond and receive assurances from him that he will purge the heretics from his lands."

"And the Lord William?" I asked, wondering irritably just how much time William had spent in the south searching for my son and how much attending to the business of the pope and the king of France. "Is he to be present at this important meeting?"

"He is to be our moderator, assigned by the Holy Father as an informal diplomat. I hope he can aid me to make Raymond see reason." The shadows around us wavered, as the door opened again and torchlight and breeze flooded our area. But the pilgrim who emerged paid no heed to our dark corner as he made his way along the corridor to the large room with pallets for sleeping.

"Père Pierre, surely you did not summon me from the refectory to discuss politics?" I was growing wary, and felt I should return to my companions. Above all, I did not want to be noticed. "Neither you nor I want to draw attention to ourselves. We must not appear to be conspiring in this place of hospitality."

"I was glad to see you tonight." He stepped closer to me, and I caught an odor, not unpleasant, like that of mixed, dried herbs. I wondered if I was imagining an odor of sanctity. "I had wanted to see you before I left Paris, but Amaury insisted on an abrupt departure. I wanted to tell you more of the politics of our mission. Amaury's actions are, in part, caused by his desire, nay, his obsession with success in bringing Count Raymond to heel. This imminent meeting will be the summit of his efforts."

"I have guessed as much." I gestured with open hands. "Indeed, it was obvious from what you told me after the tournament. As it happens, I left Paris quite unexpectedly myself. But something else is troubling you."

"When I was in Paris I did something that might result in harm to someone. I want you to know about it."

"A matter of confession, Father?" I asked, with some irony.

"I suppose it is." He paused, pondering my comment, and when he replied, it was with an unexpected seriousness. "Perhaps I should make this a matter for my confessor. But I only thought that if I told you, you could forestall any injury I might have caused."

"Père Pierre, please speak plainly." I was more and more puzzled.

"There is a cup that is of great value to the Cathars. It was once theirs to venerate and they used it in their simple ceremonies. Then, some years ago, a careless Cathar preacher, fatigued from his mountain journeys, fell asleep in a barn. When he awoke he found that his leather bag beside him had been quietly ransacked. It contained a few simple clothes and his copy of the good book in the langue d'oc."

"And something more." I felt the breath of the Fates on my neck. I knew I had to listen, though I longed to run. Pierre nodded. "A precious and ancient icon," I continued.

"So you know," he said gravely.

"I know there is a chalice called the St. John Cup, although I was not certain of its provenance or its value."

"The story of the cup is mixed. Some say it is precious to the Cathars because it was the drinking cup of John the Evangelist. Others say it is of value for its remarkable gold braid, and for its jewels. And others that there is a message wrought into the cup, perhaps in the placement of jewels around the rim, that contains a map for hidden treasure. No one is certain why it is of such value." Pierre was speaking rapidly now, casting his glance about to see if we were overheard. More pilgrims were leaving the refectory, although we were not easily observed standing in our small alcove.

"There was much talk of this cup at the *débats* held in recent years between the *'bons chrétiens'* as they style themselves, and the theologians of Rome. Some accusations of theft flew between the two groups. The Cathar Good-Men had the vessel from someone who had been on crusade," he continued, his voice low but intense. "A noble knight brought it back from the Holy Land and, it is said, gave it to the preachers after his conversion to their beliefs. The cup has a special meaning for the Cathar *credentes* because of their veneration of the gospel of St. John."

' "In the beginning was the word . . .' " I murmured. ' "And the word was with God.' "

' "And the light shineth in the darkness; and the darkness knew it not,' " he responded. "That is the part that matters to these purists. The Cathar bishops asked my family, my sister Beatrice, to help find the cup."

As a shaft of light caught his face, I could see he was nearly pleading with me. "You remember. I told you about her when we last met in Paris."

"Indeed, I do recall everything that you said that night," I responded, with warmth truly felt.

After a pause, he continued: "I heard rumors while traveling. Someone said the cup had been seen in the cathedral of Toulouse, but that it then disappeared. I heard another story that the cup had recently made its way to Paris." Pierre was wiping the sweat from his brow with the sleeve of his habit.

"When Amaury and I came to court, I sought out the Countess Constance, thinking that she might have knowledge of the cup since it had last rested in Toulouse. I know the countess keeps in touch with all the gossip of her son's court, though she has been gone from it these twenty years. And I was right. She told me she had just seen a chalice that resembled a description of the St. John Cup raised at Mass that very day at St. Denis."

"And then what happened?"

"I shared my plan with her. To obtain the cup and send it to my sister in Béziers. She would know how to get it back to the Cathars."

"And what did Constance say to that?"

"She said she would think on it. That she might have a way to obtain the cup, but she was unsure whether it should go to Toulouse or to my sister. She said that she would tell me the following day what course of action she might follow." The monk seemed near to tears now, and I was growing anxious. The trickle of servants and pilgrims passing our alcove had grown to a rushing brook. We would soon be the only ones left. "Then I had another idea.

"And that was to send it instead to her son, Raymond.

"I sought her out again the next morning, before she could finalize her decision. We spoke and I asked if she were willing to put the cup to the use of peace."

"And did she agree?" I was struggling to discern my aunt's shifting interests.

"Not at first." He began fiddling with the cross that hung around his neck, identifying him as a papal legate. "But after several conversations, deliberately held, I must say, out of sight of my colleague, Amaury, she agreed to my request that she obtain the cup from St. Denis. I did not ask how she would do this. Then, I was to take the cup south to Toulouse, when I came for the conference I will have with Count Raymond a week hence. My instructions to Count Raymond were to be that he use the cup to, umm, attract the Cathar bishops to come to Toulouse and talk with Foulques and the other churchmen of Rome. That could be the start of peace and acceptance here in the south."

"Luring the Cathar bishops to Toulouse? More like sending them into the lion's den. Not a noble use for a chalice with such a history." I shook my head. "It is one thing to debate in Béziers, or Narbonne, where the Roman bishops are more sympathetic to alternative views. But in Toulouse, where all is rigid and set . . ." I made a clicking sound with my tongue as I reflected on the folly of this plan.

"Yes, when I arrived at Toulouse on my way to Béziers, I saw the conditions in the city. I met the rabid Bishop Foulques. And I saw how fantastic my plan had been, utterly unconnected to the reality of the situation."

"But what happened in Paris with Constance? Did you get the cup?"

"After she agreed to get the cup, Constance began to avoid me. I could never manage to talk with her alone. Several times I came upon her talking intensely with the king's first minister, Etienne Chastellain, in the corridors or on the grand stone staircase. I surmised that she had taken him as an adviser, and wanted nothing more to do with me or my plans." He paused, looking about before he continued.

"I fear she may have shared my plan with Chastellain. I observed his actions when he was near my colleague, Abbé Amaury, and I believe they had many conversations I was not privy to."

"You said you thought you had harmed someone," I murmured, feeling more urgency as someone jostled me on the way past. The fellow was a monk, and muttered something, but I did not respond and he kept on walking. "Who do you think might be harmed?"

"The night before we left Paris, as we were walking to our chambers, Amaury asked me several questions about Lord William of Caen's household. He seemed particularly interested in the young clerk Francis."

"Why should that question alarm you?" I forced myself to ask, though it felt as if my throat were closing.

"Amaury seemed to believe that young Francis knew where the cup was, that somehow Constance had enlisted him in her scheme to steal the cup from St. Denis."

"But that's absurd," I exploded. "Young Francis would no more involve himself in such efforts—"

"Perhaps not in ordinary times," Pierre said sadly. "But the countess may have played on his anger over the death of his friend in the tournament. If she persuaded him that by helping the Cathars he could have his revenge on those who arranged the murder of his friend . . ." He stopped for a moment, as if choosing his next words carefully. "I may have been a party to involving this youth in our schemes."

I thought of my brother's words at the tourney, and of what William said about harm coming to his household, and I felt a quick, involuntary shudder.

"It is my penance for my sins that I must ride by Amaury's side, and sit next to him at state dinners and know that his violent ways will triumph. That his path in matters of religion is to give no quarter, to stamp out dissent, to adhere to his rigid beliefs."

"Do you know where young Francis is now?" I was having trouble with my breathing again.

"I do not. Amaury and I parted at Poitiers, at his request. He went on to Fontfroide Abbey and I was bound for Toulouse. It was south of Poitiers that I accidentally encountered William of Caen. He said the young knight was not with him, but he was terse when I asked and would not speak further about him."

The door to the refectory opened again, and this time four pilgrims made their way past us. I felt a growing concern. Someone would soon wonder what we were doing locked in conversation, a monk and a nun! "Père Pierre, we must part. To talk further would be to invite notice."

The monk bent his tall frame so that he spoke in my ear, his voice scarce above a whisper. "I ask a boon of you. Please find the young Francis, and tell him: There is no chance for peace, with or without the chalice. He should not bring it to Toulouse. It will only create more violence."

"I give you my word, Father. I will make every effort to find the young knight." The worthy priest had no idea how determined I was to do this very thing. "But if he has the chalice, where then should he take it?"

We had begun walking back toward the dining hall, and when we reached an open space where the cloister walks intersected, the monk stayed me with a hand on my shoulder. It was an act of treason to touch a royal in such a way, but he was clearly becoming agitated to the point of distraction.

"Tell young Francis that if he has the object, he should take it to my sister Beatrice of Béziers. She will see that it is returned to the Cathar bishops. I understand now that the only use of the chalice in Toulouse would have been to bait the trap for the Cathar leaders. I was sadly mistaken in what I tried to do."

And behold, another innocent who was no match for the strategies of Amaury and Chastellain, I thought grimly.

I looked closely and once again I saw tears glistening in the moonlight on the narrow face of the monk. "You have no hope for a good outcome, then, at your meeting in Toulouse, even with the Lord William there to assist?"

"If Foulques is at the conference, and he will be, there will be few options of compromise allowed the count. The bishop will push him to the wall in the name of orthodoxy. And Raymond is caught. If the Cathar leaders were to come, what chance would they have when even the Lord of Toulouse cannot elude the wolves."

I put my hand on his arm and spoke clearly in a low voice. "Père Pierre, you are a good and holy man. One does what one can. Sometimes it is not enough to combat the forces of darkness. But I will find Francis, rest assured, and if he still has the cup, I will do all in my power to see that Beatrice receives it." With an impulse, I peeled off my leather riding glove, and took the ring from my right hand. "Here, take this. It has the royal insignia on it. If you have need of safety anywhere, say you are my deputy. It may save your life."

He looked up with a face that suddenly appeared angelic and serene, full of resignation. "I bless you for that, but I have no need of safety now," he said. And he put up his hands in a gesture of regret. Then, for some reason he changed his mind. He took the ring and slipped it into the pocket of his habit.

Suddenly I recalled the picture of the priest lying by a river's bend, his blood watering the land. I knew the monk saw the image as well, for he started, then sighed.

I dared not tarry longer. "Blessings on you, Pierre of Castelnau. God knows you have done what you could." And so saying, I leaned forward and brushed each of his cheeks with my own. I left him standing with tears streaming down his face. And I could not bear to look back.

20

Fontfroide Abbey

O ur horses were as fatigued as their riders when we finally rode up to the gates of Font-froide Abbey in the morning two days later. We looked every inch the dusty and tired pilgrims we pretended to be. Even the stalwart Geralda, who had scarce complained at all since we left Lavaur, was reconsidering her decision to accompany me. I could see it in her lined, weary face. But now, of course, it was too late.

The last few days had been rainy and cold, but today the sun shone brightly as we dismounted. The sweet air was a welcome change from the rain and that, coupled with the fair sleep I had enjoyed at a nearby inn the previous night, caused my spirits to rise. I felt renewed confidence that Francis was here and that we were now close enough to prevent harm to him. If only we could move fast enough.

The hospitaler was summoned by the porter immediately after we identified ourselves as nuns from a small monastery near the abbey of Moissac. I thought that might be an address far enough away to be safe. At least days away by messenger, should the current abbot of Fontfroide decide to inquire about us.

True to our plan, we announced ourselves as pilgrims bound for Santiago de Compostela. We were somewhat west for our story to ring true, so we added that we had attended the recent *débats* in Narbonne on religion, which were, I knew, in the nature of a large convocation for many professed religious.

Our story was accepted without question by the hospitaler. He only inquired how long we would like to stay at the abbey. Geralda and I looked at each other. We had agreed in advance she would usually speak for us, sparing me any additional questions about my Paris accent. Though I had learned the langue d'oc well as a child at Queen Eleanor's knees, I now carried unmistakable evidence of my northern years in the smooth way I slid over the words. While most would overlook it, we never knew when we would encounter someone who knew the nuances well enough to challenge me.

"We would be grateful for a time to rest, before we continue our journey," she said. "Perhaps a period of a few days?"

"The abbey is quite overwhelmed with guests now," the man said. He was short, and rotund, and genial of expression, as he surveyed us. Also, it turned out, generous with information. "Our former abbot is here visiting, and he has a large retinue, which we have had to house, feed, and stable. And we have other important guests at the moment."

"It does seem busy," I murmured. There were many carts coming in and out of the gates, even as we spoke. There seemed to be enough provisions passing by to quarter an army, raising a great cloud of dust that floated even into the small porterhouse in which we stood. I stifled a sneeze.

"He's a very important man," the hospitaler confided. "He is now a papal legate, and traveling our region to persuade people to adhere to the true religion of Rome." As he spoke, he was examining a list, an inventory perhaps of cells or guesthouses available.

"Ah, here is the perfect place." He looked up and smiled, as if he had made a brilliant new discovery. "We have three small huts, er . . . guesthouses on the abbey property, and one is not in use. It should accommodate four pilgrims nicely. It is quite far from the main abbey buildings, from the church and chapter house and Great Hall, but it will provide the isolation proper for you all as women religious."

He glanced skyward, his great brows beetling against the sun. "And the weather is still clement enough, praise the Lord, so coming to and fro for worship and meals should not be a hardship for you."

"Thank you many times over, Father Hospitaler," Geralda said with excessive meekness, and I cast her a sharp look. But no sign of a smile appeared on her face and the hospitaler seemed pleased at our gratitude.

"Father Hospitaler," I interjected before he could move on to his next task. He turned in surprise, perhaps at my commanding voice, perhaps my accent. I softened my tone. "We would be happy to work while we are here at the abbey. We can work in the kitchens, or sweeping, or helping with the altar linen." Anything, I thought, to draw us into the abbey life so we can find the trail of my son.

"Thank you. We appreciate the offer of service. I will have word sent to your guesthouse before sundown as to your duties on the morrow. Meantime, please use this day to rest and pray, as you must be fatigued from your long journey."

So saying he turned to give a pull to the great bell that hung over the porterhouse.

"I'll have Brother James show you to your house. He will have someone see to your horses," the hospitaler said. Within moments another monk appeared, this one wearing the brown garb of the men who did not take holy orders, but instead joined the community to do the menial work of the abbey.

We bowed our eyes like good nuns and followed as humble guests behind the brother. It was difficult, however, to rein in our two younger companions, for each had a lively way about her, and had not learned the inhibitions necessary for safety in our situation.

"Look, yonder," said young Fabrisse, her youthful voice ringing out as we crossed the abbey close. Brother James stopped and turned abruptly, for such openness would not be characteristic of a young woman religious.

"What is it, Sister?" I said, intending a warning with my stern tone. "Have you been frightened?"

"It is the livery of the king of France," she said artlessly, and I raised my eyes from the ground and followed her pointing finger.

"How do you know the insignia of the king of France?" I asked, covering my surprise as she had spoken truly.

"When I was at my lessons, we were taught coats of arms for Count Raymond of Toulouse, and King Philippe of France, and King John of England who is also Duke of the Aquitaine."

"Hush, child," I said, but Brother James's attention was already captured and he was regarding her with some amusement.

"Well said, young Sister. You learned your lessons well. That is the livery of the king of France. His chief minister arrived only hours ahead of you this very day, to confer with the abbot of Fontfroide, and with our honored guest, Abbé Amaury of Cîteaux." Brother James chuckled at the precosity of Fabrisse. He was elderly and had a kindly face. Also, he was sufficiently ignorant of the ways of a young novice that her unrestrained behavior aroused no suspicion in him.

"What is your name, child?" he asked.

"She will be Sister Marie of the Sorrows when she makes her final profession," I interjected, before she could answer. The name Fabrisse, which was native to the rural south, could arouse suspicion even in one so lacking in guile as Brother James.

Then I cast my eyes to the ground and tucked my hands into the sleeves of my robe, as did the others. Geralda walked beside me, giving no indication that she had even heard the exchange. But it was only with restraint that I managed my insouciance. My head was spinning. Chastellain at Fontfroide! And here to meet with Amaury. How dare he come here, in the livery of the king of France, while a knight of Lord William's household might be languishing a prisoner in this very same abbey? Or could he have conspired in the abduction of Francis himself? Perhaps that was what the meeting was about.

It took some walking to arrive at our guesthouse, and I had time to ponder my disturbing suspicions. The hospitaler had spoken truly. Our quarters were well isolated from the main abbey buildings. But that did not displease me.

We were led along the cloister walks that ringed the massive church, Great Hall, and chapter house of the abbey. The brother fell silent, but roused himself to point out the church and the refectory as we passed them, and indicated in his twangy southern accent that the main meal would take place an hour after the sun was highest.

We left the main buildings of the abbey and crossed what appeared to be a sizable meadow. We followed a well-worn dirt path. Cows were grazing on either side of us, and I could see cultivated fields off in the distance. After some time we came to a little house and I assumed we would stop here, but Brother James merely continued on.

Soon we entered a forest, still within the abbey enclosure. We found ourselves at another small hut, and here he finally made us pause. He took from the rope around his waist a large ring of keys, and opened the rusty lock on the door. It creaked as he pushed it inward.

We entered to find that the house consisted of one somewhat large room filled with a musty smell that indicated a long vacancy. The fire had not been lit for some time, and the pallets for sleeping had certainly not been aired. Not for the first time, Geralda cast me a look that had significant meaning, and it was not optimistic! Ah, well, but here we are, I thought, and brightly smiled back.

"Thank you, Brother James." I turned to him with a nod. "If you would ask the porter to send our few belongings, we should be grateful. And perhaps some firewood?"

"That request is easily answered," he said, drawing me out the door and around the side of the small building. "Here is cut wood for your fire. I shall send a boy with a burning log, and he will start it for you. And he will bring watered wine as well."

"God's blessings on you, Brother," I said, as I made to rejoin my companions.

"You are not from around these parts, are you, Sister?" he asked as he placed his hand on my arm to stay me.

I looked at his eyes. Though there was no direct sunlight because of the surrounding trees, still heavy with leaves here in the south, I could see in his eyes an intelligence I had missed earlier.

"No," I said simply.

His eyelids lowered for the barest moment, as if in fatigue.

"We of this community of Cistercians do our best to follow the rule of Benedict strictly," he said.

I waited for some further sign of his meaning.

"We are people of God," he added, his eyes opening wide. He bent his tonsured head down to mine, as if to tell me a secret. "If you should need help or advice while you are here, have a care from whom you seek it. Not all here do God's will."

Then, as if nothing untoward had passed between us, he turned and reentered the small hut. So much for my disguise, I thought ruefully.

"Sisters," he announced to all our group in a raised voice, "when the large bell rings, it will be time for the Angelus. After the chapel service of the holy office, which I know you will want to attend, the dinner will be served in the refectory. God keep you." He folded his hands and then departed noiselessly.

Geralda and I looked at each other.

"What is the chief minister of France doing here?" she nearly squeaked, shading her eyes against the sun to examine the far-off flag. "Does this mean danger to you?"

"Not if I can forestall it," I said. "He is here to meet with Amaury, and his presence convinces me that there is a conspiracy between them. I wonder what story he gave my brother to allow him to ride off with a retinue of the king's men."

"We must have a care. He would know you on sight, would he not?"

"Indeed. But he has never seen me garbed as a nun. And I do not wear a wimple at court. As a *princesse royale* I am allowed certain liberties with my dress. So he might not recognize me, even if he saw me."

"You believe young Francis is here, in this abbey, do you not?" she asked, turning to me.

"I am certain of it," I replied. "The Cathar preachers said Amaury was here with a great contingent of northern knights. And Pierre of Castelnau told me Amaury was overly interested in Francis. And that he insisted on coming here when he parted from Pierre. I grow more certain by the hour that my son is near."

"Then let us air this bedding, make our fire, and attend the Divine Office. After that we shall go to dinner and then do our best to insert ourselves into this abbey life so we can accomplish our mission."

The two younger women were exhausted, and after we shook out the bedding, we encouraged them to rest until the abbey bells should summon us. And, truth to tell, Geralda and I rested also until the sun was high in the sky and a great clanging in the distance summoned us to prayer and our midday meal.

21

FONTFROIDE ABBEY

The Women's Hut and the Church Nave

We settled quickly into the rhythm of abbey life. Prayers before dawn, a spare breakfast, assigned work, more common prayers, a spare lunch, rest, work, and more prayers. One could easily get accustomed to this life, I thought. It seemed by far more productive than the way we frittered away time in the Paris court. On the third day, a fresh sparkling morning, I found myself alone in the hut, as the others were at their tasks. I had begged charcoal and a small piece of vellum from one of the monks in the scriptorium, and I decided to take these outside, thinking to sketch the birds I heard twittering in the trees before dawn.

As I left the hut, I came upon a surprise in my path not a stone's throw from the door to our dwelling. I had been out earlier to pick firewood from the forest floor, and a small object that I now noticed had not been present then. I leaned over to pick it up. On closer examination I saw that it was a ball of fabric, of a faded green color, dirty and wrinkled.

I unraveled it and saw, to my astonishment, that it was my own green scarf, the token I had given Francis at the tournament in Paris. It had the Capet royal insignia woven into one corner, as did most of my accessories. This was proof that he was somewhere on the abbey grounds! Joy leaped in my heart as I rewound the treasured object and tucked it down the front of my habit, out of sight should anyone happen by.

Despite my elation I decided it would be good to continue my plan to sketch for a while. I have long found I can contemplate as I draw if I am in the soothing presence of nature. I made my way around to the back side of our dwelling, where the absence of a path would have allowed the birds more safety. Even now they may be ready, perching on branches and waiting for my keen eye.

As I walked close to the stone wall of the hut, I saw a squirrel scramble up the chimney stones. I bent again to pick up a branch which I intended to use to harry the squirrel down from the chimney, fearing he might wind up in our fire later if I did not. As I moved quickly forward I stumbled. I peered at the ground to see what could have been the cause. A small brick ridge, scarce above the ground, was visible near the corner of the house. I picked at it with my foot, and separated the leaves and branches that had fallen around it.

In so doing, I exposed a small opening in the ground, like a miniature flue. I noted the position, close to the chimney that rose from the back that served our own small hearth.

I was puzzled. Where could this small opening lead? Was it connected to our guesthouse?

I forgot my desire to sketch and slowly retraced my steps to the front door. When I entered, I was facing the hearth. I walked toward it, my eyes scanning the floor for some sign of any stone that might have been disturbed. I walked carefully, dragging my leather shoe on purpose through the rushes. When I reached the hearth, my toe hit a loose tile. I reached down and pried it up with my finger. Then I crouched down, and began to remove the stones around it. After working feverishly for some minutes, I was rewarded by a most amazing sight.

I knew I had gone as far as I could without help, so I quickly replaced the tiles and the rushes. Then I sat down on the one chair in the room, and thought for some time.

I was called out of my reverie by the sound of the iron doorlatch lifting. That would be Geralda, back from her work in the kitchen. Her patience was fraying, I knew, for the day before when she had returned she flopped on her pallet without a word of greeting to me. Today, she did the same.

"Geralda, you seem tired," I said, addressing her supine figure, but I could not keep the excitement from my voice.

She looked over at me, as I stood winding my nun's wimple around my head. "And you, dear Sister, seem unusually animated."

"Indeed, you are observant." I smiled, playing on her interest. "First tell me how you are feeling, and then I will tell you of my morning."

She swung her legs over the bed, and sat upright, facing me. We were alone in the small guesthouse, Fabrisse and Grazide having gone to their tasks of sweeping the cloister walk and kneading the bread for the morrow's meal. Geralda's long face set, and her chin jutted forward, as a kind of preface to her remarks.

"All right, Princesse, I will speak honestly. We have been here three full days. We have swept and cooked and washed the linen of the abbey, and we still have no sign that Francis is here. We have only glimpsed the Abbot Amaury once, in procession in the church, and have not seen the king's minister at all." She sighed. "I am not complaining, but I am beginning to think our mission here misguided. I do not know how we can crack open this closed egg that is the abbey.

Nor am I even certain the young knight is being held here. We have seen no signs of it."

"And so you are thinking we should give up our cause?" A grin was spreading wider on my face.

"Why look you so cheerful, madame?" she asked, a bit irritably. "Surely, my remarks could not inspire that smile."

I came to sit beside her on the bed, and put my arm around her broad shoulders.

"Geralda, dear friend. I believe our task is nearing completion. This morning, after you and the young women left, I walked out into the forest to sketch the small animals. I had just said a prayer to Saint Barbara, the martyr, that she give me courage not to falter in my task, and my prayer was answered in the forest."

"I thought you did not believe in the Romish religion?" Geralda leaned away from me.

"Well, I do, and I don't. My desperation is leading me to old habits." I waved my hand dismissively. "But hold, and listen to me. The prayers were scarce whispered, than I looked down and saw this on the ground in front of me."

I reached down into the front of my habit, and pulled out the damp and muddy clump of green silk. Geralda who was, I had discovered, quite fastidious, wrinkled her nose.

"And what, pray, is that?"

"This, my dear friend"—and I shook out the fine piece so that she could see the corner—"is a token marked with the emblem of the royal house of France."

"How came it here?" She was genuinely puzzled, as she took the scarf—for so it was—by the corner with her two fingers.

"It is mine. I gave it to young Francis on the day of the tourney in Paris, the very day his young friend was killed, and the day before he himself was abducted."

She looked at me and understanding spread over her blunt features.

"He is here, then."

"Indeed. And I now believe that he is not only being kept at this abbey, but somehow he knows I am near. This token of mine was dropped deliberately where I might find it."

"But where can he be hiding? We have walked the abbey from front to back, almost to a point where we look suspicious, and we have discovered no trace."

"But we have not walked these broad meadows and fields, spread behind us. Remember when we came, the hospitaler said there were three guesthouses. But we only passed one on our way to our shelter."

I rose and smoothed my skirts. "That means that there is another one, somewhere out of sight. Whether in the woods or in the meadows over those hills, I don't know. But we must begin to search the grounds."

"That will be difficult. We are moving toward solstice and the light fades earlier every day." Geralda now also had risen, as if informed by new energy at my news. "We should begin now, and go out at every opportunity."

"Stay, my friend." I placed my hand on her arm, though I was pleased to see her spirit returning. "I have another plan. The darkness can be our friend. We might excite suspicion if we were seen prowling about the fields and meadows when we should be at prayer. But at night, with torches sheltered from the wind, we might make better progress."

"Yes, *vous avez raison*," Geralda said, flopping back onto her pallet. I had taught her some of the expressions we used in the north, and she enjoyed working them into our daily conversation. I smiled. She was a born learner.

"You should rest now, and I will hurry to my tasks. Today I have been instructed to change the altar cloth, instead of working in the laundry. I shall see you back here before chapel and the midday prayer. Tonight we shall explore our surroundings and find that third guesthouse." As I spoke, I tucked the small bundle the scarf had become under the covers of my own pallet, where it could not be seen through the window by some inquisitive passer-by, though in truth we had seen few of those since our arrival.

I was nearly humming as I departed our little hut, as happy as I had been since I had left Paris. My visions and my sense of the presence of Francis had been accurate. This scarf confirmed it. Francis must have seen us, though how that could be I did not know. But surely it was no accident that the scarf had appeared. It was so small, so crumpled, he could have dropped it without being observed, knowing that I would recognize it when I found it.

My first stop was the laundry, a squat pile of stones set some way from the main cluster of abbey buildings where the monks lived, prayed, and ate. The sisters who did the laundry and helped in the kitchen dwelled in a dormitory attached to the side. I passed their door and went directly into the larger room. There I found huge vats of water, heated over fires, and several women stirring them with large sticks whose bark had been peeled off. The steam filled the room, and made it difficult to see beyond an arm's length.

These sisters kept a vow of silence, so they merely nodded to me when I entered. One of them held up her hand, and disappeared into another room, returning in a moment with the white altar linen. It had been washed, laid on a scrubbed wooden table and dried under clean stones, so that it appeared flat and pristine. I marveled that such a clean-looking item could be produced from this outbuilding with its dirt floors covered by simple rushes.

I bowed to her and extended my arms. She placed the altar cloth over them, and I proceeded to the abbey church in that manner. By the time I arrived, I was grateful to bend my arms and set the cloth down, while I stripped the altar of its current covering. I had rolled up the broad sleeves of my habit and tied back my veil, the better to have freedom to work. I had been pleased to see that no one was in the chapel when I arrived. The less I was observed by anyone, no matter how casually, the better I liked it.

But some moments into my task I heard the clip of boots on the floor, and another sound, the soft clap-clap of slippers. I decided to continue my work and did not turn around. It was well for me that I made that choice.

To my astonishment, the voices I began to hear were all too familiar. Abbot Amaury and Etienne Chastellain, for it was those two conspirators, were seated well toward the front of the church where I could easily make out their comments. They paid no attention to the back of the Benedictine nun at the altar as she slowly rolled and unrolled the used altar cloth, biding for time to hear their exchange. They spoke in ordinary tones, no doubt feeling safe in that sacred space to plot any intrigue.

"I want you to go, Chastellain. I do not like it that you showed yourself here. This was never part of our agreement." It was the abbot's raspy voice.

"Our agreement was based on mutual interest." Now it was Chastellain's turn. It seemed the tone of the conversation would be contentious. "You want gold or arms and men to fight your heretics, and I was willing to aid your request to the king of France. In return, you promised to hold your tongue about the information Eugene had funneled to King John of England." He sniffed, as if sensing an unpleasant smell. "A situation you would not have known about if it were not for the loose lips of John's western guard."

The abbot grunted, but said nothing, as if contemplating his rejoinder. I dared not cast a glance backward to see the look on his face.

"But now, I tell you, you have gone too far," Chastellain continued, his tone lower and more intense. "Abducting a young knight, a favorite of the Princesse Alaïs, belonging to the household of the king's counselor Lord William, these rash actions were not part of our plan."

The church was so quiet that I could hear the rustle of the abbot's silk sleeve moving as he flung his arm to dismiss Chastellain's comments.

"Bah! As I told you, I had to seize the day. The king was not going to accede to our wishes, pope's letter or no. If we can offer William information on his young ward's whereabouts, he is much more likely to bend our way in Toulouse, where that fool Castelnau is bound for the conference with Count Raymond."

"How are you going to tell William you have information on the lad without arousing his suspicions that you were involved in his disappearance?" Chastellain's comment cause a sharp intake of the abbot's breath, followed by an audible sigh. "The man has a temper. I have seen it."

"I've already thought of that. I will let him know that we have captured a messenger who was taking word to the Cathars of the young knight's whereabouts."

"So the shadow of suspicion will fall on the Cathars," Chastellain murmured. "Elegant indeed. But won't the young man lay the blame on you when he is back with his master?"

"No, he's never seen me. He was always kept in the back of the train, with a foulard around his eyes, and I took care that he did not know who we were, nor where we were going. We could actually take him to the countryside and leave him, and he could never point a finger."

"Because if he did identify you as his abductor . . ." Chastellain left the unspoken words hanging in the air.

"I have considered that possibility. I will make certain he knows nothing. The alternative course of action would be to close his mouth forever, so there would be no way to trace his disappearance back to us." There was a pause. "I have not yet made a final decision. I will see what William's response is first. I have sent a messenger to him to tell him I have news. I expect an answer soon."

My heart chilled at these words. I realized how I had slowed in my work, and hoped the two men would not notice the inconsequential nun in front of them, fiddling at the altar, moving the tall and weighty candlesticks from left to right and back again.

"But having influence over Lord William was not the only cause of my action. I wanted the young man also because I thought Constance had given him the chalice."

"What chalice?" Chastellain sounded impatient.

"You know well what chalice! Constance met me that very evening and told me you arranged to have the cup stolen from St. Denis. You bungled that as well, your men killing that sacristan. You can't murder a monk in the sacristy of the largest abbey in Paris and get away scot-free! Now the king cannot overlook this theft, as he might have otherwise."

"And what was the chalice to you, if I had stolen it?"

"I wanted it for the same reason you did." Amaury's voice tightened. "The object contains directions for finding the Cathars' treasure lode. The clues have been worked into the jewels around the lip. Or somewhere else. I need the cup to find that gold. It could fund my entire work against the heretics." Amaury paused. "Then I wouldn't need the king of France," he growled.

"I never knew it had a treasure map." Chastellain sounded genuinely confused. I could only raise my eyes heavenward. God's teeth, as King Henry was wont to say. The only thing worse than a corrupt courtier was a stupid one. "Constance pressured me to have my men steal the cup because she said it belonged rightfully to her son's cathedral in Toulouse." Chastellain's voice had a tone of one ill-used. "She promised if I brought it to her, she would use her influence with Philippe to send men for our war against heretics. But the very night I delivered it to her, after that unfortunate sacristan got in the way of my man's sword, she simply took it. By morning, instead of meeting me as promised to finalize her strategy with the king, she had disappeared."

"And that shows what you know about the court in Paris. She has no influence with her nephew, the king," Amaury railed. "And now, where on God's earth is the damnable chalice? When I heard about the theft I sent to her, but the servant returned saying she had suddenly left the palace. Only the night before it was stolen, Constance met with me and promised I should have it when it came into her possession."

"You are angry because you think she played you for a fool?" Chastellain emitted a short bark that could pass for a laugh in some quarters.

I heard an impatient thump on the floor as Amaury pounded his abbot's staff on the stone floor. That staff was probably as good a weapon as any for a murder. "I think she played both of us for fools. But I still hold a trump. And that is young Francis of York. I'll get something out of this muddle yet."

I heard the rustle of silk again, and surmised both men had stood.

"And the young knight? He knows nothing of this treasure?" Chastellain said.

There was a pause, and I hurriedly finished smoothing the new cloth along the edges of the stone altar. I felt the hot breath of their sudden observation on my neck, and knew I was in danger if I tarried further. I made a deep genuflection to the altar, and began to walk away from the voices of the men, bowing my head to hide any accidental sighting of my face.

"No, he says he knows nothing of this cup. And my chief assistants, who have been questioning him, now believe he is innocent of any information."

His voice trailed away as I glided out of the abbey church and into the cloister walks. So Amaury took Francis, but he didn't have the chalice. Then Constance must have taken it with her when she fled the court. I had much to think on as I walked back to my guesthouse and it was only when I arrived that I became aware that I was still carrying the used altar cloth. I had forgotten to leave it with the laundry sisters. I hurried back to deposit it with the nuns, givng them a forced smile. I was grateful for their silent practice. My heart was too full for speech. When I returned to our hut, I pushed open the door to tell Geralda of my most recent discovery, and to make a plan for our evening search.

22

The Women's Hut

Geralda could see I was brimming with excitement. Fabrisse and Grazide had also returned from their work and were seated on the sleeping pallets with crossed legs, their backs against the wattle-and-daub hut's walls. They ceased their conversation as soon as I appeared.

"Princesse, you have news," Geralda said. "I can see by your face."

"Indeed," I replied. "And I now have reason to believe that our time is running short for a rescue. I overheard Amaury and Chastellain in the chapel."

"Did they see you?" Geralda was alert, as always, to the signs of danger.

"No, I never turned their way. Even if Amaury knew we were here, he would have no reason to suspect a group of nuns making a pilgrimage to Santiago de Compostela." I sat down on the only wooden chair the room afforded. Suddenly I was very tired.

"But I now know why Francis was taken. And that Amaury has not yet decided his fate. We must take action soon. My son is in mortal danger."

"I have told Fabrisse and Grazide that you found the scarf that Francis took from you the day of the tourney in Paris. And that you suspect he is being kept in the third guesthouse."

"We need to move quickly," I said. "I believe we could discover that guesthouse this day, and find out under what circumstances Francis is being held. Then, even this very night, we could go under cover of darkness and create a disturbance, and in the chaos that ensues set the lad free."

"Mother of God," Fabrisse breathed, but whether in excitement or fear, I knew not.

"What sort of disturbance?" Geralda asked ominously, as if she knew already.

"A fire," I said, rising in my agitation and pacing the length of the little hut. "It is the perfect weapon. We have never let the fire in our hearth go out. We have a torch we can light from that fire and take with us. If we can ascertain during daylight how he is being guarded, we can put a torch to a hay left in the surrounding field. Then we can raise the alarm. While everyone is distracted, we can take Francis away to our hut."

"And where will we hide him? Our place is so small." Grazide's eyes were widening by the moment. All of the adventures she had endured since leaving Lavaur were as nothing to what I was now proposing. What stories she would have to carry back to her family!

"I will show you. This morn as I was preparing to draw the small animals and birds for a diversion, I came across a peculiar thing, an opening surrounded by a set of bricks right next to our own chimney.

Come outside with me." And I led them to the door, and around to the side of our little structure. As I walked them through the events of the morning that led to my amazing discovery, I could see their interest mounting. We wound up back in the house, where I showed them the loose stones on the hearth.

I kicked the side of the stones gently, and they moved under my foot. "I removed the stones, and, voilà, something extraordinary came into view." I brushed aside some of the rushes in front of the stone hearth with my foot. "Come, help me take them up again. I'll show you something amazing."

With a willing attitude, the women came to my side, driven as much by curiosity as a desire to help. In a short time, we had pulled up the dozen flat stones ringing the hearth. Geralda came to look over my shoulder, following with her gaze the direction of my extended hand and gasped.

"By the breath of Christ and Saint John," she breathed. "What is it?"

The other two women crowded around. Set in the stone floor was a heavy oak piece with an iron ring fixed into one corner. But what was most arresting was the carving in the center of this door, for door it appeared to be.

"What is it?" Fabrisse echoed.

"Ugh," the younger Grazide said. "It is a monster."

"No, not at all." I smiled, though I had been as startled as the others at the initial sight. "It is a figure of a woman carved into oak."

"But look at her pose, and all of those breasts." Grazide was fascinated.

"It is merely a remnant of the old pagan ways, a figure to honor fertility." I tried to speak calmly, especially for the younger women, though I was excited about my find. "It is called a Sheila-na-gig in England, from the Celtic tradition. It is even worked into some of the churches that have been built since the time of William Rufus. I saw one myself at Whittlesford when I rode with King Henry's party there."

"But what's it doing here, at the abbey?" Geralda's heavy brows were drawn together. "This is supposed to be a place of Christian prayer."

I shrugged. "Many Christian abbeys were built over the old pagan sites. Surely you have heard of the black virgins? They were simply shrines to the Roman goddess Diana that were appropriated by the monks." I was amused at the expression of horror on the faces of the two younger women. "But it makes good sense, you see. The managers of the new religion let the folk keep the dark figure of the goddess of the hunt and the moon. They simply redirected their homage to the Christian mother of God."

"Does this drawing not disturb you?" Geralda asked. "Where it came from? What it might portend? It may have been carved by those who believe in witchcraft."

"Not at all. I have no interest in the history of this place. And I do not believe in bad luck or omens, not in this way." I stared down at the carving with its many breasts and it stared back at me. There were eyes carved into the face, unlike the other one I had seen. "If I were to take any meaning from its appearance at this time, I would say it is a sign from God that a mother's love will triumph."

They all fell silent. Then I continued, in a lighter tone, "But if there is no meaning beyond a convenience, then I say this image and the alcove it hides will do very well to hide my son until we can spirit him away. Help me move this heavy plank, my sisters. I am not strong enough to move it by myself."

Together Geralda and I pulled on the ring until the board lifted, and Fabrisse and Grazide grabbed the sides as they rose. We were able to drag the oak piece off and I was amazed to see a large opening scooped out from the ground.

A small rope ladder led down to the opening, which appeared quite large.

I quickly untied my veil, and unwound my white wimple. My hair fell around me and it felt good to have it unbound, even for this brief time.

"What are you doing, Princesse?" Grazide, ever curious, came right up behind me.

"I am going to descend to the underworld, little one, and I do not want to get my wimple dirty and have uninvited questions from the nuns in the laundry or from Brother James, should we meet him." So saying, I cast the white cloth onto my pallet and took a small torch from its holder on the wall. After I lit it from our hearth fire, I handed it to Fabrisse. Then I began my careful descent down the ladder as she held the light close to the opening. With only one good hand, I had to go slowly.

"I'll come as well," Geralda said, and began to discard her own wimple, seeing the sense of what I said about keeping it clean.

I stopped, my hand firmly grasping the ladder. I was already waist deep in the hole and able to hold my balance only by applying some strength.

"No, Geralda, I forbid it," I said sternly. "We do not know what is below. Just wait one moment." And I continued down the ladder before she could reply.

I was startled to find the space much larger than it appeared from above. Indeed, it was quite comfortable, with a sleeping pallet in one corner, a small table, and some curious artifacts sitting there. I did not have the time or interest to examine them, but thought that later—if all worked well—I would do so. I could not help but believe this oddity in the large and well-run abbey had to do with some protection that had been offered to adherents of the old religion. But who they were or why they were hidden here might remain a mystery.

I cast a glance at the far end of the little chamber, and saw an odd thing: a hearth with a small chimney built upward. There was no sign that a fire had ever been laid there, and I got down on my knees to peer upward.

As I gazed up the chimney structure, I glimpsed blue sky above and suddenly knew what this was. Rising from the hearth, dusty with ill-use if not with ashes, I brushed my hands with great satisfaction. Someone had stayed for some time in this underground chamber. And they had had the benefit of air flowing from the chimney to the outside to keep them well.

The room seemed clean, or at least as clean as an underground hiding place could be, and it seemed a miraculous answer to aid our plans to rescue Francis, for once we had rescued him, what would we have done to hide him? It was with a light heart that I made my ascent and began my report to my friends on the comfort of that space, and my discovery of the small chimney to the outside.

Suddenly we heard the large abbey bells tolling for the noon prayer, and I rushed to wash my hands and rewind my wimple. Geralda and the two young women were able to drag the oak door with the fertility goddess on its back over the hole and replace the tiles and the rushes that covered it.

We were all a bit breathless as we left the hut, once again observing the silence the abbey demanded of its guests as well as its monks and brothers, for most of the day. But my heart was beating fast as I continued to make my plans to find Francis that very night. As we walked through the short forest path, past the laundry building and toward the abbey church, my head was spinning. I did not know how I would contain myself until we were free once again after the noon meal.

We filed into the abbey church, our hands folded and our eyes downcast, as befitted our status as pilgrim sisters. We took our places at the back of the church. I was interested to watch Abbot Amaury lead the procession to the front of the church, with the current abbot, a small, bent figure, walking behind him. There was no mistake about who still wielded the power at Fontfroide Abbey! Or so I thought.

I did not see Chastellain or any of his retinue, as the monks continued to pour into the chapel in their orderly way, singing the beautiful chant in the Latin tongue as their tradition demanded. I wondered if he had already left the abbey, his mission fulfilled after his conference with Amaury. Perhaps he was already on the road to Rome.

The opening prayer was from Psalms, and it gave me great courage:

> When the Lord led back the captives of Sion
> We were like men in a dream
> Then was our mouth filled with laughter and our tongue with rejoicing.

My heart lifted at these words, and for the first time in many months gratitude filled me. I had a strong feeling now that I would be successful in my quest, and my son would be safe.

It was after Nones, the midafternoon prayers, that we finally made our way back to our hut. The November late afternoon sun was settling behind the trees, and I encouraged our little group to wander out. We need not go far, I told them. The third guesthouse must be close by. And so Grazide and Fabrisse set out toward the deeper woods, giggling softly with no one around to hear them.

Geralda and I made our way over the meadow, just down the path from our hut. We stayed close to the tree line, so as not to be observed, and when we had attained the third rise, we were rewarded.

"By Saint John's Gospel," Geralda said, as we came over the rise. And we both shrank into the bushes alongside the trees.

For before us the third guesthouse came into view, much larger than the other two. It had a chimney like ours, but appeared to consist of at least two rooms, more than double the size of our quarters.

What made Geralda exclaim, however, was the sight of two burly men-at-arms standing outside the door. They would surely have seen us had we been walking in the open fields.

One was talking to the other, and gesturing. After a moment, and a terse response from the second man, he turned and went inside.

"So there is one to keep guard outside. That means that two men are assigned here," I murmured. "If this building is so well guarded, there must be something important inside. Something that must be protected, or imprisoned."

"We can't know how many men are inside," Geralda said, as we crept deeper into the trees. We made our way back to our guesthouse inside the tree line now, but keeping close to the meadow opening so as not to lose our way.

"Nevertheless," I said with some determination, "we must go forward. I believe our only chance is to set a fire and cause a distraction. If the fire is close enough to the hut, everyone who is not bound will come to put it out."

"That's a dangerous game," she responded. "What if we can't get Francis out in time?"

"We shall get him out." I could feel my jaw tighten with determination. "It is our only chance. And I fear nothing that could attempt to stop us."

Still, after bread, wine, and cheese in the refectory some hours later and after the night prayers of Compline had been chanted in the church, I had some misgivings. As we made our way back from the main abbey buildings, I felt more unsettled than I cared to admit. We had only five hours until morning prayers, five hours to create the distraction, rescue Francis, and bring him back to the hut to hide in the recesses of the underground shelter.

According to our prearranged plan, we were to spread out. Grazide and Fabrisse were to take the torch and risk the open field. Geralda and I would keep to the forest line behind them. When we arrived at the guesthouse, the two younger women would circle around the dwelling to the other side. Since the harvest had been completed weeks earlier, the hay allowed to remain in the field had become dry and brittle. I was counting on this to make an immediate fire of interesting proportions. As soon as it was set, the two young women were to douse the flame of their torch and run for our hut, immediately scrambling into bed once they arrived there, so that they could say they heard nothing.

Geralda and I would watch to see at least two men leave the dwelling and then run for the doorway. After that, our actions would depend on what we found.

When I journeyed, I carried with me always a large knife in a scabbard of sorts. I buckled that instrument around my waist. Geralda and I wore page's clothes, leggings and a jerkin that we had packed in anticipation of the need to dress for running. We all agreed we would be better without our wimples and veils, the more quickly to attain our pallets and pretend sleeping when we were finished.

We crept along the side of the trees, and I could hear my own heart beating. To be so close now was excruciating. We must not fail.

True to plan the younger women cut off from us a short distance from the third guesthouse, and made their way to the back of the building. Geralda and I waited with bated breath.

Suddenly a horse whinnied, and then another. Sheep began baying and we saw our friends dashing across the meadow, a torch held in Fabrisse's hands, their forms scarcely visible under the melting light of the rising moon. A flare rose from behind the small house. They had been successful in lighting the hay! Smoke began to rise.

A moment later a great commotion could be heard. One of the men must have gone to see what the animals were bellowing about. A second voice joined the first, and though we could not make out their figures, we knew they were outside.

I nodded and Geralda and I streaked across the ground, glad to have our legs freed from skirts. In the blink of an eye we had achieved the door and, to our amazement, it gave when I applied my shoulder to it. What we saw inside made us pause fully a moment on the threshold.

23

In the Field and
Back to the Hut

Two torches on the far wall threw enough light to allow us to observe the scene. No guards were visible, I noted immediately, and thus our first hurdle had been achieved. But a noxious odor pervaded the room and it hit us as we crossed the threshold.

Then I saw two large sides of beef hanging in one corner, and what looked like the carcass of a pig as well. The room stank of curing meat, almost overwhelming us as we moved into the space. I could see flies, despite the late autumn coolness, clinging to the sides of meat.

Francis lay prone on a pallet in the corner opposite the butcher's wall, his hands bound behind him. He was turned toward us and he showed both fear and resolve in his expression as we burst through the door. His grimy face and his tattered clothes could not hide the noble courage with which he met our surprise entrance.

"Who comes?" he asked, in a voice parched with thirst. "How dare you enter without permission?"

His face was the dearest in all Christendom to me, and the relief that flooded through me when I saw him was like a wave. It was a sight I had thought I might never see again and yet now he was here, in front of me. I could feel the sting of tears and blinked them back firmly. All that mattered now was to set him free. Later, I could indulge my heart.

I came quickly toward him. He squinted for a moment and suddenly a look of pure astonishment crossed his handsome features. Something resembling a smile lit his face.

"Princesse," he said weakly, "is it really you?" His voice was hoarse, as if he had not enough water, and I could see by the light of my small torch that his lips were swollen and cracked.

"Indeed it is, Sir Francis," I responded gravely. "And I have sturdy companions who will help me free you."

"Come quickly, no time for talk," Geralda hissed from the door, where she watched the corners of the outside of the house.

I helped the young man to his feet. I could feel that he was almost too frail to walk as he leaned heavily on me.

"Your leg, it is wounded?" I said as I felt him buckle slightly.

"No, it is nothing," he said.

We hurried to the door as best we could, while hampered by his limp. Geralda had moved outside, her outline visible against the trees in the soft moonlight. She flagged us forward with her long arm. We made the dash to the woods, both of us supporting our prize. Meanwhile, the hue and cry over the fire had been passed to the abbey proper, and we could see a horde of monks coming over the hill, carrying buckets of water on each hand. We made the cover of the woods just in time, as the vanguard of that group was reaching the back side of the house.

It was fortunate that a stream ran just behind the structure, so further water would be readily available. I had no doubt that the fire would be contained soon. And then the guards would notice that Francis was missing.

Within a short span of time we had obtained our little guesthouse. We entered quickly and doused our torches.

Grazide and Fabrisse were already on their pallets, and looked for all the world as if they had been sleeping since the noon Angelus. But at our entrance, they both sat up and scrambled to their feet, ready to hear the tale of our part of the adventure.

"Help me with Francis. No doubt they will search our dwelling here, as soon as they find him missing." I was tense, and they responded. Fortunately there was moonlight filling the hut, and we could pull the tiles and the heavy oak door back without aid of a candle, light that might attract attention from the outside.

"Here, lad, hold my hand while you descend. It is not far, only a few steps down the ladder. There is air below, and a pallet in the corner for you to rest. We must return to our beds until someone comes to question us, as surely they will do. After that event has passed, and it is safe, I'll come to you with water and food, and we will talk."

I saw with concern how Francis's hand shook as he lowered himself on the ladder, feeling his way. The moonlight caught glints of his auburn hair, the red hair of the Plantagenets, of his father King Henry. When his foot had touched bottom, he called up softly: "I am here, and I see the pallet. Replace the door now. I mind not the dark as long as I am safe."

Brave lad, I thought, while my fury at Amaury mounted for the injury done my son. We worked quickly, dragging the oak piece over the opening, replacing the tiles, and quickly kicking rushes to hide them.

We all leaped into bed, for there were loud voices throughout the meadows, and some cursing, which I took to be the guards' expression of dismay when they found their charge gone.

It was some time later when the voices came near our little house, and I pretended sleep as they hovered outside. There seemed to be an argument about whether to disturb us, but I couldn't see the sense of that, since they would have woken us with their noise already!

Geralda rose at the peremptory sound of the knocking, and went to the door, doing her best to insert sleep into her voice. It was well that the moonlight had shifted, for the questioners surely would have noted the sheen on her face from her recent exertions.

"Sirs, who comes at this time? We've scarce another hour till Matins bells, and we would have our rest."

"Good Sister, we seek to know if you have heard anything this evening. There has been a fire near the barn where meat is cured, and of the three men living there, one is missing."

"Men living in the place where meat is hung?" Geralda sounded outraged. I stifled a chuckle. She knew the value of distraction. "I am astonished that the abbey would permit such a thing. Living with live animals is one thing; living with dead ones quite another."

"Sister, we are not come to debate these issues." A new and deeper voice, more commanding. This must be the master of the two thugs we saw earlier guarding my son. No doubt he had a comfortable bed somewhere in the abbey proper. "We need to know if you heard any disturbance this night along the path by your hut."

"No, good sirs. We have heard nothing. I see a fire in the distance. Should we be concerned about our welfare here?"

"No, the fire has been contained and the monks are bringing more water. Forgive the interruption," the man said gruffly, as he hustled his men down the path. We made our way back to our pallets on the floor, and with a collective sigh we lay down. For a long time I could hear only breathing as none of us dared speak. After a while, the measured sounds coming from the younger women signaled that they slept. But I knew Geralda was as wakeful as I.

"I am going to visit Francis," I whispered finally, swinging my feet to the floor. Just then the bells for Matins began tolling and I groaned. We were all called to chapel for the predawn prayers that marked the beginning of the day.

"Princesse, I advise you to come with us to chapel," Geralda said. "We cannot afford to draw attention. If anyone is watching us, we must continue with our usual life."

I paused. More than anything I wanted to see Francis. But I saw the wisdom of what she said. With a sigh, I acquiesced, and gently bent to shake Fabrisse, and encourage Grazide, who was having trouble rousing herself.

So we put our black cloaks around our habits, wound our wimples quickly around our heads, and pinned on the veils and made our way across the meadow we had traversed in the opposite direction and with an entirely different purpose only a few hours earlier.

The church was chill and drafty so there was little danger of dozing during prayers. The monk leading us this morn was as cold as his followers, and so he was efficient in dispatching his duties. We were soon bound for the refectory and the first, and I might add meager, meal of the day. I listened to the lector at the front of the refectory with half a heart as I nibbled my brown bread, and afterward could not have told which epistle of St. Paul was read, nor what the good saint's advice was on this day.

But I dared not absent myself, for we did not want anything to look amiss in our little group. I noted that neither Amaury nor the current abbot of Fontfroide had been present for the morning prayer, and I wondered what the conversation was in the abbot's quarters at this hour.

Finally we made our escape back to our hut, and I was grateful for the late autumn season which allowed still the cover of darkness. We were silent as we walked. When we arrived at our quarters, we all clustered around the hearth again.

"We will move the door and after I descend you must replace it. Give me part of an hour. Then move it again, and I will come up. If the dawn begins to break meanwhile, use this loose stone to tap the oak door, and I will make ready."

Geralda nodded, and we all shifted the tiles and, grunting with effort, managed again to move the heaving oak piece over the opening. The Sheila-na-gig appeared to me to be grinning, but I couldn't swear to it. The dancing candlelight and my fatigued imagination could have caused the vision.

I descended carefully, slowed by the use of only one hand. I carried a gourd of water slung round my neck on a leather strap. When I was nearly on the ground Fabrisse leaned over and passed to me a candle, a torch being too much flame for this small space.

I heard the clanking of the iron corners of the oak piece as it was laid over the opening, and thought what courage young Francis had, tired and bruised as he was, to accept his assignment to this closed space so readily.

He was sleeping now, and I crept over to him and gently shook his shoulder. When he mumbled something and stirred, I sat on the floor beside his bed. He opened his eyes sleepily and propped himself up on his forearm, his other fist rubbing his eyes as a child would. I felt a stab of fear for his safety, as if he had no more than eight summers.

"How now, Princesse," he said, some irony in his parched voice. "It appears I have merely exchanged one confinement for another."

"Only for the moment, Francis. I promise you that," I said, placing my hand on his arm. "Here. I have brought you water for your thirst. My friends are even now assembling a basket of food for you."

The young knight rose on one elbow and drank greedily.

I continued: "We have very little time, for I must not appear to be missing. If Amaury asks questions, and discovers there is a group of Benedictine nuns here from a northern abbey, he will surely want to see us. And that would be the end of everyone."

"And I would rot in here, if that happens," Francis said. The bitterness of his tone sent a chill through me.

"I will not let you," I said fiercely.

In return, he gave me a thin smile, but nodded his head to acknowledge my words.

"Tell me what happened in Paris," I said, pushing away the image of Francis trapped in an underground prison. "William said there were signs of a struggle in your chambers. He was certain you had been abducted."

"I put up as much of a fight as I could, so that Lord William would see the disarray in my chamber and know I had not simply gone off on my own. But there were three men, and in the end I was no match for them." He shrugged, as if it had been one more joust in a tourney.

"Were you not fearful?"

"I could see that they wanted me alive. They were rough, but they knew how to use their fists and feet without killing. That gave me some reassurance."

"Did you leave Paris immediately?"

"No, they hid me somewhere on the Île de la Cité, probably within shouting distance of the palace. I think I was in the lower part of the Tour Dagobert, near the cathedral building site." Francis heaved himself upward, and sat with crossed legs, his back resting against the damp wall. We were facing each other, the candle between us throwing light on each other's face. I took in his features, so like his father's, and the strong jut of his jaw. He was, indeed, a survivor. After all, the blood of kings ran in his veins. "They questioned me for hours. They thought I knew the whereabouts of some chalice, some sacred cup. What would I be doing with such a thing?"

"The Saint John Cup." I ran my hands through my hair. "A number of people want that cup. But why did they think you would know the whereabouts?"

"One of the men let slip something about Constance of Toulouse. They had seen me in her retinue in the past week, and they thought I was her confidant."

I had to chuckle. "I also noticed you with her coterie quite often. But it was usually at the side of the fair Esclarmonde of Foix."

"Yes, that is clever of you." His voice was good-natured. "Apparently the abbot does not have your acute powers of observation."

Or the abbot is not a mother, I thought, but I held my tongue. This was neither the time nor the place for that revelation.

Instead I remarked: "William found a map that had been dropped in your chambers when they took you. It showed the area around Toulouse. I was not certain the map was dropped accidentally, but William was convinced it was where your abductors planned to hide you."

"That was left to throw you off their track. They hoped you would find the map and be distracted, searching for me in the Toulouse area," Francis said. "But it was at least a full day before we set out from Paris. And it was not for Toulouse at all, but for this place."

"Do you know who was responsible for this?" I asked, remembering the threat of death I had heard Amaury utter in the chapel, only the day before.

"They kept me in the back of the train, and my eyes were bound much of the time." He smiled. "But it would have been hard to not see the colors, or glimpse the standard as we traveled. Of course I knew it was the Abbé Amaury's train."

"If he thought you knew that, your life would be forfeit." I could feel the pulse in my throat as I said this, wanting the young knight to take this seriously, yet not wanting him immobilized by fear.

"But he would have to find me first, would he not?" Francis almost managed a grin in the flickering light.

"You did not seem overly surprised to see me in the dead of night, in that butcher's building," I said. "Did you know I was at the abbey? Did you drop my scarf deliberately?"

Again that impish expression took over his face. "I heard the guards talking about some nuns taking the second guesthouse, and the danger that someone would be nearer to our barn, which is also called a guesthouse." He gave a snort. "Perhaps it was a guesthouse at one time, but now it is used to cure meat."

"I wonder that they would put you in such a foul place."

"They just wanted us as far from the abbey life as possible. Only a few monks know we are here. They did not want the general body of monks inquiring as to why an abbey of God had been turned into a prison."

"Thanks to an abbot with no scruples," I muttered.

"The same monk brings us food every day. And my captors let me out to walk once a day with one of the guards, although I must keep behind the tree line so as not to be seen. I dropped the scarf when I passed this guesthouse yesterday, hoping that the new visitors might find it." Francis stretched his arms overhead, his hands grazing the ceiling of this dirt hideaway. "I thought the emblem sewn into the silk might catch the attention of someone, and perhaps they would ask questions. Surely the fleur-de-lis, which always denotes the king of France, would be noticed."

He paused. "I did not know it would be you who found it, but nothing you do surprises me."

Now it was my turn to smile. "I suppose I should be flattered."

"No, Princesse, I meant no offense. I only know that Lord William has talked of you often. He says you have more courage than any man he knows, and that you are resourceful beyond belief. He is the one who first said that nothing you undertake astonishes him. I always had trust that if Lord William didn't find me you would." He reached out his hand to me. "I would search for you if something happened in the same way. We have a bond. I know not how it has come about."

"It is true," I said simply, taking his hand. I knew I must put down my urge to tell him the whole truth now. There was not time. "I feel it also."

We looked at each other. It was enough for the moment.

"If I am not to stay here forever, what is the plan?" Francis said suddenly, as if the silence between us had become too much to sustain.

"Geralda and I have discussed it. We are playing the same game Amaury played with you in Paris; we will hide you near while the abbot's men scour the countryside looking for you. When they tire, and believe you have eluded them, we will spirit you away."

"How will that come about?" For the first time, the practical nature of our predicament was making an impression on him. "You are four women and I am clearly not one of you."

"You shall be. After two days, we will announce that we must continue our pilgrimage. We will ask that the abbey order our horses ready early on the morning of the next day and you will dress in an extra Benedictine habit that Geralda brought with her. You must have noticed her great height, which is quite convenient." That brought another chuckle from the young man.

"When the four of you are well away from the abbey, you will split up. Geralda will go with you to Foix, by way of Fanjeaux and Laurac, where you will be sure of a welcome from the nobles as they are sympathetic to the Cathar way. Geralda is known to them. You will be safe at Foix until I join you."

"And where will the others go?"

"They will take the more traditional route toward Santiago de Compostela, and then turn sharply north just before they cross the border into Pierre d'Aragon's land." I forestalled his next question. "On the outside chance that you are followed from here, they will not know which party to keep in sight."

"It sounds like a good plan, Princesse." Francis yawned and stretched again, then stopped. "But what will you do? How can you be safe?"

"I will melt into the forest, lad. I am adept at that feat, from my years in England hunting with King Henry."

"Did you know him then?" The voice was wistful. "He is my hero, more than anyone. The Lord William has talked of him so often. He was his clerk when he was a youth."

"Yes, I knew him well," was all the comment I could muster at this. What would the lad say when I finally told him?

But our conversation was cut off by the tapping sound of the tile on the door. Then I began to hear a scraping sound of the door being raised.

"Princesse, you must come up. It is near daylight now, and you can afford no more time." Geralda's strong voice floated downward. I sighed.

"Lad, I must go. Rest now, for you will need your strength. We will come for you when the dark falls, and you and I can walk in the forest late at night. You will breathe the fresh air, and we will be safe in the late hours." Even as I spoke, my eyes pricked with tears, which I blinked back in embarrassment.

Geralda lowered a basket as I came to the bottom of the ladder, which I caught and passed to Francis. "Here is food, young Francis, that we brought in secret from the refectory. This should sustain you for some time. Try and rest so you can move about at night. And conserve yourself. The trip to Foix will be demanding."

"I shall do as you suggest, Princesse." Francis's face registered his pleasure at the basket. "What a relief it will be to eat food without the rank smell of curing animals in my nostrils." And my last sight was of the young knight eagerly tearing into the bread and gulping wine from the flagon in the basket. I knew he would sleep soundly after that. And I ascended the ladder with a heart full of gratitude.

24

In the Abbot's Quarters

For the next two days, waiting was the hard part. We went about our chores with some eagerness. After all, we wanted to appear as normal pilgrims. We also kept our ears open, and shared all of the rumors that came past us as we worked: Geralda in the kitchen, I with the laundry sisters, Fabrisse who was assigned to sweep the cloister walks, and Grazide who was busy weeding the herb garden.

Amaury did exactly as I had hoped: his men went forth that very day from the abbey, raising the hue and cry in the countryside. They had no idea that Francis was hiding under their very noses, the exact tactic Amaury had used in Paris. Though my spirit was anxious, I smiled a great deal as I went about my work and prayer in the monastic community in those days.

True to our word, we took our leave of Father Hospitaler on the eve of the second day, and promised to pray for him and all the monks of this abbey when we should arrive at Compostela. We retired after Compline. The darkness had invaded our little hut, and we kept only two candles burning.

We had told Francis I would not be visiting this night, as we all needed to sleep. We did not attend the predawn Matins in the chapel. Instead, when the bells rang, we removed the tiles, slid the heavy door away, and I descended to Francis with the extra black habit and veil Geralda had brought.

It was tight for him, and I had to push down a smile when I saw him struggle to pull the fabric across his broad back as it came down over his head.

"Princesse," he said, when his face was free of the black cloth, "I would be so grateful if you could restrain your amusement." At which point I laughed out loud and he eventually joined me, although with a quaver in his weak voice.

"Francis, some years ago you told me you loved the stage," I said after a moment of quiet. "I saw you perform in the 'Debate Between the Body and Soul,' in Chinon village. You are a gifted and convincing actor. I suggest you look upon the role of nun with the same relish, as one who loves the stage. If you do, you will attain your freedom."

After we had wound the wimple and pinned the veil, we ascended the ladder for the last time. Grazide had obtained food from the abbey kitchens and had packed the bread and olives and small flagon of wine into a basket they had also kindly given her.

We said our farewell in the center of the hut's room. I had changed into the clothes used for travel before I began my recent life as a Benedictine, the clothes of a page or messenger. I wore hose and a leather doublet and I had a short cloak as well among my other meager belongings. My hair was wound atop my head and well hidden by the cap that covered it.

"Let us review the plan," I said, placing Philippe's maps upon the floor. "You will all leave together. When you arrive at Alaric, Geralda, you and Francis will strike out for the north." I traced the way with my finger. "Grazide and Fabrisse will go straight east as if to continue to Santiago de Compostela. If anyone is following you, they will be confused."

The four nodded. "Grazide, to confound Amaury's men further, you must take my short cloak, the one with the insignia of the house of Capet on it." I handed her the folded mantle.

"You can wear this over your habit when you part company with the others. If anyone is following you, they will see the royal insignia and think you are me. I doubt that any harm will come to you if your pursuers think you are the sister of the king of France." I felt particularly pleased to have thought of this ruse. "You should discard the nun's costumes before you reach Montségur. Once there, the Cathars will give you hospitality and new clothes. After a few days' rest, you, too, may turn north and join us at Foix."

I stood up and rolled up the map. "We shall all meet at Foix within the fortnight. If you are in trouble, send word there. The Lady Philippa will respond with her husband's men, if needed."

"And will you be all right?" Geralda put her hand on my arm and looked steadily into my face. "You will no longer have the Benedictine habit to get you free food and lodging in the towns."

"I shall be fine." I pulled a leather purse from within my doublet. "I have the four gold pieces I sewed into the hem of my habit before we left Lavaur. I'll buy a horse and food at the first village I come to, and will head north immediately. I know how to travel alone."

So we embraced and said our good-byes once again. I watched the four figures make their way across the meadow for the last time. Then I took the bread and fruit that had been left for me, wrapped it into a bundle and left the hut.

This would be the most difficult task: to travel alone, not to be with Francis, not to aid him if he needed it. I must trust that he would be safe. But I knew I had made the right decision. Of the four, I was the only one who knew how to travel alone.

I headed into the woods, thinking to circle around and avoid the abbey close. I would be less noticeable if I did not cut through the cloister walks, but followed the fence around to the main gates. And I certainly did not want to become caught up in the leave-taking of the four nuns, as they mounted their horses and rode out to continue their pilgrimage.

All went well for some time. As I suspected, the forest was naught but a small stand of trees, and I soon came to the fence that I knew surrounded the abbey and kept the farm animals in the far corners of the fields. But then, as the sun was climbing, I noticed a figure making his way far behind me, slowing as I slowed and speeding up as I did the same. The man took care that the distance between us remained the same, no matter my speed.

Finally, I saw the gates of the abbey. I had come full circle round the entire meadow and was approaching from the other side, having avoided the more crowded parts, the monks in the fields, and even much of the commerce that always took place in the abbey close. Suddenly my pursuer, for that is what this mysterious figure had become, closed the space between us. It happened so fast I was taken unawares. One moment I thought I was going to achieve my freedom as I mingled with the merchants and those buying from them in the dusty little lanes of commerce set up near the gates, and the next someone was grabbing my arm from behind, and twisting it hard.

"Let me go," I cried, more in exasperation than in pain, for he was not actually hurting me.

"Not a chance, lad," the man growled in my ear. "You have an appointment with the authorities."

I resisted, but we were drawing the attention of the crowd, and so I allowed myself to be led off. I knew this would have no good end, for I would either be brought before that unpleasant man who first questioned us the night Francis disappeared, or mayhap before Amaury himself. But, I considered, if it were Amaury, he would not dare touch me. He couldn't afford to alienate the king of France.

And indeed, it appeared we were heading for the abbot's quarters. The man, who was not much taller than I, but very muscular, kept a hand on my arm. I decided to go along willingly. No need to make a further spectacle of myself.

We were admitted into the large room, after the man explained to the guards that he had found me skulking around the meadow grounds, and that I might know something about the missing knight. I was surprised at what I saw.

The room had many windows allowing the morning light to flood all the spaces. There were many leather-bound manuscripts resting on the shelves, and more lying about on tables. One old, bent man sat at one end of a large table. I knew he was the current abbot, and the man I had seen follow Amaury in the formal procession in the abbey church.

Arnaud Amaury sat at the opposite end of the table. He looked, if possible, even more degenerate than he had in Paris. His face was heavy with fatigue and the good meals he was consuming at Font-froide's expense. He had what appeared to be a permanent scowl on his face as he sat heavily in his chair reading parchment that had been placed in front of him, turning the pages with impatience and an occasional unhappy exclamation.

As we waited, I examined the face of the older man, who had not yet looked up at us. His face seemed tranquil, arranged in symmetry, as far as I could see. Several other men, not monks, loitered at one end of the room, as if at the beck and call of either man. Both the church-men were dressed in the finery of their office, as if trying to outdo each other. My sympathy, such as I had available at the moment, was all with the old abbot, who must be struggling to maintain his authority now that his predecessor had invaded his abbey with a retinue of strongmen. But his calm demeanor belied the thought of such competitive actions.

The old abbot looked up finally, as did Amaury. The man who had captured me made his bow. The abbot inclined his head with permission for him to speak.

"Your Grace, we found this young man lurking about the abbey grounds, near to the place where the horses were stolen." The man spoke in the accents of the langue d'oïl, and I knew he had ridden in with Amaury.

I stood straight and proud before my enemy, for so I now knew he was in every way. Amaury looked at me briefly, then down again to his papers, and suddenly looked up again. The shock of recognition passed over his face. I had him at a disadvantage there, as I already knew it was himself in front of me.

"Princesse Alaïs?" the old reprobate asked, his hoarse voice betraying his total surprise. "What are you doing here?"

"I had a particular errand, Abbé," I replied, adopting as cool a tone as was possible under the circumstances. "It seems a young knight disappeared from the Lord William's household in Paris. I thought he might be here."

Amaury had risen, and slowly came toward me, peering at my face, as if I were a ghost.

"What made you think that?" Recalling the threat he had made at dinner in Paris about my special gifts, I saw the fear on his face with satisfaction. Perhaps now he would be certain I could call upon supernatural powers.

"I met a colleague of yours in my travels. Pierre de Castelnau. He thought you were headed toward this abbey, and I decided you might have news of the young man, since you had both left Paris at the same time." I added meaningfully, "In the dead of night."

"Princesse." The abbot's tone was a warning. He was so close I could smell garlic coming up from him, and the heavy red wine he had already been drinking. "You take too much upon yourself," he hissed.

I had placed my feet apart and put my hands on my hips, in an attitude of deliberate defiance.

"No more than you, Abbé." We stood a breath apart.

"The young knight seems to have disappeared again," he said, his voice low. "I suppose it is no coincidence that you are suddenly on the scene at the same time."

"Make of it what you will," I said jauntily, my voice equally soft. "On the other hand, your ruffian here has laid hands on a royal person, the sister of the king of France. I should think you will have difficulty explaining that to my brother when next you are in Paris to beg him for arms and men."

"But your brother refused my request, and I'll not be going back to Paris." Amaury leered at me, his head angling and an unpleasant smile spreading across his face. "And I remind you, your brother is not king in this part of the world."

"No, but Count Raymond, my kinsman, is overlord here. You would be ill-advised to breach his hospitality, abbot or not." Suddenly I had a thought. "And Cîteaux, your present responsibility, sits dangerously close to the Île de France. You may yet have need of King Philippe's good graces."

"Bah," he spat, turning from me, and pacing back to the table. But I could see I had scored a point in this game between us.

"Amaury, what is all this about?" The surprisingly firm voice of the old abbot, Amaury's successor in office, broke into our tension. I turned my head to regard him more closely. He was hunched over the scrolls and leather-bound manuscripts surrounding him. He had been reading to himself when I was brought in, and he seemed only now to raise his gray head and take in the scene. "Who is this person? What is your discourse with him about?"

Amaury cast a quick glance my way over his shoulder. Did the current abbot not have an inkling that Amaury was keeping a prisoner on his property? At that very moment my approach and plan changed. I now had the power, if I played my role carefully, to get free of any net Amaury might be inclined to spring on me.

"My men found this man skulking about in the forest, Anselm. Nothing for you to worry about. We have lost some horses and I thought this young ruffian might have been involved."

"Your Grace." I spoke up over Amaury's shoulder now, addressing the old abbot. I made my voice as close to a growl as I could to imitate a man. "I am but a poor pilgrim from the north. I was set upon by thieves who stole my horse from me. I have been lost, wandering in the woods for these three days. If the abbey could but spare a horse for me, I can pay. I could then continue on my way."

Brushing past Amaury, I advanced toward the aging abbot, who watched me with interest. When I came close enough, I was surprised to see the ice-blue eyes, penetrating and intelligent, observing me closely. It was almost as if he knew my entire ruse. Still, I was already committed to my story, and Amaury could say nothing to contradict me, without giving away all that he had concealed from his host.

The old abbot Anselm placed his forearm on a page of manuscript in front of him, and leaned forward.

"Whence are you bound, pilgrim?" he asked. "The Holy Land, or Hispania?"

"I am making my way to Santiago de Compostela," I said. "This pilgrimage is taken to atone for sins of my wild youth." At this, the old abbot raised his eyebrows, and I thought I saw the whisper of a smile appear.

"And why on horseback, rather than on foot?" he asked.

"I have an injury to my leg from an accident," I replied readily, rather amazing myself that I could make up a story on the spot, out of whole cloth. "I could not finish the pilgrimage if I were on foot."

"Amaury," Anselm said calmly, looking to his colleague, "you have brought quite a retinue of horses with you. You can certainly spare one for this young man, dirty and tired as he is. Perhaps we can even arrange a guesthouse for you this even." He turned his impenetrable gaze in my direction as he spoke these words. "I understand the pilgrim nuns left our guesthouse vacant this very morning."

"My thanks, Lord Abbot. Nothing would please me more than to accept Cistercian hospitality. But your first suggestion was the best. If I could obtain a horse from . . ."—I gestured toward Amaury—"his lordship's retinue, I would be most grateful."

Amaury sputtered for a moment or two, but what could he say?

"Take this man to the stables," he finally said, waving at the *voyou* who had brought me in. "Find him a horse and send him on his way."

A complicit look passed between Amaury and myself. My freedom for my silence in front of the abbot Anselm, his expression said. But inwardly I rejoiced, for I had a glimmer that Abbot Anselm knew exactly what Amaury was about. He might even have guessed who I was, or at least that I was a woman. There was that spark of humor in his eyes when he offered me further hospitality. And I had no doubt that he would not be surprised if he discovered his guest abbot had arranged for a prisoner to be held in the butcher's building, though I thought he would not have allowed it for a minute. Perhaps he suspected something of the mysterious four nuns in the guesthouse. He probably knew of other covert activities taking place here in this holy place and had his own plans to redress them. I would wager little escaped this man.

"Young man." Amaury's voice arrested me as I was about to pass through the door. "Watch that you do not overreach yourself in the future. Pride is a dreadful sin. And there are many heretics here in the south. You must not allow yourself to be seduced by them as you make your way alone on your pilgrimage."

I turned to face Amaury. "I will certainly seek the company of the pure of heart," I said. "And of those who practice the charity that Our Lord in Heaven preached while here on earth. As for heretics, I meddle not in theological disputes. I watch what men do, and make my judgments. There is an old Arab fable on that very topic."

Amaury made a dismissive gesture with his hands, but the old abbot at the other end of the table raised his head, and spoke in a surprisingly strong tone.

"And what is the fable you have heard?" He asked it in a voice that would not be refused. Amaury had no choice but to listen.

"A man was walking through a field, with a bow and arrow, shooting rabbits as they scuttled about. One little rabbit said to another: 'Look at that man. He has tears in his eyes.' And the other rabbit said: 'Don't watch his eyes; watch his hands.'" I stood looking at Amaury as I spoke. There was a long silence, and then the old abbot began to chuckle, which turned into a full rolling laugh.

"There you have it, Amaury. 'Watch his hands.'" He shook his head as his smile faded and his voice became unexpectedly serious. "Well said, young pilgrim. You will be saved if you live what you speak. I agree with you. Theological disputes are not the royal road to heaven. Take heed, Amaury." This last was said as the old man picked up another scroll, his hands shaking with age, and dismissed his colleague effectively.

I bowed to him, and turned to go. Amaury was glaring in the direction of his successor but I had the feeling that in any further exchange, the Abbot Anselm would not be the loser.

25

On the Road to Foix

Once clear of the abbey, I applied my knees to my newly acquired horse and felt the fresh wind in my face with relief and something akin to joy. My son was free, and my victory over Amaury in our last interview tasted as sweet as the southern air felt. I headed north toward Alaric and then turned west. I did not believe Amaury would have me followed, for he had other difficulties to overcome. He would try to find Francis, but he would not know which route he might have taken. And I suspected Amaury was more interested in the outcome of the meeting in Toulouse with Raymond than in finding Francis who, after all, had no information about the chalice Amaury sought.

The thought of the conclave at Toulouse reminded me of William. In the rush of recent events, he had been far from my mind. My thoughts since leaving Lavaur had been for

Francis and his safety. As I sat at table the first night, grateful to have found a small inn with a fine cassoulet and a pleasant, round-faced cook who came from the kitchen to deliver it herself, I called up William's face. A sadness overcame me.

William would be furious that I had not heeded his command to stay in Paris the night we had the quarrel. He had never yet held sustained anger toward me, but there is always the first time. Would he be cold when we met? Would he see my actions as rash? Would they affect our plans for marriage when his duties to the pope were finished? I found my appetite diminishing as I pondered these things. Finally, with a sigh, I retired to my small room off the area where the animals slept. At least the rushes were clean. I prayed that I would not wake up in the company of fleas.

The trip was difficult. Alone, I fell prey to many doubts and fears about the future. I did not want to risk drawing attention to myself, so I dropped my role as pilgrim and stayed instead in smaller villages, finding an inn or asking for shelter from a woman on the street. I still had two of the gold pieces remaining, and some silver. Although I was lonely, I did not feel in danger.

All that changed suddenly soon after I had passed the château at Puivert, marked clearly on the maps Philippe had given me. The morn was bright and sunny, but I was very tired, having slept in the fields the night before. The riding was difficult as well. I was coming into mountainous country, but the hills that were so protective of the Cathar preachers did not seem welcoming to me. I had taken no breakfast that day, and so was in danger of fainting away before I could find food.

Just when I thought I would have to dismount to keep from falling off my horse, I spied a small hovel, off to the side and over a short field. I turned my palfrey from the main road, and wandered down the path to the door of this humble dwelling, little more than a mud hut.

I left my horse grazing in the meadow some small distance away, and made my way through the overgrown gorse to the front door.

There was no knocking device, and so I merely pushed in. I had little experience entering the house of strangers but this was a peasant hut and I did not feel that I needed to stand on ceremony.

The room was small and spare, containing only two chairs of wood and rushes and a table with a broken leg, propped up by a small bale of hay. There were clothes and eating utensils everywhere, and the straw on the floor had not been changed for many moons. A somewhat foul odor clung to the walls.

I looked around. Truth to tell, I was so hungry that I considered trying the biscuits I saw on the hearth, even though they resembled burned rocks. Fortunately, my attention was drawn to the table.

There lay a loaf of bread, and some hard cheese. I drew close. The cheese looked fresh, and the bread had no mold on it. I had cut a hunk of the first and a large piece of the second and had just begun to wolf down my food when I was interrupted by the sound of heavy wooden clogs.

I looked up to see a figure in the doorway, a short but broad-chested man in a peasant's smock and hose, staring at me.

"Good day to you, sir," I said, with as strong and deep a voice as my hunger would allow. "I thought the hut was deserted, and I was in need of food. I am happy to pay you for your bread and cheese."

"Hardly be deserted if the bread was fresh, now would it?" he replied saucily, as he moved his bulk slowly through the door. I became acutely aware of the small space the two of us were now occupying, and the malevolent manner of the man facing me. For the first time on my journey I felt more than a twinge of fear.

We faced each other warily. I fingered my dagger under my cloak. "What do you want?" he demanded, in a peremptory voice that I, a royal princess, had never heard.

"I told you. I was on the road and was hungry, so I stopped to see if I could beg or buy food." To make my voice strong I visualized King Henry, commanding in the fields.

"And what would a young, dirty swain, with a voice almost like a woman's, be doing with money to pay for food?" The man began to sound more accommodating when I jiggled the purse hanging from my belt.

I inwardly breathed a sigh of relief and decided to brazen it out. By moving around the table, I kept a barrier between us whilst I made my way closer to the door. He was forced to move with me, in order to keep his beady eyes on mine.

"I'm on an errand for my master. He is a noble and very powerful. So watch your tongue, varlet. And here is payment for the bread." I tossed a couple of small coins on the table. "And if you give me your name, I'll see that you get a reward from my master, the Count of Foix."

My change in tone, from commanding to civil, seemed to take the man aback. He blinked, and that hesitation was just long enough for me to reach the door. I edged out still watching him, and then broke into a run for my horse.

The man followed me to the door, shielding his eyes from the sun to watch me, but he did not give chase. I mounted rapidly, and spurred my horse back to the road, thankful that I had stuffed some food into my pockets before his arrival. I galloped off, feeling quite pleased with myself. King Henry would have applauded my performance. I didn't want to dwell on what William would have said.

The drama in the peasant's hut cost me time, but I felt buoyed by the energy from the food. Truth to tell, I had no real worry that the peasant would give chase, for I saw no sign of horse in this yard and no barn behind the house. Still, I was uneasy about something in the encounter. I rode hard for some time, and when I felt I had put a safe enough distance between the hut and myself, I decided to rest and finish my lunch.

Once again I left the road, this time after spying a small stream that looked inviting. After I found a grassy place I spread my cloak on the ground, and washed my hands in the brook. Then I sat in the dappled sunlight and ate the remainder of my meager lunch. Leaning back on my elbows, I considered my options. I knew the sun would soon wane and that I should get back on my horse. If I rode hard, my guess was that I might reach the castle of Foix by nightfall. The Lady Philippa had promised a welcome and I was sore longing for the sight of a friendly face. I had seen none since parting from Geralda and our two young companions.

Yet I was passing tired and longed for a rest, a nap, just a short one. The sun on the back of my head spread heaviness, and I knew the grove was protected from the road by a stand of trees. I finally gave in to my urge to sleep and, wrapping my cloak around me, stretched out on the ground.

The next thing I knew, there was a sharp pain in my ribs and I rolled over to escape whatever it was that made it. But it came again before I could scramble to my feet.

The sun was low in the sky and at a slant, as happens in autumn. When I opened my eyes, it blinded me for a moment. I wriggled away slightly until I was in the shade, and then tried to see. As my vision cleared I found I was looking right into the devil's eyes. They were framed by giant black brows, thick as a nest of beetles. The face pulled back and I felt a third kick to my ribs that sent me rolling down the riverbank.

The pain was a spur to clear my head and it brought me to action. I leaped to my feet, trying to get my footing on the mossy bank of the creek. The stabbing in my side caused me some difficulty in standing upright, but I forced myself to concentrate. I withdrew the dagger I carried in my belt, and held it straight out, thrusting, my wrist turned upward, as I had been taught. It glinted as it moved, catching the sun.

"So, you have a weapon, do you? Let's see if you know how to use it, little boy." I could see my attacker fully now, a large man with a shaggy, dirty beard and a snarl twisting his ugly face. His nose had been broken at some time in the past, I noted, with some satisfaction. This was not, however, good news for me. The man was a seasoned brawler. He came toward me, circling the hand that clutched his own short knife.

I did not speak, worried that my voice would brand me a woman. I tried to remember every move the swordmaster at Philippe's court had taught me, glad now that I had badgered my brother into letting me train with the young knights of his court. I shifted my weight from one foot to another, to keep my adversary off balance as to which way I would turn. I knew I had only one chance at him. After that, if I missed, he would have his way, as his was the larger and more powerful body.

He came straight on. No lessons in strategy distracted this *voyou*, which might work to my advantage. But then suddenly he surprised me. When he was only an ox length away he stopped dead in his tracks and threw his dagger directly toward me. I scarce had time to duck and, indeed, it caught me in the left arm, a searing tear. My eyes watered but I didn't stop. I lunged at him in my rage.

I sprang to close the gap between us. He was slightly off balance from his effort and surprised that I was finishing my attack. My knife went into the soft part of the middle of his body. With only a small grunt of surprise, he fell forward, his entire weight landing on me, knocking me over. The wind went out of my body, and I struggled for breath, cursing in a strangled voice, words I didn't know I had in me.

Then a respite came. Someone was dragging the load of the felled body away and I doubled up, gasping for breath. Finally I could feel some thin sliver of air start to trickle down inside me. As relief came, I took in great gulps and suddenly I rolled over and began throwing up the lunch I had been so quick to eat only a short time before.

A familiar voice came as from a great distance and someone was patting my back. I looked up through my tears to see Tom of Caedwyd bending over me with a look of concern that a mother might envy.

"Tom," I gasped, still in the grip of a heaving sensation in my stomach, though there was no more to come out of me. "How have you come here?"

"Ah, lass, more about that later. You killed this man, but he was like to smother you in revenge when he fell, it appears. I'm only glad we got here in time to haul him off you. You've cheated death today. You have a charmed life now." I glanced over his shoulder to see Roland looking down at me with an expression of great concern, although his face seemed to move somewhat in and out of my vision. I drifted for a moment between worlds, and then came once more to myself.

Tom was extending my arm to examine the wound. I could finally breathe again, but the pain in my side where I had been kicked was increasing with every slight movement.

"You've got a nasty wound here. We need to get to Foix tonight and see to it proper, Princesse. Do you think you can ride?"

"I don't know, Tom. Help me up. Let's see if I can walk first." They pulled me up from the ground and, despite some initial dizziness, I found a purchase for my feet and began to move forward, taking great care. With every step, though, the throbbing in my side was excruciating.

I glanced at the body of my assailant on the ground as we passed. His face lay one cheek up in the river mud. He was not known to me, but I stopped suddenly, and turned back. Tom was holding my elbow to keep me from falling, so he must turn with me. I motioned with my head.

We walked back slowly to the body. I pushed it with my foot, and it rolled over. There was no marking on the rogue's tunic that would identify him as belonging to anyone. On a whim, I reached down into his pockets to see what he carried and my fingers closed around a small leather bag. From the weight of it, I surmised it was full of silver.

"What would such a man be doing with all this coin?" I asked my knights. We formed a small circle around the fallen attacker. Roland had pulled my dagger from the man's stomach, and was cleaning it of the stranger's blood with leaves, even as we looked down on him.

Tom shrugged, but Roland nodded at the leather pouch. "Your Grace, may I see it?"

When I passed it over to him, he didn't look inside, as I had expected. Instead he turned it over to inspect the bottom.

"What do you think to find, Roland?" I was curious. "Some type of marking?"

"See here, Princesse. On the bottom. The stamp of the leather maker. This is made by a London leather worker. Raynulf of Surrey. Royal Guild of London Leather Makers. That mark means this guild are purveyors to King John." He tossed it thoughtfully on his hand a couple of times, the flat bottom returning easily to his palm. "What would such a villein be doing with a purse from the best leather worker in London? And with so much silver?" He tossed it back to me.

"Odd indeed," I said, pocketing the small pouch and finally turning away from my erstwhile attacker. "Still, the south is full of *routiers* who are no longer employed by the nobles to fight. They prey on any passer-by. This could have been stolen from someone. Indeed, this purse may have passed through many hands already. Although it is strange that it made its way this far all the way from London," I mused.

"Princesse, we must make haste to leave. The sun is slipping in the sky. It would not do for you to be caught on the road at nightfall, even though you are no longer alone." Tom was at my elbow, speaking low into my ear. He was right. I felt a need to find a safe harbor for the night even more than he did.

I looked down again at the man who was dead at my feet and was surprised that I felt no pity for him. Perhaps that is the gift of not-feeling men have in war, not caring when their attackers fall, especially after a narrow escape from death themselves.

"And I am right grateful that you two are now with me." I looked with relief and affection at my knights. I felt thanks, too, that they had not remonstrated with me over the trick I had played on them at Lavaur. Although all might not be forgiven, at least they did not reproach me at this difficult time.

It was so painful to mount my palfrey, even with the good help of Roland and Tom, that I wondered if I would swoon or ride. I collected myself, however, and tried to hide my discomfort. Tom was more concerned with the wound in my arm, but I knew that was not the true problem. The three kicks I had taken to my side before I could get up and fight had created a constant burning sensation, and every time my horse's hooves hit the dusty road I felt all over again the stabs of pain, worse even than the original had been.

I was determined not to show my hurt to my knights. I surmised that they had not seen the beginning of the attack, since the trees hid the clearing from the road. And I had no intention of riding into the castle at Foix slung over some knight's horse like a sack of oats. As it took all my effort to block the effects of the jostling ride I made no conversation for some time.

When we reached a fork in the road, I was surprised to see Marcel and Thibault riding toward us. "They were sent the long way round, whilst we took the road by the river," Tom volunteered, when he saw the surprised look on my face. "We knew not where we would find you." After briefly greeting their comrades, my knights insisted we continue and I complied, although the jabs of pain in my side were growing worse.

To distract myself, I asked for their story. "What brought you to this place? How did you know I would be riding north at this time?"

"When you disappeared from Lavaur, we had no way to know where you went. The Lady Blanche seemed to be in charge of the household as Lady Geralda had left to attend to her brother in Montréal, so they said. But Lady Blanche was no help to us. First she told us you were ill. After three days, we demanded to see you, and stormed the room where they said you were. But the room was empty."

"Tom," I began apologetically, thinking for the first time how ill I had used my faithful knights with this trick. But he waved my explanation away.

"We have found you, that is all that matters now, lass." I could hear a gruffness in his speech that almost signaled tears. "But you led us a merry chase."

"Why did you choose this road today?"

"We had no way to know how to begin our search, what direction you had taken. The Lady Blanche acted as though she shared our surprise, so we knew it was no use to harass her. She would not give up your plan. So we headed for Toulouse where we knew the Lord William was to come soon, for the great meeting of Count Raymond and the papal legate, Pierre de Castelnau."

"And there you found the Lord William." The clop-clop of the horses' hooves, like the sound of some relentless church bell calling peasants to pray, echoed in my head as I fought the pain. "I can guess that he was not happy to hear the news of my activities," I said ruefully.

"Ah, Princesse. He was in a state when he heard you were in the south, and missing at that. But he also had the crucial conference with Raymond and the papal legate and he must put his mind to that."

"So did he send you to look for me then?"

"No, at first he said we must wait until the conference had concluded, so he could come with us. But then two days later Pierre de Castelnau arrived at the count's palace. He was closeted with Lord William for some time. When Lord William emerged, he told us to head south at dawn and not stop until we had reached the abbey at Fontfroide. He must have had news from the Cistercian monk that gave him to believe you were near Fontfroide Abbey."

"And what were Lord William's instructions, should you find me?" For a brief moment, I allowed myself to feel these men were treating me like a lost package, but then I pushed that thought away. I knew in my heart William cared truly for my well-being.

"He merely said when we found you, we were to bring you to the château at Foix. The Viscount Raymond-Roger at Foix is someone he trusts. He said he would join us there as soon as he could."

"Hmm," was all I could muster in response.

"Lord William said we were not to tarry, but to make haste on the main road in the direction of the sea and so we did. But a few miles back, at the place where we saw a small dwelling, the road splits. We did not know which path you had taken."

"Tom, did you notice anything about that hut? Was there a man about the place?"

"Yes, some tough-appearing man came to the door. He must have heard our horses. We stopped long enough to ask if he had seen a young lad on horseback, and he said he saw a figure answering that description riding past earlier, and that the young squire had taken the road off through the fields. But we didn't trust him, so we split up at that point. I thought you would have stayed by the river."

"And so I did. It is well you didn't trust that peasant. I believe that man told my attacker where to find me. He knew I had silver on me." I shuddered. "You arrived just in time."

"Princesse, I thank our God it was not two moments later, or you may not have survived," Tom said, his usually taciturn voice full with feeling.

"Tom," I said, after a moment's consideration, "if Lord William thought I was in danger and was so keen to send you after me, why did he not come himself?"

"My lady, all the court is talking about the conference that is taking place today. Many hope that with Pierre de Castelnau in Toulouse, and with Lord William to moderate, and Count Raymond finally in a mood to listen, some accommodation can finally be made between Rome and Toulouse, some agreement that will prevent open warfare."

"Ah, yes, the important conference." I had paid little attention to William's diplomatic mission, but the news carried by Pierre of Castelnau when I saw him in the pilgrim's hostel now made sense. William's mission was an important one. And I was in error to have been thinking only of my own problems. Still, he had promised to find Francis when he left Paris and he had not done so. And so I fell silent, occupied with my pain for a time.

Daylight was slowly dying when the formidable castle of the counts of Foix came into sight. I could only pray to the saints that the lady of Foix had returned from Lavaur and would be there to greet me, and that there would be a bath with water from the hearth pot. By this time the pain in my side was almost unbearable, and even the wound on my arm had begun to throb mercilessly. My dearest hope was that Francis would already have arrived, and once more we could be united. This time I would not part from him until I had told him I was his mother.

The castle of the counts of Foix was situated much like the one at Lavaur, built into a hillside for safety. But it was much larger and more forbidding than Lavaur and set much higher with the only access a narrow path winding around the small mountain. Entry was made especially difficult by deep trenches dug at ground level, so steep that even when the mountain streams do not fill them with water they require that one must depend on the drawbridge to advance into the *redoute*. Between the barrier of the trenches and the climb necessary to achieve the entrance, I knew that I would feel secure once we had been admitted to the fortress.

My knights hailed the guards on the top of the castle's battlements. They waved back with a shout. After we identified ourselves, they bade us wait. A seemingly long time passed, during which the sun worked its way down toward the mountainous horizon at an alarming rate. I recalled with a shiver how fast the darkness fell in the mountains and wished the guards would make haste. Suddenly a tremendous clanking signaled that the drawbridge was being lowered.

Though the pain cost me dearly, I gathered myself and cantered across it ahead of my men and picked my way up the stony path that wound around the hill on which the château was built. We could only make that last piece of the journey one horse at a time, and so I was alone when I entered the grand courtyard of the castle. When I saw the round, small figure of the Lady Philippa advancing from the Great Hall to welcome me, I felt a surge of relief. I reined in my horse and began to dismount, but found my legs would not obey. Instead, I slid to the ground, only to feel a great wave overcome me. Then I passed into darkness.

26

The Castle at Foix

hen I regained my senses I was flat on a feather bed in a large chamber. The light flickered from many torches, but still it was difficult to see.

I felt for the sore spot in my side, but instead met a large cloth wrapped around my entire midsection. In truth, I was so tightly bound I wondered I could still breathe. I felt rough muslin fabric, a shift no doubt, and I knew I had been undressed and bandaged while I was in the darkness. Every breath caused a new stab of pain, and so I took in air and let it out carefully. I seemed to be alone in the room, but I dared not sit up. I would need help and anyway I was not yet ready to face the seizure of pain that would accompany me when I changed position. Without thinking, I sighed audibly.

"Your Grace?" Tom's cautious voice

seemed to come from directly beside me. I turned my head to see him, faithful servant, sitting next to the bed.

"Tom, how long have I been asleep? What hour is it now?"

"It is yet some time before daylight, Princesse." He spoke softly, through a large yawn.

"Before daylight." I spoke with effort, the rush of air creating an unexpected jab in my side. "I have been asleep since sunset of yestere'en?"

"Your Grace, why didn't you tell us of your side wounds and bruises? We would never have allowed you to ride as you did." Tom sounded genuinely peeved. I had to smile, which turned into a grimace of pain.

"I've never seen myself as a burden on my men," I retorted.

"You keep this up, begging your pardon for impudence, Princesse, and you won't be a burden on anyone for long." Tom cleared his throat to cover a quaver in his voice, and I drifted back into sleep again. I felt safe with him beside me and the pain was mercifully gone when I slipped into darkness.

When next I knew anything, it was mid-morning. I opened my eyes and turned my head slightly to look at my surroundings. There were large windows set in the stone of the east wall of my bedchamber, and the early winter light sliced into the room through them.

"She is coming round, Countess." I heard Roland's voice this time, and when I turned my head, it was he sitting beside me.

"Princesse, are you now awake?" The cheery, red-cheeked, and very welcome face of Philippa of Foix came into view.

"I am awake," I said, "and I want to sit up." I began to struggle, despite the discomfort. Roland carefully put his arm behind me and lifted me upward. With this, the pressure was released from my back and the spasms that had troubled me ceased. I found I could be upright with little pain. Philippa settled the pillows behind my back, clucking like a mother hen.

"What hour is it? What day? How long have I been asleep?" Philippa had motioned a servant forward, and was giving instructions while I was rattling off questions. "And is young Francis here? William's young knight? He is coming here for safety."

"Please, Princesse. I can only answer one question at a time. I am sending for some victuals for you. Have you a preference for your first meal? Could you manage more than bread and wine? When did you last eat?" My hostess smoothed the furs around my shoulders.

"I don't know. I think I had some bread and cheese just before I was wounded." My head felt full of clouds. "Anything will do. Bread. Perhaps some cold chicken or pheasant." My mouth began to water, although there was a queasy feeling in my stomach. "But I want to see young Francis. Has he arrived?"

"You have eaten nothing in days?" Philippa's honest face opened with surprise. She had ignored my questions about Francis. I was about to repeat myself when there was a tumult outside the door. In a moment the large oak door flew open, and, to my astonishment, the Lord William appeared. He rushed in, cloak flying, shouldering past the servant who was attempting to announce him.

At one glance I could see the anger blazing in his face. I closed my eyes against the sight, but there was still this pulse in the air between us. In my weakened condition I did not feel ready for this interview.

"Countess," William said, with barely a glance in her direction. "Knights, leave us please." There was no mistaking the order.

"Don't go," I said to my men, aware that my weak voice was no match for William's command.

"You may wait outside." He overrode me. "If your mistress needs you, she will call."

"I have sent for food for the *princesse*. She has not eaten for several days and she needs sustenance," Philippa said bravely. "Here is a bell to call the servants if you have need," she said, deliberately brushing past William, who had positioned himself beside my bed. "Need of anything," she added, casting a look back at me.

"Send the meal in when it arrives," William said with a curtness I rarely heard him use. He tossed his sword and cloak off to a side bench, and ran his hand through his hair.

Tom glanced in my direction. I shook my head weakly and shrugged. Of what use to protest? William no doubt had his men with him. With the Knights Templar at his beck and call, he could enforce his will. The knights and the countess understood, and left the room wordlessly.

William and I were alone. He stared down on me. I looked him full in the face, the face that had once been dearer to me than anything on earth. I felt tears come, and pushed them back. I refused to give in to the sentimental woman who lurked deep within me and placed demands on me when I was weak.

"And you, Lord William. Do you not want food? You must be tired after your journey," I said, trying to make my voice flat of the emotion I felt.

"I'll take food later." He turned abruptly and went to the side table, where a flagon of wine stood. I watched as he poured himself a good measure. He cast a quick look in my direction and poured another for me, which he carried back to the bed.

"I don't know if wine will agree with my empty stomach." I pulled a wry face. "I have eaten little in the past day. And I think the countess gave me a sleeping draught yestere'en."

"Drink it," was all he said. I complied, sipping a little, then resting the goblet on the bedcovers, my good hand shaking slightly as it curled around the cold stem.

William pulled up a small bench and seated himself near me. In other times, he would have sat informally on the bed, close to me, touching my hand or even my body. In those days, though the fur covers lay between us, I would have felt the heat we generated. Now, all was cold.

"What did you think you were doing, Alaïs?" He sounded like King Henry grilling his lieutenants after a rout.

I sighed. "What was I doing when?"

"Yes, you might well ask 'when.' In any of the following: leaving the safety of your brother's Paris court to come to the south, when you knew the unstable situation here. Going to Fontfroide when you knew Amaury was there. Traveling alone so that you were prey to *routiers* and cutthroats. Putting your life in danger day after day. You are an intelligent woman." His voice dripped vinegar, so tart was it. I kept a blank expression on my face, looking straight ahead. "Why did you not stay in Paris as I ordered? You were nearly killed."

"That's quite a litany of misguided actions, or at least misguided in your eyes. But I had good reasons for everything I did." I kept my voice steady. "How did you know I was nearly killed? And what brought you here to Foix?"

"As soon as you arrived the countess sent a messenger to me at Raymond's court. She thought your injuries might be fatal. She didn't want a *princesse* of the blood dead in her castle, without sending word."

I took a deep breath. "I came south to find my son. You knew I would when we parted in Paris."

"I knew no such thing. My instructions were for you to remain at your brother's court. I assumed you would follow them." He bit off the ends of his words, his tone unforgiving. "I told you I would find Francis."

"But I wanted to find him." I finally flared up at him. "You had other tasks to distract you, and I could not lurk about Paris, knowing that I might never see him again, that he might never know I was his mother."

"Impatience has ever been your Achilles' heel." William shook his head. "I heard from Pierre de Castelnau when he arrived in Toulouse some days ago that he had met you on the road heading to the sea, that you believed Amaury held Francis at Fontfroide."

"That is true. I had a premonition as you know I sometimes have. And the Cathar preachers said there was much activity apparent when they passed the abbey. Then, when I met Father Pierre at the hostel at Verdun, and he said that Amaury was suddenly interested in visiting Fontfroide Abbey, my hunch became a certainty."

William cast a sharp look in my direction. "Have a care, Princesse. Even to use an expression that implies touching the hunchback for luck could get you into trouble in this volatile time."

I made an impatient gesture with my hand, as if to toss an imaginary ball into the air. "You know that I do not believe in that sorcery. Only that my second sight sometimes appears in the guise of something I know, from somewhere deep inside. I cannot account for it."

"Yes, I do know," he said, placing his hand on my arm, touching me for the first time, though briefly.

I took another draught of the wine, feigning not to notice his gesture, nor that his tone had softened. "I was desperate to find Francis. If his life was in danger, I did not want him to die without knowing that I was his mother." I could not keep the feeling from my voice, though I was ashamed of the quaver it produced.

William shifted on his bench, leaning forward, his elbows on his knees, now holding his head in his hands. But he did not speak, so I continued.

"After you and I quarreled that evening, I was desperate to take action. So I beseeched my brother the next day to give me and my men permission to come to the south."

"And Philippe let you go?" The rising notes reflected his assessment of my brother's actions. "I find that hard to believe. He must be truly distracted with the intrigues of his court."

"It wasn't a question of permission," I responded, with heat. "I should have come whether he allowed it or no. And yet I told him all. That Francis was my son, and that King Henry was the father. At first Philippe was furious." I closed my eyes against the picture of the wrath that invaded that interview with my brother. "As king, he felt that I had betrayed him by not marrying Richard and bringing France the benefits of that alliance. But then, after a time, my brother relented. Eventually he gave me men, and maps that have been my guide."

"I wonder that he gave in, even with the news of your relationship with Francis."

"Ah, well," I said, smiling faintly, "he had another motive. Philippe is ever the king. He wanted me to deliver a message to you."

"And do you still have the letter?" William sat upright at this news.

"There was no letter. I committed his request to memory. He wants you to return to Paris as soon as possible. He needs your help to unmask the conspirators at his court." As the ache in my head was receding, I was becoming clearer in my thoughts. "He has identified the source. And through my recent adventures, I can confirm his suspicions. Amaury and Chastellain are in league together."

"With King John?"

"I am certain of it. At the place where I was attacked, a purse was found, one stuffed with silver. Roland inspected the leather marking. It came from the Royal Guild of Leather Makers in London." I lay back against the pillows for a moment. "I believe the man was sent to track me, although it seems an accident that he found me."

"So the man sent to attack you was paid by English gold. That supports what Philippe suspects, and what we discussed before I left Paris. John's silver has corrupted his chief minister. But how do you know that Amaury is involved?"

"Chastellain came to Fontfroide while I was there. In the chapel one day, when they did not recognize me, I overheard a conversation between Amaury and Etienne Chastellain."

"Chastellain at Fontfroide?" Now William was truly startled.

"What in the name of the devil was he doing there? Philippe told me he sent him to Rome to soothe the pope's ruffled feathers over his denial of Amaury's request."

"Well, he made a detour to Fontfroide. I was in disguise, but I heard Chastellain refer to a pact they had made: he would help Amaury with Philippe, if Amaury would remain silent about the information Chastellain's secretary Eugene was funneling to John of England about the movement of Philippe's soldiers."

"That proves what both the king and I suspected." William stood suddenly. "I will depart soon for Paris. My work here is finished with the fiasco of our conference yesterday in Toulouse."

"And what happened there?" I suddenly realized that I had not inquired about the outcome of William's diplomatic mission. I had been too caught up in my own adventures.

"The meeting was a disaster. Raymond was quarrelsome and Pierre de Castelnau seemed distracted through the entire meeting, as if his heart were not in the work he had to do. It ended badly with Pierre leaving in exasperation, saying he would not stay under the roof of a man who so insulted him and the office he represented." William's jaw muscles tightened. "I could do nothing."

"I'm sorry," I said, and felt it truly. He gazed down on me for a long moment. Then he sat again, and resumed his inquiry of my travels, as if his announcement of leaving for Paris had been premature.

"When you arrived here, I was told you asked for Francis. Do you have reason to suspect he will come here? What happened at Fontfroide Abbey?"

And so I told William the entire story of the rescue. Although he began shaking his head from the beginning, the story of meeting the Cathar preachers at Lavaur, then the disguise as Benedictine nuns and the adventures on the road to Fontfroide finally produced an occasional muted chuckle, immediately followed by a stern look.

After speaking for a time, I was unable to sit upright anymore in my weakness so I lay back and closed my eyes. As I did so, I could see again the details of scenes of my adventure. I began to embellish the story with the look of the brutish men who held Francis, the feel of the underground chamber where we hid him, the sight of the scary fire we deliberately set.

When I described my capture and interview with Amaury, and my final barb thrown to him as I left, William burst out laughing. He was shaking his head now, no longer in disapproval, but in humorous disbelief.

"Princesse, your most exasperating qualities are your greatest virtues."

I smiled to see his anger abated, and could not forbear to ask: "And what might those be?"

"Your impatience, your occasional bad temper, your unwomanly love of adventure, your manly courage." He reeled these off as if he had given some thought to each item in the weeks since we had parted.

"I accept those virtues, and I will give little thought to changing," I said, "though in the future I shall attempt to curb any excesses that might put my life in danger."

Then, noting the satisfied look that settled over his countenance, I added, "And I have a gift for you as well: your exasperating qualities match mine. You have a choleric temperament, quick judgment, and a high-handed way with women. And you are so used to getting your own way that you cannot see when you could be wrong."

"You have bested me again, Alaïs," he said ruefully, but smiling. Then he pulled the bench closer to me, so that he could look directly into my eyes. I could smell the heat of travel still on him, the leather of the saddle, the male scent so familiar. It somehow brought me closer to him, and made me more aware of my own travel-stained body and matted hair. But my appearance seemed to matter little to him. He grasped my wrist in his large hand, and I could feel the pressure on my bones.

"It is difficult to remain angry with you, Alaïs," William was saying. "All my soul fights me. My feelings for you pull me like an army pulling a trebuchet, forcefully tugging me a way I would not go."

He released my wrist and leaned forward to bend over me. "Wait," I said, but my words were muffled when he placed his lips on mine. The kiss was not long, or particularly passionate, but marked a union of our two selves, a rejoining, as if a peace were created after a storm.

When we separated there was silence. Then William took the goblet still circled in my hand on top of the covers, rose, and went to the side table, where he poured more wine for each of us.

He came back and offered the cup, which I took with gratitude. The pewter stem felt cold to my hand, but the spice in the wine warmed me as I let it slide down my throat.

A knock at the door, which William opened, heralded a servant with a tray of hot broth and bread and pheasant on a trencher. I picked at the food, and ate a little. But my heart was not in it. All the while William sat next to me and watched in silence as I also watched him. Soon I asked him to take away the tray, and I rested against the pillows.

Our conversation had yielded much information, but my feelings were overwhelming me. I felt a fatigue I had seldom known when my body was undamaged.

William pulled the furs around me, and leaned down to take away the cup, as he saw my eyes closing. "Sweetheart, I have tired you. You must rest. You have wounds and broken ribs that need time to heal."

"Don't leave," I murmured, although my lids were already growing heavy.

"I'm not leaving Foix." He smoothed the hair back from my brow. "But you must sleep now, and when you wake eat something more. From what you have said, if Francis is safe and all has gone well with him, he should be here by nightfall. When he comes, I will bring him to you. You may tell him you are his mother. You have earned the right, and I was wrong to keep you from doing it."

I heard the door close behind William. For a few moments I tried to recall what had been said in this long, remarkable interview, but the words were supplanted by images that jumbled in my mind as I drifted off. The images were of me falling from my horse, and William riding toward me, slipping off his destrier in time and catching me in his arms. These pictures evoked a feeling of serenity in me that was vastly comforting, even as they faded into darkness.

27

The Chamber of the
Princesse at Foix

Only once did I come to again that day, when they brought my broth and shook my shoulder to awaken me enough to drink it. I saw that dusk was falling outside the castle window. Then I pulled the furs around my shoulders and gave myself back to sleep even as I held the image of my son's young and handsome face.

When next I opened my eyes, late afternoon sun was streaming into the chamber. In a panic I saw I had slept another whole day. This time my head felt much clearer, and the pain as I attempted to sit up was not so vehement as it had been. My arm throbbed, though, where the dagger had torn the flesh. Fortunate for me that it had been my left arm that was wounded, for with my withered left hand it was of no use to me anyway.

As I looked for a bell to ring, the door

opened. Philippa, Countess of Foix, entered with a string of servants following her. Some had trays of food and pitchers of milk, some carried basins of warm water.

"My dear Princesse, you must be famished." Philippa came toward me and motioned a servant to place the tray on my lap. Others set basins on the table beside the bed, and the clouds of moisture rising from them was welcome.

"You will eat first, and more hot water will be brought for you to wash," the kind countess said, leaning down to sponge my face with warm water. She placed the cloth in the basin when she had finished and stood back, her hands folded in front of her. "I cannot tell you what pleasure it gives me to see you awake and mending," she said.

"And what pleasure it gives me, Countess, to be well cared for. And to be safe." I looked around. "But where is Lord William? And has young Francis arrived, or Geralda or Fabrisse or Grazide?" Fears began to insert themselves into my sense of well-being, as I thought of the dangers my comrades might have experienced on their journeys.

"Young Francis and Geralda arrived last eve. Lord William thought it best not to wake you. Geralda is quite fatigued and still sleeps, but Francis and the Lord William should be in to see you soon. They are conferring with my lord Raymond-Roger even now." And this rejoinder satisfied me that all was well. My heart swelled with gratitude that my son was safe.

"And Grazide and Fabrisse?" The faces of the young women rose in front of me, as if accusing me for my comfort whilst they might still be sleeping in fields. But Philippa shook her head. "No word yet from them."

Despite my worry, I felt famished. After I had happily eaten warm game, a broth soup of leeks and turnips that created heat all through me, and a delicious almond cake, I finished off the meal with cheese and wine. I could feel life returning to me with the nourishment I had taken.

"Countess, I would welcome that tub of warm water for washing."
I was especially aware of my gritty and matted hair. I did not want
William to see me this way again. It put me at a distinct disadvantage
as a woman in our relationship. The countess snapped her fingers and
two servants hustled from the room.

Within a short time a wooden tub was brought, along with pails of
hot water. With help I hobbled over to the steaming vessel, and, after
removing the cloths that had been wound tightly around my battered
ribs, I submerged myself in it gratefully. A servant appeared at my
side with soaps and pitchers of water. I wished to frolic and splash as
a child, so relieved was I to lay aside the dusty traveler I had been for
weeks and become once more clean as a woman of my station ought
to be.

The maidservants had carried in the scented oils and creams of the
countess, and their gentle hands on my back brought a further sense
of well-being. They helped me from the tub and rubbed my body with
perfumed unguents as I lay on the bed. A small, wrinkled old woman
arrived with yards of muslin, the light cotton that had come back with
the Crusaders from the east, and she wound it around my midsection
tightly. When she was finished I felt somehow lighter and safer, and
the pain eased. Then I donned fresh linen and a gown belonging to the
Countess Philippa, which nearly fit, although the skirt was too short
to brush the floor in the current fashion. To finish all, the servants
bound up my still wet hair with a circlet of jewels.

I settled myself in a large, carved chair with many embroidered
cushions around me to prevent my sore ribs from hurting. I found that
I could avoid almost all pain in this position by moving little, turning
my head rather than my body. The absence of pain is only noticed by
those who have the recent experience of pain itself, I reflected.

While our womanly rituals were under way, the countess sat in a
companion chair entertaining me with stories of the women I had met
at Lavaur. Finally, when I was ready, she stood.

"La, I nearly forgot. Lord William asked to see you straightaway when you woke, but I told him you must first be made ready. He seemed impatient, but in my house, even when my lord Raymond-Roger is here, I rule the servants and the protocol of dress."

"The Lord William not only seems impatient, he is impatient," I commented, thinking of our duel of words the day before. "But my thanks go to you, Countess, as I would not for all the world have had him see me again in that state of disarray." I smiled my gratitude, and the countess's sunny face told of the age-old conspiracy of women that was beyond the ken of any man.

The words were scarce uttered than the door was flung open, as if to prove my statement, and William strode in.

"I hope the women have had sufficient time for their *toilettage*," he said, a tinge of good-humored irritation in his voice.

"And so we have, Lord William," I greeted him happily, feeling I appeared once again the *princesse royale* who might hold appeal for him. I felt the stronger for it. "You were kind to indulge us."

He glanced at me sharply, as if he knew I made fun of his impatience, but then a smile spread. "Ah, Princesse, had I known this hour would restore your customary loveliness, I would not have begrudged it so."

"You see, Countess. An impatient man, a soldier and commander, but also one who can use fine words when necessary." I grinned, and he came to me in one movement, bending down to kiss me hard.

"And I have brought someone to see you, as I promised," he said.

Then I saw behind William the only face that was dearer to me than his, that of my son, Francis, his auburn hair longer, fuller, and more unmanageable, his face burnished by the southern sun. He stepped forward with the same assurance William showed, a new manliness about his presence. His expression was inscrutable, his features settled into a calm state. But lines had appeared on his forehead and around his eyes, lines that I did not remember, even though it was only a fortnight since we parted at Fontfroide. It appeared that the events of these past few weeks had taken the impetuous youth, so enraged at his friend's useless death in Paris, and made a man of him.

"Your Grace," he said, bending over my hand as it lay on the coverlet beside me, "I owe my life to your courage and resourcefulness." As he came close, I pulled his head down and pressed his cheek to mine. I could not speak, for my heart seemed to have worked its way into my throat. It was a moment before I released him.

"Princesse, the young knight and I must have a conversation with you. Countess, could you leave us please?" William's tone was far more politic than it had been the previous day.

"With all good wishes, Lord William. I will be in my chambers. Servants are just outside the door, if you need anything. Even though I believe they are to be trusted," Philippa added, in a lower tone, "have a care not to speak with a voice that could carry."

Francis stood, his legs apart, his hand on his sword hilt, regarding me gravely. William stood at a slight distance, as if the conversation belonged to me and my son.

"Princesse, Francis has told me what happened to him. It is clear Amaury arranged the abduction under the illusion that Francis somehow had possession of the St. John Cup, from Constance." William paused, and gave a wintry smile. "And perhaps to hector me as well. My young knight has explained to me that all of this occurred because of his dalliance with a young woman of the house of Foix."

The color rose in my son's face at this remark. I watched Francis all the while, and I knew I could never gaze too long on that dear face, now safe not only with me, but with William.

"But now, Princesse, I think you owe young Francis the true story of why you were willing to undertake such danger for his sake." William paused. "Now it is time, Alaïs," he added softly.

I raised my hand to rub my cheek and turned my head to look out the window. I could see the clouds mounting, and yet the sun shone brightly overall. Happiness and sadness seemed to vie for a place in my heart.

Then I turned back to my son. "Francis, as the Lord William knows, I have something of significance to tell you," I said, keeping my voice even. "Perhaps it is best told in the form of a story. It may take some time, so please, sit here beside me."

"Lord William said you had important news, but it would be difficult for you in the telling." He nodded as if to encourage me and that touched me more than anything. He lowered himself into the chair beside mine, turning it so that he could look full upon me. I noticed that he sat on the edge, though, as if he might suddenly be called into duty and must be at the ready. He leaned forward, elbows on his knees, chin in his hand. I was reminded so of William.

"Long ago there was a young girl, living in a foreign land. She had few friends, and although she had a large family, they often quarreled among themselves." I watched his face, which held a look of puzzled bemusement.

"She had a stepmother, of whom she was fond. But then the stepmother went away."

"Did this young girl have a mother of her own? Or a father?"

I cast my glance toward the ceiling, as if in thought. "Her own mother died when she was quite young, and soon after the young girl was sent away. Her father was a powerful man, but in another country."

This seemed to satisfy him, or perhaps he was coming into the knowledge that I must tell the story my own way, for he waited, watching me intently.

"This girl was strong-willed, but she was really a pawn for her father and stepfather. She was told whom she would marry, where she would live, how she would learn."

"Was she a captive, then?" He broke in again, almost in spite of himself, I could see.

"Not exactly, but because her family was important many decisions about her life were not her own. But to continue: She was in awe of her stepfather when she was young, for he was a powerful man, as powerful as her father in another realm. But she had a memory of him once, when she was a little girl, and he came upon her drawing. He noticed what she was doing, and he told her that, in a way, he envied her gift. He saw that she could draw images that were called up from inside, and he—a man of action—could see only what was before him. It was a brief exchange, but from that moment on, she had a warm feeling for him, almost of sympathy."

I waited for a moment, for, in truth, I felt my own heart swelling with the memory of the events that had brought me to King Henry's bed. After a moment, I continued.

"When I was older, my stepmother, Queen Eleanor, was sent away, and King Henry was lonely, as was I. Because we had shared a moment once, when he had revealed to me his vulnerability, we came to an uneasy joining at that time." I suddenly saw Francis's eyes widen, and realized that I had switched into saying "I" without thinking, and to say the king was Henry and the queen was Eleanor. So be it.

"I had a child. There were . . . circumstances at the time that prevented me from . . . taking the boy away. Then I was told the child had died, and thought so for many years." My voice began to cloud over, as if a fog were descending inside me. But I pressed on, for now was the time. And I must be equal to the task.

"Years later, I discovered the lad still lived and had been well cared for by an old friend. And it was for the best of reasons, not the least of which was the safety of the child, that I had not been told the babe had survived. But when I knew, I moved heaven and earth to find the young man."

Francis was staring at me, his mouth open with a quick intake of breath, but he said nothing.

"When I found my son, I saw he was a delight. Learned, bright, adventuresome, and brave. All that I hoped a son could be. And I no longer thought it was necessary to tell him I was his mother. Not then. Perhaps later."

"And why now?" Francis's voice was unsteady. I could not tell if it was anger or tenderness. "Why tell him now?"

I glanced at William, but I knew I could not lay all this at his door. "Because the times are turbulent, it seemed better to delay telling you. We . . . I thought that perhaps later, when things were more settled and he . . . you might have some ease in which to make your decisions . . ." My voice trailed off as I watched the young knight's face darken.

"The *princesse* does not tell the entire story," William interrupted. "I insisted she not tell you while you and I had our final mission for the pope. I thought it would distract us from this work I had promised to do. And I did not feel I could protect you if I were far away."

"But what has changed now?" he asked, after clearing his throat.

"Your abduction changed everything for both of us. I saw the point of what the *princesse* was trying to tell me. Life is uncertain. I had no right to make her keep this news from you. It is too important." William's voice was quiet and I gave him a look of such thanks that his face relaxed from its tight expression.

"When you disappeared, and I thought you might die, I regretted that I had never told you the most important news of your life." I picked up the story, dropping the pretense for good. "And told you the story well. I wanted you to know that I love you and I am proud of you. And other things. That you could be proud of your father. That the person who protected you still watches over you, even as you grew to knighthood. That royal blood from two kingdoms runs in your veins."

There was a long silence. Francis threw his head back and stared at the ceiling for a long moment. Then he faced me again.

"I am that son." He said it as a statement, not a question, but I answered anyway.

"Yes, you are that son."

"And that story of Lord William finding me at a village outside of York? That was a fable?" Yes, I could hear the anger now, but I could assign no blame for that. We would just have to weather the storm. "Could no one have told me before this time, in all these years, who my parents were?"

"Why?" I asked, suddenly wondering if I had made a mistake in my son. Could he care so much that he was a bastard of a king? "What would have been different for you had you known?"

Francis rose and looked about, somewhat wildly. His glance landed on William who had remained leaning against the wall behind Francis's chair, his arms folded.

"How could you not have told me all the while I grew up in your household? Why did you even take me in? Did they pay you? Has that been my life . . . My past hidden, dependent on the kindness of strangers!"

He backed away, and looked from one to the other of us.

"Francis," William said, so sharply I winced. "You forget your-self. You have just been told your parentage, for now it is time. The *princesse* had the right to decide that, for you were her child. It is hers to tell."

"But do you know, do either of you know, what it is like to grow up thinking one thing about your family, believing you came from a poor village, an orphan, and to suddenly discover that none of it was true . . . that you don't know who you truly are?"

William moved to the young man so quickly I scarce saw his feet touch the floor. He grabbed his shoulders and shook him, as if he were a schoolboy. Suddenly the youth, who was near as tall as his master, threw his arms around the older man and began to sob. William held him closely for a long moment, then released him.

"You are yourself, lad," William said. "All the rest matters not."

After a long pause, William spoke again. "You have a kinship with the *princesse* that is so obvious I sometimes wonder why others don't see it," he said, and young Francis gathered himself and wiped his eyes with the back of his sleeve, a boyish gesture that nearly undid me. He looked into William's face and the mixture of emotions, which I could see from my chair, made my own heart ache. "Both of you are headstrong and rebellious. You should have seen it yourself that night you escaped into Chinon, against my orders. I found you both in the town square, where you could have been harmed. But neither of you had a thought for the practical things."

Francis smiled gamely as he turned to me. "I do recall that night. And the wonderful conversations we had as we continued our journey into France, where you came to visit Queen Eleanor."

"Yes, I remember. I was then so impressed with all you knew, of philosophy and poetics, with your curiosity and your liveliness." I paused, and then took a chance. "I cannot tell you how proud I am to be your mother, young Francis."

"And your mother loves you above all things," William said gravely. "She risked her life to save yours. You would not be alive without her, not then and not now."

The youth came quickly and gracefully and fell on his knee in front of my chair. "Forgive my outburst, Your Grace. It is so startling to have one's life, all the things one has come to believe about oneself, overturned. I lost myself for a moment."

"My son, you will never lose yourself. You are Francis, no matter who your parents, nor what they did." I placed a hand on his unruly auburn mane, and caressed his head with a feeling of great love and relief.

"But how did I come to Lord William's household?" the youth asked, insistently but this time without hostility.

"Lad, that is a tale of its own and I will tell it myself," William interjected, pulling up a small stool for himself and one for Francis. "It is simple. King Henry, for he indeed was your father as you now know, feared for your safety, and the safety of your mother. There were vultures at the courts of both France and England who would have taken you and used you for their own ends. So the king asked me to take you away and see to your upbringing. And he kept that news from your mother, for he knew she would never rest until she had you, if she thought you lived." He clapped his hand on Francis's shoulder.

"Raising you like my own son was a labor of love for me, my young knight. I had loved your mother, although she knew it not in those days, ever since she was my childhood playmate." William paused, his glance meeting mine. "It was my way of serving her as well as my king."

"Did you love my father?" He turned to me directly. The question was not unexpected, but still caught me with my guard down. I could only answer truthfully.

"With all my heart, at the time."

"It matters not that I am a bastard," he said, with gravitas. "But how my father was to you, that is important. I would hate him until the day I died if I thought he had mistreated you."

I saw before me the young man who had entered the room earlier, and knew that his words were a kind of benediction for me, both a forgiveness and the statement of a proud son.

"And besides," he continued, "Lord William is my guardian and always has been. He has been all that a father could be to me."

"I know that," I was beginning to say, when William interrupted.

"King Henry, your father, also loved your mother for her gifts and her active nature, so like your own, Francis. I know. I was there. I saw it all." And then his voice became brisk again. "Since I have been all that a father could be, you will be pleased to know that I am about to marry your mother."

A smile spread across the young man's face, erasing any clouds that had gathered during our conversation.

"Splendid," he cried as both men rose, Francis knocking over the

three-legged stool near my bed. Francis clapped his guardian on the
back in return. In truth, he was so joyful I thought he might clap me
on the back as well, but instead he reached for my hand, and bent low
over it, first brushing his lips and then holding my hand against his
dear cheek.

And when William edged him aside so he could raise me up and
embrace me, we three were joined.

It was William, ever practical, who broke our touch with a brisk
statement. "Alaïs, we need to make a plan for your safety, now . . ."

Francis took the opportunity to move to the window, and stood
looking at the very clouds I had watched earlier, lost in his own
thoughts. William began restlessly walking to and fro, but never out
of my eyesight as I lay back against the pillows of my chair. As he
was beginning the litany of actions we three must undertake, the door
flew open and the Countess of Foix stepped inside the door, highly
agitated.

"Princesse, Lord William, my husband's sister has just arrived
and when she heard you were here, she demanded an immediate audience." Whereupon she stepped into the room and behind her appeared
the mysterious Lady Esclarmonde, framed in the doorway. She was
dressed in traveling clothes laden with grime, her boots dusty, her formerly lustrous brown hair matted and hanging in clumps. She had a
small, leather travel *sac* slung over her shoulder. I could not have been
more surprised if it had been Abbot Amaury himself.

I saw William turning abruptly, angered at the interruption. I
saw Francis spin from the window, an expression of disbelief coming
over his features. I sank back into my chair and prepared to watch the
scene.

28

The Chamber of the Princesse at Foix

Francis, thank God in heaven that you are safe!" The intense exclamation from the young woman was a total surprise to all of us. She stood, cheeks flushed, hovering on the threshold, as if once she had breached the privacy of our council she did not dare go further.

But then she did. After her slight hesitation, she ran to Francis and sank on her knees before him. William and I stared in astonishment.

"Can you forgive me for putting your life in danger?" she asked. Francis looked as startled as we did. But he rose to the occasion in a knightly way, gently taking the young woman's elbows and raising her to face him.

"What are you talking about, Lady?" he asked, true confusion filling his voice. "I have no knowledge of your efforts to put my life in danger." Perhaps he did not, but once my initial amazement subsided I began to have a glimmer.

"I had no suspicion when Constance proposed a flirtation with you that it would end in your abduction," she said. At least she had the character to look Francis in the face as she confessed.

"Constance of Toulouse proposed a flirtation with me?" Francis's eyebrows rose and I could hear a sliver of sadness fill his voice. He looked crestfallen. Her interest in him had all been part of a game.

"I am so sorry for my part in this mischief," she sniffled, as she finally turned from Francis to face me.

"It was Constance behind the entire plan, *n'est-ce pas?*" I asked, as the young woman paused.

"Yes, she was at the center of the intrigue in Paris," she sighed. "And certain mistakes were made. May I sit now, please?" With the sun full on her face, I could see the weariness and dust lining it. But she had still a pert, cheerful look and the aura of youth surrounded her.

William dragged a chair from the corner, muttering: "I am happy to have you sit, Lady Esclarmonde, if you will only clear up some of the mysteries regarding the activities of Constance of Toulouse."

"This is the story," she began. "Countess Constance knew Abbé Amaury was coming to see King Philippe to beg for money and men to fight in the south. She has a network of spies that is quite large. She advised my brother, the Count of Foix, to send me north to Paris. I was to engage the king's attention and use whatever influence I had to keep the king from committing arms and silver to Amaury's plan." Esclarmonde sat down, casting a glance at Francis as she did so. "I must say, I was mildly successful in that endeavor."

"Hence your performance at the royal reception the day Amaury made his formal request," I noted, and she nodded in response.

"Yes, the king persuaded me ahead of time to play such a part. He said it would help people accept his decision if I pleaded in front of his courtiers." She smiled ruefully. "I was well prepared, you can be assured. All the while, Count Raymond was sending couriers to his mother, Constance, for reports on the political climate of Philippe's court."

"Those were the secret meetings at Créteil my brother asked me to investigate." I turned to William. "Remember how concerned he was that one of his varlets was murdered when he sent men to follow Constance?"

"Constance did not intend for anyone to get hurt. Raymond's men were overzealous in trying to protect the meetings from the knowledge of the king," Esclarmonde said.

"Instead, they simply caught his attention where otherwise he might not have bothered about her affairs." I managed a wan smile. "You see how the best laid plans go awry. So continue, Lady Esclarmonde."

The young woman took a deep breath. "It seems that Raymond does not fully trust his mother, for he never told her that he had possession of the golden chalice, or that he had given it to Philippe to keep safe at St. Denis, far from the eyes of the Cathars who claimed it as theirs."

"And when she saw the cup at Mass, she recognized it and wanted to retrieve it, to restore it to the cathedral at Toulouse." I filled in the story. "And she concocted a scheme to steal it from the abbey."

"She hinted to me that one of the close councelors of the king helped her by having his men steal it. But she would not say what she gave in return."

"I suspect that she knew about Chastellain's treason, funneling information from the king's council to John's captains in the west," William remarked as he leaned against the wall, arms folded. "Perhaps arranging the theft was the price of her silence."

"Or else she made a lucky guess, and he gave in to her demands on the chance that she would betray him," I interjected.

"Or, for Chastellain, it could have been just plain greed for the gold of the chalice," Francis offered, and we all nodded.

"Whatever it was, it seems he was the instrument by which the chalice was stolen. But in addition to Chastellain, Constance had the problem of Amaury," Esclarmonde said. "Constance told me Chastellain confided their plans to Amaury. The abbot approached her, and told her he knew all."

"When I stumbled upon them in a tête-à-tête the last night I was in Paris, she must have been busy seducing him with stories of the jewels in the chalice that could be pried loose. She knew he wanted the cup for its treasure, and so she told him that young Francis would be her messenger to take the cup to the south." I recalled the image of Amaury and my aunt outlined against the night sky. "She thought, and rightly so, that his interest would shift to Francis and he would leave her alone."

"Yes, but I couldn't understand why she would do that." Now it was Esclarmonde's turn to look puzzled in my direction. "There was no need to involve Francis. That was not part of the plan."

"Oh, but it was," I said, stretching my arms as they had grown weary. The sharp pain in my side recalled to me my condition, and I dropped my hands into my lap. "She wanted Amaury to think she was on his side. And she didn't want him to know she was keeping the chalice. If he knew she had it, he would find a way to wrest it from her, either by coercion or force. She also knew he needed gold for his wars, so all she had to do was mention the chalice's supposed treasure clue and Francis in the same breath, and he was off to find it, leaving her with only Chastellain to deal with."

I continued with what I had gleaned from Francis when I rescued him. "And I am sorry to say she was successful. The abbot took Francis. He hid him in the ancient tower near the building site of Notre Dame. He stayed on a day or two at my brother's court to avoid raising suspicion, then left with his prisoner. By the time he found out Francis did not have the cup, he decided to keep him anyway, in case he needed to press Lord William to get tough with Count Raymond."

William nodded. "It all makes great sense. But what did she do about Chastellain? After all, his men stole the icon. He must have wanted his share of the treasure."

"I know the answer to that from what I overheard in Fontfroide Abbey," I said quickly. "When she saw the king receive that message, she guessed it was about the chalice, that Chastellain had carried out their plan. She simply got up from the table then and disappeared. She probably went directly to Chastellain and obtained the chalice under some pretext. Perhaps he was afraid of discovery. He might have been glad to be rid of it for the night. He knew, with the killing of the monk, whoever had the chalice would be found guilty of that crime. Chastellain thought they would finalize the plans on the chalice in the morning. But she fooled him. She left quietly in the middle of that night after obtaining the object."

"Chastellain must have been furious," William interjected.

"Yes, he hadn't counted on Constance disappearing immediately, and with the prize. To judge from what I overheard at Fontfroide, he must have been beside himself in a rage the next day when he discovered her flight. He had taken the risk, indeed killed a monk, for no reward at all."

Esclarmonde continued with her part, speaking in the langue d'oïl, but with her clear, southern lilt. "I knew of Constance's design to steal the chalice from the beginning of my visit at the court. But I did not think those plans concerned me. My only task was to prevent the abbot from getting the king's support. Then, that last night after the royal dinner in the Great Hall, Constance caught up with me in the drafty corridor. She told me the king had received a message that the cup had been stolen. And she said she had told Amaury that Francis was to be the messenger to take it to Toulouse. I was appalled. She had placed Francis in grave danger." The young woman turned to Francis and extended her hand to him: "You were not at the banquet that night. So I knew I must find another way to warn you."

"So did you go to his chambers?" I reclaimed her attention.

"No, I sent a note. Because it was late, I told the servant to deliver the note at dawn. I did not dream the abbot would act that night, spiriting Francis away from his chambers." Now she raised her head and looked directly at Francis. "The servant I sent to you returned at once. He said that you were gone, your chambers in disarray. It was then I feared the worst. But I knew not whom I could trust in that hotbed of intrigue." She pulled from her sleeve a crumpled, small scroll. "See here, I still have the note I wrote you."

"I would see that note, Lady," I said, holding out my hand, for Francis had moved forward to take it, no doubt as some proof of her affection for him.

Francis passed it to me without reading it, rather reluctantly it seemed. I unrolled the dog-eared scroll and glanced at it. I was not interested in the message, but in the handwriting. It proved as I had suspected.

"You are the one who sent the note to my brother's chief minister, warning him about the impending theft of the St. John Cup, and also one to me, about following the trail of gold to the south. The handwriting is the same on this note to Francis." I looked over at her as I passed the paper back to Francis. "Why did you send those warnings?"

The young woman raised her small, pointed chin bravely at that question. "Just before his public audience that day I had sent that note thinking it would reinforce the king's desire to stay out of our troubles here. I hinted at the imminent theft of the chalice, which I knew Constance planned. I thought such a message would further dissuade."

"And also confuse the issue?" I asked pointedly.

She nodded, but added, with a somewhat saucy air: "I did not think it would endanger our plans, for by the time the king heard of the theft of the chalice, it would already have left Paris with a trusted courier."

"And Francis was to be the courier?"

"Oh, no, madame. It was never to be Francis. That was Constance's ruse with Amaury, a trick gone bad, certainly. We meant him no harm." She looked to my son, who had remained standing near William. "Truly, Sir Francis, my attention to you was not only that the countess wished me to entertain you. It's true, I began it as a dalliance to provide distraction, but I grew genuinely fond of you. I had never a thought to place you in danger."

"But when Amaury heard the false news from Constance, he thought Francis had the cup," I asserted.

"And so he was abducted. When the servant brought me back my note that night, and said that the room was in disarray, Constance and I realized what had occurred. We knew we were no match for Amaury, so we decided to set out at once for the south. Constance for Toulouse, and myself to Laurac to spend some weeks before coming here." She cast a glance at Francis under lowered eyes. "Yestermorn a messenger came from this house, to tell me you were here, Sir Francis. And I made haste to see for myself that you were safe."

Francis rewarded this new confession with another blush, to my amusement.

"So Constance took the cup to Toulouse after all," I murmured, thinking of the conversation I had overheard at Fontfroide.

"No, Your Grace. That would have been too obvious," the young woman said. "Constance never had the cup, except to receive it and pass it to another for safekeeping before dawn that very night."

"But why, after all of the intrigue, would she not take it herself?" I was astonished.

"Because, as you correctly surmised earlier, she feared that Amaury would find out where she was, hunt her down and take it from her. I do believe she fears him greatly."

"Where is it then?" William's tone reflected his impatience. He pulled a small oak chair to him, turned it so the back was facing us, and threw his leg across it to sit astride. "All of this conniving and scheming was to distract everyone from the theft of this gold cup. Where is it now?"

"I find it passing strange that the icon has value so different for each person," Francis said thoughtfully.

"That's true. For Amaury it is the gold, or the treasure it could lead to; for Chastellain it was a way to buy Constance's silence, and perhaps secure her help with the king," I mused.

"And for Constance, a prize to bring back to Toulouse," William added.

"And for Raymond, a bargaining tool with the Cathars," Esclarmonde volunteered. "But of all of them, the only players in this drama who desired the chalice for its own sake are the Cathars. For them it is a sacred object because it belonged to Saint John, their patron and guide."

There was a silence in the room, each of us occupied with our own thoughts.

"So, if Constance did not take it to Toulouse, where is it now?" Francis asked the question.

"Oh, it is with me," Esclarmonde said simply. "I promised Constance I would never let it out of my sight until we could reinstall it in the Toulouse Cathedral. I have it even now in the travel *sac* I brought from Laurac."

All of our faces turned toward her.

"You have it here?" I sounded stupid with amazement. After all of the peregrinations and actions, lies and deceits and adventures, the cup was here, in this château.

"Yes," she said. "As I said, in my travel *sac*." And she slipped the strap from her shoulder and let the *sac* slide to the floor.

.29.

The Chamber of the Princesse at Foix

For a moment, time stopped. Finally I found my voice.

"Lady Esclarmonde. I understand why you would come here to see Francis, but why did you bring the Saint John Cup here today? Why not just leave it at Laurac until you were able to deliver it to Toulouse?"

She hesitated for a long moment, then held my gaze as she spoke.

"Princesse Alaïs, although I owe loyalty to the Count of Toulouse, for my brother is his liege man, I also admire you. I watched you at your brother's court, observed your courage, the way you stood up to the abbot at the king's audience. I watched you after the tourney, in conversation with Francis, though you did not see me. I saw you calm him with your very words. You are royal not only in your title, but in your actions."

"I thank you for your kind words, Esclarmonde, but I still do not see why you brought the chalice here."

"I owe a debt for putting Sir Francis in danger. And, to be sure, although the cup was stolen from Toulouse, before that it was taken from the Cathars." She assumed a slightly defiant look, her features hardening somewhat. "I am of the Cathar sympathies myself, and so are my brother and his wife. And I have wondered if perhaps the cup should be returned to them, instead of to the Count of Toulouse."

"So you want me to make the choice?" I asked, with some amusement—which I dared not show, as she was so solemn. Then I sighed inwardly. With the responsibility would go the blame.

"Yes, Your Grace. I have been dithering for days over my course of action. When I heard you were here, at Foix, I knew this was the answer for me."

"Let us have it, then," I said. Esclarmonde reached into her travel *sac* and pulled forth a substantial package, wrapped in folds of soft material that might once have been a lovely gown.

I unraveled the muslin cloths that bound the cup, and it rolled out easily, as if it were any everyday drinking mug. Ah, but what a fine goblet it was. We all, even William, drew in a breath at the sight.

It was as I remembered from the Mass at St. Denis, but even more stunning close up. The heavy, solid gold was hammered to a fine, thin state and jewels dotted the cup just below the rim. There were rubies and emeralds in various shapes, some as large as rocks in a riverbed. And diamonds from Africa were scattered in between the other precious gems. Indeed, part of the cup seemed to be winking at us as it caught the fire from the sun cutting into the room.

More jewels formed a second ring around the bottom of the swelling cup, and the long, thick stem, braided round with gold, attached it to the gently spreading pedestal. I turned the icon over carefully, and noticed a tiny ring of diamonds around the very base, but carefully placed so that they did not interfere with the balance of the cup when it was set on a table. This cup had been used by someone of note, even if it was not Saint John.

"Probably some sultan's cup passed off as a Christian relic," William said, as always knowing my thoughts.

"Take care, my lord, that you do not become a cynic," I murmured as I examined the cup.

I gentled the cup in my good hand, letting my fingers feel it as if I were a blind person. Indeed, I looked away for a moment so as not to be distracted by what I saw. It was then I felt it. Three tiny rubies were set right at the base of the stem, as the pedestal widened out. Two of them were at the same height, but the last was placed below the others. I fingered them each, rubbing them back and forth.

I felt a little movement from the oddly placed one as I nudged it, and I pressed harder. Nothing happened.

"What are you searching for, sweetheart?" William asked. But I shook my head, intent on my task. I tried the rubbing action again. And again there was movement.

"William, have you a knife?" I queried, unable to keep the excitement from my voice. He looked at me quizzically, but handed over the small knife he always carried at his belt.

I rubbed the ruby again, feeling a bit more movement than before. I took the knife and began edging it under the ruby, coaxing it to the left, and felt nothing for a moment. Suddenly the ruby moved a discernible distance and the bottom fell away from the stem.

I looked up. Both men were wide-eyed. Even Esclarmonde was riveted.

I turned the cup upside down and squinted into the hollow of the stem. Then I turned the stem toward the floor and shook. A yellowed piece of dried but intact parchment fell out. We all stared.

"Well, well, Princesse," William finally said. "You found it. You open it."

I carefully spread the crinkled parchment and we gathered around it. The handwriting was indecipherable.

"It's Arab script." I said. "I can't read it."

"I can make it out," Francis said quickly, reaching for the cup, which I yielded gladly. "I know some Aramaic."

William smiled at me over the bent figure of the young knight. "Before he trained for tournaments, you will remember, he was my clerk. His specialty was language study. He did some translations of Aristotle that compared favorably with Averroës' work."

"It is ancient, and the calligraphy is so ornate I can't be certain. But I think this is a copy of a very old version of the gospel of Saint John."

"'In the beginning was the word,'" I murmured.

"Yes, that's it. I'm sure of it." Francis had the scholar's love of discovery, and he was narrowing his eyes to help decipher the text. "This is very exciting."

"Alaïs, how did you know that something was hidden in the stem?"

"When I first saw the chalice raised at St. Denis, I was curious about the length and thickness of the stem. It did not have the ordinary form of a chalice used for Mass. It has been clear, from what everyone surmised, that something was hidden on it or in it. When I saw no special engraving that could signal a message, I tried the only part of the cup that could hide something."

"So now what do we do with the cup?" Francis said, looking from me to William to Esclarmonde. "And with this gospel fragment?"

"Princesse, what is your advice?" asked Esclarmonde.

"When he saw me in the hostel near Verdun, Pierre de Castelnau begged me to divert this cup to Béziers, and back to the Cathar bishops," I said, without hesitation, for my mind was already firm.

"Who should have it in Béziers?"

"His sister, Beatrice."

"Beatrice of Béziers! So she is the sister of Pierre de Castelnau." William let out a low whistle. "That explains much about the good monk's actions at the court of Paris. I wonder if Amaury knows."

"I fear he does. But Pierre is beyond being threatened by his colleague," was my rejoinder. "I think he has allegiance to a higher power than the abbot or pope. He is committed to doing what is right."

"And do we keep the parchment?" Francis inquired, the acquisitive nature of the scholar now showing.

I shook my head. "I want to keep faith with Père Pierre. Everything goes to Beatrice." I began carefully rolling the parchment into a small scroll, and sliding it into the stem. "Do you agree, Esclarmonde?"

"Yes, Your Grace, with all my heart," she said. "It is the parchment the Cathars will reverence. They care little for the gold and jewels."

Suddenly there was shouting somewhere below. I stopped in midsentence and we all listened. "William, help me up. I want to see what is happening." I struggled to rise.

He lifted me up and I leaned on his arms as I moved awkwardly to the window. There was a great ruckus in the courtyard below us. Two men had just ridden in, dusty and breathless. Servants' calls for the Countess Philippa were echoing inside the castle. As we watched, the men disappeared into our building.

"Do you recognize those men, William?"

"If I mistake it not, it is the Count of Foix and his eldest son," William said, with concern in his voice. "And they appear to be in a great hurry. I heard while I was in Toulouse that the viscounts of the south were in conference together at Albi. I wonder what has driven him back in such haste."

Even as we continued to watch the chaos of the arrival in the courtyard the door to my chamber was thrown open with a loud bang. The countess flew in, followed within moments by the two men.

"Lord William," the elder man said, wasting no time moving toward William. William clasped the man's forearm with his free hand, whilst he kept me encircled. "It's good to see you. It has been too long since you have stopped to visit us."

"The press of business, as you might imagine, has determined my journeys in recent months," William said tersely, but his smile was amiable. "May I present the Princesse Alaïs, sister to the king of France."

"Princesse." The count stepped back and bowed to me, gesturing to the man at his side. "My eldest son, Raymond-Guillaume." His son bowed also, and then looked at me with a frank inquisitiveness. I noticed how like the little boy I had seen at Lavaur he appeared, only older and fuller faced. This was the elder brother, and the mold and model for Roger-Bernard in the future.

"My host. Thanks to you for your hospitality," I said.

"Count Raymond-Roger. You are in a great hurry, sir," William said, as he helped me back to the chair I had occupied earlier. With care, and his support, I lowered myself into the chair. William, standing, turned to face his host.

"Lord William, I have news." The Count of Foix was a man with a hard look about him. His narrow, spare face was tanned with sun and lined with liberal amounts of Armagnac over the years. His legs were bowed, showing hard days in the saddle. His gray hair, worn much longer than was the style in the north, stood out around his head like the halo around the statue of St. Denis. Grizzled is the look I would seek to represent, if I were to make a drawing of this man, I thought. And his son the perfect copy, only with a softer face and more color in his hair.

"I believe you can say anything in front of the *princesse* and the countess," William said quietly. I was privately pleased he had included the countess, although she struck me as quite capable of speaking for herself. "And certainly you trust your sister, the Lady Esclarmonde."

Raymond-Roger nodded to Esclarmonde, who smiled at him. It was obvious there was affection between them, which gladdened me, for I had taken a great liking to this young woman.

"First, we had news at Albi about two of our young women. They were with you at Fontfroide, Princesse, I believe." He bowed in my direction. Although his voice held no accusation, I feared what he was about to say. "They were attacked on the road near the château at Montgaillard. One was killed, the other wounded. She lingers at Montgaillard, but she will live. Her companion was not so fortunate."

"Dear God in heaven," I thought, recalling the vivacity of the adventuresome young women who left Lavaur with me weeks earlier and shared the danger of my trip to Fontfroide.

"Princesse, the one who was killed wore your cloak with the insignia of the royal house of France," the count said gravely. "There is no question that those who attacked thought it was yourself."

"Amaury!" William exploded. "How dare he."

Yes, I murmured, indeed. But I knew how he dared. The man was possessed by a devil of power and anger. My heart was sore for Grazide, who took my cloak so innocently. I had a bitter taste in my mouth, for I had urged her to take it, though I thought to ensure her safety with it, not her demise.

"But there is other news, even more grave," the count was continuing. "There has been an unfortunate incident, William. It will affect all of us. I only heard about it this morning, as we were lodged overnight near Montgiscard. Pierre de Castelnau, the pope's legate, left Toulouse after a quarrel with Count Raymond two nights past. It was the day of your conference. Pierre swore he would spend not one more night under Raymond's roof."

"I know that," William said. "He left while I was still at Raymond's court."

"His party crossed the Garonne and camped on the other side. The next morning two horsemen caught up with them and rode in with swords up. They killed Pierre and one of his monks and rode off. No one has been able to identify the killers."

"God's bones." William spoke in awe. "This will do it. Now the excuse for Amaury to invade the south is overwhelming."

"It's like Thomas à Becket's murder all over again," I murmured to myself, recalling all that I had lived through as a child as King Henry's ward when that tragedy occurred. I noticed no one asked if Raymond had ordered the killing. It mattered not. The charge was all that was necessary to set in motion events that could never be called back. And this time, I knew from my visitation, flames would engulf everyone.

"Raymond will be accused, of course. No one will believe he did not order this. Every noble in the south is already making ready for war."

"I must leave for Paris immediately. Philippe must be told what has happened here." William was buckling on his sword even as he spoke.

"I'll go with you," I said, beginning to rise from my chair, albeit with difficulty.

"No." William gently pressed my shoulder and I acquiesced in the movement, for I felt a sharp stab of pain. "Paris is more dangerous for you than the south, at least for the present. We need to clean out that nest of vipers surrounding Philippe, the very ones who mean you harm." He stood looking down at me, emotions flickering across his face that made me yearn to put my body against his. "Besides, you are in no condition to ride."

He read the displeasure on my face, for suddenly his demeanor changed and the arrogance disappeared from his face. "Please, Princesse," he pleaded in a voice I had not heard before. "I beg of you." I must have registered surprise, for he gave me a most winning smile, as would a boy who had just won the prize for learning!

Suddenly an unexpected voice intervened.

"Princesse Alaïs should stay here, with us," Philippa said, in a surprisingly commanding voice. "We can protect her. Southern women have many resources, and safe places that are not known to others, not even to our men. And we gather frequently. Even this day, several of the women who were at Lavaur are on their way here. If it seems unsafe, we shall move the *princesse* to another castle. It's easily done."

This caused her lord and husband to cast a sharp glance her way, as he muttered, "Not known to your men?" William and I exchanged raised eyebrows. But the interlude was momentary, as we all turned our minds back to the very real threats of the present.

"Will the *princesse* be safe? She could be taken hostage." Raymond-Roger frowned as he spoke. William stroked his chin as he listened.

"There is no problem. Our group of women weavers will congregate here in the next few days. When they leave, we will see that the *princesse* goes with Geralda, back to Lavaur. There is a small house of women outside of Lavaur. Princesse Alaïs can convalesce there. If danger comes, we can move her again. No one will think to look for her among the daughters and sisters of the *petits nobles* here in the Toulousain. When she is strong enough to ride, you can come to fetch her."

I felt like a ball in a field game as my head moved from one speaker to the next while they discussed my fate, but the plan made sense.

"Alaïs, will you agree?" William now knew better than to order me. The lessons of our exchange in Paris and its disastrous results for all our family were still fresh.

"Yes, I agree. It seems a good plan. But what of Francis?" For the first time, all eyes turned to my son, who had been standing within our circle of conversation silently following it.

"I should go to Béziers, as you ordered a moment ago." He spoke firmly, but I shook my head in his direction.

"What need is there for a trip to Béziers?" The count looked alert, ever ready, mayhap, to see conspiracy against his countrymen.

"We need to have something carried to Beatrice of Béziers. It is a sacred object, and it was the last wish of Pierre de Castelnau that it be delivered to her. But I do not think Francis should take it."

William caught my glance. "No," he said quickly. "Francis must come with me to Paris. He is, after all, still my secretary, even if he is a knight. And I have need of his translation skills."

"If something needs to be taken to Béziers, I can do it." The young, frizzy-haired son of our host spoke up, for the first time. His voice was as strong as his father's and we all turned to look.

"This is a relic of a sort. It may be sought by some who know of it, for its value. But if you can ride swiftly, you may outdistance those who would find and take it," I said.

"Beatrice of Béziers is our kinswoman and a dear cousin of my wife," Raymond-Roger said. "Raymond-Guillaume knows all the back roads. He has loyal young men who can ride with him. This relic would reach its goal, I can assure you."

"Then it's done," William said firmly. "Francis, prepare to depart for Paris within the hour. Alaïs, give the cup to Raymond-Guillaume, please, and he can start now as well. The entire south will become one fortress when the news of Pierre's death is known. We must move quickly. And now," he said in his commanding way, "I would like a word with the *princesse,* alone."

The hosts of Foix bowed and withdrew without another word, as did their son and the two servants who had entered with them. Francis came to me and leaned down to kiss my hand, but I drew him to me in a full embrace. "My son," I whispered, "you are dearer to me than life itself. Safe home to you. We will see each other soon."

Esclarmonde had hesitated to leave until Francis had bidden his adieu to me. She stood now, next to the chair, although her hand was on the back as if to steady herself. She was waiting to see what Francis would do.

He came to her, looked down from his height, and then solemnly offered her his arm on which to lean. She took it and her expression was of such blinding relief that I was assured they would have much to discuss after the doors had closed behind them.

William raised me from the chair into his arms and held me, gingerly it seemed. "My dearest love, do not worry for Francis. He will be safe with me. And you will be safe with these good women, until you can make the journey back to Paris. I will come for you within a fortnight."

"William, are we never to be together in an ordinary time? I have just found you, my love, and now you are gone again."

He put a finger under my chin and turned my face up to his. "I only ask this. Do not put your life in danger again. There has been no woman for me but you since I found you again at Canterbury. And, in truth, not since I saw you at Henry's court all those years ago. And there will be no one for me in the future but you. If anything should happen to you, I know not what would become of me."

I nodded, and was ashamed that tears were coming. "What will happen now?"

"Now, my love, you will see a vicious war the length and breadth of this land, unless a miracle happens." He sighed and wearily leaned down to put his forehead against mine. "The fanatics of religion have won. War will come."

"And Raymond, our cousin?"

"Alas, this crime, whether he did it or not, will be the final excuse to excommunicate him. Then they will use that as a bargaining chip to get him into the camp of the army that is sure to come from the north."

"And afterward? How will it end?"

"There is no way it will end happily for the Count of Toulouse." He held me close for a long time, resting his chin on my head. I could hear his heart beating and feel the warmth of him through our clothes. But we both knew there was no time for lovemaking now.

Then William picked me up as if I were a feather and brought me gently to the bed.

"William," I said, my voice hoarse with my returning fatigue and a leave-taking sorrow that would not be denied. "I pray for the day we will be together."

He held me close for a long time.

"I have to go," he murmured.

"You are always going," I whispered in his ear.

He pulled away from me and looked at my face. "And you, my dearest love, you are always with me. And I will come back to you soon, no matter what happens."

I had no words for this parting, no more to express to him than what I had just said with my body. I closed my eyes. He kissed me once more and I felt him close. Then his hands brushed the length of my body down under the fur, as if that touch could rouse my spirit to trail after him as he departed.

After the sound of the closing door reached me I recalled the dream and vision I had the day William came to Paris, only a few short weeks earlier.

And now I saw a new meaning unfold before me. The excommunication in the vision was that of Raymond of Toulouse. Pierre's murder would be the cause and Amaury would be the hammer, standing at the side of the pontiff, just as he had in my vision. And Francis was in the vision because Amaury had taken him prisoner. But thank the heavens, he was now restored to William and to me.

Then I pondered the dream of the gryphons.

My task in the dream at the start of this adventure was to retrieve the gryphons and to put them back into the glass bowl. But the relevance to these events leading up to war still eluded me. Perhaps I was only meant to play this small part, with the aid of Pierre de Castelnau. It was with my help that the St. John Cup would be returned to those who would value its spiritual meaning, not its jewels or its bargaining power. If that was the purpose, I had played my part well. If there were a larger task assigned to me, it would be revealed.

My body, though sore, was warm and safe under the fur. There was a sense of William being with me still and that feeling stayed with me as I slipped into new dreams.

Afterword

THE ROMANCE

These stories of Princesse Alaïs of France, of the house of Capet, are set at the beginning of the thirteenth century. They could be called of the genre of romance, not the romance of bodice ripper fame (so-called for the partially disrobed, sexy females in costume on the covers), but the true romance stories of which the grail series, begun by Chrétien de Troyes at this very time, was the initial and still greatest model.

The characteristics of the romance are several: stories of faraway people and events (the original Arthurian legends, written in the twelfth century, were about the exploits of fifth-century knights), stories concerning mystery, heroes, quests, adventures, passion, and sometimes even death.

The modern detective story has many of the elements of the romance about it. A hero, a quest, a death, perhaps a love interest. While some may call it escapist literature, it satisfies a need we have for reaching out into another life, another time, and a story beyond ourselves.

These stories of Alaïs Capet are such tales of adventure, mystery, and love.

THE HISTORY

Many of the characters and events in this story are real. Others are fictional. Part of the challenge of writing historical fiction is to decide how true one ought to remain to the actual history while weaving a fictional story through it.

The chapter of the Albigensian Crusade (sometimes called the Cathar Crusade) is one of the most bloody and vicious of European history. The wars wiped out an entire culture in the south of what is now France. It changed the map of Europe forever. And it was the first crusade proclaimed by the Christian church against its own members. This book is a story set against the run-up to this war.

On the side of history, I have telescoped a number of events that actually extended over three or four years. Pope Innocent III sent to Philippe of France three times to beg him to intervene in the south. The king refused each time, although later his son, Louis, led the second crusade against the south.

Arnaud Amaury's portrait in history is close to what I have described in this novel. While I have invented his words, his actions are recorded and speak for themselves. There was indeed a circle of women in the south at this time who were the mainstay of the initial Cathar movement. Many of their names survive, and I have woven them as characters in the tapestry of this novel. As for Pierre of Castelnau, he did exist and was Amaury's co-legate. There also lived a Beatrice of Béziers who was rumored to be an early Cathar, but there is no evidence, and it is unlikely that she and Pierre were at all related. Finally, it was indeed the murder of Pierre de Castelnau in January 1208 on the banks of the Garonne that set off the bloodletting in the south.

Constance of Toulouse was married to Count Raymond V and had a bad time of it. Her son was Raymond VI and he was, in fact, excommunicated as the story relates. Joanna, favorite sister of Richard Lion-Hearted was married to the Count of Toulouse and she did leave her husband to go north to Eleanor when she was ready to give birth and died there. However, in historical real time it was actually in 1199 that this occurred. Charlotte of Fontevraud is entirely a figment of my imagination. It pleased me to make her royal and an abbess. Fontevraud Abbey has an interesting history of its own. It was founded by a man, Robert d'Abrissol, more than a century earlier. The abbey had religious houses for men and women, as well as a hospital and poorhouse. It was the first abbey in Europe to have a woman abbess rule over men.

Hervé de Donzy, Count of Nevers, and Eudes, Duke of Burgundy, were among the first knights to go to the south to fight a few years after my story, with Philippe Auguste's acquiescence, but not his support. They went in search of land and fortune.

Alaïs, sometimes called Alix in the genealogies, was a real person and the story recounted in the first book of her adventures, *The Canterbury Papers*, was based on the chronicles of the time, which hinted at her alleged affair with King Henry II of England, and the child that was supposed to have been born to them both. That son, Francis, figures in this story. There is no record, however, of his survival in real history, nor of Alaïs's intervention in the "matter of the south" as I have related here. Still, it makes a good story.

THE CATHAR CRUSADE

The Albigensian Crusade of the early thirteenth century was one of the bloodiest in history. It also gave rise to what has become known as "the Inquisition," not one of Christianity's finest hours (or centuries). Saint Dominic rose to prominence at this time; it was his idea to institute the "inquisition" to determine heresy, and to root out the enemies of God. The Inquisition later came to be associated especially with the persecution of the Jews and Moors in Spain. Indeed, some histories have it that it was Dominic's accidental meeting with Pierre de Castelnau and Arnaud Amaury outside of Marseille, while traveling with his bishop from Spain, that caused the papal legates to revise their strategy to win back the south for Rome.

The Cathars (a term generally thought to be from the Greek, "to purify") did have the practices outlined in this novel. They also had a special devotion to Saint John the Evangelist. While many scholars consider them dualists theologically, I am indebted to Emmanuel Le Roy Ladurie, famous French scholar and former director of the Bibliotheque Nationale, who spent some pleasant hours with me explaining patiently that the new scholarship (since 1950) indicates that the Cathars were more Christian than Manichean, and were the first of a long line of "reformers," forerunners of Martin Luther and John Calvin. They were purifiers (hence their name) intending to return the Roman church to its original state of grace, found in the early Christian period.

The Cathars had their own brand of nuttiness, but they were, overall, treated brutally not only by Rome but by the knights of northern France. The gracious culture of the people of the langue d'oc disappeared under the sword of Abbot Amaury and his followers.

For those interested in Cathar history of this period, I recommend Jonathon Sumption's *The Albigensian Crusade*, Malcolm Barber's *The Cathars*, and the best popular history which talks about all the women, Stephen O'Shea's *The Perfect Heresy*. For those who want to delve deeper, I found Henry Lea's nineteenth-century work *The Inquisition of the Middle Ages* very useful, and also Sir Stephen Runciman's *The Medieval Manichee*, which has a good theological background.

The Cathars were a movement among the nobility when it became prominent enough to attract the attention of Rome in the early thirteenth century. A hundred years later, after many wars and much bloodshed, the only *credentes* who remained were in the hill country and villages. For a look at Catharism in its waning years, readers might like to read *Montaillou*, by Emmanuel Le Roy Ladurie, *The Yellow Crosses* by Rene Weiss, and the great other classic, *Montségur*, by Zoe Oldendorf.

Finally for popular history, and sheer fun (think *The da Vinci Code*) take a look at *Holy Blood, Holy Grail* by Henry Leigh et al., and a more serious work, *Coming to Our Senses* by Morris Berman. On page 303, the Princesse tells the abbots an old Arabic fable. This is an adaptation of a fable given in one of Dorothy Dunnett's marvelous stories in her historical series, *The Lymond Chronicles*.

FANATICS

Our time is attempting to come to terms with fanatics. But who or what are fanatics? Who will define fanaticism? Who are the enemies of God? And who knows the mind of God clearly enough to say?

The human race is no more certain of the answer to these questions than those characters who created history in the thirteenth century were. But while we consider these deep questions, we might as well also look at adventure, heroism, jealousy, mystery, murder, and very strange vision, all the things humans get up to while history is happening. It makes a good story. That is what I have tried to present in the new adventures of the Princesse Alaïs.

Acknowledgments

Many friends and writers have helped by reading and commenting on various versions of this story. I am indebted to Alice and Lance Buhl, Dee Ready, and Mary Logue, whose editorial and overall comments were most helpful. I owe a debt of gratitude to Marolyn Downing and Michel Charpentier for their hospitality while I was in France, and the use of their fine French library as well as the invaluable comments Michel provided in early drafts of the manuscript, regarding language and history. I have already acknowledged the important role of M. Le Roy Ladurie and his views on recent historical scholarship that revised my thinking on the Cathars. I would not have completed the project without the monastic hospitality of the Studium program of the Sisters of the Order of St. Benedict in St. Joseph, Minnesota. Sisters Colman O'Connell and Emmanuel Renner, my dear friends, were especially helpful with their multiple readings, comments, and support. And thanks to my lifelong friend Ruth Murphy, who accompanied me on an early trip from Toulouse to Béziers, and who shared many adventures on the way.

No book comes to fruition without agents and editors. I want especially to thank my editors at HarperCollins, Wendy Lee and Carolyn Marino, and my agents Marly Rusoff and Michael Radulescu. Without Marly's support and belief in the book as it was developing, there would be no *Rebel Princess*!

THE HISTORY

BEHIND

THE STORY

A Conversation with Judith Koll Healey

Both The Canterbury Papers *and* The Rebel Princess *are set in the late twelfth and early thirteenth centuries. What is it about this time period that fascinates you?*

Part of the reason I am drawn to this period is that I grew up as a Catholic. The Catholic Church was at that time (pre–Vatican II) still very medieval in its liturgy. There were costumes, the use of Latin, and many saints as well as set prayers. In addition, when I was very young—about nine years old—two elements were inserted into my world. For Christmas, my brother received a book about Robin Hood, which I found much more interesting than the Louisa May Alcott books I had been given, and a year later, when we had moved to the north shore of the Chicago area, my parents took me to see a movie called *The Crusades*. It starred Loretta Young and some English actor. I was hooked on the period. It seemed to me to embody all the story-telling and history one could desire. I never recovered.

Later, I began reading history more widely, traveling to France and England, and my tastes became a bit more sophisticated. But I never lost that love of story from my early experiences.

Your books are full of rich historical detail. How do you conduct your research?

For many years, I simply read history. I was particularly drawn to biographies of people at the forefront of that historical period: Eleanor of Aquitaine, Henry II of England (originally of Anjou), Richard the Lionheart, and Philippe of France, along with Thomas à Becket. I discovered that whereas historical works covered political changes and battles, biographies told who did what, making a much better human story. It was out of this reading that *The Canterbury Papers* grew.

I amassed a fine library, much of it as a result of haunting used book stores in Sarasota, Florida, on Cape Cod, and in other places—bookstores that had out-of-print books from the estates of retired, educated people. I bought many books in France and England while I was traveling. After some years of interested reading, a story began to form around the central characters of the time. I asked the question that every writer of stories asks: "What if?"

I did, however, do regular research at the library on food and dress. Detail is important to draw in the reader.

How closely is Princess Alaïs based on the historical figure?

There was definitely a character in history named Princess Alaïs, born about 1157, who was the daughter of the second wife of Louis VII, King of France, and half sister to Philippe Auguste. She and her elder sister Marguerite were betrothed to the two eldest sons of Henry and Eleanor. This betrothal arrangement was conducted by Thomas à Becket on Henry's behalf. It was strange because Eleanor had been the first wife of Louis and had divorced him to marry Henry. But thereby hangs another tale. Alaïs was to marry the younger son, the man history calls Richard the Lionheart, who was eventually king of England.

The two girls were raised at the court of Henry and Eleanor and schooled by Eleanor when she had the royal children with her at Poitiers. Some chronicles hint that Henry took Alaïs as his mistress out of pique when he had Eleanor imprisoned after she fomented rebellion among their sons.

Richard refused to marry Alaïs, or Henry refused to let him. History is not clear on this point, but the failure of the betrothal led to a break between Philippe and Richard and a fight over the Vexin, a key region near Paris that had been her dowry.

Early genealogies from the Cluny museum in Paris give the name as Alaïs. More recent genealogies from the same museum use Alix, which would have been easier for people to pronounce, but I had to work with what I had at the time.

There is no evidence that Alaïs had a withered hand or any special gift. I made that up. That's what fiction writers do!

Including Princess Alaïs, there are quite a few strong female characters in the book. Were women back then more powerful than we might think?

In the history of the south of France, especially in the Cathar times, women were quite powerful. Because the distribution of titles and lands was made to all the sons, not just to the eldest as was the custom in the feudal north, a smaller amount of power was held in the hands of many men. Therefore, many women had a chance to exercise power as well, as doyennes of their husbands' estates when the men were away.

In particular, the Cathar culture honored women, and they, in turn, became the hosts of many of the preachers who roamed the countryside of what is now southwest France and northern Spain. In *The Perfect Heresy*, Stephen O'Shea highlights the role of women in the Cathar culture and names many of those who became characters in my book. I have also presented the actual, unfortunate ends of some of them in the "visions" that Alaïs has from time to time.

But we should not forget that many women were powerful in their own right at this time. Eleanor of Aquitaine took her lands with her when she left Louis and married Henry. Part of their fight, and the Hundred Years' War to come, was as a result of this exercise of power.

My novels are also set near the time of Eleanor's granddaughter Blanche of Castile, who was a powerful regent of France for years. And let's not forget Hildegard of Bingen and other abbesses who ruled their particular realms without interference from men. We are also not far from the time of Ferdinand and Isabella of Spain, who were called the "Catholic Kings." As Queen of Castile, Isabella was the more powerful monarch.

Can you tell us about Alaïs's next adventure?
The third novel in the series will be set during the Cathar war itself. Francis and his beloved will feature more prominently in this, as will William, whom I have quite grown to like! But war is tough. There will also be a child. Stay tuned.

Discussion Questions for
The Rebel Princess

1. Princess Alaïs has a withered hand, a defect from birth. What does medieval superstition say about such a defect? Do you agree with this belief? How do you think Alaïs's "gift" would be interpreted today?

2. What role does Alaïs play in her brother's court? How does the arrival of the two monks compound this role?

3. Why is the St. John Cup considered important? Do you think it is worth all the intrigue that surrounds it?

4. Alaïs is often caught between personal and political events in this story. What are some of these situations, and do you think she handles them well?

5. How would you describe Alaïs's relationship with William of Caen? What do you think will happen to them?

6. When Francis learns that Alaïs is his mother, did you find his initial reaction surprising? Why or why not?

7. What do you think of the Cathar women who assist Alaïs? How do they represent a culture of the south different from that of the Paris region?

8. Do you sympathize with the Cathar cause? Is there anything about this religious conflict that seems similar to modern events?

9. What do you think is going to happen to Alaïs in her next adventure? What do you hope will happen?

10. How does Alaïs compare to the other heroines you've read about from this time period or other heroines in historical fiction?

The lighter side of HISTORY

* Look for this seal on select historical fiction titles from Harper. Books bearing it contain special bonus materials, including timelines, interviews with the author, and insights into the real-life events that inspired the book, as well as recommendations for further reading.

AND ONLY TO DECEIVE:
A Novel of Suspense
by Tasha Alexander
978-0-06-114844-6 (paperback)
Discover the dangerous secrets kept by the strait-laced English of the Victorian era.

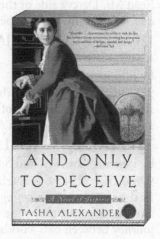

ANNETTE VALLON:
A Novel of the French Revolution
by James Tipton
978-0-06-082222-4 (paperback)
For fans of Tracy Chevalier and Sarah Dunant comes this vibrant, alluring debut novel of a compelling, independent woman who would inspire one of the world's greatest poets and survive a nation's bloody transformation.

BOUND: A Novel
by Sally Gunning
978-0-06-124026-3 (paperback)
An indentured servant finds herself bound by law, society, and her own heart in colonial Cape Cod.

CASSANDRA & JANE: A Jane Austen Novel
by Jill Pitkeathley
978-0-06-144639-9 (paperback)
The relationship between Jane Austen and her sister—explored through the letters that might have been.

CROSSED: A Tale of the Fourth Crusade
by Nicole Galland
978-0-06-084180-5 (paperback)
Under the banner of the Crusades, a pious knight and a British vagabond attempt a daring rescue.

A CROWNING MERCY: A Novel
by Bernard Cornwell and Susannah Kells
978-0-06-172438-1 (paperback)
A rebellious young Puritan woman embarks on a daring journey to win
love and a secret fortune.

DARCY'S STORY
by Janet Aylmer
978-0-06-114870-5 (paperback)
Read Mr. Darcy's side of the story—*Pride
and Prejudice* from a new perspective.

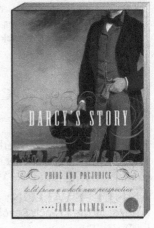

DEAREST COUSIN JANE:
A Jane Austen Novel
by Jill Pitkeathley
978-0-06-187598-4 (paperback)
An inventive reimagining of the intriguing
and scandalous life of Jane Austen's cousin.

THE FALLEN ANGELS: A Novel
by Bernard Cornwell and Susannah Kells
978-0-06-172545-6 (paperback)
In the sequel to *A Crowning Mercy*, Lady Campion Lazender's courage,
faith, and family loyalty are tested when she must complete a perilous
journey between two worlds.

A FATAL WALTZ: A Novel of Suspense
by Tasha Alexander
978-0-06-117423-0 (paperback)
Caught in a murder mystery, Emily must do the unthinkable to save her
fiancé: bargain with her ultimate nemesis, the Countess von Lange.

FIGURES IN SILK: A Novel
by Vanora Bennett
978-0-06-168985-7 (paperback)
The art of silk making, political intrigue, and a sweeping love story all
interwoven in the fate of two sisters.

THE FIREMASTER'S MISTRESS: A Novel
by Christie Dickason
978-0-06-156826-8 (paperback)
Estranged lovers Francis and Kate rekindle their
romance in the midst of Guy Fawkes's plot to blow up
Parliament.

JULIA AND THE MASTER OF MORANCOURT: A Novel
by Janet Aylmer
978-0-06-167295-8 (paperback)
Amidst family tragedy, Julia travels all over England, desperate to marry the man she loves instead of the arranged suitor preferred by her mother.

KEPT: A Novel
by D. J. Tayler
978-0-06-114609-1 (paperback)
A gorgeously intricate, dazzling reinvention of Victorian life and passions that is also a riveting investigation into some of the darkest, most secret chambers of the human heart.

THE MIRACLES OF PRATO: A Novel
by Laurie Albanese and Laura Morowitz
978-0-06-155835-1 (paperback)
The unforgettable story of a nearly impossible romance between a painter-monk (the renowned artist Fra Filippo Lippi) and the young nun who becomes his muse, his lover, and the mother of his children.

PILATE'S WIFE: A Novel of the Roman Empire
by Antoinette May
978-0-06-112866-0 (paperback)
Claudia foresaw the Romans' persecution of Christians, but even she could not stop the crucifixion.

A POISONED SEASON:
A Novel of Suspense
by Tasha Alexander
978-0-06-117421-6 (paperback)
As a cat-burglar torments Victorian London, a mysterious gentleman fascinates high society.

PORTRAIT OF AN UNKNOWN WOMAN: A Novel
by Vanora Bennett
978-0-06-125256-3 (paperback)
Meg, adopted daughter of Sir Thomas More, narrates the tale of a famous Holbein painting and the secrets it holds.

THE QUEEN'S SORROW: A Novel of Mary Tudor
by Suzannah Dunn
978-0-06-170427-7 (paperback)
Queen of England Mary Tudor's reign is brought low by abused power and a forbidden love.

REBECCA: The Classic Tale of Romantic Suspense
by Daphne Du Maurier
978-0-380-73040-7 (paperback)
Follow the second Mrs. Maxim de Winter down the lonely drive to Manderley, where Rebecca once ruled.

REBECCA'S TALE: A Novel
by Sally Beauman
978-0-06-117467-4 (paperback)
Unlock the dark secrets and old worlds of Rebecca de Winter's life with investigator Colonel Julyan.

THE SIXTH WIFE: A Novel of Katherine Parr
by Suzannah Dunn
978-0-06-143156-2 (paperback)
Kate Parr survived four years of marriage to King Henry VIII, but a new love may undo a lifetime of caution.

VIVALDI'S VIRGINS: A Novel
by Barbara Quick
978-0-06-089053-7 (paperback)
Abandoned as an infant, fourteen-year-old Anna Maria dal Violin is one of the elite musicians living in the foundling home where the "Red Priest," Antonio Vivaldi, is maestro and composer.

WATERMARK: A Novel of the Middle Ages
by Vanitha Sankaran
978-0-06-184927-5 (paperback)
A compelling debut about the search for identiy, the power of self-expression, and value of the written word.

THE WIDOW'S WAR: A Novel
by Sally Gunning
978-0-06-079158-2 (paperback)
Tread the shores of colonial Cape Cod with a lonely whaler's widow as she tries to build a new life.

9 780061 673573